Brushfire Plague: Reckoning

by

R.P. Ruggiero

Your Survival Library

www.PrepperPress.com

Brushfire Plague: Reckoning

ISBN 978-0615919577

Printed in the United States of America.

Prepper Press Trade Paperback Edition: November 2013

Prepper Press is a division of Kennebec Publishing, LLC

--To my wife of twenty years. You believed in me before I did. For that, I am forever grateful. And, together we have a family that is worth surviving for.

Acknowledgements:

First, I wish to thank the many readers of *Brushfire Plague* that reviewed the book or contacted me directly. Your positive support is always an encouragement that cannot be underestimated.

My family deserves my eternal gratitude as well. I already work in a field that is demanding and intense, so the additional time to write is another sacrifice they make for me to pursue my dreams. Their support is immeasurable and it fills my heart with gratitude.

Many thanks to Prepper Press for supporting my work and providing the professional editing from Sarah Cairns. She has improved *Brushfire Plague: Reckoning*, as she did with the original!

Finally, to my readers, I offer these words that inspire me.

"A human being should be able to change a diaper, plan an invasion, butcher a hog, conn a ship, design a building, write a sonnet, balance accounts, build a wall, set a bone, comfort the dying, take orders, give orders, cooperate, act alone, solve equations, analyse a new problem, pitch manure, program a computer, cook a tasty meal, fight efficiently, die gallantly. Specialization is for insects."

-Robert A. Heinlein

About the Author:

R.P. Ruggiero lives in Colorado with his wife and two sons. He spends as much time as he can in the outdoors and strives to live by Robert Heinlein's credo that, "Specialization is for insects." When he is not outdoors, writing, or learning a new skill, he works coordinating people to achieve their common goals. He brings his two decades of experience in group dynamics--particularly when people are under stress--to good use in writing *The Brushfire Plague* series.

Contact the author at rpruggiero@gmail.com with your comments about the novels, visit **www.brushfireplague.com**, "like" the Brushfire Plague Facebook page, or follow him on Twitter @rpruggiero.

Chapter One

Startled, Cooper Adams shuddered awake and bolted upright in bed. His rifle was in his hand without a thought. His heart thundered in his chest, revving up for action as adrenaline raced into his veins. Alert eyes darted about, scanning for danger. His ears fixated on any noises coming from outside or inside his home. They told him nothing was amiss and he emitted a long exhale. He relaxed his nearly six-foot frame, put the rifle against the wall, and laid back into the bed. He stared at the ceiling for a long moment, deliberately slowing his breath and collecting his thoughts. He couldn't tell if some random noise had woken him or if it had been another fitful dream.

Next to him, his eleven-year old son, Jake, lay sound asleep. His chest rose and fell in a steady rhythm, while his eyes moved rapidly about, underneath closed eyelids. *Dreaming. I can only hope for sweet ones.* A chill ran down his spine as he thought about his son's encounter with the Brushfire Plague. The fever had broken just last night. Without thinking, Cooper put the back of his hand to his son's forehead for reassurance and smiled in relief.

His gaze drifted back to the white, monotonous ceiling. For a moment, Cooper wistfully thought the last twenty-four hours could have been a dream, but the distant crackle of gunfire belied the thought. The fact that his son, instead of his wife, slept next to him burned it out of him. The plague had merely scared his son, but it had taken his wife, Elena. It had only been two weeks since she breathed her last breath, but the world was already so different that his life with her was steadily turning into a dream-like memory. Now, he realized what had jolted him awake. He *had* been dreaming of Elena and was terrified that he could not recall her eye color. If the world had somersaulted in just two weeks, it had added a barrel roll in the last twenty-four hours when Cooper learned that the calamitous Brushfire Plague was a deliberate act of men and not some dreadful accident of nature. *A deliberate act that will end up slaying one billion people.* Ethan Mitchell, a zealous CEO of a biotech company, had argued that his actions served the greater good by saving mankind from the civilization-destroying effects of climate change and a ravaged planet. Cooper's mind still whirled at the facts and arguments made by the man who had released the Brushfire Plague across the planet. Luckily, Mitchell's brain thought about these things no more. Cooper had made sure of that. He gritted his teeth at the thought. A pained, wry smile

1

crept onto his face, as he thought of Mitchell's body, cold now, lying in the man's mansion.

A billion dead. The thought staggered Cooper and his breath caught in his throat. Unlike anyone else, Cooper had had the satisfaction of putting a bullet into the brain of the main progenitor of this horrendous act. He did not doubt that Mitchell deserved death for what he had done, but revenge had not lightened his heart nor dulled his pain. He also uniquely carried the burden of having told the world the truth of what he'd learned, with consequences still unknown. The magnitude of those possibilities gnawed at him like a lazy rat nibbling rope.

Cooper was also perplexed by his feelings toward the woman, Julianne Wheeler, who had assisted Mitchell in all that he had done. He wanted to hate her and failed to understand why he didn't. He desperately hoped it was simply the lingering effects of the deep, primal, connection he'd felt toward her when they had met. He could not deny the instant connection. He remembered an oft-quoted line; *the heart wants what it wants.* However, this instant connection happened before he knew anything about her role in the conspiracy to unleash mass death on humanity. So far, this knowledge had done little to sever the bond. While his brain warred with his heart to make it so; the heart kept winning.

Next to him, Jake stirred. His eyes fluttered and opened. He saw his father and smiled. Cooper curled his arm underneath his son's head and pulled him closer.

"Mornin', boy."

"Good morning, dad."

"How are you feeling?"

"Tirrrr-ed," he yawned with a gaping maw. "I feel really tired, dad. But, I *do* feel better. For a while, I thought I was gonna catch on fire!"

"Yeah, you had the fever bad. But, it's passed now. Lisa says you're going to recover," Cooper said, sharing the report he'd received last night from the woman who was their friend, neighbor, and nurse.

Jake smiled incredulously, eyes twinkling and moistening, "I'm not going to die...like mom." His words were caught between question and statement by the force of wonder.

Cooper pulled his son into an embrace, "No, you're not going to die like your sweet, sweet mother." His own heart swelled with a torrent of love for his son and his dead wife; sorrow for the latter and unbridled newfound hope for the former. They held each other for a long time. Finally, curiosity grabbed ahold of Jake.

"So, what happened last night?"

Cooper burst out laughing so loudly it echoed off the walls of Jake's bedroom. When he finally caught his breath, he blurted out, "What *didn't* happen would be a better question, son!"

Jake grimaced in annoyance and returned with mockery in his voice, "Alright then...what *didn't* happen last night!"

Cooper tussled his son's hair. As he did so, levity fled the room like animals fleeing a wildfire. Cooper breathed deeply and looked his son squarely in the eye. "I learned last night that this Plague wasn't an accident, son. It was started by some stupid, stupid...and misguided men."

Jake's eyebrows furrowed in confusion. Tears welled up in his eyes. His breath came in fitful gasps. His lips quivered. "You mean...they...someone *killed* mama on purpose," he wailed between pain-wracked sobs.

Cooper pulled his son in close once more, allowing him to bury his head into his chest. He rocked him back and forth in a vain attempt to comfort him. He breathed more and then said, "Yes, son, they did." His stark words of confirmation sent Jake into another round of deep sobs. Like any father, his son's pain cut him to the core. His fists clenched and his jaw grinded his teeth as rage against Ethan Mitchell surged once more. Then, listening to his son's sobbing, it hit him.

With one billion dead, almost every single person on earth is going to feel this newfound confusion, pain, and fury when they learn this wasn't some malevolent act of Nature...but a calculated act of Man. A man who lived in America. In Portland, Oregon. It slowly dawned on him that a grief-fed rage would consume the world just as the Brushfire Plague was receding.

The realization stunned him. His stomach turned and saliva filled his mouth. He fought back against the presage to vomit. *How did I miss that?* Cooper knew the answer before the question had finished flashing through his mind. *The truth blinded me to everything else.* His fists became tight balls and his nails dug into his palms. He grimaced, trying to steel himself to the decision he'd made just hours before. His heart and mind roiled in a tug of war over right and wrong and what he had done.

"Damn the consequences, the world deserves to know the truth," he shouted defiantly, his voice thundering across the walls.

"What?" Jake asked and only then did Cooper realize he had yelled what he'd been thinking.

"Nothing, son. Nothing," Cooper responded laconically, his eyes downcast.

Jake continued, "Why? Why'd they do it?"

Cooper's unwavering penchant to the truth led him to do his best to relay the thinking that had driven Ethan Mitchell to his deadly act of destruction, "You've heard of global warming, right, son?"

Jake's eyebrows raised in confusion, "Yeah. What has that got to do with anything?"

"Well, this guy, Ethan Mitchell, believed that we weren't going to deal with it and that it would have eventually wiped out civilization."

"What?" Jake mouthed in disbelief.

"I can't fully explain it. But, he believed that, left unchecked, global warming would have heated the planet so much that agriculture would have become near impossible, weather would have become extreme, sea levels would have risen so much that it would have put many major cities underwater. In short, civilization would have ended. So, he thought it was a better idea to *intentionally* kill hundreds of millions *now* to prevent this."

Jake shook his head in disbelief, "But...but, that's wrong." Cooper watched as his son struggled to understand. "How could he decide something like that all on his own?"

"That's exactly what I told him." Cooper weighed his next words carefully. Then, he decided to go forward. "That's exactly what I told him, right before I killed him." His words trailed off.

Jake looked up at Cooper, his eyes wide open in shock, and "You killed him?"

"Yes, I killed him. What he did was wrong. So wrong, that he deserved to die," Cooper's words rolled off his tongue, slowly, deliberately.

Jake absorbed the words even more slowly and a long silence hung in the air. His eyes searched his father's face for understanding or meaning. "How do you feel now?"

"Empty," he said flatly. He paused, drawing a deep breath. He continued with tired words. "It had to be done. He deserved it. It wasn't his *right* to decide the fate of so many. But, it isn't bringing your mother — or anyone else — back."

Jake simply nodded, with vague understanding. "Well, I'm glad he's dead." His son spat on the ground, acting the grown-up. Cooper did not like the snarl that latched onto his face when he did so.

"There's something else you need to know. It's more important than any of this." Jake nodded once more, sitting up straighter, readying himself for what was to come.

"Last night, I told the world what I learned, too. I told the world everything. And, I very much fear the consequences. "

Jake interrupted him, "What consequences? The truth is always the right thing. You've taught me that." His last words were laced with the certain truth of childhood.

Cooper nodded slowly, "That's right. The truth is always right. But, I've also taught you that the truth isn't always easy. And, this truth is probably the most difficult of all."

"What do you mean?"

"Think about it, Jake. Think of how sad and angry it made you to realize that your mother didn't just die—but that she was *killed* by this terrible act. The *whole world* is going to get very, very angry. Our country already teeters on the edge. There's *already* been so much chaos and violence. I fear there will be much more."

Jake's eyes slowly morphed from being clouded with confusion to the clarity of understanding. His voice trammeled, "Then, why'd you do it?"

Cooper's eyes wrinkled and his lips curled into a skeptical smile, "Son, I'm not sure I had much choice." Cooper paused and rubbed the stubble on his chin, "But, I guess I did have some choice. At the end, I have faith that we will get through all of this…even knowing the truth. It might be painful and likely worse in the short-term, but the world must...it *must* know the truth. What we do with it is *our* choice. *I* couldn't deny the world that choice. Otherwise, I'd be just as bad as Ethan Mitchell. You understand?"

Jake's mind sorted through his father's words, "I think so. I think so, dad. I just hope it doesn't get too much worse. It's already been very, very bad."

Cooper began to nod in agreement, but a furious pounding on his front door caused his heart to race once again and his mind to doubt his son's hope would be proven true.

****

As Cooper neared the door, there was no mistaking the familiar timbre of his friend, Paul Dranko's, voice yelling from the other side, "Cooper, it's me, Dranko. Open up, brother, open up!"

Cooper yanked the door open and burst out laughing as he caught Dranko in mid-yell, his mouth twisted half-open, "With an

5

adorable face like that, I can see why you've always had trouble with the ladies, my friend."

Dranko scowled and brushed past him, "Screw you. I had problems with the ladies because no one wanted to believe our precious civilization would ever hit a bump in the road…until now, of course." Cooper knew this was true. Since he had known Dranko, the man had been consumed with all manners of theorizing and preparing for the myriad ways that civilization might collapse. For Cooper, it had been an endearing idiosyncrasy. He could only imagine the problems it had caused Dranko in the pre-Brushfire Plague dating world, however. Now? Well, now Cooper understood very well that Dranko's preparations had saved his life and those of many around him.

Cooper turned to follow his friend inside, closing the door behind him, "Just look on the bright side…" Dranko's cocked eyebrow interrupted him, but Cooper bludgeoned onward, waving his hand, "Yes, I know! For a dyed in the wool pessimist like you, looking on the bright side is damn near impossible. But! Try it out. Just imagine how all of the beautiful women whom you dated over the years are, right now, wishing they had stayed with that crazy bastard who was preparing for the end of the world!"

Dranko returned Cooper's beaming smile with a deepening grimace, "Like I said, screw you. You're an ass. Are you ready to get down to what I came to talk about or do you want to discuss my romantic life's prospects in the post-Plague world?"

"Fine, fine," Cooper said, turning serious. "What have you got for me?"

"First, how's Jake doing?"

"Fantastic. Still a little weak, but he's looking good."

Dranko clasped his hands together in excitement, "That's great news. Great news, brother!"

"Don't I know it? We got lucky. Very lucky he caught it as the strain was deliberately mutating itself to a weaker form," Cooper answered.

Dranko nodded. "That's good. I'm afraid I have some bad news for you. You ready?"

Cooper nodded in return, "Yeah. Shoot. I figured you had something bad from how you were banging on my door."

"Well, the world has been on fire with the news you dropped on them. Half the world seems to be calling what you've said the biggest hoax since H.G. Wells' *War of the Worlds*."

Anger at being called untruthful, even by strangers, flashed across Cooper's face, "And, what are the other half saying?"

"The good news is that they believe what you've put out there."

"What's the bad news?"

"They are really pissed off about it." He paused, his eyes squinting, "And, I mean pissed off on a Biblical scale."

Cooper's eyes dropped to the floor, "Yeah, I was thinking about that very thing as I told Jake about what I'd learned and what I had done."

Dranko nodded in agreement, "Losing a loved one is bad enough. When it's been done on purpose, revenge is the first...and often last...thing people feel."

Cooper moved past his friend, striding toward the kitchen, "I had to do it. The world deserves to know the truth, dammit!"

Dranko turned to follow him, "Look, brother, I ain't arguing with you. I am just here to tell you the reaction to that truth, mainly so we can be prepared for it."

Cooper drew his pistol from its holster, laid it on the counter, and leaned back against it, facing Dranko, "Yeah, I know. Keep going."

Dranko settled in, legs in a wide stance and arms folded, "Like I was saying. The other half is pretty damn upset. On the foreign front, recriminations and demands for justice have already started pouring in to our government." Dranko paused and averted his eyes from his friend's.

Cooper looked exasperated, "C'mon. What's the worse news? I can handle it."

"So far, that's been the official reactions. You have opposition parties in many countries screaming for retribution. Some of the most radical have already started calling for nuclear strikes on us. It's already being called an unprecedented 'worldwide genocide' that an American thrust upon the world."

Cooper exhaled loudly; his left hand ran raggedly through his black hair, while his left grasped the countertop until his knuckles turned white, "Jesus. I didn't see that coming." He shook his head once, as if to clear it.

"Yeah, me neither. On the domestic front, it's similarly bad. There are renewed outbreaks of violence and rioting. However, they've shifted from happening near medical and food facilities to anything that is government related. Hell, the funniest has been a report of a firebombing at the U.S. Patent office!"

"I wish I was in the mood to laugh, because that *is* ridiculous,"

Cooper intoned. "How's *our* government responding?"

"As you might expect. They are denying any knowledge of the events in question, promising a swift investigation and severe and unprecedented punishment if they discover a shred of truth about the allegations against Admonitus and the Mr. Ethan Mitchell."

Cooper's eyes grew quizzical, "They haven't announced that he's dead?"

"Nope. But, you'd better be happy about that!"

"Why?" Cooper asked.

"Haven't you thought about it? They'd tie it to you and add murder to the list of charges against you."

Cooper's face went slack in surprise, "I hadn't thought about that. I guess I didn't think of a lot of things that might happen by telling the world the truth." Inwardly, he cursed himself for not having thought it all through. A wave of dizziness hit him and his arm cast about until it found a wall to steady himself with.

Dranko watched him and waited until he was all right before going on, "Well, friend, you can be impulsive sometimes. But, that's why you have me around, to worry about all the angles for you!"

Cooper's smile returned to his face, "Thanks, brother. But, you are the ugliest nursemaid I've ever seen."

"Funny." Dranko quickly held up his hand. "Oh, I almost forgot. The President is holding a full press conference in about a half hour about all of this, too."

"Really? Well, we'll have to tune in," Cooper said, as a wry grin spread across his face. *I wonder how they will try to spin themselves out of this one.*

****

The sharp rap of a cane against his door interrupted Dranko's response. Cooper walked to the door and before he could call out, a raspy voice shrilled from outside, "Let me in Cooper, or I'll have to blow your door down!"

Cooper and Dranko exchanged bemused smiles. Lily Stott's voice was unmistakable and the old woman's wit and wisdom were legendary in the neighborhood. Her reputation had only grown since the outbreak of the plague.

"Coming ol' darlin'," Cooper said, doing his best to mimic Lily's accent from her native Kentucky.

He opened the door and her diminutive frame greeted him, as

did her expansive personality, "Ya know, if I was a few decades younger...or you a few decades older, that accent just might get me into a friendly way with ya, Coop." Her piercing blue eyes lit up as she lilted the last few words.

Cooper couldn't stop the blush that ran into his cheeks and he flashed a smile at his embarrassment, "Lily, I know you didn't come over to charm me, so what can I do for you?"

"I came here for this," she said as she rapidly closed the space between them and wrapped Cooper into a tight embrace. It was far tighter than he would imagine an eighty-something woman could pull off. He burst out laughing in surprise.

"What's gotten into you, Lily?"

She held him in the bear hug for several seconds longer. Cooper cast a "help me" gaze at Dranko, who only smiled in return, arms crossed.

"You're on your own, brother. I ain't crossing swords with Ms. Stott," he exclaimed.

At that, Lily released him, "Oh, fool's feathers, you young boys can't handle something you ain't planned or predicted, can you?" She stepped back from Cooper so she could look him directly in the eyes before continuing, "*That* was to thank you for what you done. Paul told me this morning it was you who sent the world the truth about this terrible thing. Plain and simple. What you done was right. And, I know it didn't come easy to go on and tell that truth."

Cooper shrugged nonchalantly, "You know me, Lily. After what happened to my dad, I can't do anything *but* tell the truth." He choked on the last word, as he did every time he was reminded of how deceit had destroyed his father's life. As a boy, he had watched his father wither away in prison, put there by the lies of other men. That wrenching experience had led Cooper to a life of absolute honesty; even in the most difficult of situations.

"Pig doodles! Don't hand me that. You coulda *kept quiet.* I seen you do that, Cooper, because that ain't the same as lying. At least to you it ain't. I believe the good Lord would take a different view. No offense," she said waving her hand dismissively.

"None taken. That's true, I thought about just keeping quiet. I thought about it quite a bit."

"I bet you done. So, don't try to shirk off your hero name tag. I'm planting it on you. And, you know what?"

"What?"

"You know me. Once I aim to do something, it sticks like a

dried up bug's wing to flypaper!"

Cooper and Dranko both laughed at that, "I won't even try to deny the truth of that, Lily."

"Alright, so thank you for telling us what really happened. It was mighty difficult to swallow, with so many dying and it being done *on purpose*. That is a bitter pill to choke down," her voice rising to mimic that of a Southern preacher on Sunday. "But, it says so in the Bible, 'the truth shall set you free', so what you did was the *only* thing a righteous man could have done. Yes indeed, Amen!" She clapped her hands in exultation as she finished.

"Well, you're welcome," Cooper said awkwardly. "I don't feel heroic or righteous. I just did what I knew I *had* to do to wake up feeling right about myself and my boy." His eyes gazed into the distance as he talked, "People deserve the truth, even when it's tough to hear. In fact, when you think about it, that was a problem in the country before the plague...no one wanting to tell unpleasant truths."

"You're right about most regular people. But, people like me were always telling you all the truth about what might happen. You just didn't want to hear it," Dranko contravened.

Cooper pushed him with an open palm in the chest, "Can you give it a rest? How many more times do I have to hear some version of 'I told you so' from the great Paul Dranko? Sometimes, I think you helped Mitchell out just so you could be right about *one* of the versions of the end-of-the-world you were always spouting off about." He turned to Lily, "Can you help me put a stop to this and give *my medal* to Dranko instead? I think it might shut him up!"

Dranko pushed him back, "Alright already, I made my point and you made yours. How about we leave it there?"

"Good enough for me," Cooper returned.

Lily wagged her head deliberately back and forth and moved to the door, "You two remind me of my boys, always bickering like they say old women do. But, take this as the truth, when it comes to fussin', you boys are far worse than the worst of any withered up old women I ever did see!" She exited the house and took deliberate care descending his front steps. When she reached the bottom, she looked back, "You all have a good night now, hear?"

Cooper gave her a warm smile, "Sure thing, Lily and thank you for stopping by. You are very kind."

Lily just nodded her head and ambled off back towards her home. Cooper closed the door and turned to Dranko, "So, we can fire up my radio in a little bit and listen to the President?"

Dranko stepped towards the door, "Better yet, come over to my place. I can get it up on the computer most likely."

"Your internet is still working?"

"It is. I don't know how much longer, but my satellite link up is still working its magic."

"Okay, I'll be over on the hour."

Dranko opened the door, left, and then shut it.

Cooper decided to spend the remaining time with Jake before listening in to the President's message.

****

Later, they'd gathered at Dranko's place. Cooper, Dranko, and Jake huddled in his basement room where Dranko had stockpiled all manner of communications equipment over the years. When they'd arrived, Dranko had surveyed the spectrum for their benefit. He had old vacuum-tubed radios that could survive the Electro-Magnetic Pulse he feared would eventually happen from a nuclear device detonated above America. He had several solar and hand-cranked radios that could operate without batteries. However, his most elaborate set-up was reserved for the myriad of ways he could stay connected to the Internet: satellite, cable modem, and satellite phone topped the list. Dranko's small battery of stockpiled weapons had enabled the neighborhood to defend itself during the chaos thus far. Now, Cooper was thankful for his friend's communications equipment that had allowed him to spread his message to the world about the Brushfire Plague and, now, listen to the President's response.

The familiar podium and Seal of the President greeted them as Dranko secured a live streaming telecast of the speech over the Internet. Cooper tuned out the familiar greetings and the platitudes of sorrow the President offered his fellow Americans. His ears literally perked up when he got to the meat of the speech:

"In this trying time for our nation, a time of horrendous loss for so many, a time of unfathomable grief, a time when the strength of our country is being tested like never before, I first want to share that the hopeful rays of God's mercy are shining once again. That's right, my fellow Americans, the first signs that the scourge of the Brushfire Plague is finally abating."

"I receive briefings from the Centers for Disease control three times daily. It pleases me beyond measure that over the last forty-eight hours, those briefings have told the same story: both the infection rate

11

and the morbidity rate from this terrible plague have been falling steadily. In short, this means that the number of those becoming infected is falling. More importantly, the rate of those who do contract this disease and then die from it is declining rapidly. At the conclusion of my remarks, Dr. Charles Holmes, the Director of the CDC will speak to the specifics. But, the layman's version is that the virus is mutating to a less lethal form. These developments mean great hope to those who are now sick, and even greater hope that our nation has passed through the darkest hour of this devilish calamity. Rest assured, we will be monitoring this situation carefully, but the best medical minds are confident that this trend will continue."

The President paused as his face turned from one filled with hopeful and sympathetic lines to ones far grimmer. The transformation was slow, subtle, but complete. Despite himself, a riot of goose pimples erupted across Cooper's body.

"However, amidst this moment of enormous hope and guarded relief, I must also respond to a new threat to our great nation. Most of you have probably seen the scandalous and unfounded reports spread across the Internet and some irresponsible media outlets that the Brushfire Plague was no accident. That it was *intentionally started* by a company called Admonitus, based in Portland, Oregon. Yes, I know, my fellow Americans, it is a shocking allegation that is beyond the pale." Cooper felt the others' eyes on him as the President recalled Cooper's email to the world's media detailing the devastating truth that he had learned about the genesis of the Brushfire Plague. The email sharing Mitchell's darkest confessions.

"I want to assure you all that once this administration learned of that frightful rumor, we launched a full scale investigation to determine its veracity. In the reports, you may have also heard that my administration was *aware* of this diabolical plan *and* possibly assisted its implementation."

His face grew angry, dark lines outlining his eyes and his jaw firmly set with muscles twitching, "You may only guess how outraged I was when I first heard of this nonsensical drivel. But, let me state plainly, and for the record, *no one* in my administration knew of such a plan, if it even existed. It is an affront to the honor of my family that such a thing has even been uttered. My family has suffered losses, as well. We were not spared from the death that has spread across our nation. It is incomprehensible to me that any madman *would* have done this on purpose. But, I swear on the word of God, that my administration had no warning of it nor did we enable or abet any such crazy plan."

"We have found no evidence, thus far, that this plague was intentional. But, our investigation will continue, and we will transparently share with the American people any, and all, results that we learn. As I talk to you, officials are on the ground in Portland and we are moving to secure the offices and facilities of Admonitus and the home of its CEO, Ethan Mitchell."

"I wish to say to my fellow Americans, and our neighbors around the world, *America* did *not* start this terrible plague of biblical proportion. *We*, as a nation, did not do…or even conceive…of any such thing. And, I promise you, if we learn that a crazed man or a company led by a madman *did* this, the punishment will be swift and unprecedented. You can know *this* as truth!" He pounded his fist against his desk with a loud thud.

"Now, let me turn to our efforts to track down the origin of these dreadful rumors. The potential harm of these unfounded reports is already evident. Sadly, they have already sparked attacks against innocent government officials and the wanton destruction of property. For that reason, our efforts to track down who started these vicious rumors are being conducted under the auspices of the Patriot Act and this is being treated as an act of terrorism against America."

Once more, he paused for effect. "This decision was not taken lightly, as we deeply value the right of Freedom of Speech within my administration. However, the spreading of these unconfirmed reports at a time of great trial for America *is* a dangerous act. Already, this rumor has resulted in violence upon the innocent. I'm sure that the decent and God-fearing people of America will agree with me that the threat to our shared national security posed by these lies trumps any right to free speech."

The camera now zoomed in further, almost imperceptibly, but the effect was dramatic. Cooper felt the hair on his neck rise. "I wish to announce that we have a person of interest in this investigation. Our evidence indicates that this person may know about, or have been directly involved in, a series of dreadful acts including the killing of Mr. Ethan Mitchell, the CEO of Admonitus. Most importantly, we believe this person is responsible for spreading panic and violence by proclaiming these irresponsible — and unfounded — allegations. This person of interest is Mr. Cooper Adams, of Portland, Oregon."

The President's words sucked all the air out of the room where Cooper, Dranko, and Jake sat. Silence engulfed the room. Both Jake and Dranko looked at Cooper in shock.

"As you might imagine, prior to this crisis, we would have this person in custody before I would make such an announcement. However, our resources are already taxed beyond heroic measure and I refuse to allow the apprehension of this person to take precedence over tending to the greater, and more immediate, needs of our nation. I am coordinating efforts with the Governor of Oregon to apprehend Cooper Adams and to bring him in for questioning. In the meantime, I urge anyone with information on his whereabouts to contact their local authorities. I also wish to remind my fellow Americans of their power to make a citizen's arrest in the event they encounter Cooper Adams and can secure him until the authorities arrive."

Dranko let out a low whistle, "Christ, Cooper. He just declared open season on you!"

Cooper's face gave Dranko a sharp rebuke as he inclined his head slightly to remind his friend that Jake was in the room with them. Dranko continued undeterred, "I know you don't want to hear this, but we need to get out of here. As soon as they can get themselves organized, they will be coming for you."

"Dranko, we've been through this before. I won't leave my home. It's all I have left of Elena."

Dranko sprung to his feet, "Cooper, don't be ridiculous! *This* changes everything. Hell, yes, we've survived against some teenage hoodlums, some disorganized thugs, and even that squad of National Guarders. We've been far beyond lucky! Tell me you think we can survive the full weight of the U.S. Government, even if they are disorganized and weak right now!"

Cooper stood in turn. His own head was swirling in shock at hearing the President call for his arrest to a national audience, "Damn it, Dranko. Just give me a minute before you start telling me what I *have* to do!"

Dranko knew his friend's lack of outright rejection was his best chance, "I'm sorry, brother, but I have to tell you because you need to think straight right now. You know what I'm talking about! They are figuring out how to land a couple Blackhawk helicopters on your front lawn and send a couple teams of Navy Seals to round your ass up! If the world wasn't a stinking pig pile of shit, it would've *already* happened."

His words deflated Cooper and he sank back into his seat, "Damn you Dranko! How can I leave her?" Cooper's head came to rest in his hands.

Now, Jake jumped up, "We can't leave mama! We can't!" His

shrill words, laced with grief as his eyes filled with tears, cut both men to the bone.

Dranko took a step back and his voice calmed, "I know it's hard, for both of you. But, Elena would want you to both live. *She wouldn't want you to sit around waiting to be taken by the government and put into a prison...or worse.*" His eyes pleaded back and forth between Cooper and Jake for understanding.

Before either could respond, loud banging on Dranko's front door caused both men to look upward to the basement stairs and reflexively reach for the pistols on their hips.

Cooper welcomed the interruption, "Stay here," he directed Jake. Dranko nodded to Cooper, drawing his .45 caliber pistol to show he understood what he wanted. Dranko barred Cooper with his left arm to prevent him from going first. Cooper drew his own pistol and they began ascending the stairs. Cooper's body tensed, as his mind raced trying to figure out who was at his door. *Could someone already be coming for me after the President's speech? Had some new threat emerged against their neighborhood?*

When they reached the main floor, the pounding had not let up. Dranko moved silently to a side window and looked out. He caught Cooper's gaze and mouthed, "Gus." Cooper breathed a sigh of relief learning that it was Gus Varela, a lawyer who lived in the neighborhood, and not someone more dangerous.

They both put their guns back in their holsters as Dranko opened the door.

Gus' face was red and contorted in rage, "Damn you," he shouted at Cooper as soon as he saw him. Gus tried to bull rush towards Cooper. Dranko quickly overcame his surprise and threw an arm out to bar him.

Cooper welcomed his own anger to push back the confusion Dranko had aroused in him earlier and he moved forward, to put his own face inches from Gus', "What the hell do you mean, Gus?" Cooper deliberately let scorn drip off his name.

Dranko strained under Gus' weight to keep the two men apart. "What the hell do I mean? Why the hell did you put all those lies on the Internet?"

Cooper's rage flushed higher at being called a liar. His arm shot up and caught Gus by the throat, "They *aren't* lies you dumb bastard. It's the truth. Every last word of it!"

Gus choked as he gasped for air. Cooper's firm grasp prevented him from speaking, but he rasped out, "Le...t...me...g...go!"

Cooper waited until Gus' face went from crimson to the first shades of purple and then he abruptly released his grip.

Gus gasped for air and would have collapsed to the ground, but for Dranko's arm catching him, "Breathe in. Take a deep breath, you'll be fine," Dranko said.

Cooper stood in front of him, defiantly, and offered no such words of comfort. A minute later, Gus recovered and stood up straight again. He glared at Cooper, but made no effort to close the scant gap between them. "I don't care if it's true or not. It's either lies or its truth we'd all be better off *not* knowing."

Cooper stared straight back at him, unyielding, "People deserve the truth!"

Gus shook his head, "Not, this. Don't be such a damned naïve Boy Scout! You've caused a lot of damage with what you've done. *More* people are already dying because of what you said!"

Cooper glared at him.

Gus strained once more against Dranko's arm, "Well, we can stop debating this. But, one thing isn't open for debate. You better get the hell out of our neighborhood!"

Cooper exploded, "What the hell are you talking about?"

Gus assumed a self-assured tone, "What I mean is plain. You are now a clear and present danger to our neighborhood. You are going to have to find a new place to inhabit."

"Inhabit?" Cooper said, digesting what Gus had just said.

Then, Cooper lunged at him. Dranko shifted his body to keep the two men separate as Gus backpedaled in surprise, "How dare you! You pompous fat bastard! *I'm* the one who kept you all safe the last few weeks! I ain't going nowhere!"

Gus shook his head and his lips curled up in derision, "We'll see about that!" He retreated down the steps, being careful to keep facing Cooper as he did so. Finally, he turned and walked quickly back towards his own home.

Dranko turned to his friend, "See?"

Cooper just shook his head, "Aw, shut up, will you?" Despite his words, a chill ran down his spine as he realized that anyone might turn on him now. He knew the truth would be hard for the world to hear, but it was dawning on him that even those who knew him well might now become an erstwhile ally…or worse. He turned and made his way back toward the basement where Jake was waiting for him. Dranko paused, shaking his head, and then followed his friend downstairs.

****

The trio spent the next hour making small talk and listening to Dranko's Ham radio. Dranko pensively wrung his hands. Cooper knew he wanted to talk about the dangers facing him now, but that discussion led to only one conclusion: leaving his home. He reflexively dismissed the idea, so he avoided the topic.

Then, the radio caught his attention.

"...reports, reliable ones, have filtered in about the dangerous rise in gang activity. In Detroit, Cleveland, Los Angeles, New York, Boston, and several other cities, gangs are engaging in outright control of entire sections of the cities in question. With the loss of central authority, organized criminal enterprises are filling the gap..."

"I'm glad we haven't seen that here," Cooper intoned.

The corner of Dranko's mouth curled upward, "Not yet, anyway."

Cooper smiled, "That's right Mr. Sunnyside, not yet indeed!"

"I'm just sayin'...it can still happen here. When you think about it, it has already started."

Cooper's eyebrows drew together, "What?"

"Look at the craziness in Sellwood. Hell, they nearly burned the whole city down! Then there's the Vietnamese Protection Society that we talked to. He's getting organized. And, I worry about that church around the corner."

Cooper nodded, "OK. You have a point with the Sellwood and the Vietnamese group. But, they haven't started taking over and running parts of the..."

"But, they damn well could if they wanted," Dranko interjected. "You've seen their firepower. They're organized when so many are not. What's stopping them?"

"No, you're probably right. What's stopping them is Michael Huynh is more interested in profit than power."

"That's true, too," Dranko returned.

"Now, what do you mean about that church?"

"I just mean that any organized group is going to have power now. Gangs are criminals organized with guns. Churches are people organized and bonded together tightly by faith. They may or may not have guns. Most, from the reports I've heard, are doing good with it. Keeping people fed, helping with security, organizing self-help between people. But, right here, we have that one around the corner is using their access to food to win converts, right?"

"Yeah. Despicable," Cooper spat the word.

"I agree. But, those kinds of things are happening, too. All I'm saying is that, throughout history, some churches have used access to resources, like food, to expand. And, sometimes, conversion has come at the end of the blade of a sword…"

"Or, the barrel of a gun," Cooper finished the thought. "Yeah, I see what you're saying. I agree, we will need to keep close tabs on the other organized groups around. Let's hope that Mr. Huynh stays focused on making money in a semi-legitimate way. And, let's hope our churchgoers next door keep their proselytizing based on the reward system."

Dranko nodded gravely.

"What's that?" Jake asked, cocking his head to the side.

"What's what?" Cooper responded.

"Don't you hear that?"

Dranko moved quickly and turned off the Ham radio. Then, they heard it.

Muffled shouts coming from outside. Seconds lingered as they struggled to make out what they people were shouting. Then, one word hit Cooper as clearly as if it was being shouted out from inside the room.

"Fire!"

Cooper was to the stairs and rocketing up before Dranko had reacted. Then, he and Jake bounded up the stairs in his wake.

****

Dranko's door banged on its hinges as Cooper flung it open and leapt over the front steps. He landed harshly, letting his knees buckle to absorb the shock. He swiveled his head toward where the crowd was shouting from.

His throat tightened when he saw the group gathered around his house. In slow motion, his head kept turning until he saw the black smoke billowing angrily skyward.

"No!" Cooper yelled in fury as he raced towards his burning home.

He quickly rounded the corner. Several neighbors were racing toward his home, buckets and containers of various origins in hand. Mark Moretti, one of his friends, was using his home's garden hose to spray the flames.

As he ran headlong toward him, Mark saw the determined look

on Cooper's face and handed him the hose as soon as he came up.

"I'll go and get the neighbor's hose going," Mark shouted.

Cooper nodded and concentrated on dousing the flames before him. He breathed a sigh of relief as he realized the fire was, so far, confined to his small detached garage.

Seconds later, Mark brought a second hose to bear and Cooper realized they would get the fire under control before it spread to his house.

Out of the corner of his eye, he spotted Dranko and Jake running across the street to join the makeshift bucket brigade that was coming together.

Within ten minutes, the fire had been put out. As Cooper relaxed, he surveyed the scene. A messy mixture of steam and smoke curled lazily upward from his wrecked garage. The structure was a mishmash of undamaged wood alternating with boards scorched black by the flames. From the heat, most of the paint had blistered or peeled. Then, his gaze fell to the base of the garage. Like a diamond amidst a coal miners' convention, a glistening object jumped out and grabbed his attention.

A mostly melted glass bottle lay broken in half at the foot of the garage.

His heart raced and rage filled his veins as he clenched his fists. "Molotov cocktail," Cooper muttered vehemently to himself before realizing that Dranko and Jake had come to his side.

"What's that?" Jake asked.

"It's a bottle filled with gasoline," Dranko answered.

"You mean someone *wanted* to burn our house down?" Jake asked incredulously.

"Yes, son."

"But, why?"

"Because some men are too weak to handle the truth," Cooper fumed.

He turned to the group of neighbors still clustered about. "First, thanks everyone for helping me get this thing out. This sure looks intentional," he said pointing at the glass bottle. "Did anyone see anything?"

"I saw a white pickup full of teenagers racing down the street just before I saw the flames," Mark offered.

"You've got to be kidding me," Cooper said, remembering the trouble he'd had with Woody and his ragtag band of teenage troublemakers in the first days of the outbreak. After they had broken into his home in the dead of night, two had left humiliated and forced, by Cooper, to carry their dead friend home. Apparently, they had not been chastened enough. *Or, maybe just emboldened with the President calling me out by name.*

At the edge of the crowd, having just walked up, Gus weighed in, "Yeah. Those teenagers coming back is a pretty dangerous thing for our neighborhood. And, it looks like they came for you."

Cooper glared at him, but Mark responded, "Does it matter? We defend each other here. That was our agreement when all this started."

Unrepentant, Gus continued, "It matters if things have changed so much that one man endangers us all."

"What do you mean?" shouted an anonymous voice from the group.

"Didn't you hear the President? Cooper here has told the world a tall tale that the plague was deliberately started by a man hell bent on crashing the world's economy as a way to stop global warming. He's also said the government knew about it and did nothing to stop it. Just an hour ago, the President declared Cooper a liar and asked for the nation's help in bringing him in for questioning."

Gasps and exclamations emanated from half the crowd who had not heard the news yet. Mark was one of them. "Is this true, Cooper?"

Cooper nodded gravely, "It is true, except it isn't a tall tale. Everything I've said is true. You all know me. Tell me you've ever heard me say anything but."

His challenge was greeted with silence.

"Nonetheless, others will be coming for you Cooper. You've put us all in grave danger!" Gus barreled onward in his attack.

Mark turned on him, "Maybe. But Cooper's also the one that's kept us alive so far!"

"Old news," Gus' words dripped with scorn. "This is a new reality now."

"You know, maybe Gus is right." Michelle's voice was soft, but her words sounded to Cooper like they'd been shouted through a bullhorn.

"What?" Dranko's response was flustered.

Michelle spread her feet, standing firmly, "It's not just that Cooper has become a danger to us."

"What do you mean," Mark asked.

"Well, if the government knew Cooper was here in our

20

neighborhood, I bet we'd all get attention and protection from them," Michelle kept her tone flat, but her eyes betrayed a dark and sinister look that shook Cooper to his core.

Mark's reaction shocked him in the other direction. He pulled his pistol and pointed it directly at Michelle, "And, if anyone turns Cooper and Jake in, it will be the last thing they do."

Gus gasped. Michelle took a jagged step backward and fell to her knees.

A dark hand took Mark's into his own and slowly lowered the pistol; the President of the Neighborhood Association and recently elected neighborhood's Captain of Defense, spoke up, "Look. That *is* enough from both of you. I am the chief of security, so let me worry about that. Let us all either help Cooper clean up or go on home. And, *no one*, is turning anyone in. We clear?"

Gus and Michelle slowly nodded.

Cooper gave Calvin a look of appreciation and then turned toward the larger group. When Cooper surveyed the crowd, what he saw disturbed him. Up until that point, the group had looked at him; eyes laden with respect. Now, in at least half of those eyes, he saw fear. Gus and Michelle had poisoned the well and it was spreading outward. *I'm a threat now. Worse, I've become an opportunity.* It was glaring how few people stayed behind to help clean up. Cooper shook his head in disappointment as he went to find a shovel.

****

A few hours later, as they were almost done cleaning up the debris and salvaging what they could from the fire, Dranko put his hand on Cooper's arm and motioned him away from the group. Cooper looked up in surprise, but followed.

"How bad is it?" he asked his friend.

"Well, I'm glad no one was hurt, but I lost most of my tools. Our bicycles and fishing gear, too. Stuff that will be hard to replace now," Cooper responded, as he absentmindedly cleaned his soot-blackened hands with a rag.

Dranko shook his head, "Sorry, brother. This shouldn't have happened."

Cooper chuckled, "I couldn't agree with you more."

"I want to bring up a sore subject," Dranko said, his eyes pleading with Cooper.

Cooper stared right back at him, "Yeah, I know. And, the

answer is still no."

Dranko's eyes flashed, "Are you kidding me, Cooper? Your name has been on the wire for less than an hour and you've already been attacked! What do you think tomorrow is gonna bring? Or, the next day?"

Cooper spread his feet and straightened up defiantly, "I can handle some teenage punks. I did last time."

Dranko's eyes rolled, "Really? What about when the military finally has enough resources to come and *get* you? Yeah, we got lucky and took out those two HUMVEEs. What about when they send in a Bradley or a *tank* for God's sakes!"

"I'll figure it out," Cooper glared.

"Haven't you noticed that, already, half of the neighbors are now *scared* of you, too?"

Now, it was Cooper's turn to roll his eyes, "Sure. But, the ones that count, their eyes haven't changed."

Dranko paused for a moment, thinking. Then, he grabbed Cooper harshly by both shoulders and only inches separated their faces, "What about him?"

"Who?" Cooper asked him, confused.

"Jake. You know, in your foolish, stubborn, quest to keep him in this house, you are going to get him killed. Just as sure as it rains all year round in Oregon, you're going to get him dead!" Dranko shouted the last words and spittle flew onto Cooper's face.

Cooper pushed Dranko back so hard that he stumbled backward and slammed into the fencepost behind him. "Now, you listen to me! I *can* handle it!" Cooper's voice strained with desperate emotion and Dranko knew he was trying to convince himself as much as Dranko.

He pursed his lips, "You're wrong, Cooper. I know you. You're not thinking straight. You had to *know* the world was gonna come down all around you the moment you hit 'send' on that email! I just assumed you knew that you and Jake would have to go on the run!"

He gave him a blank look.

Dranko pounced, "You've got to be the silliest optimist in the…"

Cooper punched him in the shoulder, "Look, damn it! Yeah, I thought about it. I know it will be rough. But, I think those who can handle…or want…the truth can help me stay safe. Hell, I expect a CNN truck to roll up here any minute. You think the military can just come and get me with that kind of scrutiny?"

Dranko cocked his eyebrows, unimpressed, "Yeah. I do."

"What?"

"Brother, don't you remember Waco, Texas? The feds rolled in on those guys with the whole world watching."

Cooper shrugged his shoulders, "Ah, hell. This is different. I ain't holed up in some compound with a bunch of kids. I told the world about the biggest crime in the history of mankind."

Dranko looked back, unconvinced, "We'll see if your vaunted CNN truck shows up before the next attack does."

"Yeah, we'll see."

"At least stay over at my house tonight. Just to be safe."

Cooper eyed him for a moment, "Sure. That makes sense. Thanks."

"And, one more thing," Dranko said, his eyes twinkling mischievously.

"What now?"

"After it's dark, drive your truck around the block and leave it at the far side, in between here and the barricade. If anyone does come looking for you, maybe they will think you've flown the coop."

Cooper scratched his chin, "Not a bad idea. My car is already on the south barricade, so moving the truck makes sense."

Trying to lighten the tension, Dranko made a display of making a deep bow, "Glad you recognize my genius, kind sir!"

Cooper welcomed the overture and chortled, "Brother, there's a long way from an idea that isn't moronic to genius status. Just be happy that today you're a couple steps above idiot."

Dranko smirked, "See?"

"See what?" Cooper asked, confused.

"Once in my life, I try to be optimistic and see things just a tad better than they are and you just go and shoot those dreams all to hell." As Dranko finished, he mocked a wounded tone.

Cooper didn't miss a beat, "Hey, I'll encourage you to be optimistic every day of the week. But, when it comes to your mental prowess, it's a wide gap between optimism and just plain losing touch with reality!"

Dranko's hands clutched to his chest and his face pantomimed pain, "You wound me!"

"Well, I'll see you tonight if you do not succumb to your grievous wounds!" Cooper turned on his heels and left, chuckling to himself.

****

"Wake up!" Dranko's breath was hot and urgent as he whispered into his ear.

Cooper, instantly alert, sat up in bed and began reaching for his boots, his eyes pleading for an explanation.

"Your house. It has company. I saw four men, maybe more. In civilian clothes, but they move like they are military."

"Damn!" Cooper cursed.

His boots laced, Cooper rousted Jake who lay sleeping next to him in Dranko's guest room. Jake's eyes fluttered open as Cooper motioned for him to remain quiet. "I need you to get dressed quickly and then wait here for me." Jake nodded and went into motion.

Cooper followed Dranko to his living room where they could get a good view of the front of Cooper's house. He saw multiple figures moving around his home, securing the perimeter. Like Dranko, he counted eight men, likely an equal number deployed around the back, where he could not see. Movement caught his eye from the shadows across the street.

As it registered, his hands balled into fists and a fierce scowl slashed onto his face. Venom dripped, "Gus."

In the shadows, he could see the unmistakable portly figure of Gus Varela standing next to another man, dressed in dark clothing, pointing towards Cooper's home. Moments later, Cooper almost ducked when Gus' finger shifted and pointed towards Dranko's house.

Next to him, Dranko exhaled, "Bastard."

Cooper's vision returned to the activity in front of his house. "They are planning to breach," he whispered to Dranko.

"Yup," his friend agreed.

Cooper wasted no time and returned to where Jake was waiting.

"Son, gather your stuff. From Dranko's back yard, I want you to make your way to the third backyard up the street, away from our house. Then, go over that fence to the backyard behind that one. There are no dogs between here and there, so you shouldn't be noticed. Then, huddle in your sleeping bag and wait for me or Dranko. Got it?"

Jake stared at him with wide eyes and nodded. Only his father noticed they weren't nearly as wide as they were just a few weeks back. *He's getting used to this chaos.* Cooper's insides protested against the necessity of it.

"Don't come out 'til morning if I or Dranko don't come for you.

And, you *will* hear gunfire. But, you wait. You hear me?"

Jake nodded, more firmly this time, "Just one thing."

Cooper eyes grew quizzical, "What?"

"Don't die. Please," The innocent sincerity in Jake's eyes stunned Cooper and his knees nearly buckled. He grasped his son's shoulders as Jake's eyes filled with tears.

"I'm not planning on it, son." It was the best he could offer his son in the way of comfort and still tell the truth. "I don't want to, but I gotta go. And, you need to get moving!" Cooper swatted his son to spur him into action. He threw his bulletproof vest on, grabbed his rifle and a bandoleer full of ammunition and ran out. He felt as if he'd left his heart on the floor for abandoning his son.

Angela and Dranko met him at front door, Dranko apparently having awoken her. When they abandoned Cooper's home for the night, Angela had joined them. They were kitted up and ready to follow him into battle.

Cooper saw them and emphatically shook his head, "You wait here."

Both Dranko and Angela shot him furious looks.

"After they find out I'm not home, one of three things happens. They leave. We get into a firefight. Or, they come here looking for me. If it's a fight, join in. If they come here looking for me, you can tell them I hightailed it out of town after the attack today. Got it?"

Angela and Dranko nodded.

"What are you going to do?"

"Watch. But, if it's a fight, there are two people that won't survive it."

"Who?" Angela asked.

"Their commander and that traitor lawyer, Gus Varela." He spat the man's name as his lips curled into a baneful snarl.

****

Cooper closed Dranko's back door quietly just as a furious banging came from his home a few doors down. *They'll make a racket up front, but breech from the back.* He'd learned enough of breeching tactics to guess that.

He circled behind Dranko's house, so that he could exit from the far side and minimize his chances of being seen by the commander or Gus. From the backyard, he saw Jake's backside slipping over the fence into the neighbor's yard and then out of view. When he reached the opposite side of Dranko's house, he heard the battering ram smashing his back door. He imagined the team moving into his deserted home, clearing each room. It would only be a minute before they had swept the house and learned he was not there.

Cooper went prone and crawled forward, until he was at the front of Dranko's porch. He inched his rifle out, sighting in on the commander, still standing out in the open next to Gus. He was relieved to see the man did not appear to have any night vision equipment with him. He silently chambered a round.

Moments later, the commander put a finger to his ear and listened intently. Cooper expected he was getting word that the house was empty and his men were asking for instructions. The commander conferred with Gus, who quickly pointed toward Dranko's house. Although his cover was good, Cooper couldn't help sliding even lower behind the porch and plants.

The commander was mid-sentence when the first shots rang out from behind Cooper's house. The shotgun blast followed by a single rifle shot told him it was the people from their neighborhood patrol who were firing first.

He quickly eased out half a breath and fired at the commander's groin; hoping to avoid his body armor. When he crumpled to the ground, he knew he'd hit him somewhere good.

Cooper shifted his aim and rushed a shot where Gus had been standing. To his surprise, Gus had reacted quickly and disappeared from view. *Moved fast for a big man.*

The cavalcade of gunfire from the rear of Cooper's house told him all he needed to know. He only heard the sharp pops of 5.56mm rounds being fired. The absence of a booming retort of a shotgun or the deep roar of a hunting rifle's round made it likely the pair on patrol lay dead or, at best, wounded. Then, silence, filled the night.

Cooper kept scanning for any sign of movement from the commander or of Gus Varela. To his left, he heard Dranko's back door open and close. Seconds later, he saw Angela and Dranko take positions on opposite sides of the driveway and then crouch down. The seconds drifting past felt like an eternity. Cooper practiced breathing deeply and scanning the street in front of him from left to right. He saw Dranko make some hand motions to Angela and then she moved toward the back of his house once more. *Dranko must be guarding against them coming across the backyards towards us.*

Just then, two figures scurried across the road, running toward the commander. Without thinking, Cooper fired and dropped one of them as his .308 round found purchase. The man was sent sprawling onto the pavement and his rifle clattered across the asphalt. His partner took two more steps and then dove for cover near where the commander lay.

The men covering this pair opened fire in Cooper's direction. Bullets stitched across Dranko's lawn, clods of dirt and grass were flung into the air as angry rounds landed around him. Cooper knew they were laying down suppressing fire because they didn't know exactly where the shot had come from. Thankfully, Dranko was outside their line of fire. On the other side of the street, the man who made it across joined the fray. The front of Dranko's house took his abuse. Wood splinters rocketed out as the man methodically pockmarked the doorway with gunfire.

Just as methodically, Cooper sighted in on him. The man was obviously well trained because he presented very little in the way of a silhouette to target. Cooper took what he could and fired. The man disappeared from view, but Cooper didn't know if he'd hit him or if he'd just scampered back behind the half wall that shielded most of his body from view.

This shot brought a renewed fury of gunfire at him. Now, the men had a better idea of where he was. Bullets impacted very close to him and he heard the whine of several just over his head. Cooper scooted himself behind Dranko's porch to take cover.

He heard Dranko fire a controlled burst, but couldn't tell who he was shooting at. A flurry of gunfire responded and Cooper hoped his friend had found cover. Then, silence descended once more upon the night. He waited a while before pushing himself forward, past Dranko's porch, to survey the scene. He could see Dranko crouching to his left. The street was empty; the man he'd shot previously had either moved off or had been carried away. Likewise, the commander's body was gone. There was no sign of the men.

Dranko motioned for Cooper to come to him. Cooper switched to a crouched position and moved quickly towards him. Angela arrived just as he did.

"What's the situation?" Cooper asked.

"I think they've moved out. After they lit my position up, as I came back up from cover, I saw the tail end of them disappear down the road."

"Makes sense that they would try to be surgical."

"I hope," Angela began but Cooper cut her off with is hand. He cupped his other hand to his ear, to tell the others to listen. From down the block, the deep-throated roar of an engine came to life, revved, and then faded as it moved away from where they were.

"Must have parked outside our barricades and infiltrated through the yards," Angela observed.

"Right," Cooper agreed.

"Good thing you stayed at my place, eh?"

"Sure thing. But our excitement isn't over yet."

"What?" Dranko asked.

"I need to pay a visit to Mr. Varela."

Dranko nodded but looked chagrined, "You won't find him home, I bet. No one is that stupid."

"I know he ain't stupid, but I'm hoping fear will overwhelm him and have him panicked. He did just see someone shot right next to him. That can take the stuffing out of a lot of people. Scared people make dumb decisions all the time."

"I won't argue that," Dranko intoned. "Let's go, then."

The trio moved out. They searched his house from top to bottom, but found it empty. Coming back outside, there was no sign of him, either. The oddest thing that struck Cooper was that no neighbors had come outside of their homes after the gunfire had ended. *Did they know? Or, did they see that it was focused on me so they don't care?*

Cooper retrieved Jake, who he found curled up shivering in his sleeping bag in the neighbor's backyard. His eyes were wet, but they alighted with relief when he saw his father's face.

Taking precaution, the group joined the northern barricade until dawn.

They called out to the guards as they approached the barricade while giving the coded sign that the neighborhood used and that changed every few days. Mark and Freddie were there and they answered their rapid questions about what had happened.

"We wanted to go see what the hell was going down, but we know our job is to stay on the barricade, no matter what," Freddie said excitedly. Cooper could tell Freddie was stressed because typically, the young man in his twenties could barely breathe without telling a joke or performing some antic to make others laugh.

"Your discipline was spot on," Cooper said, still thinking about the many that had *not* come out to help, but weren't constrained by duty like Mark and Freddie had been. Cooper stroked his chin and his stomach felt empty realizing that the world was shifting under his feet yet again.

****

When the sun rose and fought in vain to pierce the gray clouds that were so common in Portland, Cooper and his group gathered away from the barricade.

"Let's survey the damage at my house and then we need to pay Gus another visit," Cooper commanded more than said.

They moved down the street, weapons at the ready. As they neared his home, he saw spent shell casings scattered about. He picked up several and noted they were all the same caliber, the size used by the military.

The front door had been battered off its hinges and the frame splintered. His house struck him as a man missing his two front teeth. Jake let out a gasp when he saw it. Cooper clenched his jaw.

He steeled his voice, "Let's clear the house to make sure it's empty." He chambered a round and Angela and Dranko did the same. He motioned for Angela to stay with Jake on the front lawn as he and Dranko entered the home.

They stepped over the front door that was lying on the ground and noted muddy footprints scuffed across the floor. They moved from room to room, being careful around corners. Dranko had once explained to him how to 'pie' the corners to minimize your exposure while you searched a building. He let Dranko take the lead in doing so. The two quickly fell into rhythm moving through the house. They moved through the front living room, then the dining room, before coming to the kitchen. The back door, which led into the kitchen, was also knocked off its hinges and lay sprawled on the floor. A burn mark in the middle of the room was evidence that a flash-bang grenade had been thrown inside. Fury surged within him, seeing his home violated like this. He grunted and tried to push it aside. Within minutes, the rest of the house was cleared and they moved back to the front lawn.

"Worse than being burglarized," Cooper said, as they gathered once again with Jake and Angela.

"A burglar just comes to steal something. These guys game to steal you," Angela said. Cooper just stared at her, nodding slowly.

"We were lucky they tried the stealth mode first. That gave us the fighting chance. Next they will come in with a tank or an armored vehicle of some kind. Or, maybe a damned Blackhawk!," Dranko added.

Jake's face flashed in alarm and Cooper gave Dranko a stern look. "But, your dad is too smart and too good for these bums,"

29

Dranko offered quickly.

"And, we were lucky they sent in some second-rate crew. These guys didn't have night vision, for example," Cooper added.

Dranko nodded slowly, "That might also explain why they *didn't* roll in with tanks. Not sure they have them on hand. I think they are stretched beyond belief with what Brushfire's wrought."

"I'll make some breakfast while you guys clean up. Jake, do you want to help me?" Jake nodded to Angela in response.

A half hour later, Cooper and Dranko had managed to reattach the front door and enable the door to close, albeit awkwardly. Angela and Jake offered up an equally awkward breakfast of beans, canned fruit cocktail, and crackers. A pot of weak coffee completed the repast. They had barely begun eating when Gus' voice assaulted them.

"Coo-oo-per! Come out!"

Angela fumbled her coffee cup, spilling some of it. Cooper's fork crashed against his plate as he threw it down in rage and disgust, "That bastard!" He leapt to his feet, grabbing his rifle and made a beeline to the door. Dranko and Angela were quickly on his heels.

Cooper nearly tore the hastily rebuilt door from its hinges as he flung his door open, weapon at the ready. What he saw shocked him.

In front of him, stood Gus. A smug look lashed to his face. Behind him stood about twenty of his neighbors, armed, with hostile eyes glaring at Cooper. The shock at seeing such a crowd arrayed gave him a momentary pause. The contrast with the prior times he'd stood on his stoop and addressed his neighbors, guiding them through their fear or instilling hope, struck him to the core. He stopped in his tracks.

Gus saw the muzzle of Cooper's rifle pointed at his stomach and he waved his hands, "Calm down, Cooper, we just came to talk!" Cooper heard the fear in voice in marked contrast to his earlier shouted orders.

Cooper grimaced and barreled into Gus, pushing him backward and off his front steps. Gus backpedaled and barely kept his balance.

"What's this about," Cooper called to the crowd, ignoring Gus.

No one spoke, but instead, heads turned to Gus.

He recovered more than his footing, "Don't play dumb, Cooper. You know what this is about. After last night, you are a clear and present danger to this neighborhood. So..." Cooper's glare made Gus choke in fear.

"So...what," Cooper dared.

Gus coughed once, "So, you need to leave."

Cooper's wry grin unnerved Gus, "Oh, yeah?" His grip tightened on his rifle as a fulsome rage burned inside. "And, what are you gonna do when I say no?"

Gus steadied his feet, "Well, the good people gathered here are hoping you will be reasonable."

Cooper laughed aloud, "Reasonable? Do you mean reasonable like when I've risked my life over and over again to save this neighborhood?" Cooper noticed how half the group looked ashamedly at their feet while the other half tightened their hold on their weapons.

Gus was unfazed now, "Cooper, I know I speak for everyone when I say how much we appreciate what you've done for all of us. But, even you must admit that what has bound us together in this time of crisis has been our mutual desire for safety. It's not any of the prudent people here's fault that you are *now* a danger to that very security." Many in the crowd nodded enthusiastically at that.

Cooper shook his head, "Damn, you're good, Gus. I'll give you that. You know how to tell the people just what they want to hear." He directed his attention back to the group, "So, these cheap words from a lawyer are going to absolve your consciences of putting me and my boy out of our home? Is that all it takes?" Not a single pair of eyes would meet his gaze as he scanned the crowd while talking. "Well, guess what? I have a better way of keeping your consciences clear. I ain't leaving."

"Damn you, Cooper! This isn't our fault. You brought this on yourself! We have to protect our children — those that are still alive!" The voice from the back of the crowd belonged to Michelle Jamison, a homemaker who had lost one of her three children in the plague. Her voice cracked as she finished and tears ran down her face.

"So, you want to throw me out because I told the truth to the world? Told the truth to *you*?"

"Whether your words were truth or not, only time will tell. But, what is clear right now is that you've brought untold danger to us all," Gus fired back. A brief silence hung in the air.

Then, Cooper heard it. A sharp metallic click, followed by another, as someone chambered a round on a bolt-action rifle. Instantly, his rifle was to his shoulder and flashed across the group. Behind him, he heard Angela and Dranko doing the same. In front of him, half the group fumbled with their weapons because of fear while the other half shouldered theirs without hesitation.

Gus moved frantically to the side, to get out of the line of fire. He flashed his palms up, open, "Calm down, calm down, everyone."

Cooper shouted, "Lower your weapons, now!" Very few in the crowd complied. Seeing their neighbors still keeping their weapons trained on Cooper, they quickly raised them once more.

"Cooper, please. Be reasonable," Gus pleaded.

He pointed his rifle directly at Gus, "You say that word 'reasonable' one more time, Gus, and I will blow you to hell, so help me God!"

From the corner of his eye, he spotted Calvin Little rushing down the street. The President of the Neighborhood Association was unarmed, save the pistol he wore on his hip.

"What is this? What is going on here," he shouted as he came up.

"Gus here and this...ah...lynch mob are telling me I need to move out of my home," Cooper answered first.

"What?" Calvin asked, in surprise.

Gus turned to face him, "We're doing this for everyone's safety, Calvin. Surely you understand that, as the neighborhood's Defense Captain?"

Calvin continued to move through the crowd until he stood in front of Cooper, "Yes, Gus, you are correct. I take security seriously. But, if anyone wants to drive Cooper from his home at gunpoint, they will have to shoot me first. This is not how we do things in *our* neighborhood."

Cooper tried to conceal his shock at Calvin putting himself in harm's way to protect him. Calvin's words had many in the group looking at one another in confusion. The seconds ticked by.

"Goddammit! Lower your fucking weapons!" Calvin exploded. It was less the vehemence of his words, but more the shock of the normally well-spoken man using profanity that commanded compliance. *I'm not sure I've ever heard him swear, Cooper marveled to himself.* He lowered his weapon first, and slowly, everyone else did, too.

"Good, that is more like it," he said and turned to Gus. "Look, you want to discuss Cooper's residence here, we will do it properly. Let us have a meeting here at five o'clock today. *That is* how we make decisions here. Not like *this*," his infused the last word with scorn.

Cooper took a long look at his neighbors, including a few who he would have called friends. At best, he saw fear in their eyes directed towards him. Among the worst, he saw fear and hatred. He took a deep breath and shook his head in disgust, "I'll save you the damned trouble. Jake and I will be leaving. And you, Gus, can go rot in hell."

Gus reacted to Cooper's pointed finger as if he'd been shot.

Cooper turned sharply on his heels and brushed past Angela and Dranko. Dranko's mouth was agape in shock.

Chapter Two

Cooper paced his living room in silent fury. His fists were balled and a dark glare adorned his face. Angela and Dranko followed him inside, looks of disbelief still plastered across their faces. They watched Cooper for a long while.

Finally, Dranko broke the quiet, "What happened, brother?"

Cooper looked up at him for a moment, eyes still burning. He wilted under his stare. Cooper inhaled deeply, and then fought to control himself as he spoke. Still, the rage laced every single syllable, "Those sons of bitches out there, that's what. Seeing them turn on me like that. How *dare* they?"

Angela moved to him and put a hand on his shoulder, "This isn't about you, Cooper. They are scared. Scared people do stupid things, you know that."

He shirked her hand off, as if it burned him, and continued striding around the room, "Screw that. I kept these people together. I risked my ass for them. How can they forget that so quickly?"

"Angela's right. You could have been Christ Almighty and they would've done this, given how scared they are. Hell, the people *did* turn on Christ, too," Dranko intervened.

"Whatever. Bottom line is, I don't want to stay here. I don't want Jake to be around people like this. You just can't trust people," Cooper's shoulders slumped, as hope melted away from his words.

Dranko stepped in front of him and grabbed him by the shoulders, "C'mon, Cooper. You just can't trust these people, right now. Fear is driving them. But, you *can* trust us."

Cooper glared, "Yeah, I know I can trust you two. As for the rest, you are too kind. If these people would turn on me at the first sign of trouble, how can you trust them? Ever?"

Dranko laughed, "Damn, brother, you sound as negative as I normally am!"

Cooper stared back, "A man's true character comes out in crisis."

Dranko turned serious, "Your father would never have said what you just said. You know better. Don't go all dark and negative on us!"

"My father," Cooper began, but then stopped himself. "No," he said shaking his head. "You're right. My father took people through a lot of struggles and they hung together. But, this. This," he stammered. "I just don't know anymore."

"Just take your time and let it sit. Let's focus on getting ready to leave," Angela said.

Cooper nodded and refocused, "Yeah, you're right." He turned back toward Dranko, "Your cabin still have a vacancy sign out?"

A wide grin opened across Dranko's face and he clapped his hands together once, "Finally! The man talks sense. Yes, of course. We will be infinitely safer out there. Especially now."

Cooper stopped short, covering his face with his hands.

"What's the matter?" Angela asked.

His voice choked with emotion, "I can't believe these bastards are forcing me to leave. To leave my home, to leave Elena." He sat down on the couch, hands still shielding his face.

Angela glided down next to him and put her arm around him, "We know it's hard. But, you'll carry your home, and Elena, in your heart no matter where you are." Cooper dropped his hands and rubbed his chin with his left hand, nodding once, slowly.

Dranko looked him in the eye, "Brother?"

Cooper met his gaze. Dranko went on, "Yeah, this sucks. But, you of all men know that the truth often carries a high price."

Cooper nodded, "Yes, it does." He rose from the sofa, "I've got to go tell Jake now." He took several deliberate strides across the room and then turned his head over his shoulder, "Then, we need to get ready to leave."

****

He found Jake reading a book in his bedroom. He looked up when his father opened the door.

"I heard," he said, his face somber.

Cooper moved to his bed and sat down next to him, "What do you think?"

"I'm sad."

"What are you sad about, son?"

"Leaving mom," he said as his eyes filled with tears.

Cooper put his arm around him, "Yeah, me, too."

"It's like losing her again. We won't even be able to come back and visit her here, will we?" His little body wracked with sobs.

Cooper pulled him closer, "Not for a while. But someday, I hope we can." He choked back his own tears, "But, we can see her

36

every day, right here," he pointed at his heart.

Jake folded himself into his father's chest and hugged him tightly, "I know, but I want her here, with us."

Cooper hugged him back tightly, "I do too, son. I do, too. She was the best woman I've ever known. And, God, I loved her more than any man has loved his wife."

Jake pulled back to look at his father's face, "I know, dad. I could tell. She was the best mom." A new round of sobbing took him and he buried his head in Cooper's chest again.

They held each other, as Cooper rocked him slightly back and forth.

"We will take pictures, too, as many as you want."

Jake wiped his tears, "I'm angry, too."

"At what?"

"At our neighbors. I was at the window. I heard all of that, too. How could they?"

Cooper stiffened, "They are scared."

"And stupid," Jake nearly shouted.

"Yes, stupid too. Scared people do stupid things sometimes, son. In fact, they usually do," he chuckled.

"I hate them!" Jake's voice echoed across the bedroom's walls and his hands balled into tiny fists.

"Yeah. I don't blame you."

"We have to get ready to leave, don't we?"

"Yes. Yes, we do. Today."

"Damn them," Jake cursed.

"Hey, it's okay to be angry, but I don't want you using language like that," Cooper mildly rebuked him.

"You talk like that when you are mad."

Cooper smiled, "You're right. But, I shouldn't. I want to raise you better than that."

Jake stood up, "Why? It doesn't matter anymore. The world's screwed."

"Now, watch it," Cooper looked sternly at him.

"Why? I gotta carry a rifle. I gotta be scared all the time. I've had to be ready to kill people. There isn't school anymore. My friends are probably all dead. My mom's dead. You could die any day. What the hell does it matter if I say damn? Or shit. Or fuck!" Jake's voice reached a loud crescendo as he finished.

Now, Cooper stood up and grabbed him by the shoulders. He lowered himself so he could look directly into his son's eyes, "You wanna know why? Yes, the world's gone to hell. But, *we* don't have to go to hell along with it. The true test of a man…and, yes, you're having to become a man much sooner than is right or fair…but the true test of a man is how he acts in crisis. How he acts when things are hard. I want you to hold onto as much of your childhood as you can. So, how you talk *does* matter."

Jake looked back defiantly, "If I have to become a man now, why can't I talk like a man?"

"First, not all men talk like that. I'm not proud that I do. Second, your mother wouldn't want you to talk like that."

"She's dead," Jake said flatly.

Cooper raised his voice and spoke urgently, "Yes, she's dead, alright. But, do you want to honor her memory and live up to how she raised you or throw that all down the drain?"

Jake recoiled at that and paused. His eyes burned looking back at Cooper. After several tense seconds, he took a deep breath, "Okay. I will try."

"That's all I ask, son. Try not to let this world ruin what your mother raised up. We *have* to hold onto as much of that…of all of it…as we can."

Jake nodded, stepped in, and hugged his father again.

"Cooper, someone's here to see you," Dranko's voice rang from the other room.

Cooper pulled back from Jake, "C'mon. Let's see what this is about."

****

Cooper and Jake walked down the hallway, back to the living room.

Calvin stood waiting for them. He stood over six feet. His dark skin and solid nature conjured an image of granite for Cooper as he looked upon him. Their relationship had started out very tense during the first days of the plague, but Cooper had formed a deep respect for the man. After Calvin's actions this morning, his respect had grown to admiration.

"Thank you, for that," Cooper said in greeting him.

"It was the least I could do. Gus was smart enough *not* to tell me about that gathering he organized. Fortunately, I received word."

"Just in time, I think," Cooper returned.

"Yes. Just. Pack of fools."

38

"I couldn't agree more."

"So, are you really leaving?"

"Yes, we are. I don't think it's a good idea to stay here now. Frankly, I don't want to. It's clear too many would leave me hanging. And, to be true, I wouldn't raise my rifle for too many of 'em anymore."

Calvin nodded in understanding, "Where will you go?"

"Somewhere safe," Dranko responded, still unsure of the other man's intentions.

"Is there room for one more?" Calvin asked.

Cooper's face fell open in surprise, "What? You want to come?"

"Yes I do, if you will have me. I do not have anyone here, and after what I saw this morning, I am disgusted."

"You are surprising the hell out of me," Cooper said, laughing.

Calvin remained serious, "It should not surprise you. I respect what you have done by risking everything to tell the world the truth about this plague and how it started. Besides, it is clear things will be bad for a while and it is more important than ever to be around people you can trust."

"And, who are handy with a rifle," Cooper joked.

"Yes, that, too," Calvin smiled.

"Well, it's beyond fine with me for you to join us. But, it's Dranko's place," he said, turning to his friend.

The corner of Dranko's mouth upturned, "Let's see. Lily's coming, too," as he began counting on his fingers.

"Lily?" Cooper quizzed.

"Yeah, she came by while you were talking to Jake. Her son is out in Estacada."

Cooper nodded, allowing Dranko to continue. He dropped the charade of counting, "Of course, it's fine with me. I wasn't looking forward to trying to get that AK-47 back from you, anyway," he said, laughing.

Calvin grinned, "That part was simple. You could have had it when you had pried it from my cold, dead fingers!"

Dranko smiled for a second, then turned serious, "One thing you should consider, Calvin, where we're going, there are very few people who are....well...umm...not white."

Calvin looked at him in disbelief and then burst out laughing, "Really, Paul? I have lived in Portland a long time. Going from seeing my fellow black folks once a week to maybe once a month will be an adjustment I think I can handle."

The others fell in, laughing.

As it subsided, Cooper grasped his hand and pulled him into an embrace, "Thank you." After the tense morning, Calvin's support washed over him, like a tonic. The two men exchanged a warm look of camaraderie.

"We need to make a list of what to take with us and get moving on packing," Dranko said as Cooper and Calvin separated.

Cooper turned to him with an impish grin, "I'm guessing you have such a list typed up and ready to go?"

Dranko looked back sheepishly, "I do have something we can work off of for this situation."

Cooper burst out laughing, while wide smiles graced the faces of Angela and Calvin, "You do think of everything, don't you? I bet you had a list ready to go even before the outbreak of the Brushfire Plague, didn't you, you sorry bastard?"

"Sure as shit, I did! And, if you don't like it, sue me…once the courts open up again, that is."

"Oh, I like it. It just cracks me up that you are ready for everything; including fleeing your home," Cooper returned.

"That's funny, because I think it's absurd that you'd live in the Cascadian subduction zone and within range of Mount Saint Helens and you *haven't* thought about how you might have to leave your home for an extended time!"

Cooper cocked his head to the side, "Point taken. Why don't you grab your list and we can all meet back here in five minutes and divide up responsibilities for the gathering and packing?"

The group nodded in agreement, as Dranko moved toward the door to exit.

****

When Dranko returned, he had a copy of his list for each of them. They gathered around the large oak table that dominated Cooper's dining room. He distributed the lists and each person began intently reviewing them.

"You will see that the list is divided into sections by the Survival Triangle," Dranko began. Noticing the blank stares that looked back at him, he hastily added, "The Survival Triangle is a basic concept in being prepared to survive natural disasters or other breakdowns of normal life. There are three major things you need to stay alive: food and water, shelter, and a means to protect yourself and your supplies."

Cooper nodded, "That makes sense. We should go through this list and identify if one of us has the item, who is on point to get it, and any changes or modifications we need to make as we go through it, right?"

Everyone indicated agreement and Dranko added, "This list was also designed for a unit of four people. Given we have five, we will have to make allowances."

"Let's try and double things, just to be safe," Angela offered.

"I agree, that is a good idea," Calvin answered. Cooper and Dranko nodded, as well.

They set to work and began the tedious task of reviewing the list and taking assignments. Not surprisingly, Dranko already possessed most things on the list. They agreed that Angela would help Dranko gather the items on his list, since it was much longer than everyone else's.

The discussion over which firearms to bring, and which to leave behind, quickly turned into a debate. Dranko kept pushing for 'caliber standardization'; meaning that their weapons should all use the same ammunition to make supplying them easier. Cooper argued strongly for a wider variety of weapons so that they had the 'right tools for different situations.' After ten minutes of back and forth, Calvin offered a compromise that everyone was satisfied with. They would standardize on two rifle calibers: 5.56mm for the battle carbines that most would carry and 7.62 for the FAL that Cooper carried and two hunting rifles that could double as poor man's sniper rifles in a pinch. For pistols, they would standardize to the common 9mm round, except Cooper insisted on retaining his pistol that fired the fast moving, and penetrating, .357SIG round. Finally, they agreed to bring three shotguns that fired the ubiquitous twelve-gauge shell.

"This means I'll have to swap out the AK-47 for one of the AR-15s, right?" Calvin asked.

"Actually, we can swap it for an M4. After we had defeated those soldiers who attacked us before we hit Ethan Mitchell's place, I distributed one M4 to each barricade, but I kept four on hand in reserve. I haven't had time to distribute them."

"What's an M4?" Jake asked.

"It's what our soldiers carry. It's an updated version of the M16," Dranko answered.

Cooper stroked his chin, "So, we can easily take those four M4s without even having to argue with the neighbors about it?"

"I think so," Calvin answered.

"That will be some good firepower to have on hand as those are selective fire," Cooper added.

"Selective fire?" Angela asked.

"You can fire it semi-automatic; one pull of the trigger means one bullet downrange. Or, you can put it on 'burst' fire and one pull will send three bullets at the bad guys," Cooper offered. Angela and Calvin both nodded in understanding.

They continued reviewing the list until Calvin had a question, "Paul, you have on this list not one, but two, portable bucket toilets. With only five of us, why take up the space of having two?"

Dranko smiled, "It's a little gross, so I'm glad we aren't doing this over breakfast. The reason for two is that if you keep your liquid and your solid waste separated, it doesn't stink as bad as when you mix them."

Calvin let out a deep laugh, "Yes, that is gross. But, I agree, it's worth having two on hand!"

After the laughter subsided, Angela asked a different question, "I'm noticing that for so many things...water and water purification...things to start a fire with...tools...first aid supplies...your list has at least three different things that do the same, or similar, things."

Dranko's face lit up, "Good observation. When you are getting prepared for providing for yourself, there's a saying that 'one is none, two is one, and three is best'. It just means that if you only have one way to provide something, you are screwed if you lose it, so at least have two ways to do things and, hopefully, three."

Angela smiled, "Wow. I guess *that's* prepared!"

Dranko shrugged his shoulders, "If you're gonna do something, you might as well do it right. And, truthfully, it's not usually that hard to have a back-up or two. I'll give you an easy example. Take having the ability to start a fire. Some guys I know have a lighter, waterproof matches, and then some expensive fire-starter piece of gear. Me? I just bought a bunch of packages of cheap lighters and spread them throughout all my gear. Plus, I have two good lighters that will work in the wind. I carry one on me all the time and the other is in my vehicle. I feel pretty confident that I will *always* be able to start a fire, as long as I have fuel available."

The others were staring at him, "None of that sounded simple, but we'll take your word for it," Cooper said.

They continued down the list. "Holy shit, you have night

vision," Cooper exclaimed when he saw that on Dranko's list.

Dranko frowned, "Sadly, no. I never got the funds together for that. It's very expensive, but *very* good to have."

"*What* are you guys talking about, please?" Jake interjected.

"Sorry. Night vision is equipment, either a scope on a rifle or like binoculars, that lets you see at night," Cooper explained.

"Wow, that sounds cool," the boy exclaimed as his eyes lit up.

"Trust me, I wish we had it. It can be a huge advantage, especially now with the electricity out. The nights are *very* dark," Dranko said. He stroked his chin, "When the lead starts to fly, and if one side has it and the other doesn't, it's a true force multiplier."

Cooper pre-empted the next question, "That just means something that doesn't just add to the effectiveness of your force, but *multiplies* it." His eyes drifted for a moment, "Like when Hank Hutchison used that light machinegun when those HUMVEEs attacked us."

Angela nodded and looked askance at Dranko, "I appreciate the translation, Cooper." Dranko merely shrugged in response to her acerbic gaze.

The team agreed to use Cooper's pickup and Dranko's Jeep Wagoneer as their vehicles for the trip. They would also take one of the motorcycles to use for scouting duties. No one was surprised when Dranko produced maps with three different routes to reach their destination. Everyone agreed that roads would likely be a mess as everyone had heard various reports over the last few weeks about people attempting to flee the plague by heading for the rural areas.

"We need to leave in four hours. I'm worried about another attack," Cooper said as the conversation winded down.

"We know what we need to do. It is time to get to it," Calvin added.

****

The loud clang of metal hitting metal made Cooper whirl around from his pickup bed, where he had just finished loading a box full of foodstuffs. His pistol was in his hand and at the ready.

Angry steam hissed from the cracked radiator from a late model BMW that had crashed into the "No Parking" sign in front of Cooper's house. He scanned the inside of the vehicle for potential threats. The backseat and passenger seat appeared empty. The driver lay slumped over the steering wheel. Black hair flowed haphazardly over the driver's head, shielding the face from view. The muted sound of the crash told Cooper that the car had not been speeding when it crashed. In turn, he deduced that any injuries the driver may have were likely sustained earlier.

Cooper moved in a wide arc to flank the driver's side door, covering the driver all the while. "Out!" He yelled to the driver. The driver's head lolled briefly, but then came back to rest on the steering wheel. Cooper grunted in frustration.

He waited several seconds before suddenly moving adroitly to the driver's side door, jerking it open, and grabbing the driver by the shoulder. Still, the driver did not respond. Cooper, fearing injury to this individual more than to himself, pulled the driver slowly back from the steering wheel. The hair fell back to reveal a face soiled in blood. Some was fresh and running crimson, surrounded by splotches that were dried and dark. Cooper let out a gasp when he recognized the driver. Julianne Wheeler's eyes were only half-open and she appeared barely conscious. Even so, her eyes conveyed electricity to his own. He fought, and lost, against the tide of tenderness that washed over him.

He grimaced as he cupped her chin in his hand, "Julianne?" Cooper willed his voice to be steady, but unwanted tenderness leaked through. He immediately clenched his jaw and castigated himself.

Her eyes drifted open. Just like the first time they met, those large pools of brown drew him in and sparked something deep inside him. He saw the faintest flash of recognition across her face.

"Coo...Cooper? Is that you? Did I make it?" Her voice cracked with emotion and warbled in disbelief.

He knelt so he could look at her directly and holstered his pistol. He took her shoulders with both hands to steady her.

"Yes. It's me."

Jake appeared at his elbow, "What's going on dad? I heard the crash." Cooper turned to him and saw Jake stiffen as he recognized Julianne.

"Get me some water and bandages," Cooper commanded.

Jake shuffled his feet, caught between obedience and surprise.

"Now!" Cooper barked and Jake took a last look at him and then sped towards their home.

Cooper turned back toward Julianne and began inspecting her injuries more closely, "What happened?" Fortunately, the injuries were on the surface only and appeared grievous because the head and face bled so easily.

Julianne's eyes looked intently at Cooper as she gained lucidity, "Attacked. I was attacked. In my home."

Blood flushed up across Cooper's neck and face, "Who?"

"I don't know. I barely escaped. Only place…only person I could think of for safety was you." She looked up at him with glistening eyes. His heart filled with warmth towards her and her plight. She dropped her gaze and continued, choking the words out past a flood of tears, "They came to *kill* me, Cooper. The worst is…" she paused, gathering herself, and her body rocked in sobbing, "The worst is, I *deserved* it for what I've done." His emotions roiled, caught between the deep pull she exerted upon him, his sympathy for her, and the rage against the role she had played in unleashing the Brushfire Plague and the death of his wife. That she was overcome with guilt and now understood her folly undermined his anger as it readied itself to boil. After several long seconds of indecision, her deep grief overpowered him and he pulled her into a tight embrace to comfort her.

"Only God or someone much wiser than I, or you, knows if you deserve to die. You should not think like that," Cooper offered in the way of comfort.

She regained herself and wiped her hand to smudge the tears across her face, "I don't know. Part of me wishes I had just given up and let them kill me. The other part is happy to still be breathing and to be here," her eyes probed his. Then, she added, "To be here with you."

Cooper pulled back, "Don't talk like that."

Her anger met his, "You can't deny what connects us, any more than I can!"

"What connects us is that you helped kill my wife," Cooper yelled, grabbing her shoulders to tight that she grimaced.

Julianne jerked her shoulders to free herself and then slumped back into the seat, "You're right. I did." Her shoulders drooped and her eyes fell to the ground.

He tried to maintain his glare, but softened as long, awkward moments passed. Finally, he shook his head in frustration, "Look. I shouldn't have said that."

Her eyes met his once more, as he continued, "But, let me be clear. I don't want to speak of anything 'between us'. Do you hear me?" He demanded as he squeezed her shoulders and shook her body. Julianne heard, and Cooper resented, how his words were laden with the tones of desperation a man uses to convince himself of something he knows is not true.

"Yes, yes. I hear you!" Julianne shouted back at him. "Goddammit! Stop shaking me. It hurts!"

Jake arrived with a handful of rags and their first aid kit. Cooper softened his voice, "Let's get you fixed up. I need to finish packing."

****

The sky had clouded over as the day wore into late afternoon and a chill had returned to the air. Dranko's Wagoneer was in the lead position, with Cooper's well-worn pickup parked behind it. Absentmindedly, Cooper peeled a fleck of paint from its body, adding to the paint's losing battle against age. Jake stood right next him, angry eyes fixated on Julianne who leaned up against the tailgate. Jake had voiced his displeasure at his father's decision to allow Julianne to join. And, voiced loudly. Cooper didn't fully understand his decision. With desperately conflicting emotions about her, his sense of obligation had tipped the balance.

Angela and Calvin returned from his home with their armloads of gear to be loaded. Their steps hiccupped when they spied the stranger, Julianne. Cooper saw Angela's eyes flash in anger as she guessed who the mysterious woman was. They continued to the pickup and dumped their loads into the bed.

Calvin extended a warm smile, "And, whom do we have here?"

Angela crossed her arms, "I'm guessing, Julianne Wheeler, the right-hand woman to the man who *started* this whole mess?"

Calvin's eyes flew wide open and his mouth dropped open as his smile disappeared.

Cooper straightened up, "Yes, the very one. "

"And, I doubt it matters, but I'm very sorry for what we did," Julianne offered meekly.

"Sorry! You're damn right you're sorry! That's real. What, are we supposed to do? Forgive you?" Angela shrieked.

Julianne met her gaze, "I don't ask anything of you. I don't even have that right. I'm just telling you that the words 'sorry' or 'regret' don't nearly capture how I feel about what I have done. Most days, I just wish I was dead," her voice cracked as she uttered the last words. The depth of her sorrow was such that Angela's face shifted for a moment from rage to sympathy.

Angela turned to Cooper, "Please tell me you aren't thinking of

46

letting her come with us?"

"That's right. I'm not thinking about it. I've already decided. She *is* coming along."

Angela threw her arms down in disgust, "What? Are you serious? That doesn't make any…"

Cooper cut her off, "Look, she was attacked this morning. Nearly killed. Leaving her here is a death sentence and…"

"And just what is so wrong with that?" Angela interrupted.

Cooper glared at her, "It's wrong. I don't want it on my head. Her being dead won't bring anyone back."

"You put a bullet in Mitchell's head for what he did. Tell me how she's any different?"

"She just is," Cooper blurted.

"I see," Angela said, her eyes burning cold.

"You ain't saying the best reason to bring her along," Lily Stott's demure voice made them both turn in her direction in surprise.

"Yeah, what's that?" Calvin asked.

"I fear we ain't heard the last from the government types," Lily said and then stopped, smiling wryly.

"And?" Angela asked impatiently.

"Ms. Wheeler might know some things we can use."

"What if she doesn't?" Angela demanded.

Lily's smile grew to a shade just shy of sinister, "She'll make a good bargaining chip."

Julianne's face flushed crimson, while everyone else raised their eyebrows in surprise. Jake burst out with a loud cackle. Cooper didn't like what he heard in his laugh. "It sure is nice to be welcome," Julianne mumbled as she scrambled to the pickup's cab, got in, and slammed the door shut.

Angela stepped towards Cooper and jabbed her finger into his chest, "You're a damn fool, Cooper Adams. She ain't some stray dog. That woman killed your *wife* and millions more." Before he could respond, she brushed past him and deposited herself in Dranko's Jeep.

Dranko approached, carrying a rifle in each hand. Freddie was in stride behind him, also carrying two rifles. "I need to let you know that…" Cooper began.

Dranko waved him off, "Julianne Wheeler is coming along?"

"That's right, how'd you guess?"

Dranko grinned, "Two things. Even just catching a glimpse of her, I recognized her. Beauty like she's got is a rare thing. And, nothing else would get Angela storming around like that. *That* woman is *the* most unshakeable woman I've ever met."

Cooper shook his head, "I can't argue either point."

"I guess I should tell you that you picked up a stray and so did I. Freddie wants to come with us, too."

Cooper clapped Freddie on the shoulder, "Glad to have you! Thank you."

Freddie shrugged, "No need to thank me. I know who's held this place together. With you and Calvin going," he paused. "Well, let's just say I've always wanted to live in the booming metropolis of Estacada, Oregon!" The others laughed at Freddie's deft sarcasm in calling Estacada a city of any size.

"We about ready to roll?" Dranko asked.

"Yeah, I'd say so," Cooper answered.

Cooper saw Mark and Peter approach and nodded to them. "We wanted to say goodbye. Been on guard duty all afternoon," Mark called to him. They both wore easy smiles and had their rifles slung across their shoulders.

Cooper grinned, "That's real good of..."

His last words were drowned out by the sharp staccato of machinegun fire from the barricade to the north, the one Mark and Peter had just been relieved from. He watched their faces devolve into surprise, and then shock. Once again, the sound of HUMVEE revving motors was unmistakable.

Cooper began to lunge into a run toward the barricade when Dranko grabbed his belt to hold him back.

"Go! Cooper, go!" Peter yelled at him as he spun on his heels and unslung his rifle. Mark and Peter both ran back up the street from where they had just came.

Cooper and the others clambered into their vehicles. The motors roared to life as the sounds of gunfire escalated from behind them.

In his rearview mirror, Cooper caught a glimpse of a HUMVEE at the far end of the street, but it was growing rapidly in his mirror as it sped towards them. Dranko's tires squealed as he raced to the intersection and jerked the Jeep to the left. Cooper revved his motor and followed.

Machinegun bullets splintered the pavement to the right of his truck and began stitching closer as they sought their target. He shot another glance into his rearview and cursed in disgust.

Peter had run into the street and now stood in the middle of it without any cover. He was firing round after round at the driver of the

HUMVEE. It bore down upon Peter as he pumped rounds into the windshield, which was already pockmarked from previous bullets hitting home. Everything slowed as Cooper saw the machinegun pivot on its pintle mount and fire at Peter from a mere dozen yards away. Cooper marveled at how he simultaneously looked naked, exposed, and small against the hulking HUMVEE coming at him, but also heroic and larger than life standing his ground on the asphalt.

A burst of rounds from the heavy machinegun pulped him. His body twitched about like a shredded plastic bag in a gusty wind. Red clouds of misty blood peppered the air all around him. Then, the HUMVEE crashed into his body and Cooper heard the crunch of bones breaking. He fought the bile that rocketed from his stomach at such a horrible scene. He could see the HUMVEE's machinegun slowly searching for him once again.

Just then, the HUMVEE swerved to its right, collided with a parked minivan and rolled. That's when Cooper registered that Peter had not died in vain; he had killed the driver and enabled them to escape. The driver's side windshield was riddled with bullet holes and was painted red. As the first HUMVEE came to a screeching halt, it neatly blocked the road and prevented the one following from pursuing them.

Cooper cranked his steering wheel hard to the left to get themselves out of the field of fire from the second HUMVEE. He breathed easier once his house on his left shielded them.

He mumbled, "Thank you, Peter Garcia. *Thank you.*"

Out of the corner of his eye, he caught sight of Jake who was turned around in his seat and had seen the whole thing. His eyes were haunted, unblinking. Automaton-like, his body shifted back toward the front; his face frozen in shock. He stared off into the distance while a lonely tear descended down his left cheek. Cooper, in turn, stared at him in disbelief. His stomach fell out and he ground his teeth in frustration.

Damn this world to hell! Cooper cursed without uttering a word.

Chapter Three

Dranko had expertly guided the vehicles through the eastern barricade. He had waved at those remaining at their post, but their attention was consumed by the sounds of battle coming from behind them and they didn't see him. Once free of the obstacles, they drove at breakneck speed eastward on Division. Angela rode shotgun in Dranko's Jeep, while Lily and Peter sat in back. Next to Cooper, Calvin sat, cradling an M4 rifle. Behind him, sat Julianne and Jake; a look of shock still gripping his face.

"Keep a good lookout," Cooper said unnecessarily as they passed a burned-out minivan. Calvin grunted and tightened his grip on the rifle.

"If you are doing aimed fire, keep it on single-shot mode. Flip it to burst only if you are just spraying and praying," Cooper advised.

Calvin laughed, a deep baritone, "Can you please speak English to me? I did not serve in the Corps like you did!"

Cooper smirked, "That's Dranko who served with the wet boys. I was in the Army. But yeah, sorry, I just mean only use burst fire if you are trying to keep the other guys' heads down. Until you get used to it, one shot per pull is best if you're actually aiming."

Calvin nodded, "Alright, *that* I understand."

Dranko's Jeep took a sharp right onto 82nd Avenue, which was a major roadway heading south. From the news reports during the first days after the Brushfire Plague hit, they knew the freeway was hopelessly blocked when it had appeared that the entire city had decided on the same day to flee the plague by *getting out*. It had made the worst Los Angeles traffic jam look like a lonely desert highway in Arizona. Traffic became snarled on every lane, the emergency lanes, and the medians. Eighty-second had its share of abandoned vehicles, likely refugees from the freeway disaster, but it was still navigable.

"I think what saved us was that people waited too long to exit, and even those routes were blocked, and most people were trapped on the freeways," Calvin offered.

"You could be right," Cooper agreed. "Michael Huynh's group is headquartered not far from here. I wonder if they've kept this area cleared out, too."

Calvin recoiled at the mention of the name of the leader of the Vietnamese gang that Cooper had sought assistance from, "You mean gang? We shall see. As we go further south and away from that *gang,* we will see what happens to the roads." Calvin managed to pack a truckload of derision into just one word. Cooper would never forget how vehement Calvin had been in discussing the idea of having the gang assist them with security. The neighbors had deadlocked. *Of course, if I'd lost a brother to gang violence, I'd probably feel the same way.*

"That's true. We'll find out."

They drove on in silence for several minutes, winding their way through the abandoned, or destroyed vehicles, they encountered. *Looks like a war zone.* The vehicles alternated between those that had simply run out of gas or broke down and had been left, to those that had been burned, to those that were riddled with bullets. Too often, those were metal coffins, holding dead bodies, some of which had begun to decay.

When they encountered the first car with dead inside, Cooper told Jake to get down on the floor so he wouldn't have to bear witness.

This woke him from his torpor and he yelled, "Why? I've seen *everything* already!"

Cooper's heart broke at the words and the wounds they held. He stifled this and lowered his voice, "Just *do* it, son." Jake obeyed, but with a defiant look upon his face.

It pained Cooper to know his son was likely right. Suddenly, he felt exhausted, like the Dutchman trying to plug the holes in the dike without enough fingers *or toes.* As if he needed another reminder about his futile efforts to protect his son from the horrors all around them, they soon passed a Chevy sedan riddled from stem to stern with bullets. Inside, a woman at the wheel and two kids in the rear were dead from gunshot wounds. Decay had set in and, despite their closed windows, the foul smell found them. Seconds later, Cooper heard Jake whimpering. Julianne reached down to comfort him, but he slapped her hand away. She looked out the window and tears rolled down her face.

Cooper wrenched the steering wheel toward himself in futility and wished it would all just go away. Calvin offered a look of sympathy to Cooper. He appreciated the effort but realized it was as inadequate as trying to wipe with one square of toilet paper. *Thanks, but there's just too much shit for it to matter.*

****

A bit later, they all tensed up as they approached a mother and

52

two young children who were sitting on the curb next to a minivan. They looked dirty, and tired. Cooper imagined they were very hungry, as well.

"Keep an eye out, could be a trap," Dranko warned over the radio.

They parked their own vehicles about a hundred yards away and Cooper, Dranko, and Calvin approached with their weapons out and ready.

"What's going on?" Cooper called out.

The woman's head turned toward him listlessly, "Nothing."

The men looked at each other in confusion, but kept approaching. When they were within talking distance, the woman clutched her kids a bit closer. She looked up at the men facing her. Her face was dirty and tear-stained. Her eyes were sunken and hollow. *Already dehydrated,* Cooper thought.

"Whatcha want?" The woman queried belligerently.

"What happened to you?" Calvin asked first. Dranko drifted around to look inside her van.

The woman's head spun lazily from side to side, "What hasn't happened?" Her laugh was as hollow as her eyes. "I was just trying to make my way to my Aunt's place in Salem. I ran out of gas."

Cooper jumped when Dranko's voice thundered from the other side of the minivan, "Your van is full of crap! Toys and knickknacks! Where the hell is your food and water?"

His words roused her and she fired back, "It's our stuff, mister! Look, it's only a forty-five drive from here to Salem. How was I to know we'd get stuck in the worst traffic jam of the century?"

"By watching the news maybe," Dranko said sarcastically.

The woman stood up, unsteady on her feet, "Look, mister, I don't know who you are, but I don't want to hear it from you."

Dranko couldn't wipe the sneer off his face fast enough and she exploded, "We haven't eaten in three days. And that was only two cans of soup I got by having sex with some foul-smelling redneck who had less IQ than teeth. I can't even remember how long we been stuck here." When she finished, she collapsed onto the pavement and began wailing. Cooper noted how the children didn't even flinch at their mother's description of trading sex for food. *They either already knew about it. Or, worse, had seen it.* He shuddered at the thought.

Cooper began to motion to Calvin to get some food out of the truck for her, but Dranko's blazing eyes stopped him.

They retreated from the woman, Dranko still fuming, "How

53

could someone be that stupid? Setting out without any thought to food or water? Never mind gas!"

Calvin's voice was soft, "Look, Dranko, not everyone can adjust as fast as you when the world dramatically changes before their eyes." Dranko scoffed.

"She said it all. 'I had a forty-five minute drive'. She was prepared for *that*."

Dranko was undeterred, "That's just it. You gotta be prepared for when things don't go as planned. Hell, I had a 'get home' bag in my Jeep *before* Brushfire hit. But, seriously, to set off at the beginning of a crisis with *nothing* but toys, bobbles, and some clothes? It's amazingly stupid!"

They walked the rest of the way back to their vehicles in silence. When they drove past them, Cooper winced when one of the children looked up at him with plaintive eyes. He was looking at a little girl, probably eight or nine, with brown, dirty curled hair framing deep green eyes. With a washcloth and some soap, Cooper knew she'd be darling cute. Instead, he felt as if he was looking at a child's corpse. He damned Dranko and threw a protein bar he had on the truck's dash to her. The girl fell onto it like a ravenous wolf.

****

Dranko led them into the parking lot of a looted Home Depot and Cooper followed, wondering. The lot looked like a flea market and a demolition derby had been thrown into a blender, whirled around, and then tossed back out. Shattered cars and a plethora of discarded and broken goods competed for his attention. That's when he noticed it. The dead lay here, too. A limp arm, hung lazily from a Honda sedan. Crow-pecked. A woman lay sprawled across the black pavement, half her body underneath a minivan. She'd clearly been there for days and flies harried about her. The entrance had been riddled with gunfire and several men lay dead about it.

A whimper from behind made Cooper spin his head around. Jake's vacant eyes and gaping mouth told him the damage had been done. *Damn, how could I've forgot!*

"Son, lay down in the back seat there, please. You don't need to see this," Cooper's voice was soft, pleading, and miserable.

Trance-like, Jake folded himself into the seat. Julianne started when he placed his head in her lap. She recovered, and began stroking his hair gently. When she saw Cooper's look of surprise, she shrugged her shoulders to tell him she didn't know, either. Cooper shuddered to think about where Jake's mind had gone; that he would overcome his hostility toward Julianne enough to seek her comfort.

Dranko was at his window, rapping knuckles on glass. Cooper yanked his door open, "I'll be right back." He stepped out. Calvin joined him.

"Why' the hell did we stop here?" Cooper asked.

"Supplies."

"The place has been looted already."

"You wanna bet there are still good hand tools in there?" Dranko replied. "Electricity's only been out a few days. I'm guessing...and these bodies likely prove...that the looting happened before that."

Cooper nodded in understanding.

"So, that looting would have taken the high end stuff that works with electricity, like power tools and such."

"You got it. We might even get lucky and there might be a generator in there left over."

Calvin took a step closer, "I will come with you."

Cooper nodded, "Alright, why don't you take Calvin and either Angela or Freddie. I gotta stay here. Jake's on the edge."

"Right."

"But, be quick. Ten minutes until I come in after you."

"You are the optimist, brother. When's the last time you been in a Home Depot? You can't even get from the entrance to a freakin' aisle in ten minutes!"

Cooper chuckled, "That's true, but only by half. I'll give you fifteen. Any sign of trouble though, fire a weapon. One shot means come and help. Two shots means get the hell outta here. Got it?"

"I don't mean to show you up twice in one day, but why don't you just use this instead?" Dranko asked as he took something off the backside of his belt and tossed it to Cooper. "Channel's already set."

Cooper looked admiringly at the walkie talkie. "Nice. I must be slipping because I saw that on the list earlier!"

"Don't worry, I won't tell anyone about it," he smirked.

Dranko walked back toward his vehicle and Calvin followed. Dranko motioned for Angela to get out and Cooper watched as the trio moved towards the entrance, wary eyes on watch and weapons at the ready. Cooper saw Dranko talking to Angela and Calvin on the way, briefing them on his plan.

Cooper poked his head back into his pickup. Jake still laid, eyes closed, with his head in Julianne's lap. Cooper informed them of what was happening. Julianne's smile told him she understood, while Jake remained silent.

"I think he's asleep," she whispered.

"Probably for the best," Cooper responded.

Cooper grabbed his rifle from the front seat and cradled it as he stood watch, constantly scanning in all directions. With their force divided, the last thing he wanted was any hostilities now. The FAL, a rifle that fired the robust .308 round, felt reassuring in his hands. Every time he hefted it, he admired the quality design of the rifle and the good workmanship that had gone into it.

The creak of a door opening on Dranko's Wagoneer told him Freddie was getting out. Freddie paused, lit a cigarette, and came over to join Cooper.

"I didn't know you smoked," he commented.

Freddie laughed his infectious laugh, "I didn't, until all this started. I figure cancer is the least of my worries now!"

"You picked a bad time to start. Those are going to be hard to find mighty soon," Cooper said, a grin alighting across his face.

Freddie's cigarette bobbed up and down as he rocked onto his heels, "I suspect you're right about that!"

At the edge of the lot, Cooper saw him before he heard the rattle of a shopping cart on pavement. A homeless man was ambling in their direction, his cart burdened with goods.

"Keep your eye on our rear, in case he's a distraction for something else," Cooper told Freddie as he moved in the homeless man's direction. Cooper remembered reading somewhere, even before the Plague, that distraction was a favored tactic of criminals and con men. "And, make sure your safety is off," he added as he flicked his own to 'off'.

"Right, got it," and he heard Freddie's click, as well.

As the homeless man drew closer, Cooper squinted to get a better look. The man was in his sixties with a mane of gray hair flowing in all directions. A few moments later, he was surprised to see it was the same man that he, Jake, and Dranko had encountered on Hawthorne Boulevard several days ago. At that time, the man had been giving away bottled water and dispensing his own brand of wisdom to those he'd encountered.

"Well, I'll be," Cooper muttered to himself. Then, he called back to Freddie, who was now ten yards away, "I think I know this guy! But, keep a lookout still."

56

"All right," Freddie called back.

Cooper's walk became brisk until he'd closed to within twenty yards of the old man, "Howya doin'?"

The old man jerked his head up, as if he hadn't seen Cooper until just then, "Howdy to you, stranger," he said, stopping about fifteen yards from Cooper.

Cooper offered a broad smile, "We aren't exactly strangers. I believe we met a few days ago on Hawthorne, when you were passing out bottled water."

The man looked intently at Cooper, studying. Suddenly, his head jerked backward, "Oh, yes! I remember you. You had a boy with you, right?"

"Yes, I did. How are you? What are you giving out these days?"

The man's face grew long, "I'm afraid I'm back to what I'm more familiar with, asking for help, rather than lending it."

Cooper's eyebrows kneaded together, "What do you need?"

The man loosed a loud guffaw, "I need what no one is giving these days! A gun. That's what I need. Right after I saw you, I was robbed of my last few cases of water and the other meager things I had. I even lost my last picture of my darling deceased wife." He choked on the last words and wiped a dirty sleeve across his face to catch the tear that fell from his eye, smearing grime on his left cheek.

Cooper thought for a moment and then decided, "You taught us all a good lesson about charity. And, at the worst of times. I think I can help you out."

The old man's face alighted, "Really?"

"Yeah," he said and then directed his attention back to Freddie. "Grab that .45 we have in the supply box and a box of ammo for it, will ya?" He waited, watching the old man, as Freddie retrieved the items and brought it to him.

Cooper took the pistol, made sure it was unloaded, replaced the magazine into it and approached the old man.

"Here's a .45 pistol and some ammunition for it. Just don't try to load it until you're ought of sight. I'm sure you know this rifle has better range than this pistol, right?" Cooper said, only half-joking.

The old man took the pistol and the box, and then looked Cooper square in the eye, "Thank you. Thank you, for this." His eyes were misty.

Cooper's heart tugged, "No need to thank me. We have this one to spare. You deserve better than to be defenseless at a time like this. You've done good, and I'm sure you'll keep doing more good down the line."

The man's eyes grew distant and he paused for several seconds before responding, "I don't think anyone is 'good'. Especially these days. Darkness is always there and sometimes it's what saves you. Problem is, too many forget their light side." He paused, his free hand washing over the pistol as he thought. Then, his dark face turned bright once again, "But, I do thank you. I try to keep my ledger balanced out on the good side."

Now, it was Cooper's turn to contemplate for a few moments. He stroked his unshaven chin, fresh images of those he'd had to kill these last few weeks. He squinted to keep the emotions at bay as his thoughts drifted to what Jake had been forced to endure; some of which Cooper had ordered on him. "I think you're right about that, old timer. Hell, I had to ready my boy to kill so he could defend himself when this all started. I don't know if it gets darker than that."

"True. Darker. But, what lightens it is *what* you readied him to defend himself against was surely darker still. Right?"

Cooper nodded gravely, "Yeah, certainly."

"Then, forgive yourself! Those of us who are still holding our humanity in hand *must* survive. Otherwise, it isn't just our electricity and cable TV that goes *kaput*. No, then everything would go to hell on earth."

The corners of Cooper's mouth turned up, once more astounded by the old man's wisdom. Shaking his head, "I have to ask you. How did someone as wise as you end up like this?"

"Homeless you mean?"

"Yeah."

The man's eyes grew wistful, "I wasn't wise enough to stay away from the bottle, plain and simple. Well, not 'til I'd lost everything, anyway," he said as his eyes grew wistful, thinking of days past.

"Oh, you're sober now?"

"Yup. Proudly so. Do you want to know what's funny as all get out?"

"What?"

"My anniversary of being sober for one year was the exact day when the Brushfire Plague broke out."

"Really?"

"Ironic, ain't it? And, you wanna know what's funnier? I haven't had a sip of liquor *since* this all started, either. I like to think

God started this whole thing just to give me one more test to pass!" At that, he exploded in riotous laughter, doubling over and rocking back and forth on his heels.

Cooper couldn't help but laugh, too, "That is funny...in a crazy way...it's funny as hell."

The old man kept laughing for a long time, tears rolling down his face. Finally, he regained himself, "Thank you. I needed that. It *is* lonely out here. Worse than it was." He raised the pistol in his hand, being careful to keep the muzzle pointed downward, "And, thanks for this, too. I can't even tell you."

Cooper waved his hand, "Don't mention it."

"I should get going. I've bothered you enough and I see your friends are coming out now," he said turning and stashing the pistol into his cart.

"Sure. What's your name old timer? In case we meet again."

The man looked flummoxed for a moment before he beamed, eyes glinting, "You know something? No one ever asks me that anymore! It's Ed. Ed Sjowski."

"Mine's Cooper Adams," he said extending this hand. Ed took his hand and shook.

"You take care of that boy. And, be easy on yourself for the things you'll have to do to keep him alive."

Cooper locked eyes with his, "I'll try. You know I will."

Ed grabbed his cart and ambled away, continuing south down 82nd Avenue.

Dranko, Angela, and Calvin approached with a large dolly cart in tow. The cart was piled high with hand tools of all sorts, rolls of wire, and a shiny generator.

Dranko called out, "Is that who I think it was?"

"Yes. Yes it was. And I gave him that .45 we took off of Mr. Porsche."

Dranko shook his head, "While I'm sure you had a good reason. I wish you hadn't."

Cooper cocked an eyebrow, "I knew you wouldn't. But, he *needed* it more than we did. And, charity can't die. Even in times like this."

Dranko only grunted derisively and began loading the new supplies into the pickup.

Angela shifted her feet, "I don't even know the guy, but I agree with Cooper. We cannot abandon kindness. Otherwise, what *are* we surviving for?"

Calvin nodded his agreement, "My grandmother always said charity doesn't even count unless it hurts some."

Dranko just grunted even louder, "Speaking of charity, why don't you guys help me load this stuff up. We'll have room now, given that we're lighter by a pistol."

Cooper rolled his eyes in mockery at him, "Whenever you're being sarcastic, I know you aren't too pissed off."

"That's been the key to our success, *darling*. You just *know* me so well!"

They all laughed and then set to loading the supplies in earnest.

****

Minutes later, they resumed their path south down 82nd Avenue. He honked his horn playfully as they passed Ed, pushing his cart. Ed waved enthusiastically as they drove by. For a moment, Cooper's heart felt light as he recalled friendlier times before. The bleak road they travelled quickly tore that from him.

The road became successively more clogged the further south they went. Abandoned and destroyed vehicles blocked their path. Once more, Cooper ordered Jake onto the floor. *If this keeps up, he'll be living down there.* A Ford pickup was riddled with bullets, the driver dead and slumped halfway out of the shattered driver's side window. A Toyota minivan had been burned down to its metal frame and its occupants were entombed as grotesque charred husks. A Buick sedan had somehow flipped onto its side, a red splash across the pavement and a crimson trail leading away from it telling an unfinished story of injury, death, or survival. *Was the person dragged away or did they crawl away?* The litany of vehicles and the destruction to them and their passengers was unending.

Debris clogged the road, as well. Bodies. All manner of bodies. Young. Old. White. Black. Impoverished. The well off. *Unless you owned a helicopter, I guess an apocalyptic plague proved a great equalizer,* Cooper thought. Some were strewn about the streets, sidewalks, and parking lots. Others lay entombed in their cars. Some bodies had been subjected to such horrible violence; he could barely recognize them as a person. Others lacked any kind of visible mark. Cooper speculated these had died from heart attacks or some trauma that he simply could not identify. Some had clearly died from the Brushfire Plague itself, phlegm, blood, and spittle staining their clothes and mouths.

"Poor bastards, sick and stumbling down a roadway, for God

60

knows what purpose," Cooper involuntarily mumbled.

One vehicle forced itself into Cooper's attention. A white car had slammed into another car. The ground all around the vehicle glittered in the late afternoon sun and every window in the car had been shattered. Bullet holes ripped the car from stem to stern and all along the side facing Cooper. Those holes told him the car had been hit with a mixture of shotgun shells, pistol bullets, and at least one high-powered rifle. It wasn't the three bodies inside the vehicle that drew his eye — he'd already seen far too much of that.

It was the moppy brown hair and the small forlorn arm that hung just below the rear passenger door. Cooper shuddered, knowing what he could not see. A thin object was clasped in the hand. Cooper flashed his lights, to tell Dranko he was stopping, and abruptly braked.

"Stay here," he ordered, his voice heavy with grim sadness. Julianne simply nodded and Jake didn't move at all.

Cooper's steps were leaden as he approached the car. He knew what he was going to find. He knew it was going to break his heart. Still, he trudged onward, drawn to the grasped object like a suspecting husband coming home early from work one day. Glass crunched underfoot as he came closer to the car. His stomach tightened as he reached out and slowly pulled the door fully open.

A boy's body slumped further out of the car, the head bumping itself against the asphalt. Cooper reached out to stop the boy from hitting the ground, but failed. The boy was stiff and he landed with a thud. Cooper cringed, his eyes narrowing and his lips curling. The boy's face was serene and unmarked. His chest had a single neat hole. Right where the boy's heart was. *A small hole. A circle of red. And, a dead little boy.* Cooper's thoughts ravaged his mind and a vise closed upon his chest. *Is that all it takes?*

Cooper's eyes drifted down to the object in the boy's hand. The hand was smeared in blood. He couldn't tell if it was his own, or someone else's. Cooper saw a rectangular cylinder of blue peeking out from between the boy's fingers. He knelt down to get a closer look. He grabbed a rag from his pocket and pulled it from the boy's unyielding fingers.

Cooper wiped the object and then opened the rag. *Captain America.* The head of Captain America was staring him straight in the eye. *A Pez dispenser.* Cooper remembered them from his childhood, unaware that they were still made. Cooper stumbled backward, sitting down hard and awkwardly onto the cold asphalt. He tightened his grip on the bloodied Pez dispenser. His eyes raced all around him, as if looking for something. His eyes stung and big fat teardrops began falling, dotting his shirt with dark spots. His left hand smashed into the side of his head. His right grasped the Pez dispenser. He wanted to crush it into dust in a vain hope to make it all just go away. He began rocking back and forth. Then, he exploded.

"Why!" He wailed futilely. He stretched that one word for what seemed like an eternity to those who were either standing next to their vehicles or who'd remained inside. By the time he finished, he was sobbing. Cooper felt like a broken man. The dead boy reminded him far too much of Jake. The tragedy of a boy dying while holding onto a cheap plastic toy was a brutal talisman of the death of their old world and the painful, bloody birth of the new. A new world, still unformed, but already scarred by blood and death. *Too much death,* Cooper lamented.

"You know how I'm different than him?" Jake's voice right next to him made Cooper's body jerk in surprise.

He could only stare upward. His boy towered over him, the emotional gulf between them having a dramatic effect. Cooper furiously wiped away the tears from his eyes. His voice fled him and he could not respond.

"Two ways." Jake's voice was distant. He sounded like an old man. "One. I ain't dead," he paused. His lips curled into a wry smile that made Cooper cringe. Then he added, "Yet."

Cooper frantically rustled himself onto his knees. Instinctively, he sought to comfort his son. Hearing such cold, calculated words from his eleven-year-old's mouth left his own agape and unmoving.

Jake continued, as if unaware of his father's desperate movements. "Two. When I die, I'll have a gun in my hand, not some stupid ass toy." His cold words had turned to ice. Jake diffidently shrugged off his father's seeking hands. He walked slowly back to the truck. His steps plodded, crushing glass and debris that lay in his path. Cooper stared after him impotently.

Jake ignored Julianne who was staring at him in shock and sought to catch his eye. Her arms reached out halfway to offer a comforting hug, but fell back to her side when she saw the stern features that now owned his face. The door shut quietly. He never turned around, so he couldn't see the look of disbelief and sadness that crested across Cooper's face. Cooper knew a door had just closed on his son's life. *He's a child no more.* Cooper's heart ached at the fact. He stifled the emotions welling up from deep inside.

He stumbled to his feet, dazed. His eyes met Julianne's, looking expectantly from the car. All she could see was hatred. Cooper saw her shudder, as if a cold wind had just blown through the truck. He didn't care.

He wanted to know when the butcher's bill for the Brushfire Plague would ever be fully paid. *My wife, dead. Rotting in the ground. My boy, becoming hard at age eleven. Me, driven from my home and on the run. What else am I expected to pay?* If Cooper could have seen into the future to answer that question, he might never have arisen from the pavement he had settled upon.

****

They resumed their slog southward. Cooper's truck was ruled by silence. He didn't know what to say to his son. He doubted words would matter now. Now, more than ever, he wanted to be away from everything. He hoped that getting into the country and away from so much death might be the tonic that could cure what ailed Jake.

As they drove, Julianne fidgeted. Her eyes would furtively try to connect with Cooper's in the rearview mirror. Each time, she shrank before the fury she saw in his eyes. She broke the silence first, "I'm sorry, Cooper. I'm so sorry…"

"Don't," he spat through gritted teeth. Rage owned his heart now. Julianne's role in this disaster and his son's lost childhood made his mind whirl and his gut wrench. But, try as he might, he could not hate her. And, he wanted to hate her. It would make everything else so much easier. *I'd like to dump her on the side of the road and let her fend for herself in this world that she helped create. That would be justice.* But, he could not. Mercy tugged at him, too. The bond he felt toward her was powerful. Involuntary. Messy. A tenderness she had no right to had wormed its way into his heart and wouldn't let go. It mocked Cooper, as if to say, *your rage will pass, but this will remain.* Its truth enraged him further and he managed a harsher glare at Julianne.

His confused and angry thoughts were periodically interrupted as they had to stop their vehicles and push one out of the way to make passage. Calvin had his rifle at the ready, riding true 'shotgun'. His eyes were alert and scanning. He was always the first out when they stopped so he could take a look in all directions to ensure their safety. In between, he knew Cooper was not in the mood for conversation and left him be.

After another hour, they were reaching the junction of the road they wanted to take east. Dranko radioed for him to stop and they gathered.

"Jake and Lily can you guys keep an eye out and let us know if you see anything?"

"Yes, darling," Lily responded while Jake simply shuffled off a few paces to take up watch.

The others huddled in a semi-circle.

Dranko motioned into the distance, "Just around that bend, about a mile down the road, is the crossing over I-5 that we need to get on to head east. It's a dangerously exposed position and we need to think about our approach."

"Shouldn't we scout it first?" Calvin asked.

"That's exactly what I was thinking," Dranko agreed. "It's the most prudent approach."

Cooper exploded, "We don't have time for that! On foot, it will cost us at least an hour to scout it. By then, the sun will be setting and we won't have time to get across and set up camp."

Angela raised her hands to try and calm Cooper, "That's a good point. Why don't we just camp on this side, scout and cross in the morning."

"Because staying on 82nd is a mistake. Who knows what will come down this road overnight. We need to get across and get some distance off the road. There is cover on that side of I-5. We don't have it here."

"But, rushing across a vulnerable position without scouting it is a mistake, brother, you know that," Dranko pleaded, his eyebrows knitted in confusion.

Cooper turned on him and looked as if he was about to pounce, "I'll tell you what is a mistake. It's a mistake to see a disaster around every corner and a two-headed monster behind every bush. I...we need to get out of the city and into cover and away from all of this," Cooper said, waving his arms about to indicate the death and destruction that surrounded them. Deep down, he knew he had slipped into an emotional and irrational state and he hated himself for it.

"Can't we clear out on these empty businesses and bunker down there tonight?" Calvin asked.

"There are certainly a lot to choose from," Angela added.

Cooper surveyed the group gathered around and saw the nodding heads, the arms folded, and the expectant eyes looking at him. His mind turned and thought of one unfinished piece of business that had clawed at the back of his mind since the other night when they'd been attacked. "Fine, you guys clear a building, I've got something else I need to get ready for," he grunted and strode back to his truck and began absentmindedly checking their supplies. The others let him go without intervening.

****

An hour later, they had settled into an auto parts store that was set back from the road and gave them a good vantage point over the road in front of them. They barricaded the back door with boxes of heavy parts. They left a side door locked from the inside with a heavy chain, but which could become an escape route if they needed it. They decided to park their vehicles in front where they could keep an eye on them. The group unloaded the supplies so that they wouldn't invite prying eyes of anyone that might come along. As added camouflage, they parked Cooper's truck over the curb and popped the hood, feigning a breakdown. They left Dranko's Jeep angled in the middle of the parking lot and dumped a few gallons of anti-freeze underneath it to make it look like its radiator had blown out. They carefully made sure the coolant made a sloppy trail toward the street.

When their preparations were complete, Cooper pulled Dranko aside.

"I'm going to take the motorcycle and head back to our neighborhood tonight."

"That your unfinished business? Gus?"

"Yeah, that's right. I owe him a visit. I don't want to waste my time sitting on this side of the 205 tonight," Cooper's eyes flamed, anger flashing from his lost argument earlier.

"I think that's a stupid risk, but I know you well enough to try and talk you out of it," Dranko replied, folding his arms.

He ignored the barb, "You do know me well. I'll leave right after we eat. Hole up over there until dark and take him down at three AM. If I'm not back by sunrise, go on without me," Cooper said, clipping his words.

"Good luck, I hope you don't make Jake an orphan," Dranko's words burned.

Cooper turned and went to work readying his weapons. When he told Jake his plan for the night, he had only one word in response, "Good." Such a cold reply made him shudder more than what Dranko had said.

65

Cooper took a different route home on the motorbike and squirrelled himself away in a cluster of bushes off the road, about a mile from his neighborhood. He laid out his sleeping bag, put his pistol next to him, set the alarm on his watch, and was asleep in minutes.

The soft beeping startled him hours later, at two in the morning. He was instantly awake, adrenaline pumping. He packed his sleeping bag and readied himself. He would travel light, only his pistol in hand and a borrowed revolver from their supplies as a backup, holstered. He wore dark clothing and smudged grease from the auto parts store to darken his face and neck. He donned a black baseball cap that he had also liberated from the store. It had previously advertised Jack Daniels whiskey, but he'd removed the patch that held the white lettering. He turned it around so the brim faced rearward. He drank deeply from a water bottle and double checked his weapons one last time.

He moved to the edge of the bushes and surveyed Division Street. The moon was just a sliver in the dark sky. The streetlamps were all dark, the electricity having failed several days ago. Here and there, moonlight glistened off shiny metal on the many cars that littered the roadway. Cooper smiled to himself, knowing how hard it would be for anyone to see him.

He decided it would be safer to go most of the way right down the middle of the road, leapfrogging from car to car in silent sprints. This would be safer than using the yards and potentially happening upon a dog or someone awake and alert. He spotted the first car he would make and ran to it in a crouched position. He sat next to the BMW and listened for a long minute. He smelled the stench of a body, or bodies, inside and willed his nostrils shut. Hearing nothing, he made it to the next car. This he repeated over and over until he was near his neighborhood.

Now, he changed tactics. Inside his head, he had a map of which yards he could traverse, without dogs, from the edge of his neighborhood to Gus' house. He had chosen a route that began between the barricades. He knew this and the roving patrol were his most dangerous obstacles. But, he had a plan to distract those on the barricade. At the edge of a building that housed a pizza parlor, he laid out a small canister filled with gasoline and unrolled a long fuse he had fashioned with cotton rope. He sprayed WD40 along its course, hoping it would be enough to keep the fuse lit without making it burn too fast.

He lit it, sprinted behind the building, and hopscotched across a vacant lot and several yards until he made it to the midpoint of the barricades.

A little earlier than he'd hoped, he heard a muffled roar and caught the glimmer of light from the gas can igniting. He'd positioned it so that just a little light would be seen from the barricades. His plan was that they would at least focus on their attention to the light. If he was lucky, they'd send a man or two to investigate. He sprinted across Division, running low, and made it to the first yard he'd chosen. He paused here, listening and scanning for any evidence that he'd been seen. Finding none, he continued.

He was in Gus' yard five minutes later. The house was black and silent. He found the side door entrance and tried the handle. Unlocked! He couldn't believe his luck. *Even now, he leaves his door unlocked? What a fool!* He turned the handle slowly, opened the door without a sound and crept inside.

He had once been over Gus' house for a dinner party and had a good idea where the master bedroom was. Since then, Gus had divorced and now lived alone. He ghosted through the kitchen, being careful to walk on the balls of his feet so he moved almost noiselessly. He pivoted to the left and moved down the hallway. He found Gus' bedroom door open and went inside.

He heard Gus' heavy breathing from the bed across the room. Cooper paused again to listen. Silence. He glided alongside his bed. He punched the pistol's muzzle against Gus' head.

Gus awoke with a start. His eyes squinted trying to see what was going on as Cooper shined his flashlight into his face, blinding him temporarily.

"It's me. Cooper."

He choked in fear, "Coo…per? Whh..aaa..tt?"

"I only have one question for you. Why?"

As he regained his sight, Gus' eyes flew wide when he saw the pistol's bore looming an inch from his head. Cooper heard the man's bowels let go and quickly smelled the stink.

"Whhh---yyy, what?"

"Why did you betray me?"

"I ddd—didn't betray you!"

"You turned me in. I saw you that night when those men attacked."

Gus averted his eyes, looking down. He paused, breathing rapidly. "I'm sorry, Cooper. I really am."

"Not as sorry as you're gonna be," Cooper fumed.

"I just thought what you did was wrong. Lying about this whole thing."

Cooper drove the pistol into his forehead so hard it pushed Gus' head back into the pillow, "I didn't lie! You dumb bastard! Have you ever known me to lie? About *anything?*"

Gus body shuddered, "Well-lll, no. But...it is so hard to believe."

"So, you doubt me and call the military? Send them after me...and Jake!"

Gus's eyes darted back and forth, searching, "I'm sorry, Cooper. I guess I didn't think. I hope..."

"There's only one hope of yours I'm going to fulfill. Do you want to know what that is?"

"Wh...aa...t?"

"The hope you had that you'd never see me again. You won't. But, you won't ever see anyone again either," Cooper said and pulled the pistol back a few inches, readying to fire.

His finger began depressing the trigger when a whimper to his right stopped him. He looked.

In the light from his small flashlight, soft blond curls framed a terrified face. *Gus' daughter.* Her eyes shone wet and her body was shaking. She looked like she had seen a monster.

"Please, don't hurt her," Gus pleaded meekly.

"Leave!" Cooper yelled at her.

She remained unmoved. Instead, she let go with loud sobbing. She pulled a pink blanket to her mouth. Her eyes grew wider and looked him in the eye. Cooper saw something in those eyes that shook him to the core. Innocence. Her terror spoke volumes about the innocence she still had. *Like Jake used to have. She hasn't seen too much. Yet.* Cooper lowered his head for a second and the pistol drifted a few inches lower. Then, he inhaled, and looked once more at Gus.

"I'm going to leave now. I want you to remember two things, Gus. I want you to remember what you did to Jake and I. Driving us from our home and exposing my boy to horror after horror. I wish I could make you see what we've seen and do what we've had to do." The pistol shook in his hand as he raised it once more to point to Gus. He willed himself to lower it, "But, I won't do that to your daughter."

A stricken, weak, smile crept onto Gus' face, "Thh...ank you."

Cooper's lips dripped scorn in response, "Don't thank me. Thank *her.* The second thing I want you to remember is that I can come back someday to finish this. You better hope nothing happens to Jake that makes me think about coming here again," Cooper's eyes blazed and Gus' body shivered, the blankets quivering.

He continued, "And, I need you to do one thing. The authorities better believe I'm heading to Sacramento to hide out with my family down there."

"Yes, sure," Gus gulped excitedly. "They will."

Cooper looked at him sternly, "If they come after me toward the coast, I *will* come back and next time, you won't even wake up. You got it?"

Gus' head nodded furiously. Cooper stifled the urge to smile as Gus bought the misdirection—Estacada lay toward the mountains to the east of Portland; while the coast was to the west.

Cooper turned and walked to the door, he paused and whispered to the still shaking girl, taking her chin in his hand, "You just saved your father's life. You understand that?"

Her wonderstruck eyes looked up at him, "Yes," she breathed.

"There's still mercy in this world, will you remember that for me?"

She nodded gravely.

He gripped her chin harder, his voice louder in desperation, "Will you?"

"Yes. I will. I promise."

With that, Cooper was gone.

****

Cooper made it back to where the others were holed up without incident. He found Dranko on guard duty, about an hour before sunrise. He pulled the door open for him and he looked at Cooper expectantly.

"No, I didn't kill him. And, no I don't want to talk about it."

Dranko nodded, "You better get some shuteye."

Cooper bedded down and was asleep in minutes; he'd never forgotten the soldier's trick of being able to sleep whenever, and wherever, the opportunity emerged.

After what seemed like minutes, Dranko's boot was jostling him awake, "I let everyone sleep an extra hour. You need to be alert today," he said as he continued moving about the room and waking the others.

Cooper stretched himself out. *Not as young as I used to be. Few hours' sleep after a night of action is telling me that this morning!* He mused to himself and rolled onto his side so he could watch Jake wake from his slumber.

Jake rubbed his eyes lazily and let loose a loud yawn.

"How'd you sleep, son?"

Narrow eyes looked back, "Pretty good." His voice was still flat, but Cooper's heart rejoiced at the trace of the boy he heard within it.

His joy was short-lived, as Jake's tone turned harsh once again and his eyes became slits, "You kill him?"

"No, I could have. But, I let him live."

"That's too bad," Jake scoffed.

Cooper softened his voice further and looked with concern at Jake, "His daughter came into the room. I couldn't do it in front of her. She reminded me of you, son."

Jake's face fell flat and he laughed morosely, "I ain't like that no more. You shoulda killed that bastard. He drove us away from mom." Anger laced his words as he rustled out of his sleeping bag and scampered onto his feet. Cooper recognized someone trying to make an escape when he saw it. Cooper did likewise, and caught him by the shoulder just as Jake was trying to walk away.

He grabbed him by both shoulders and lowered his face so that they were eye to eye, "You don't have to do this, Jake."

"Do what?" he fired back, defiant.

"Become hard. I went through war and didn't do that. I saw lots of men *not* do that. Men who fought. Who killed. Who saw horror. Who *didn't* do what you are doing."

A long pause hung in the air. Jake's eyes filled with tears and he barely managed a raspy whisper, "Were they eleven?"

His words ripped Cooper's heart open. The painful truth was piercing. Defeated, his voice fell and he cast his eyes at the black and white tiled floor, "No. No. They weren't eleven."

Another long pause passed between them.

Jake grabbed his father's shirt and tugged hard, "I don't know *how* not to, dad!" Hearing the helpless pleading of his son, his heart sundered anew.

He pulled himself back so he could look at Jake in the eye, "Won't you at least let me help you? Trust me, what you're doing will just burn you up. I've seen it a million times."

Jake's eyes were confused, hesitant. His words were stilted, "I don't know, dad. I'll try. It hurts too much. Everyone dying. Mom dying. Peter. Worrying about you dying. Me dying."

Cooper yanked Jake into a tight embrace and stroked his son's hair, "I know, son. I know. Just let me help you. Don't go away. Please." Now, it was Cooper's turn to beg.

Jake nodded his head vigorously against his father's chest and sobbed. His little body wracked against Cooper's. "That's right, son. Just let go. It's alright."

Soft footsteps caused Cooper to look up. Angela's eyes were full, dripping with sympathetic tears. She moved behind Jake and embraced Cooper, with Jake in the middle. Jake's head turned rapidly to see who it was. Expecting Julianne, his eyes raged. Seeing Angela, he relaxed and buried his face once more in his father's chest. Her act of tenderness, and its effect on Jake, filled Cooper's heart with hope. He caught her gaze and offered a warm smile. Her eyes glinted and her lips upturned. The three stayed in this welcome oasis until Dranko interrupted them awkwardly.

"We need to pack up and get ready to move," he said softly, placing his hand on Cooper's shoulder.

As the three disengaged, Cooper caught sight of Julianne. She stood off in a corner and averted her eyes as soon as he looked up at her. Still, he saw the fresh tears spilling down her face. Even the briefest glance into those eyes stirred him from some place deep he could not name. Despite himself, his heart longed to comfort her. *Why do I feel this way toward her?* He summoned anger to push it aside. *She doesn't deserve it.* Nonetheless, the question plagued him as they prepared to leave.

Chapter Four

With their gear repacked into their vehicles, they gathered in the parking lot. This time, Jake was posted as their guard, making sure they were not caught unawares.

"Alright, we need to scout the bridge to make sure we aren't ambushed," Dranko opened.

"Right. Lily, can you drive?"

"Can a cow shit," Lily deadpanned and everyone laughed. As the laughter died, she continued, "I might be old, honey, but I ain't dead. If you didn't already have two women here jostling for your attention, I'd probably show you what else I can still do." Cooper flushed a shade just shy of fire engine red. Angela and Julianne looked at one another, exchanging an awkward mix of humor and competition. Freddie doubled over. Calvin and Dranko grinned widely.

"Hell, Lily, you could still show Dranko," Freddie joked. Now, Dranko blushed and he flipped Freddie the bird, "No offense, Lily."

"None taken. Actually, Freddie, I was thinking you and I could do the whole Cougar thing one better. I'm so old, I could be your sabre tooth tiger." Another round of laughing rocked the group. Cooper let it go on, knowing laughter was a great stress reliever. He knew they needed it every chance they had.

"Alright, already. Let's get serious," Cooper stated to bring some order to the lighthearted chaos. "Lily, you and Julianne will be drivers in the vehicles, parked just out of sight as we near the bridge. Jake will be in a vehicle, too. The rest of us can scout across the bridge on foot. Typical leapfrog. But, Angela, I want you with a scoped rifle on this side scanning the other. If there is trouble, we could use some accurate fire laid down. Make sense?"

Everyone nodded. Dranko stirred, "I've got a radio for each of us, set to Channel 15. If we get cross-traffic or interference, we will move to 16. Also, grab extra mags for your rifles. If we get into a scrape, we don't want to run out of ammo. Finally, Freddie and Calvin, since you don't have much experience with firefights, if we get into one, just remember…breathe…let it halfway out and hold it…and then squeeze the trigger. Don't jerk it."

The two nodded. Cooper noticed the clenching of their hands and neck muscles. *Nerves.* "Don't worry. If you can manage to aim the best you can and fire, you will be doing well. He clapped both men on their shoulders as he stood between them. "Alright?"

"Yeah, I got it. Set the expectations low to take the pressure off us, right? Smart," Calvin responded.

"I ain't worried about pressure from Cooper, I'm worried about someone shooting at us," Freddie exclaimed and laughed hollowly.

"Dranko and I will take lead. You'll both do great. Hopefully, this will just be a good practice run."

Ten minutes later, they had outfitted themselves with weapons and extra ammunition. Cooper and Dranko donned body armor, and once again Cooper thanked him for storing an extra set during his preparations for the end of the world. Dranko held one set of binoculars and gave the other to Angela. Finally, they ensured the radios were working before heading out toward the overpass over I-205.

"Angela, if you see movement or anyone on the other side, first radio to us the location. Then, fire. I doubt anyone waiting on the other side isn't doing so to offer us a morning tea or cup of coffee."

"Or a delicious donut from Voodoo's. Mmmm..." Freddie quipped, alluding to the almost-famous donut shop in Portland, while patting his belly.

"Damn, why'd you remind me of those? They are so good," Lily exclaimed.

"You mean *were* so good," Dranko intoned as smiles disappeared around him. Cooper just shook his head.

Calvin brought them back to the task at hand, "Right. We got it."

They piled into their vehicles and drove the short distance to the last of the buildings that could conceal their vehicles while they scouted the overpass.

They parked behind a Burgerville restaurant, a popular fast food chain in the Northwest that, before the plague, would have been overflowing with customers. *I wonder if I'll ever get to taste one of their fresh blackberry shakes again,* Cooper thought. His mouth watered at the thought.

"Jake, it's up to you to protect these fine women," Cooper began before being interrupted.

"Please, Cooper. I was hunting squirrel and possum before you were a glimmer in your father's eye. I'm quite sure Jake and I will make a splendid defense team, won't we?" Lily said, hefting a hunting rifle as she got out of Dranko's Jeep.

A hesitant smile crept onto Jake's face. *That's the best thing I've seen in days!* Cooper thought as his heart leapt.

"And, I'm sure I can hit something with *this,*" Julianne said, raising a shotgun over her head with both hands, and smiling meekly. "And, before you say a damn word, Cooper, I know to keep it tight against my shoulder when I fire."

Cooper smiled, "OK. You both got me. I'll shut up now." Jake's smile was replaced with a grimace as soon as Julianne began speaking. He moved a few paces closer to Lily. Seeing this, Cooper pursed his lips.

He turned to address the others, "Let's move."

****

Bright sunlight cascaded down from the cloudless sky, which was rare for a late spring morning in Portland. The group formed a loose diamond pattern, crouching and running from one cover point to the next and leapfrogging one another. To an untrained eye, their movement would have looked martial. Cooper saw the many flaws as his group moved: covering distances that were too far from one another, picking up and running before the person had settled into their new firing position, and leaving firing lines uncovered. *We'd get wiped out by a trained force while crossing into new terrain.* He pushed the negative thought aside. *Do your best, that's all you can ask of anyone,* his father's sage words came back to him. Cooper longed for the familiarity of his own ground and the easier task of *defending,* rather than attacking.

As he moved, he did his best to model for the others how to do it. Occasionally, he'd bark across the radio to try and correct the most egregious misstep or use it as an educational moment. But, he knew there was no replacement for training and the repetition of drilling.

He was about halfway to their 'jumping off' point that would be in full view of the overpass when it struck him. *I've probably passed at least a half dozen cars with one or more bodies, most of them stinking to high heaven, and I haven't even noticed.* That thought brought a bitter taste to his tongue. His lips curled and he spat to rid himself of the foul taste. *Damn, I can't stop seeing. I can't lose touch.*

Light glinted off the cars as they moved. Dranko was the 'point' of the diamond, while Cooper brought up the rear. Calvin, Angela, and Freddie were spread across the middle of their formation. They figured that this formation would give them the best way to control and direct the untrained trio.

Soon, Dranko called them over the open channel, "Form up, on me. The overpass is in view." The diamond collapsed upon him. When Cooper arrived, Dranko passed him the binoculars without needing to be asked.

Cooper started at the far side and worked his way back. Across the overpass was a wooded hill that was pockmarked with houses that had been cut into the steep hillside. Around the homes, the Evergreens were packed tightly. *Damn fine cover for anyone on the other side. Could be in the houses looking out from behind the windows or could be bunkered in the woods.* Cooper deliberately scanned this area, looking intently for a reflection off of metal or the glass from a scope. Finding nothing, he passed them to Angela, who spent several minutes looking over the area, too.

"Well, what do you think," Cooper asked, breaking the tense silence.

"It's dangerous. They could be in any of those houses, looking out with a scope or binoculars right at us. But, with the windows, we aren't likely to see inside from here. It's too far," Dranko answered.

"I was thinking the same thing. Angela, focus your attention on those houses. Look for any sign of movement. A window that shakes could mean something is pressed against it. A bird that takes to flight could mean a noise startled it. If you see something, take your best guess and just open fire. At the worst, we'll get an unneeded scare. At best, you'll hit someone or at least force them to fire before they want to. Make sense?"

Angela nodded, and licked dry lips.

"Calvin, I think it makes sense for you to stay back here with Angela. Scanning the same with the binoculars. Same advice to her. You see anything, tell her just where to fire. You'll do more good here than running across the overpass. Got it?"

"Sure. Easy enough," Calvin said, taking the binoculars from Dranko.

Cooper turned to Freddie, whose face had lost all color, and Dranko. "Take a deep breath, Freddie."

"I can switch roles with Freddie," Calvin offered, his deep voice an octave higher than normal.

Freddie bent over, placing his hands on his knees, and drew air deep into his lungs. He waved his hands, "I got this. Ain't gonna be scaredy Freddie!" His forced laughter rang hollow and died of loneliness.

"It is not about that. No one here would call you that," Calvin continued, his eyes sympathetic.

Freddie looked up, his face pale, "Nah, I know that. But, I'd call myself that. And, that's what matters. You know, what you call yourself. Besides, in the post-BP world, I gotta be able to deal with the threat of violence. Didn't you guys read Cosmo this week? Violence is the new black." His joke elicited a few chuckles from his friends. His own smile was thin.

"Okay, here is what we do. Dranko, you have point again. My .308 has better range, so it's best at the rear. Freddie, you got middle. Move the shortest distance you can from one cover to the next. Don't *ever* pass up cover. You got that, Freddie?"

Freddie nodded and spat dry spittle to the ground. Cooper continued, "Make sure the last man moving is settled and in a good firing position. Believe me, if you are moving and are fired upon, you want everyone able to return fire immediately."

"OK, mom. You told us all this when we did our briefing this morning," Freddie exaggerated his whine.

Cooper grabbed him by the shirt collar and pressed his face close, "Yes, I did. And, I saw you violate this basic rule twice just crossing to where we are now. My nagging might save you from getting your ass shot off."

Freddie stepped back and upraised his hands, "Alright, Coop. I got you. Chill."

Cooper's face still flashed red and his lips were tight, "I'll chill when we are across this ground. Until then, *you* best be on edge. On your toes. Got it, Freddie?"

"Sure thing, boss," Freddie answered, irritation creeping in. *Always let the other guy save face. It's the rare man that will forget or forgive a slight. Too many and your best friend can turn your worst enemy.* Cooper's father's voice rang inside his head.

Cooper softened his face deliberately, "You know. You're right, Freddie. Thank you for the reminder. Good advice. How about I calm down a bit and you ramp it up a bit? We do need to be *on* our toes, but not over the edge. Deal?"

"That's all I was saying," Freddie offered meekly.

"Yeah, I know. It just took me a minute to hear you." Freddie perked up and his typical smile replaced the scowl. *Glad I fixed that.* "We ready, team?" Once more, his father's advice came to him: *build the team every chance you get. A team that trusts each other will kick the butt off one that doesn't.* Cooper surveyed the group standing around him

77

and saw the fear and the confusion in their faces. "C'mon, bring it in," he barked, while cocking his eyebrows playfully.

"Right, coach," Freddie joked. The others clustered about him. Cooper put his hand in the middle and waited for the others to join him. "On three, muffled yell of 'shoot straight'. One…two…three!"

"Shoot straight!" They yelled together softly, so that the noise would not carry very far. Angela was grinning in delight. Calvin had a wry smile on his face. Freddie was chuckling and breathing easily. Dranko was smirking at Cooper. *Scared men make bad decisions,* his father had told him repeatedly. *That's how you tell a real leader from an imposter. The real ones lessen the fear of those around them, the bad ones stoke it.*

"Well then, team. Let's roll," Cooper commanded. Despite his efforts, he hadn't finished the words when he sensed the tension spike all around him. Faces tightened and muscles tensed. Jaws clenched. It was palpable in the air. The corner of Cooper's mouth curled upward. *The best efforts can fail, can't they?* He was thankful that Jake would be safe, remaining in the rear with the vehicles with Julianne and Lily.

****

Angela and Calvin moved across the roadway to his right so they were aligned with the same side of the road as the houses that they sought to cover on the wooded hill. The trio waited for them to be in position and actively scanning before they moved.

Dranko went first, scurrying at a crouch about ten yards before he came to rest behind a bright yellow Volkswagen bug. Next to him, Freddie rasped a frantic breath before he ran onto the overpass, his feet clattering loudly on the asphalt. In front of him, Dranko had his rifle trained onto the opposite side. When Freddie drew parallel to him, he turned towards Dranko and his eyes were white saucers. He kept running for a few seconds before crashing hard against a black sedan that had careened sideways, blocking the left two lanes.

My turn. Cooper breathed steadily, filling his lungs to capacity. Then, he crouched and began running. His eyes were alert and scanning the ground before him. He didn't want to trip while crossing ground that might be under enemy observation. Quickly, he reached Dranko and passed him. Then, he was past Freddie and sliding into the spot he'd chosen opposite of him. He was behind a red pickup that had also blocked the right side of the road, just a few yards past the black car that Freddie had sought cover behind.

They continued across the overpass like this. The road was littered with vehicles of all sorts. Some were pristine rather than being dirty. Some had burned, while others had crashed. It would have been barely passable to get one vehicle through at any given point.

They were three-fourths of the way across the overpass when Cooper's mind clicked. *Just enough room for one vehicle to get across? This is too neat. Like it's been set up this way.*

Freddie was rushing at full speed to the next cover point.

Cooper's eyes flew wide, "Get down," he screeched.

It was too late.

The shots rang out almost simultaneously, coming from in front and behind him.

His eyes were fixated upon Freddie. He saw it all in slow motion. Freddie was mid-stride, his hair dancing in the wind, his feet churning gravel and broken glass from the road's surface, when he was hit. The impact ripped his shirt, sending bits of cotton exploding into the air. Freddie took two awkward steps, his legs crashing into themselves, before smashing into the ground, his rifle clattering and bouncing across the pavement.

Dranko was in front of where Freddie had fallen. Before he could react, a tinny voice bellowed from what Cooper guessed was a bullhorn, "Don't fire! We will negotiate!"

Cooper's temper flared, "Negotiate? After you shot our guy!" He yelled. Cooper's eyes were still trained on Freddie, looking for movement. His heart leapt into his throat when all he saw was stillness.

"We got your attention, don't we? We got you dead to rights."

Cooper's mind raced, "What do you want to cross safely?"

"Our terms are fair and the same for all who cross," the voice's smug tone grated on Cooper.

"Where the hell are they?" Now, Cooper was frantically scanning the opposite side of the bridge. That they could hear his unamplified voice told him the voice on the bullhorn was close. Then, he saw it: a spot of white waving just above the roof of a red Mini Cooper.

"Half. Half your food. Half your guns. And, half your women."

Buying time, as he sighted in his rifle to punch through the Mini's doors at where he thought the bullhorn person was, "OK! Half our food and half our guns. But, we gotta keep our women. They are our wives!" Lowering his voice, he called to Dranko over the hand held radio, "Behind the red Mini. Spray."

Cooper waited until the tip of the bullhorn rose above the

79

Mini's roofline once more, he breathed, exhaled and then held his breath. He squeezed the trigger slowly. The rifle barked once. The bullhorn dropped out of view.

Dranko opened fire and the harsh staccato of the M4 on full auto was punctuated by the shells finding home, punching sheet metal, shattering glass, and the sharp *thwick-thwick* as they tore through plastic and sheet metal on the cars. From behind him, Angela fired again at a target he could not discern.

Cooper instinctively ducked as a fusillade of gunfire splattered the Chevy Malibu that he was hunkered down behind. Above the din, he heard a plaintive groan from Freddie. Quickly, he got onto all fours and scrabbled toward him. The gunfire remained focused on the car, as the other vehicles must have blocked his movement from his adversaries. Ricochets bounced angrily about him, however, and he crawled away as fast he could, his knees rubbing raw in the process.

In front of him, Freddie was clutching at his shoulder and rolling from side to side. He was moaning and his left hand, the injured side, was clawing at the ground. *It's good he's still feeling pain. It means he's not in shock yet.*

Cooper closed the last few yards with a furious scramble. Freddie's eyes lit up when he saw him.

"I'm shot," he muttered, grinding his teeth.

"Yeah, I know. You'll be fine. I'm going to move you behind cover so I can patch you up. Alright?"

Freddie gave a curt nod. Cooper grabbed him by his shirt collar and began dragging him across the rough pavement, grunting at the effort. Freddie groaned even louder, his jaw muscles clenching to hold back the pain. Cooper kept scooting along the ground, pushing with his legs, and pulling Freddie along. A splinter of concrete stitched across his cheek from a nearby bullet ricochet. He ignored it and kept sliding along the ground. His back bumped into the reassuring steel of the cement truck's frame and he pivoted to slide Freddie alongside, parallel to it. He stepped over him and knelt beside him.

The bullet had punched Freddie squarely in the shoulder, just below the collarbone. The bleeding wasn't heavy, as Freddie had kept his hand pressed up against it.

"Keep your hand there," Cooper said as he gently lifted him up and slid his hand underneath his back. He felt dampness and pulled his hand back to find it stained red.

"You have an exit wound, which is good. The bullet isn't stuck inside," Cooper relayed as he pawed open the makeshift first-aid kit that Dranko had given each of them. Using his teeth, he tore open the packaging to a maxi-pad. He used his pocket knife to slice it in half and quickly positioned one on each side of Freddie's body; covering both the entry and exit wounds. Before he could reach for his own, Freddie handed him a roll of gauze from his pack and Cooper used it to fasten the pads in place, looping around his neck to fix it in place. When finished, he patted Freddie on the opposite shoulder, "You'll be okay. I'll be back."

The gunfire continued in sporadic fits as he was bandaging Freddie. He spotted Dranko swapping mags, still in the same position. He fast crawled to his side.

"Got Freddie patched up. He'll keep," Cooper apprised him.

"I got one more. Someone who popped up a little too much for his own good health! I think we got at least six still spread out among those cars at the overpass' edge and one sniper up in those houses we saw before the jump-off," Dranko relayed, rapid fire. Cooper's mind raced. He swapped a fresh mag into his FAL. He slid to the edge of their cover and caught a quick glance at their enemy's position.

"You still got that grenade?" he asked.

Dranko padded his vest pocket as an answer, a grin growing on his face, "What do you have in mind?"

"Use our one advantage, the magic of suppressing fire against untrained men. Get on the radio and call Calvin up here."

"He's already on his way. Angela told me. As soon as the bullets started flying, he was moving our way."

Cooper's eyebrows drew together, "Really? Impressive. Takes a lot of cajones for a civvie to move toward gunfire!"

Dranko nodded in exaggerated agreement.

"Hey," Calvin called to them from behind a beige sedan, waving his arm to be seen.

Cooper motioned him forward and he crawled to where they were.

"Thanks for joining the party," Cooper exclaimed.

Calvin was out of breath, panting, and sweat cascaded down his bald head, "Came...as...soon...as I...could!"

"Here's what we are going to do. You and Dranko will put down suppressing fire on the line of vehicles where our *friends* are hiding and waiting to kill us. Suppressing fire means you fire as fast as you can in the general direction of the bad guys. Don't waste time aiming. We just want their heads down. Got it?"

Calvin nodded, still breathing deeply to refill his winded lungs.

"What...are you..."

Cooper saved him the effort, "I'm going to work my way to range where I can use *this!*" He opened his palm to reveal the olive drab grenade. Calvin's eyes opened wide in surprise. Slowly, a thin smile crept across his face.

"Calvin, we will fire in tandem. I'll empty a mag, and while I'm reloading, you fire," Dranko instructed.

Cooper punched the call button on his walkie talkie, "Angela, I need you to keep the sniper's head down once you hear Dranko firing again. Read me? Out."

A moment later, his radio cackled, "Read you. Out."

Cooper looked at Dranko and Calvin, "Ready?"

Cooper crouched. He breathed deeply several times, filling his lungs as fully as possible. He caught Dranko's eye; he was positioned at the front of the vehicle they were hidden behind. Cooper raised himself onto his haunches and pivoted so he could run out from behind the vehicle and make his way to the enemy position.

As he turned, time slowed. Dranko's rifle swung into position toward the enemy. Flame spat from his barrel as he fired at them. Dranko's face was tight, eyes squinted, jaw clenched, and nostrils flaring. Then, bits of blue flannel erupted from his chest as bullets struck him. His eyes went wide, calling out in shock. Dranko abruptly sat down, thudding into the asphalt. The last thing Cooper saw was Calvin taking Dranko's position and his rifle coming to bear.

Cooper's mind cried out to go to his friend's aid, but he was already in motion. It had all happened too fast. Cooper duck-ran to the nearest car, which was a silver sports car. He heard the rapid fire of Calvin's M4 raking the enemy's position. Cooper didn't hesitate and ran head-long toward a white panel van. He took the risk, knowing that with Dranko down, it would be tougher to keep their opponents under cover long enough for him to get within range.

Silence descended upon the overpass as if a pair of earmuffs had suddenly been slapped onto his ears. Cooper could hear his own breath and it sounded like a jet engine sucking air into a vortex. *Calvin must be reloading.* He knew it would take several seconds for someone untrained under the stress of combat. *Fine motor skills go first and fast when your adrenaline is pumping.* The seconds ticking by seemed like an eternity. What he heard next made his blood chill.

A loud *boom* from the enemy's line. Then another. And another. *Damn! They're back into action. Will be tougher to get them back into cover a second time. And, I hope they don't get Calvin!*

82

The harsh staccato from Calvin's position began again. Cooper knew this was his best chance. He ran from out behind the van and sprinted headlong. He skipped taking cover. He knew he couldn't count on getting through another reload by Calvin. As he passed the inviting cover of a burned out sedan, his body cried out for him to take advantage; like it used to plead for nicotine when he'd quit smoking after Jake was born. He kept going.

A bullet smacked into the asphalt a few yards behind him. He flinched, swinging his arm up in futile defense. *They see me now. Just ten more yards!* Calvin's firing ended abruptly as his magazine must have run dry. Bullets whistled past Cooper and he was instinctively ducking and waving his free hand about him; as if brushing off an attack of angry flies. Sweat stung his eyes, his stomach was doing somersaults, and his loins were desperately trying to crawl back inside. His FAL jerked hard in his hands and he almost dropped it. A splinter of wood dug into his thigh and he momentarily winced. *Damn! A bullet hit the stock!*

Cooper slid behind the safety of the last car between him and where their enemies were strung out. He took a careful minute readying himself and checked the magazine on his rifle, ensuring the safety was off. He pulled the grenade from his pocket and hefted it in his hands. He knew he only had one chance to get it right. The explosive encased in cold metal was comforting in his hand. He kissed it for good luck, pivoted, and threw it over the car's roof and hoped to God it landed for good effect. He crouched once more and waited for the interminable seconds to pass.

Boom! Concussion pushed past him. Sharp cries of agony rose to the sky, chasing the deadly shrapnel's wake. Cooper didn't hesitate. He rose up and surveyed the enemy's line. The grenade had gone off nearly in the middle of it. He saw no one else visible. He ran quickly to his right, toward the far end of the overpass and reached it without return fire. Feeling like a soldier from the Great War jumping into the enemy's trench, he crossed in between the small gap between the last car in their barricade and the overpass' steel girder.

As he did so, he swung his rifle barrel and trained it to his left. Barely ten feet away, someone was curled up into a ball, rocking back and forth. Stick legs in black pants were scrunched up against the person's chest. Cooper's trigger finger squeezed twice before he could even process what he was seeing. Puffs of down fluttered through the air as the bullets ripped through the other person's chest. The body toppled and fell onto its side. Cooper had kept moving; his eyes

83

quickly looking further down the barricade's line.

Toward the middle, he saw two bodies sprawled out. One was lying face down in a pool of blood. The other must have been very close to the grenade's blast. A bloody stump adorned the body while a severed arm was lying off to the side. The man's eyes stared serenely skyward. Cooper inadvertently marveled at the destructive power packed inside something that could be held in one hand. Then, jerky movement at the other end of the line of cars caught his eyes. Arms were thrust into the sky.

"I surrender, sir. I give up," a thin voice rang out.

Cooper kept moving toward him, stepping carefully past the debris and bodies lying about. The man's bolt-action hunting rifle lay at his feet. He was dressed in a dirty mélange of civilian and military clothing, black jeans, combat boots, and a woodland pattern camouflage smock were capped by a Burton-branded red knit cap. His head had been recently shaved, as the scalp was two shades lighter than the rest of his skin. Cooper's face grew puzzled. There was something was familiar about him. He closed the space until just five yards separated them.

"You hear me, old man? I give up," he called once more to Cooper, in a reedy, nervous voice.

Then it clicked. *Woody!* Cooper was momentarily shaken that he was, once again, face to face with the leader of the teenagers that he had already confronted twice. The last time had been a bloody affair in his own home.

A devilish smile alighted on Cooper, "You don't remember me do you?"

Woody's eyes intently looked Cooper over. Recognition flashed, "Holy crap!" Woody took a step backward and brought his arms down, hands upraised, in front of him.

"What am I gonna do with you?" Cooper's tone was flat, deadly.

"Please, mister! I learned my lesson this time! I swear it!" Woody was trying to back away, taking careful steps. Cooper followed him, like a wolf cornering his prey. His mind raced. It was people like Woody who caused all the violence that had followed in the wake of the Brushfire Plague. *Opportunists. Evil men. Wolves. These are the men who've stolen Jake's childhood from him.*

Cooper feigned relief, "Don't worry, boy. I'm going to take you to jail. That is all."

Hope came into Woody's eyes and he ceased his retreat. "Yeah, jail is where you belong."

Woody's voice gained strength, "Sure. Which one is working now?"

Cooper's face grew hard once more, "The kind you won't ever get out of. You see, my boy could have been OK. Even dealing with his mother dying. But, it was people like you, Woody. People like you who messed him up and stole his childhood with your fucking killing and robbing!" Venom laced his words, spray flew from his lips and he slowly, relentlessly, stepped toward Woody. Each step made Woody's knees tremble more.

"What the hell are you talking about?" Woody shrieked, "Just tell me which jail you're taking me too, okay?"

Cooper's rifle barrel jabbed Woody in the chest. "Hell. That's the jail I'm taking you to." Woody's eyes opened wide. His lips started to form the word, "No," but Cooper pulled the trigger first. Blood spray plastered Cooper's chest and face. He spat and wiped his sleeve across his face, as Woody's body slid to the ground. Woody's mouth worked wordlessly for a few seconds and his eyes pleaded with Cooper's. Then, his jaw fell slack and his eyes went blank. His body folded onto itself on the rough asphalt.

Cooper spent a long second staring at Woody's dead body. He appeared so frail and small, much more so now. The witch's brew of grieving rage at Jake's forced march from innocent childhood to harsh maturity was sated, but only for the briefest of moments. By the time he turned and began running back toward Dranko, it was perched firmly once more in the dark recesses of his belly.

****

Cooper reasoned that since he'd been able to clear the enemy's line without being shot by their sniper perched in the house, Angela must have wounded or killed him. He sprinted back to where he'd left Dranko, his mind tortured by worry. *I've paid enough, please don't take Paul away, too.* He covered the ground in a matter of seconds, though it felt like hours.

He rounded the edge of the vehicle's bumper. Calvin was kneeling, blocking his view.

"It just hurts, like a sonofabitch," Dranko was complaining.

Cooper's free hand clasped to his heart and he let loose a long sigh of relief, "You're alright," he blurted as he arrived, next to Calvin.

Calvin was beaming, "Yes! He had a bulletproof vest on! Can

you believe it?"

Cooper's eyes met Dranko's for a moment and they exchanged a look that conveyed his relief and his love for his friend all at once. He didn't need words. Dranko simply nodded.

"I'm going to check on Freddie, then," Cooper intoned.

Calvin waved his left hand, "I already did. Angela is with him. He will be fine. He took one through the shoulder, but Angela said it was a clean wound."

Cooper nodded, "Good. I'll radio the vehicles to come up. With all this gunfire, we need to get out of here as fast as possible."

Calvin's head drew back and confusion clouded his features, "Why?"

"You ever see a vulture?"

Calvin nodded, his eyebrows remained drawn together, "Sure. And?"

"Some vultures walk on two legs."

Calvin drew back once more, but this time in recognition, "Ahhh!"

"Will you help Angela get Freddie ready to move?"

Calvin drifted away as a response.

Cooper fumbled his radio out of its pocket and radioed Julianne and Lily that they should come as quickly as possible. He then turned his attention to Dranko, who was seated on the ground, his rifle lying next to him.

"You alright?"

"Yeah, I think so. I don't think anything's broken, but it hurts like hell," Dranko responded, a grimace on his face, and his right hand massaging where he'd been shot.

"Calvin did well. Very well," Cooper commented.

Dranko nodded enthusiastically, "I was disoriented for a few seconds after I was hit, but I kept hearing steady gunfire."

"He was a fool or brave for stepping into your spot and just letting loose."

"That line is always a very fine one, isn't it, brother?"

Cooper chuckled, "It is, for sure."

"What are you guys laughing about?" Calvin's deep voice rang out from behind him.

Cooper turned to face him, "The thin line between bravery and foolishness. You did really well just now. You saved us all."

Calvin's lips pursed, "I just followed the plan."

"The plan didn't include Dranko getting shot at jump street.

Many people woulda panicked at that. You didn't." Cooper returned.

"It was nothing. You two would have done the same."

Cooper nodded, "Maybe. But, we've both been trained. And, I've seen trained men wilt under fire. You did very well, Calvin," Cooper finished by clapping him on the shoulder.

"Sure, thanks. Glad I held up, alright." Calvin's eyes grew worried. He staggered and dropped to one knee. Cooper followed him down so he could maintain eye contact.

"You alright?"

"I...I...feel sick," Calvin said as his body began trembling.

Cooper clasped him by the shoulders, "You'll be okay. It's the adrenaline. You're coming down from the rush of combat."

Calvin's face was flushed, sweating, and it had lost its pallor, "I'm gonna be..." A splash of vomit across the asphalt interrupted him. Cooper curled his nose at a smell he abhorred and averted his eyes.

He looked into Calvin's eyes, "Listen to me. You're going to shake for a while. It's normal. And, it's far better to get the shakes *after* a firefight than *during* one!" Calvin mustered a feeble smile and dipped his head in agreement. "Just stay on your knees or sit down, but keep taking deep breaths. It'll pass."

The revving of his truck's engine made him turn his head. He patted Calvin on the shoulder once more and moved toward the sound. He arrived at where Freddie and Angela were waiting just as the vehicles carrying Julianne, Jake, and Lily pulled up. Lily and Julianne dismounted and clustered about him. Jake sat, disinterested, in the truck.

The two women checked in on Freddie's condition. Reassured, they turned to Cooper, who briefed them on what had happened. Minutes later, they were loaded into the vehicles and snaked their way past the barricade. Cooper stopped his truck on other side.

"What are you doing?" Julianne asked him.

"We need to gather up their weapons. Can you help?" He responded as he got out. She nodded and followed him.

He quickly made his way to the end of the line and began grabbing the discarded weapons and ammunition from the dead. He was back near the truck when he found Julianne staring blankly at the first body she had come to. She was motionless, her eyes fixated on the torn and bloody man that lay at her feet. Her right hand was clasped to her mouth. He kneeled down and rummaged through the man's pockets, taking the magazines for the rifle he'd carried and the loosened the belt that held the man's pistol. He reached up, handing the loose magazines to Julianne. She recoiled, stepping back.

He looked up at her, "I need your help. I can't carry all of this."

She remained stock still, her eyes unseeing.

Cooper recalled his father's words. *When they're in shock, sometimes you have to shock them out of it.* His father had been talking about his experiences from a bloody strike where he'd helped the longshoremen in Longview.

"C'mon! Snap out of it! I need you," he barked.

Julianne's eyes fluttered. Her gaze fell upon him and his outstretched hands. She shook herself and then grasped the magazines he held. He then pulled the man's pistol belt off of him and handed it to her as well.

Rising, "There you go. Thanks."

He led her to the pickup's bed and they deposited the weapons there. Julianne stumbled, still in a daze, back into the cab. He rounded the truck and lurched back in. He found the handheld radio.

"Lily, let me take the lead. We will get a bit down the road and find a place to hole up. We all need to rest."

"You got it, sweetie," the old woman's voice came back.

They drove down the road for a few miles until he spotted what looked like an abandoned house atop a hill. It was in an area where houses were spread out, most having at least a few acres to call their own. The front door was open, shifting in the wind. It looked to be a refurbished farmhouse. The finely manicured lawn and the lack of any garden area, despite the ample land surrounding the home, told Cooper it was likely a professional's home.

Cooper, Calvin, and Angela approached carefully. As they got closer, they saw scattered bullet holes and partly broken windows across the home's front. Fortunately, they cleared the home without incident and ensured its vacancy. The home's furnishings confirmed Cooper's intuition that this house belonged to someone better off; possibly someone who commuted to Portland. He saw no evidence of firearms being in the home: no safe, empty ammo boxes, or an abandoned rifle case. He shuddered to think what it must be like to be out on the open road without a single firearm. His stomach rolled as he thought about the bodies he'd seen on 82nd Avenue. Without question, some of those poor souls had met their demise without a means of protection.

A wall adorned with family photos, some missing, told him a family had lived here. The pictures gave Cooper pause. *Will families ever pose again for family photographs? Hell, will we have pictures at all anymore? He doubted photographic paper was on anyone's priority list for whatever remained of the disintegrating supply chain.* He sighed as he shouldered his rifle and stepped onto the porch to motion the others that it was 'all clear.'

After the vehicles were pulled behind the house and out of sight from the road, the rest of the group made their way inside.

Chapter Five

Angela cleaned and bandaged Freddie's wounds more thoroughly. He was soon asleep on a couch in the living room. Calvin did the same in a bedroom upstairs. Julianne fell into an easy chair and just stared into space. Dranko set about cleaning his rifle, moving stiffly, as Lily set up a portable stove in the kitchen and began brewing hot water.

"It's a mess in here," she called from the kitchen.

Cooper felt the fatigue, which always hit him after a firefight, begin to consume him.

"Angela, can you keep guard for a while?" Cooper asked.

"Sure. What are you going to do?"

"I'm gonna catch some shuteye. Can you wake me in two hours?" She nodded.

He turned to Jake, "Rest if you want, son. When I get up, we should scout the area and see if we can scavenge fuel or other supplies." Jake simply stared back at him and nodded numbly.

Cooper ascended the stairs. When he made it to the landing, the plaintive sounds of Julianne sobbing found his ears. He shook his head. *One firefight and most of us are spent. A firefight we barely survived.* He found an empty bedroom. A pennant for the Seattle Mariners adorned the space above the bed. Posters of a singer he didn't recognize plastered the wall opposite the bed. A desk, papers and books strewn across it, sat in the corner. The drawers had been emptied and clothes were haphazardly scattered throughout the room. He stood over the desk and looked at an unfinished sheet of math problems. *I think this family bugged out in a hurry. Probably when it first started.*

He unburdened himself of his gear. He checked the FAL's stock and saw the clean hole the bullet had made. Thankfully, it was in a place that wouldn't interfere with its operation. He set his rifle leaning against the wall, and collapsed into the bed. He was asleep in minutes.

****

Cooper's eyes flew open. He'd been dreaming about running across open ground, bullet whizzing by his ears. Jake had been wounded, fifty yards ahead. In his dream, a rifle round smashed into his chest, his arms outstretched helplessly toward Jake, when he awoke. He was panting, his body damp with sweat, when his eyes jerked open and saved him from his nightmare. He startled backwards, seeing Jake asleep and curled up next to him in the bed. Jake rumbled at his movement, but fell back into easy breathing.

His face was placid. Cooper watched him in earnest. His face was soft in slumber. It was the look he had seen on his son's face countless times when he had looked in on him before he had left on one of his many trips for work. Emotions welled up inside him. *He looks like Jake again. He's a boy once more.* Tears ran down his face. His heart began to race. He was terrified because he knew that when Jake woke up, the boy would be gone. His hands clasped together and came to his face. His fingers kneaded in anxiety. His eyebrows drew together, knowing he was powerless to stop the transformation that was so quickly overtaking his son. He desperately wanted to remain in this place forever. *Like it was before all this started.* He thought of Elena's body moldering in a cold grave, miles away. He wished that he and Jake could descend these stairs and find her making them a warm breakfast. Instead, he knew they would leave here and confront a world determined to rob them of their lives. His jaw clenched. *It's already taken his mother. It's already stolen his childhood.* His hands became fists. Inside, he raged against his impotence to protect his son. *All I can do now is make sure he lives. At least I can do that.*

"Time to get up," Angela yelled into the room.

He jerked his head around, glaring at the intrusion. She startled.

"You said to wake you in two hours," she protested. He nodded gravely at her, his eyes dropping in defeat. He turned back toward Jake.

His eyes fluttered open. Cooper's heart broke watching him transition from the boy, peaceful in sleep, but growing stiff as he stumbled toward alertness. Cooper watched the transformation with growing despair. Jake's lips drew tight. His jaw muscles tensed. His eyes reduced themselves to narrow slits. His breath grew shallow. In seconds, it was complete.

"You ready to go?" Jake asked. His voice was flat, but it cut Cooper's insides to ribbons. In vain, he brushed a lock of hair from Jake's forehead. Jake's face remained hard as he shook his head to free himself from his father's touch. Cooper grunted, sat up, turned away, and his feet fell heavily to the floor. They sounded like weights being clattered to the floor by an exhausted weight lifter.

Cooper and Jake stood in the living room, equipped and ready to go.

"We're going to survey a few houses I saw as we were coming in. We'll see what we can find. I'm hoping fuel. We can never have too much of that."

Dranko nodded, "You know where the siphon is, right?"

"Yup. I'll fuel our vehicles with one of our five gallon cans and see if we can refill it. I'm sure we burned at least that much in our slow going so far. We'll move back to the west, no more than a mile. We'll have our radio. Call us if anything happens back here."

"You do the same," Dranko responded.

He turned to Jake, "You ready?"

He shrugged his shoulders, "Got nothing else better to do."

After refueling the vehicles and finding the siphon, they were walking down the driveway toward the main road. Cooper had his rifle at the ready, while Jake carried the jerry can. His Ruger .22 rifle was slung across his shoulder.

Cooper noticed the deep silence all around them. In Portland, the clamor of city life had declined enormously within a few days of the plague's outbreak. Still, the noise from vehicles of various kinds and generators could be heard at most times. Here, the stillness was pervasive. It reminded him of times he'd been in the forest hunting. Things were so quiet he heard not only the calls and whistles of birds, but the buzzing of insects flittering about, as well. He drank it in as their footfalls thumped along the asphalt road. He and his son walked like this for several minutes.

They came to the first house. It was a white mobile home, the joints stained by rust. An old pickup truck was parked in the driveway, its left front tire flat. Cooper hoped the vehicle has some fuel inside it. He further hoped that the place was deserted.

"I'm going to approach the place, slowly. You cover me from…"

Cooper hadn't finished his sentence when the metal can clattered to the ground and fell onto its side in the dirt next to the road. Jake had taken off at a full run toward the mobile home, unslinging his rifle as he did so.

He stifled his urge to call after him, fearing that it could alert anyone who might be residing there. Instead, he ran after him, keeping his rifle at the ready. Inside, he cursed his son's recklessness. Within seconds, Jake arrived at the door to the home. Cooper scanned the windows in a frenzy, looking for any sign of movement.

His heart leapt into his throat when Jake reached the door, yanked it open, and disappeared into the dark inside.

"Damn," he cursed and strained to run faster.

He crashed into the doorjamb and ran his eyes over the interior, while flipping his flashlight on. It revealed a living room with a rundown couch, a brown leather easy chair, and a wooden coffee table. A huge flat screen television dominated the room, made larger by the small room it occupied. He heard Jake slamming doors open down a hallway to the left, presumably where the bedrooms were. Cooper crossed the room and looked into an empty kitchen, with dishes and containers scattered across the yellow Formica countertop. He ripped the curtain off its rod and peered out into the backyard. It looked similarly deserted.

Satisfied, he returned his attention back to the living room, just as Jake sauntered back in. He wore a wide, cocky grin. Cooper's face flushed red and he closed the gap between them in giant strides.

His open backhand slammed across Jake's left cheek. "What the hell were you doing?" He yelled, as spittle flew from his lips.

Jake fell to one knee, and Cooper did not know if it was from shock or the force of his blow. His cheek glowed red and bitter tears cascaded down his face.

The blow had sapped his rage. He'd never struck his son before. Remorse raced in to fill the empty space. He dropped to one knee, so he could look Jake in the eye.

"Why did you do that, son?"

He struggled to find breath in between his sobs, "I…didn't…want…to be…afraid."

"You coulda been killed!"

Jake's eyes went cold, "So?" Cooper recoiled in horror, his eyes going wide. His rifle fell from his grasp and bounced on the floor, its metallic ring filling the room. He grabbed Jake's cheeks with both hands.

"What do you mean? So?" His face pleaded along with his words.

Jake's eyes fell to the ground. "I mean. I mean," he stumbled as he looked back up to his father. "I'm going to die, dad. Everyone's dying. What does it matter *when*?"

Cooper's eyes stung and his heart joined his rifle, lying on the floor, "Oh my Lord, Jake. You just can't think like that."

Jake's response was cold, unyielding, "Why not?"

"Because it isn't true. You survived the plague."

"Brushfire didn't kill that boy back there. That boy with the Pez dispenser. It was bullets, dad. Bullets!"

Cooper's hands fell to his son's shoulders and he shook them, "That boy didn't have me at his side. Or, Dranko or Calvin. There are a lot of people here to protect you. Don't you see that?" He pleaded.

Jake paused, thinking. "Dad, I'm just tired of being scared. And, I don't know what I'm living for. The world is gone. It's gone," his last words rising to a shrill scream. A new round of sobbing shook his small body.

It was Cooper's turn to think. "You live for your mama, son. You live for her. She's *in* you. Yes, the world has been turned upside down. But, as long as you are alive, you live for her legacy, you hear me!"

Jake's eyes were impassive, his jaw set, "She's dead." His words dripped with a bitter finality that no eleven year old should ever know.

Cooper's heart felt like it was being sawn in two by a dull, rusted blade. It burned in pain. Tears piled down his face and he pulled Jake into a tight embrace, "Then, live for *me*, son. Live for me. I can't lose you, too. *Please.*"

The seconds ticked by as Cooper clutched to pull Jake in tighter still. His mind raced to find words that he could not. His breath came in ragged gasps, as desperate as his heart. He felt it before he heard it. It was a tension in Jake's belly that moved up his chest and erupted in a long wail of despair and grief. Cooper felt as if the mobile home's walls were shaking under its fury. Jake's body rocked back and forth as the agony was unleashed. When it ended, Cooper's ears rang in the silence.

"I miss her," Jake rasped in a silent whisper.

"Me, too," Cooper breathed into his son's ear. "Me, too."

Minutes ticked by as they sat holding one another, both crying.

Jake broke the embrace by drawing back, "I'll try."

"Try what?"

"To live. For her." He paused, as a fresh round of sobs enveloped him. He squeezed his father even harder, "For you, too."

Cooper's heart skipped a beat. He breathed it in. Then, he cupped his son's chin with his right hand until their eyes met, "Thank you. Someday soon you will see that you can live for yourself, too. There *will* be a future worth living in, son." Jake's unmoving face told him he didn't believe him. Once again, he recalled words of wisdom from his own father. *Sometimes you can't get everything you want in one conversation. If you get halfway there, accept it. Wait for another day.* With that, he fought his compulsion to argue with Jake about it.

"I'm sorry son."

"I know, dad. The hitting. It hurt."

"I know. It won't ever happen again."

"And, not just here," Jake said pointing to his cheek. His hand fell to rest over his heart as fresh tears welled up. "Here."

Cooper felt a vice over his heart and his eyes offered remorse, "I promise never again. And, I ask for your forgiveness, son."

Jake simply nodded in response. Cooper saw tenderness in his son's eyes that melted his heart. He grew wistful when he saw something else in those eyes that he had not seen in a long time. The sympathy held in Jake's eyes was reminiscent of the forgiveness he'd often see in Elena's eyes after he had wronged her in some way. *God, do I miss her.* He felt relief at pulling Jake back from a deadly precipice of despair. Worry clawed at him and chilled his insides. *Can I keep him away from this edge with everything all around us is pushing him towards it?*

"You ready to get back to work?"

"Yup," Jake said, and a smile that Cooper would have sold his soul to the devil for crested across his face.

Cooper returned it, "It's good to see you smile, son." Jake blushed, but the smile just grew wider.

They quickly searched the mobile home, looking for items of use. It had been stripped of most things useful to a group on the move, but Jake found a forgotten box of 9mm pistol cartridges in the back of a dresser drawer. They moved outside, this time in tandem. Cooper went first and Jake covered him from the back door. After double-checking that no one was in the immediate area, he motioned for Jake to join him next to the disabled pickup truck.

Cooper had to strike the gas tank's lid with his rifle butt to get it moving. Freeing it, they found it able to easily fill their five gallon can.

"We have to hope that the gas ain't gone bad," Cooper intoned as he fastened the lid onto the jerry can.

"What do you mean? I thought gas lasted forever?"

Cooper shook his head, "Nope. It only lasts for a year at most before becoming unusable in a car. Only if it's treated with the right additives will it last longer."

Jake shrugged, "Weird."

"It does smell good and strong, so I think it will work," Cooper said as he handed the can to Jake.

Upon first grabbing it, his arms didn't hold the weight and it fell to the ground. Cooper laughed, "Heavier now, isn't it?"

Jake laughed too, but steadied his feet and hefted it again, this time successfully.

The cackle from the radio caught their attention, "Cooper, you there?" He recognized Dranko's voice.

"Yes. Here."

"You better get back here, fast."

"Why?"

"There's news on the ham radio. You aren't going to like it."

The smiles faded from their faces. "On it. Back in ten."

"Let me carry the can so we can move faster. I need you on point, eyes sharp and your rifle ready to go." Cooper couldn't help but think about the absurdity of such an order being given to an eleven-year-old just a few weeks ago.

Now, in a different world, Jake took it in stride, "Got it." He handed the gas can to his father and unslung his rifle. He marched out ten yards before looking back to make sure he was following him. Cooper shook his head in disbelief and began following his son back to where the others were holed up.

****

Everyone was gathered around Dranko's portable ham radio in the kitchen, except Calvin, because he was on watch and Freddie, who was sleeping on the nearby couch.

"They're still talking about it," Angela exclaimed just as soon as Cooper pushed open the door.

"What?"

"Just listen," Dranko ordered.

"...of Oregon and California are welcoming the aid, while the Governor of Washington is calling it, and I quote, 'an unprecedented act of underhanded aggression at a time of perilous need.'"

Cooper shot Dranko a confused look. Dranko responded by motioning him to keep listening by extending his index finger and drawing small circles in the air with his hand.

"...the President has said that our nation needs any assistance that can be lent and that his administration will 'fully investigate' the allegations that Chinese troops have accompanied the medical and police personnel."

"In other news related to the Brushfire Plague, the reports of reduced *lethality have now been confirmed in all corners of the globe. Medical and scientific personnel report that the Brushfire Plague is now no more dangerous than the common flu to most people. Casualty figures have proven impossible to determine as many governments are either unable, or unwilling, to provide accurate figures. However, our statistical department has extrapolated the casualties from three cities on three continents and we estimate that close to 1.2 billion have died worldwide from the Brushfire Plague. The dead and those wounded from widespread violence in the wake of the disease is impossible to responsibly estimate. We now go to an interview with Doctor Zhao on the likely path of the Brushfire Plague in its new, less deadly, form…"*

Cooper and the others let loose a collective exhale. Angela's hands went to her mouth and tears filled her eyes. Julianne collapsed into a chair and laid her head on folded arms, weeping. Lily remained stoic, merely shaking her head in disbelief. Dranko caught Cooper's eye as he surveyed the room.

"There's worse."

"Of course there is."

"They are talking about you quite a bit."

"I bet. What are they saying?"

"Just that you are a crazed liar. And, that every American should look for you and turn you in just the same. The one thing I can't figure is that they say they have 'reliable information' that you are headed from Portland to southern Oregon. Your ultimate destination is for you to rejoin your extended family in the Sacramento area."

Cooper burst out laughing and slapped his leg, "Really? It worked! The goddamn chickenshit did it!"

"What the hell are you talking about," Dranko demanded.

"When I didn't put a bullet into Gus' brain, I found another use for it. I told him to tell the authorities that I was going back home, to my family in Sacramento. That I could be protected and hidden there."

"Who are you talking about?" Angela asked.

"Gus! I had Gus feed them that line, to try and throw them off our trail."

First, Dranko smiled, and then he chuckled, "You are a sly son of a bitch! I wouldn't be surprised if we still get a visit out at my cabin, but this just might throw their main search efforts in the wrong direction."

Cooper's laughter faded, "Well, thanks for raining on my parade! But, I misled Gus even there. I couldn't trust that weasel, so I told him to tell the authorities I was heading to Sacramento and *not* the coast!"

"The coast? Nice, that's the opposite direction of here. So, you covered yourself on both sides of the misdirection," Dranko finished, pride creeping into his voice.

"Yup!" Cooper returned.

"Ssshh," Lily beckoned their attention by pointing to the ham radio.

"*…the Russian government is calling for 'retribution and justice' for the 'gravest sins committed by the Americans that can only be said to be worse than what the Nazis did in the Great Patriotic War'. They are demanding that an international community tribunal agree to surgical nuclear strikes against select U.S. cities. It is threatening unilateral action in the absence of such an agreement. Our President has promised swift retaliation for any such attack. Meanwhile, governments of twenty-seven other nations are calling upon the United Nations to investigate whether the release of the Brushfire Plague was the act of a small group of madmen or whether the United States government was complicit or had foreknowledge of the plan.*"

Cooper rubbed his temples, "My God. I opened a Pandora's box, didn't I? What have I done?"

Silence from around the table confirmed his fears. A chill ran down his spine. Angela circled the table to come to his side. She put her arm around him.

"You only did what you thought best, at the time you did it. You can't blame yourself."

Cooper thought for a moment and then looked at her, "Really? Would you say the same thing to Julianne?"

"That's different!" Her eyes were sharp, angry. Julianne looked up tentatively, while keeping her head resting on her arms.

"Is it? She did what she thought best given the information she had at the time she did it."

Angela thrust her hands into the air, "Christ, Cooper! Why do you defend her so?"

"It's not about her, it is just logic. If the Brushfire's blood is on her hands then…"

Lily's soft voice cut him off, "He's right. If that blood is on her hands, then any blood spilled because of Cooper telling the world the truth is on his hands. *Or*, their hands are both washed clean by the cleansing power of forgiveness."

"You're both impossible!" Angela fumed as she strode out of the kitchen.

Cooper saw the expectant look on Julianne's eyes, "Don't look to me. I think we're both guilty as sin for what we done. Good intentions don't change a damned thing."

The hope faded from her face, as quickly as it had sprouted, "You're right," she mumbled. She rose slowly from the table and almost stumbled out the back door into the yard. Cooper reasoned she did not want to take the same path as Angela and risk meeting up with her.

He turned to Dranko and Lily, "Well, isn't this a horrible mess?"

Lily snorted, "It's what my people would call a fine fiddled mess. I'd add it's also balancing just so on a hungry bear's nose."

"You sure have a way of putting it, Lily, I'll give you that," Dranko stated flatly.

"Let me see if I've been keeping score in this game. Point one, the Chinese may, at this very moment, be conducting some semi-covert invasion of America and our own leaders can't, or won't, tell us if its heads or tails. Point two, I'm a no good liar which every red-blooded American is looking for. Point three, me telling the world the truth might just set off World War Three. Oh, and point four is that said war might be happening when there are already 1.2 *billion* dead?"

Dranko crossed his arms and grunted his agreement.

"You forgot two points, dad," Jake offered from his perch on the kitchen counter. He had been so quite up until that moment, Cooper had forgotten he was even in the room. He twisted his body back to see him.

"And, what's that?"

"Point five, the plague *has* stopped killing people. And, point six, you made me smile again." His voice choked on the last words. Cooper felt his heart in his throat and a smile beamed across the room. He got up fast, nearly toppling the chair, and plucked Jake off the counter and lifted him into the air. Jake squealed with delight.

"Stop! Stop! Put me down," he yelled as Cooper twirled him around in the air. Cooper ignored his pleas and kept spinning in fast, tight, circles. Lily wore a wide grin and Dranko started chuckling.

"I'm gonna be sick," Jake moaned.

That stopped Cooper in an instant. He plopped him back onto the floor, steadying him as Jake swayed. He looked straight at him, "Thank you, Jake. You reminded me that no matter how bad things look, there's always something good, too."

"You taught me that dad!"

"Really? How?"

"I've just watched you keep setting Dranko straight and

100

figured it was my turn!"

"Ouch! That hurt," Cooper said, pantomiming a dart hitting him in the back.

"Welcome to the *dark side*," Dranko said in a voice mimicking Darth Vader. He paused, resuming in his regular tone, "And, let me be clear. By dark, I mean realistic and objective."

Cooper mocked him with a deep bow, "Of course, master of reality. Please humor us fools with our heads stuck up our..." He shot Jake a playful wink.

"Arses!" Jake yelped in an English accent, which he was very fond of impersonating.

Dranko stared at them, feigning annoyance. Cooper and Jake looked at one another and shrugged their shoulders in exaggerated innocence. Cooper couldn't remember the last time he'd had such a playful moment with his son. It warmed his heart and he ached to hold onto it. He managed to pull Jake into playing cards and they exchanged some laughs while playing Crazy Eights. When lunch was made, it pulled them back to their stark reality.

Lily and Dranko had boiled water and made a bounty of pasta. They had found only random condiments and a few dented cans of food left in the house, so they had to use their own supplies. Cooper had looked at the different muddy footprints about the house and how disheveled everything looked to guess this home had been picked over multiple times already. Dranko had taken what little remained.

As they gathered to eat, Cooper eyed Jake numbly chomping his noodles. There was no sauce on them. Scattered drops of oil adorned them, as did scant specks of salt and pepper. They couldn't afford the weight of sauce in their supplies. To say it was the blandest bowl of noodles Cooper had ever eaten would have been an understatement.

"These are yucky," Jake complained.

Cooper gave him a sharp look, "It's not polite to criticize food someone else has made for you."

Lily laughed, "I'm not offended. I know this tastes drier than a cactus planted in hell. But, you know what, boy?" Her gaze stiffened as her eyes burned into Jake's.

"What," he gulped.

"I bet there are a lot of folks that are going hungry right now."

Jake's easy smile returned and he rolled his eyes, "Yeah, yeah. Dad's told me about the poor kids in other countries a million times."

Lily's continued, unblinking, "I'm not talking about other

countries."

"Huh?"

"Really. I'm talking about kids here. In Oregon. Kids in Portland. Kids you went to school with. Hungry."

Jake's face went white and his smile collapsed.

"That's right, Jake. We're just over two weeks since the grocery stores were picked clean. Far too many Americans have, at most, two weeks of food in their homes. That's all gone now." Cooper added.

"That includes people scavenging the homes of the dead," Dranko piled on. Cooper gave him a sharp look.

"Well, I've read places that Portland always has at least one ship full of grain in dock that can feed the city for a year," Dranko stumbled, trying to soften what he'd just said.

"Oh," was all Jake said. Then, he fell back into eating his spaghetti. After several more mouthfuls, he spoke once more, "These don't taste too bad. You get used to it."

The adults around the table exchanged knowing smiles.

****

After dinner, they gathered in the home's living room. Angela was outside, patrolling the area and keeping a lookout. Freddie was awake, reclining on a sofa in the corner of the room. Lily had made everyone tea, as they'd decided what coffee they had left would only be brewed in the mornings. The group sat in silence for a long time, each left to their own thoughts. The mood slowly descended to an oppressive one. Cooper watched it for a while, sipping the weak tea. Once again, his father's words came to him: *when in crisis, don't let others descend into despair.*

He mustered a lively tone, "So, what's everyone looking forward to most when things return to normal?"

"You mean the things we'll never see or experience again?" Dranko muttered in between sips of tea.

Chagrined, Cooper looked at him and shook his head, "Whatever. Just what you miss the most."

Several seconds of silence passed, no one wanting to speak first.

"For me, it's having choices. I used to complain about how there were thirty-seven brands of toothpaste at the store. Now, to see that again, I'd feel like I won the lottery!" Freddie offered from where he lay.

"I second that! Now, it looks like I will be using Colgate for the rest of my life since that is what Paul stockpiled. I hate Colgate!" Calvin exclaimed.

Dranko looked up, a sour look on his face, "They were having a big sale once, so that's what I got."

"Well, if I had known you were getting ready for the end of the world, I would have given you a few extra dollars to spring for Crest!" Calvin said, laughing deeply.

Undeterred, Dranko continued, "I couldn't tell anyone what I was doing. I couldn't trust anyone. Otherwise, they'd all beat down my door the moment something happened and I couldn't supply everyone."

Cooper let loose a guffaw, "Hell, you didn't even trust me. And, I'm your best friend."

"I'm careful."

"Damn, Dranko, you wouldn't trust your mother if she was walking hand in hand with Jesus Christ himself!" A round of guffaws echoed off the walls.

When it died down, Dranko looked up from his tea, smiling slyly, "Well, you never met my mother now, did you?" The room erupted in laughter once more.

"Calvin makes a good point. If you'd figured out who you *could* have trusted and talked to some of us, we would have all been better prepared for this. Hell, the whole country would have been better off," Cooper said, turning serious.

"I guess I'll know better for next time, right?" Dranko rebuffed him. He thought for a few seconds, stroking his chin, "I guess that's a good question."

"What?" Calvin asked.

"How could I have figured out who to trust without telling you all I was a diehard survivalist?"

After a pause, Julianne replied, "That would have been easy."

"How so?" Dranko asked.

"You could have asked people if they were worried about an earthquake here. Ask them if they had thought about getting ready for it. See what they say and go from there."

Cooper rubbed the side of his face, feeling the whiskers of several days growth, "That's good. You could have also asked people how they'd deal with being unemployed for a long time. Having some extra food on hand would be a good idea in that event."

"Or, asked them what they would do if something like Katrina ever happened in Portland," Calvin added.

"Yeah!" Julianne sat up, getting excited, "That would be a good way to find out if they were ready to think about civil disorder, too."

Dranko grunted, "True. I guess we'll all be better prepared next time Julianne helps someone upend the world." The air left the room. Cooper stared him down with a ferocious gaze, his eyes asking his friend, "Really?"

Julianne sank back into the armchair where she sat. She fixed her eyes on her teacup and slipped into heavy thought.

"Who's next?" Cooper asked, hoping to lighten the mood.

"Mine's easier than trapping a rat with peanut butter and molasses," Lily said. "I'm gonna miss that sweet Kentucky bourbon. I'm down to a few sips and then I trust I won't see it for a good long while."

"I thought all you white folks from Kentucky came out of the womb with the tubing for a still instead of an umbilical cord!" Freddie shouted, before coughing.

Lily looked at him with mock sternness, "While that's a true fact, moonshine ain't the same as the nectar of God brewed up by St. Jack Daniels!"

Smiles resounded throughout the room.

"You know what I miss?" Jake asked from where he lay on the floor, looking up at the ceiling.

"What's that, son?"

"Video games!" He shouted with glee.

"You'll be happy to know that I have a solar-powered Gameboy up at the cabin," Dranko said.

Jake sat up, "Really?"

"No. I'm just kidding."

Jake's face fell and he abruptly went back to lying down.

"That was cruel!" Calvin rebuked Dranko.

Dranko looked sheepish. "No, it wasn't. I *do* have the ability to charge batteries with solar. So, we'll see what we can do."

"Whatever." Jake said, feigning disinterest.

"Well, I am looking forward to a cup of fine roasted Stumptown coffee. They could brew it up like no one else," Calvin continued. Several in the room took a long pause, inhaling, as if the coffee lay before them.

"Who wants to tell me I should have stored a...what do you call those fancy coffee makers?" Dranko responded, sarcasm lacing his words.

"A French press," Julianne offered.

"Yeah, that," Dranko deadpanned.

"What are you looking *forward to?*" Cooper directed his question at Dranko.

Dranko sat up, forcing a wide smile onto his face, his voice unnaturally chipper, "Gee, Beave, I'm looking forward to getting ready for the next apocalypse!" As soon as he'd finished, his face went sour once more and he sat back into his chair.

"You're an incorrigible ass!" Cooper fired back. "The worst part is I *do* think that is what you're looking forward to!"

Dranko pursed his lips, "Seriously, brother? This is much worse than I ever thought it would be. I'm glad I prepared. But, I would never wish this again."

Cooper nodded in a half-apology, "I hear you."

Silence once again claimed the room. The only sounds were the occasional slurping of those drinking and the intermittent cough or grunt.

After several minutes had passed, Jake piped up, "It's your turn, dad."

Cooper looked up, startled. *I want to tell them I miss the peace. I miss sitting in my home with my woodstove fired up and soaking in its warmth. My wife under my arm and my boy playing at my feet. That's what I really miss. Simple quiet. The contentment of it.* He knew saying something like this would bring everyone else down again. Once again his father's words came to him, *"Leadership means not always saying what you feel. Be true, but be honest with a purpose."*

"I'm looking forward to having a Snickers bar again."

"Really?" Dranko asked.

"Yeah, really."

"Out of all that civilization has to offer, you want a cheap candy
bar?"

"Okay. Fine. There's something else. I will miss the chance of seeing AC/DC ever play in concert again!"

Calvin fell out laughing, "Weren't those old guys *already* dead!"

Cooper looked at him askance, "They weren't *that* old! I just saw them a few years ago."

"Where? At the morgue?" Freddie deadpanned. The room fell into raucous laughter and Cooper had to endure several more rounds of joking at this expense. *Mission accomplished,* he thought, easing back into the couch and taking it all in good humor.

****

Cooper was on guard duty in the dead of night. He conducted what they called a 'loose patrol', which meant he would walk about thirty yards, wait silently for ten minutes listening, and then walk again. Over time, he would circle the farmhouse several times during his watch. Dranko and he had devised the system because their limited manpower meant they could not afford to have two people on duty at a time. They also thought it was a good system to make sure their untrained crew did not fall asleep. It wasn't perfect, but it was the best that they could manage to protect those sleeping inside. *Don't let the perfect get in the way of good enough.*

The air was chilly, as it often was during spring in the Northwest. Cooper made a mental note to dress warmer the next time he drew this shift. His breath frosted into the night air as he exhaled. He had come on at midnight and was due to be on guard until 4:00am, when Dranko would relieve him.

After the first hour passed quietly, he heard a high pitched whine as a bevy of motorcycles screamed down the road in front of the farmhouse, heading for some point west—back toward Portland. As they approached, Cooper tensed and made ready to let the fog horn wail as a warning to the others. The fog air horn had been one of the more clever things that Dranko had stashed away in his supplies; a neat twelve-pack of them. When Cooper asked what they were for, he was sanguine, "Poor man's warning system. We can use them as an easy 'all warning' system. And, when our batteries run out on our walkie talkies, they will be our *only* good way to warn each other!" At the time, Cooper had laughed. But, the more he'd thought about it, he understood the wisdom behind it. The system they had developed was simple, easy to remember. This was critical when working with the untrained. One long wail meant to come running and be ready to fight. Two long blasts meant to approach cautiously, but be ready to fight, as well. Three long blasts meant to flee at all costs. As the motorcycles passed by at full-speed, he replaced the horn into his pants pocket.

Completing his second circuit, Cooper approached the front of the house. He saw someone standing on the porch, so the whisper didn't surprise him.

"Cooper," Julianne's hushed voice barely reached him.

He made a wide circle with his hand, indicating she should come to him.

She ambled towards him, wrapping her arms tightly around herself, to ward off the chill. As she drew near, Cooper noticed how even in the dull light of the moon, her hair and features were striking. Her eyes glinted and found his. *She looks right through me.* The instant intimacy that her eyes conjured made him uneasy. He looked out towards the road to avoid them.

"What is it?" he asked, forcing gruffness into his voice.

"I need to talk to you."

"Well, make it quick. Even whispering is dangerous if anyone is coming toward us quietly."

"I'm not sure where to start. It's just that…I need…" Julianne fumbled, shifting her feet, and rubbing her arms vigorously.

"Just spit it out," Cooper commanded, his voice rising just above a whisper.

She grabbed his chin, forcing him to look into her eyes, "I need to know if you'll ever forgive me?" Her tone was firm, almost more of a statement than a question. Her eyes burrowed into his and he had no escape. He felt like she could look into his soul and he could not stop his heart warming, the ice he wanted there so badly, melting.

"That's a lot to ask."

She lowered her eyes to the ground, her whisper grew softer, "I know. We were right on the problem, but very wrong on the solution. I see that now. But, I couldn't see that…I was blinded by…"

"Passion. You were a zealot, Julianne. Zealots only see one thing clearly and it makes them miss the other things. It's a great strength and a great weakness," Cooper finished, now pulling her face up toward his.

"So, what does that mean? Will you forgive me?" Her eyes pleaded with his. It was an act of will for him not to blurt out "Yes!"

Instead, he shook his head, averted his eyes, and cocked his eyebrows, "I don't know. I understand what you did. That's for sure."

"You do?" Julianne's quizzed, as her face grew confused.

"Of course. I'm a zealot, too! For me it is the truth. I'm beginning to see that telling the truth about Brushfire may cost many, many more lives. I didn't think much about it before. So, I understand what you did."

"You do?" Julianne's face alighted, a tiny, hopeful smile growing.

"I do. It doesn't mean I agree with it. And, then I think about my wife Elena lying buried in the ground. I think about what Jake has had to endure since all of this. How he's lost his childhood," Cooper's voice cracked on the last words. He paused before continuing, "And, then I hate you like I've never hated anyone." His voice grew cold and his eyes burned into her as he spoke. "I don't hate easy, either."

Julianne's face became crestfallen and her eyes glistened in the faint moonlight. Once again, she lowered them. "I understand," she mouthed more than whispered.

Cooper grabbed her by the shoulder and pulled her towards him, their eyes locking once more, "But, the worst part is. I *can't* hate you. Not for long, anyway. I don't know why. It's just…" Now, it was Cooper's turn to be at a loss for words. Julianne stared at him, bewildered.

"I'm drawn to you, Julianne. I don't *want* to be, but I can't help it," Cooper pleaded, his voice plaintive.

Julianne's eyes searched his face as her hand fell upon his cheek, caressing it. His face turned into it, seeking a deeper grasp. She bit her lower lip, as the anticipation sparked between them.

His eyes mimicked hers, scanning her face, soaking up every detail. He felt lost in her eyes; the deep pools of brown felt like they were swallowing him. The touch of her hand on his face was electric, especially as it glided down to his neck.

His hand reached for the back of her head and pulled her toward him, fingers twining into her hair. His lips found hers and their lips grappled with each other. She found his full lower lip and pulled it into her mouth, teeth nibbling it. Cooper exhaled. He shifted and enveloped her upper lip, his tongue sliding along it lightly. Their bodies pressed against each other. Her arms wrapped around him, pulling him in tightly. He felt her breasts push into his body and the play of her fingers on his back. Rank arousal coursed through him.

The effect was dramatic. Cooper recoiled and drew away. They stood just feet apart, their arms still extended towards one another, the tips of their fingers almost touching. Cooper shook his head vigorously, "I'm sorry. I can't." He turned on his heels and walked briskly toward the road. *What was that?* His mind roiled as he turned the question over and over, without answer.

Julianne stood in the gravel driveway for several minutes, watching him walk away into the dark. Finally, she shook her head in confusion and went back inside.

Chapter Six

In the morning, Cooper did his best to avoid Julianne. Sensing his discomfort, she did the same. They ate a hurried breakfast of boiled rolled oats flavored with brown sugar and leavened with some raisins. Cooper knew Jake hated Quaker Oats, but after last night, he kept his mouth shut. He winked at him and Jake dealt a knowing smile back. The adults had coffee, but Dranko did his best to ruin it by repeating what he'd said the day before.

"Don't forget, this'll be gone soon. So, enjoy it."

"Yes, we get it. Now, can you just shut up and let us enjoy it?" Cooper snarled at him.

Dranko drew back, "Well, ex-cuuussse me for telling the truth. I thought you liked that sort of thing?"

Cooper just glared at him and loudly sipped his coffee. The others stayed out of it.

They packed, faster than the day before as they gained proficiency with the routine and Dranko's system of organization. Freddie still moved slowly, but he was in much better shape and color than the day before. With Freddie in Dranko's Jeep, Cooper took point. Jake went into Dranko's vehicle, while Angela joined Cooper. They were on the road by six a.m.

"When we get two miles east of Carver, let me take the lead for a minute. We need to make a pit stop there," Dranko told him, with an impish smile splashed onto his face. Cooper decided not to bother asking why.

They covered the few miles to Carver quickly. Apparently, the local residents had pushed the vehicles off the road with efficiency, as the shoulders and fields alongside the road were littered with abandoned vehicles.

"I bet someone has a tow truck in town," Angela observed.

"And, they are organized," Calvin added. Cooper nodded at both comments. He picked up the radio as they neared the town.

"We have a family sitting next to their car about a mile up," he informed Dranko. He spotted something else and clicked the call button again, "You see that field turned up on the right?"

"The long rectangle?" Dranko responded.

"The same. Looks like a mass grave to me," Cooper added.

He heard Dranko whistle over the walkie talkie, "Damn near. Could be. We better be on the alert going in."

"Let's stop and talk to this family, maybe they can tell us something."

"Good."

Cooper stopped the truck about twenty yards away from the family and their idled Chevy Malibu. *Twenty yards is a pistol shot most people can't make. And, if they have rifles, it probably wouldn't matter. If they'd wanted, they could have fired on us as soon as we'd come into view.*

Cooper stepped out of the truck, and Calvin and Angela exited the other side. The family was bedraggled. The father was in his thirties, dressed in dirty jeans and a grease stained sweatshirt. He looked like he hadn't slept in days. His wife was plain-looking with no remarkable features. She was cleaner than her husband, wearing brown hiking pants and a North Face black jacket. Two children lay huddled underneath blankets in the back seat. It looked like they had been camping there for several days, as garbage and cooking paraphernalia lay scattered about.

"Mornin'," the man grumbled.

"Good morning. What's going on here?" Cooper asked.

The man stood up angrily, throwing a tin cup to the ground, "You can see can't you? You gonna help us or not?" The man had taken a step toward them, but Cooper's hand quickly found the grip of his holstered pistol and the man stopped just as abruptly.

He raised his left hand, palm out, "Why don't you take a step back?"

"C'mon Josh. Calm down," his wife pleaded.

Josh's face lost a shade of red and he stepped back and resumed leaning against the car. He lowered his head, "I'm sorry. We've just been asked twenty million times in the last week what's going on or what do we need and no one has helped us."

"What help do you need?" Calvin asked.

Josh laughed mockingly, "What *don't* we need? Hell, we need gas, food, and water."

"Where are you from?" Dranko asked, coming up from Cooper's left side.

"Beaverton. I got relatives in eastern Oregon."

"And you left home with just what you had in your tank?" Dranko blurted in shock.

"Actually, just three-quarters of a tank. That's all I had when this whole thing started," Josh said, the mirth of the hopeless clouding his voice.

"What's the deal up ahead? I'm assuming you just didn't

happen to run out of gas right outside of here," Cooper asked.

Josh nodded, his face growing foul once more, "Yeah. These bastards charge a toll. Ten gallons of gas or one hundred pounds of food to get through town. They call it a 'road mainteance' fee. I didn't have either. I burned what gas I had left trying to keep my kids warm at night."

"Why didn't you just siphon gas from all these cars around?"

"I'm not a moron. All these ones here were empty. This Carver crew is thorough."

"We can't spare gas, but I think we can..." Cooper began.

Dranko grabbed him by the arm, jerking Cooper around. He pulled him away from the group, "We can't give them food, Cooper."

"Why not? Just a little?"

"Because we don't have any to spare. We have no idea how long our stores will have to last. I stocked my cabin, but only for me. It might be months before we're producing enough food for ourselves."

"But..."

"But, nothing. These people are dead, anyway. He'll never...*never*, make it to his relatives. He's a dead man. And, he killed himself and his family because he didn't think, didn't plan, didn't do *shit!* You want to see Jake go hungry six months from now on account of this guy?"

Cooper grimaced, knowing his words were true, but liking it none the more. He briskly turned back toward the group and strode there, "Sorry, Josh. We can't help you."

Josh let loose an eerie cackle that grated on Cooper's ears. His wife fell out sobbing and rushed toward him. She grabbed Cooper by the shoulders. Her foul breath made him curl his lips, "Please, Mister! Help us! We're gonna die!" Her words pierced his heart, the desperation calling upon him.

He scowled and pushed her arms off of him. She fell to ground and collapsed. Her hands found his ankle and she pulled on them, rising to her knees, "Please. At least take my kids. You can save them. They don't deserve this!" Her cries wracked her body as she feebly grasped her hands to his legs.

Dranko stepped forward, "You're right. They don't. You should have planned better than this. Getting in your car and thinking you'll find gas and food along the way!" His words were laced with ice. Dranko's rage surprised Cooper as he yelled at her. The woman howled as he spoke. Josh stood up again, "Fuck you!" He looked ready to charge right at Dranko. Cooper drew his pistol and pointed it straight at Josh.

"We're going. Don't try anything stupid." He kept the pistol trained on him as everyone loaded back into their vehicles. Getting in, they drove off without incident, and witnessed Josh standing in the middle of the road flipping them off with both hands.

****

Minutes later, they approached the barricade outside of Carver. When their vehicles were within a hundred yards, a voice rang out over a bullhorn, "Stop right there."

Cooper stopped the truck and Dranko pulled along, forming a V across the road. Everyone emptied out of the vehicles, except Freddie and Jake.

"One man approaches. No weapons," the bullhorn called once more.

Cooper began taking off his weapons, smiling widely, "Negotiation time. Get the rifles ready to go and have your aim on them. I need some leverage, after all." Dranko, Calvin, and Angela nodded and moved into action.

Leaving his rifle behind, Cooper approached the barricade slowly, hands raised. He couldn't shake the feeling of just how *vulnerable* he was. *One jumpy finger on a trigger and I could be dead and Jake an orphan. Just like that.* The thought sent a cold chill run down his back. As he drew closer, he saw four men on the barricade; three with scoped hunting rifles and one with a shotgun. Off to his left, he spotted another, ably camouflaged on the top of a panel van, a rifle poking out from underneath a white tarp that made him blend into the van. He noted that they had positioned the van in front of a white building, which added to the concealment. *I'll have to remember that trick.* About a hundred yards behind the barricade, he spied six men lounging around a pickup truck, with weapons in various states of readiness. *Must be their 'reserve' ready to go to wherever needed.*

About twenty yards out, the apparent leader called out, "What do you want with the fine town of Carver?"

"Passage," Cooper called. "That's all."

The man bellowed, "That's all? I'm betting that's everything to you. That's why you're on the road at a time like this." *Posturing. That's good. That means he's getting ready to bargain.*

"We have a Plan B, but passage through would be easier," Cooper retorted, keeping his voice calm, in control. The words of his

112

father echoed in his mind: *never let the other guy know that he's the only game in town. Once you do, you're stuck and dependent on his charity – which means you are no longer negotiating.*

"I'd like to hear your Plan B."

Cooper shuffled his feet easily and held a steady gaze, "Well, I could tell you." He paused ror effect, "But, then I'd have to kill you." *Make the other guy laugh whenever you can. People at ease are better negotiators.*

The other man let loose a howl of laughter, "A joke. I like that. I haven't heard a joke from anyone on the other side of this barricade since all this started. Just a lot of moaning and crying."

"Well, we're not like the others you've seen."

The man stopped laughing slowly, "I see that. Shall we get down to business?"

"I thought you'd never ask," Cooper said lightly and the other man smiled again.

"The cost of passage is either ten gallons of gas, a hundred pounds of food, or a functioning rifle with one hundred rounds of ammunition," the man paused to let his words sink in. "Per vehicle."

Cooper purposefully let loose a guffaw, "Good one. I haven't heard a good joke like that since before all this started." *Whenever possible, ridicule the other's position and watch closely how he responds. It will tell you a lot.*

The other man spoke quickly, "I'm not joking. That's the price." *There it is, his voice sounds not nearly as sure as his words.* The trammel gave him away.

"I'll give you a few choices. First, we'll give you a twenty-five pound bag of rice or one hunting rifle that we have a handful of shells for. Second, we can have a little dust-up right now that probably leaves half on each side dead or wounded."

The man paused for several seconds before responding, "I don't like your threats, so why don't we knock that shit off?"

Cooper pursed his lips, "Agreed."

"You're gonna get me fired, but I'll do half our normal rate. One hundred pounds of food or the rifle and one hundred rounds. I like you; you made me laugh."

Ah, now we're negotiating. Just a matter of time now before a deal is reached. Cooper breathed easier.

It took five more minutes of relentless back and forth, blustering, and moaning, but he finally agreed to give them passage in exchange for the rifle, the handful of rounds for it, and a six- pack of

113

canned peaches. The rifle was the one that Angela had used when they'd attacked Ethan Mitchell's compound. With just a few rounds left for it, it was nearly worthless to them. Fortunately for Cooper, he learned this group had an ample supply of ammunition of this caliber, foraged from a hunter's stash after the hunter had fled with the rifle and they had yet to find a replacement.

As they drove past, the man called out to Cooper, "When things get back to normal, you wanna sell my used car for me?" Peach juice dribbled down his bearded chin as a wide smile crossed his face, revealing several missing teeth.

"If it doesn't have too many bullet holes in it, sure!" He called back.

As they drove through, they noted the town looked more like a small military encampment than the friendly hamlet they recalled from before the Brushfire Plague had struck. Very few children ambled about. The ratio of men to women appeared to be about two to one. The biker bar that had hugged the right side of the road was burned to the ground. Cooper noted boarded up windows and bullet holes on the other buildings on the flanking streets. Cooper imagined the bikers may have made a play to control the town, given the strategic location of their hangout at the crossroads. *I guess the bikers lost this contest of power. I wonder what force rallied them to do so?* Cooper had already seen that organized groups had an enormous advantage over scattered individuals as society unwound. *Maybe the local church?*

As they continued, he saw further random destruction. Some houses alongside the road looked just as before, pristine as ever. He marveled at those with blooming flowerboxes, probably planted just weeks before. The contrast with others was startling. Next door to one such house, Cooper saw another burned to the ground, only a lonely chimney scrambling skyward remaining. As the wheels on their vehicles slowly churned through Carver, he saw another house that had been subjected to a bitter firefight; hundreds of bullet holes scarring the home's walls and shattering its windows.

Then, it struck him. About a fifth of the people could see in Carver wore yellow armbands. Unlike the others, each of them looked downtrodden and was engaged in some form of manual labor: hauling wood, doing laundry in large open kettles, dressing an animal, or cooking. Cooper felt his stomach churn. While he could guess, he had to know. When they pulled alongside the barricade on the eastern edge of Carver, he called out to one of the guards.

"Hey, what's with the yellow armbands?"

The guard smirked, "They are our workers."

"What's that mean?"

"People that got into trouble or couldn't pay their debts to the town. They gotta work it off."

"How long does that take?"

"Depends on what got them into trouble in the first place. Some just a few months. Some we're thinking a few years." He spotted the tight look on Cooper's face and continued, "I'm surprised you didn't ask about the pink armbands."

Cooper cocked an eyebrow, as he hadn't seen any of these, "What are those for?"

"Heavier debts or crimes. The sentence is shorter, but you gotta be a looker, if you get my drift," the guard's smile became a leer. Cooper grunted and his face flushed. His lips curled in disgust. Next to him, Angela clawed her fingers into his leg and bit down on her lips.

"Disgusting," she breathed through tightened lips. Calvin banged the side of his door with a loud *whack.*

The guard saw it all and called after them, "Sure, get all high and mighty. You'll be doing the same in no time!" The man's leering smile made Cooper's stomach turn.

Cooper felt powerless to do anything except gun his motor and put as much distance between himself and Carver as possible.

"Don't hot rod. Save gas," Dranko scolded over the walkie talkie. Cooper cursed, but let the pedal off of the floor.

****

East of Carver, they made good time. Carver had been a chokepoint. Cooper guessed that few cars could afford their 'toll'. After driving through that despair, the road was mostly clear. They only encountered the occasional abandoned or destroyed vehicles.

As they drove, the implications of what they had just seen sank in. Someone, or some people, in Carver had already made the leap that things were not ever going to return to 'normal'. And, they had already organized themselves—albeit in an exploitative way—to deal with it. Within weeks of the outbreak of the Brushfire Plague, they had set up a system of indentured servitude and pressed women into sexual slavery. He wondered if some of the 'armbands' were working off their passage through town? *They just might all become slaves, permanently working there to survive.* The thought chilled him. *How could this happen so fast? I know things have unraveled but I still believe the remaining threads*

115

can be rewoven. Cooper's mind struggled to maintain his optimism but what he had seen in Carver struck at the core and made his stomach feel hollow.

Cooper welcomed the freedom of making highway speed and, despite the cold, rolled down the window so he could feel the wind whipping past him. Angela gave him a wink as they drove, the speed elevating her mood, as well. Calvin's face softened, though he kept a sharp lookout down the road.

"Keep it at 45. That's the most efficient speed to save fuel," Dranko advised once again via the walkie talkie.

"Party pooper," Cooper bemoaned to those next to him, but complied.

"Still feels like we are doing ninety, compared to what we were doing," Calvin offered. Cooper nodded, grinning.

****

Soon after they left Carver, Dranko sped past Cooper to take the lead. Almost exactly five miles east of Carver, he pulled off the road on the left side, next to a distinctive clutch of three white birch trees. He stopped his Jeep, grabbed a shovel from the back and ran do the middle area between all the trees. Before Cooper could even reach him, the dirt was flying in all directions as he dug furiously.

"What *are* you doing?"

Dranko stopped. When he looked up, he looked like a kid on Christmas morning. "I'm digging up my cache!"

"What?"

"I stored some supplies here. They were meant for walking *out* of Portland, so no gas though."

"You mean you have stored some gear out here, buried?"

Beaming, Dranko continued, "Exactly! I knew I might need to walk to Estacada if I'd had to flee my home without proper supplies. Wouldn't have made it."

Cooper shook his head in disbelief, "My Lord, you *do* think of everything!"

Dranko's shovel clanked metal, "Here, help me."

Together, they finished dragging out two metal bins that each weighed about thirty pounds. "What's in here?" Cooper asked as they freed the second one from its hole.

"Some sealed food, water, some first aids supplies, and a Glock 9mm, with three full magazines."

Cooper stroked his chin, "I guess that's worth stopping for."

"It sure was! I'm just happy we're driving to my cabin instead of having to hoof it. I'm still surprised the roads weren't hopelessly clogged."

"Not enough people thought they could flee this thing. They didn't all get on the road at the *exact* same time. That's what saved us."

Dranko nodded and hefted the first metal bin and began walking back to their vehicles. Cooper grabbed the second and followed him. He was still shaking his head at his friend's thorough preparations when he deposited the bin marked "food" into the pickup.

****

In less than an hour, they were approaching Estacada. "There's a gas station a few miles coming up. Let's stop there and see if we can fill up," Dranko informed him.

"Roger that, wilco," Cooper responded.

As the gas station came into view, Cooper immediately knew it was occupied. Two pickup trucks were parked at either entrance, like watchdogs. At least one man stood up in each pickup bed, rifle in hand. Several men were loitering across the parking lot.

"It's controlled," he called to Dranko over the radio.

Cooper decreased his speed, so that he could approach slowly. The men on the ground motioned for him to stop just outside the gas station's parking lot. A man dressed in a hodgepodge of military clothing approached. He was young, in his twenties, with long, dirty, blond hair that contrasted sharply with his military dress. A sidearm was affixed to his hip, and he carried a large bore shotgun.

"What can I do you for?"

Cooper rolled down his window, "You have gas for sale?"

The man rolled the toothpick in his mouth, "That depends."

"Depends on what?"

"Are you a registered resident of Estacada?"

Dranko had walked up just then, "Sure. I have a house just outside of town."

The man eyed them derisively, "I figured as much. You aren't from around here?"

"We're fellow Oregonians and I have land up here," Dranko said, doing his best to sound friendly.

"Well, you gotta register with our Sheriff if you want to buy anything in this town."

Cooper's eyebrows knotted, "What does registration mean?"

"You know, the usual. Sign up, keep your nose clean, pay your taxes, and swear loyalty to the Man."

Cooper's jaw tightened, "What's the name of the Man and where can we find him?"

"Sheriff Hodges is the man. He's gotten us through this mess. Gotten us organized. You can likely find him at the Thriftway, that's what used to be the supermarket. That's where most of the trading happens these days."

"Much obliged. We'll do that," Dranko said.

They piled back into their vehicles and drove off.

"Let's go to your place first. We can figure out what's going on with Sheriff Hodges tomorrow," Cooper radioed to Dranko.

Dranko responded by accelerating his Jeep and taking the lead position. In twenty minutes, they were driving up the long driveway to Dranko's cabin.

****

The driveway was a skinny affair. Only one vehicle could pass at a time. Gravel crunched under Cooper's tires as he twisted his steering wheel this way and that making his way up the slight incline. About twenty yards in, out of sight of the road, Cooper spotted something odd. A rusted and graffiti-riddled dumpster sat alongside the driveway. It looked like it belonged on the streets of New York, not in a peaceful, green forest.

He thumbed the walkie talkie, "What's that?"

He could hear the delight in Dranko's voice, "My temporary roadblock. It's filled with rocks, but a man can move it into position to block the driveway. I have a carjack I can use to prop it up and remove the wheels."

"No one can move it after that, I'd guess."

"Pretty close. And, if I want to block this driveway semi-permanently, I will fell those two large trees on either side."

Cooper could tell which ones he meant. He smiled wryly, "Effective, friend."

"The only way to be, brother," Dranko's glee came through loud and clear.

Dranko's Jeep made it halfway through the next turn before he stopped his vehicle and jumped out. Cooper idled while watching

Dranko drop to one knee while examining something very near the ground. He couldn't make out what he was looking at. After a few seconds, apparently satisfied, Dranko clambered back into the Jeep.

Cooper's curiosity couldn't wait, "What was that about?"

Cooper's radio cackled once again, "I put a lightweight line of fishing line across the road, near tire level. Unless someone is being very careful, I can tell if a person has been through here in a vehicle."

"Got it. So, I'm guessing we're clear?"

"Yes, but when we get up there, we should clear the area, just to be safe."

Cooper smiled once more to himself, "I'd expect nothing less from you."

They continued driving onward. After two more steep S-turns, they emerged into a large clearing. Off to his left, Cooper saw the cabin. It was truly a *cabin*, made of logs and gray wattle in the joints. It was small, Cooper guessing twenty by twenty. It was made to appear smaller because the logs themselves were large, thick and out-of-scale to the dwelling's size. *Hmmm, let me guess. Dranko chose logs big enough to stop up to a .50 caliber round?* Cooper didn't have to ask his friend; he was convinced beyond a shadow of a doubt that he was right.

The cabin's front door glinted gunmetal gray and appeared heavy and thick. It weakened the rustic nature of the cabin, though its windows destroyed it. The "windows" were more like firing ports. Scattered on each of the two walls, he could see three or four small circles of glass, at various heights. He noted that each wall had one that was barely a foot off the ground, so someone could fire out from the prone position. As he completed his survey of the cabin, Cooper noted the metal roof had a skylight cut in. A ground-mounted solar array lodged where it had ample access to the south sky.

His eyes drifted across the clearing. Almost an acre of ground was prepared as a gardening area. The ground lay fallow. Next to that were several neat rows of fruit trees. Given the elevation and knowing Dranko's no nonsense approach, Cooper guessed they were hardy apples. He spotted a cluster of white beehives set at the edge of the clearing. Finally, a derelict silver bullet-shaped Airstream trailer was grounded opposite the wooden cabin. Sunlight sparkled off its distinctive metal shell.

Dranko was already out of his vehicle, rifle in hand and moving adroitly toward the cabin. Cooper felt remiss, his mind having drifted as he had taken the scene in. Hastily, he grabbed his rifle and raced to catch up to Dranko and take up the supporting position. He covered Dranko as he approached the front door. Dranko checked it and found it locked. He motioned Cooper forward. Within seconds, Cooper joined him at the door. Dranko fished out his key and prepared to unlock the door. Cooper made ready to clear the cabin as soon as the door was opened.

"Don't shoot me! Don't shoot," a muffled voice rang out from behind the door. Dranko's eyes flashed and he dropped his keys in shock. His mouth fell open. His jaw moved, but no words came out.

"Unlock the door!" Cooper shouted.

"Promise you won't shoot, first," the voice on the other side pleaded.

"Sure, I won't shoot you." Silence ensued. Then, Cooper heard the metallic snicks as multiple locks were disengaged. Cautiously, the door inched open.

Dranko's face grew crimson, veins bulging on his forehead. He recovered and slammed the door open. Cooper followed quickly enough to see a man pushed backward by the door and falling in a heap on Dranko's cabin floor. He was a skinny, young man. Pimples still dotted his face, which he was frantically shielding with waving arms.

"Don't hurt me, Mister. You know me! You know me!"

Dranko and Cooper exchanged looks of surprise.

"Get up, then. Let me see you!" Dranko's face was a contortion of rage, curiosity, and impatience.

Clumsily, the man gathered himself to his feet. He wore blue jeans and a white Budweiser t-shirt. Tan work boots adorned his feet. Disheveled blond hair fell to his shoulders. His facial muscles were tight, in a bewildered and frightened grimace.

"You remember me," he nervously croaked. "I can't remember your name. Mr. Dinko or something like that. But, I helped you install that solar unit a few summers ago."

Dranko's face fell and his body deflated like a fast-leaking balloon. "It's Dranko. Yeah, I remember you. Tim or Tom, right?" He dropped his rifle onto a nearby couch.

"That's right, Tim," the man said.

Dranko began pacing the room, agitated hands ran through his hair. In a few moments, he was animated again, "Are you kidding me! I can't believe it!"

"What?" Tim asked.

Dranko drew up in front of Tim, looking him in the eye. "I only had *one* person ever help me build up this place. I did *everything* right to keep a low profile here. And, the *one* person that knew about my hideout is already *here* when I make it!" He threw up his hands in exasperation and paced a tight circle once again. A scant smile crept onto Cooper's face. Dranko spotted it and leapt upon him for it.

He wagged a finger in front of Cooper's nose, "You see! You call me a cynic! What are the odds? I even hired this kid from two towns over so he wouldn't be blabbing to locals."

Cooper fought the laughter bellowing up from inside, but lost. His chortling made Dranko grow apoplectic. He grew a deeper shade of red, "Sure, laugh at me! This is the story of my life! If it *can* go wrong, it will. It should be called Dranko's Law and not Murphy's." He ranted as he strutted about the room, arms flapping in exaggerated self-pity.

Tim remained stoic in the middle of the room. He looked happy to be ignored for a moment. His bulging eyes tracked Dranko around the room as best he could, while remaining still.

Dranko continued grumbling, but the ferocity began fading.

"Why don't we find out what damage has been done?" Cooper asked. Dranko stopped in his tracks, thought for a moment, and nodded his head once. Then, he returned to where Tim was standing.

"When did you get here?"

"A week ago," Tim said, nervously.

"Anyone else with you?"

"No, sir. My girlfriend died early from the Plague."

"You bring your own food or did you eat mine?"

Tim's eyes grew wider, "Both. I didn't have much at my place when all this started. But, I'll pay you back, I swear!"

"With what," Dranko returned, his voice flat.

"I'll work for you. Whatever you need!"

Dranko squinted, "We'll see about that. You mess with my guns?"

Tim's eyes darted back and forth, "I tried. I was scared with everything that's happened. I didn't have one and was scared up here by myself. But, I couldn't open your lock."

"Did you try to break it?"

Tim shook his head frantically, "No, sir! I didn't break anything here. I figured you'd show up eventually and I wouldn't want to, anyway."

Dranko cocked his head, suddenly thinking of something, "How'd you get in here, anyway?"

"That took me two days. Your locks were impossible to pick. I searched all over this place and I finally found your extra key after two days. Putting it under the beehives was pretty clever."

"You slept outside those two days?"

Tim grew sheepish, "No. I did jimmy open one of the windows on the Airstream."

Dranko glared at him, "So, you *did* break something then."

"Not really, the lock wasn't fully engaged. So, I got it open without breaking it."

Dranko looked chagrined, "I see."

"Look around. I kept your place clean and in order."

"I bet that's true. I didn't see any trash outside," Cooper intervened.

"How'd you *get* here?"

"I drove into Estacada, but ran out of gas and couldn't lay my hands on anymore gas for neither love nor money. So, I left my car and walked up here."

"Alright, we need to discuss what to do with you," Dranko said, and motioned Tim to move outside.

They followed him.

"Go stand over in the garden area so we can talk." The others in their group were milling about the vehicles. Cooper and Dranko walked over to join them. "Don't do anything stupid," Cooper called over his shoulder to Tim. Tim nodded fervently.

"Who's that?" Angela asked.

"Proof that optimism is stupid," Dranko groaned.

The corner of Cooper's mouth downturned, "He's someone who worked on installing the solar unit, so he knew about this place and showed up."

"He's the *only* person I *ever* had up here to work on anything! So, naturally and of course, he shows up!"

Cooper grew impatient, "Yes, but let's stop complaining and *deal* with it."

"He looks harmless enough," Calvin observed.

"What do you remember about him? Behavior. Character." Cooper asked.

Finally, Dranko calmed down and grew serious, "Honestly. Good kid. Worked hard. Fair rate. Always on time and stayed late to finish the job."

"Anything else?"

"He did have a brother who was a Meth head. Totally hooked on that stuff. He was really pissed off about it and complained to me about it."

"We know he has electrical skills, what else?"

"He mentioned hunting as a kid with his dad. We should ask him, though."

"Did he tear your place up?" Lily asked.

Dranko shook his head. She continued, "So, you got yourself the world's best trespasser?"

He pursed his lips in response.

"So, let's make sure his brother or parents won't be a problem. And, if he's willing to work, we let him stay?" Cooper asked the group. Everyone nodded, Dranko joining reluctantly at the end.

As they walked back to finish the interview with Tim, Cooper pointed to the Airstream, "What's that all about?"

"It was my temporary structure up here, as I was building it up. I got it cheap because it needed some work. It's the world's best-kept secret. RVs and trailers make the cheapest and quickly set up bug out shelters."

Cooper cocked an eyebrow, "Best kept among the one-tenth of one percent of people like you who were getting ready for all this!"

Dranko chuckled, "Just remember you said it."

His eyebrows drew together, "Said what?"

"That I'm part of the smartest one-tenth of one percent!"

"Smart? I never said that. Maybe just lucky? Tell yourself what you want."

His words failed to wipe the self-satisfied smile off Dranko's face.

Tim was kneading his fingers when they came upon him. "So, did I get voted onto the island?" His smile was tentative, nervous.

"Dunno yet. We have a few more questions."

"What about that brother of yours, with the meth problem?"

Tim tightened his lips, "He's dead."

"Plague too?"

He shook his head, "Nope. 'Bout a year ago. Knifed in a bar." His head wagged back and forth, "Dumbass."

"What about your parents?"

"They moved to Arizona last year. After my brother died, they wanted a change of scenery and a warmer climate, anyway. I talked to them the day after all this broke out. But, not since."

"You willing to work?"

"Yes, sir. Mr. Dranko knows I bust tail." Dranko cocked his head and raised an eyebrow to show he agreed.

"You might have to work harder than the rest. We all brought something to this party and you haven't," Dranko added.

Tim looked him straight in the eye, "No problem. I know I got some debt I need to work off for you, anyway."

"Can you shoot?"

"I haven't hunted in a couple years, but I punch paper targets with friends a couple, three times a year. I'm still a decent shot."

Cooper feigned thinking for several seconds, stroking his chin for good measure, "Alright you're in. But, we'll be keeping an eye on you."

The tension left Tim's face, he grasped both men's hands in succession, "Thank you! You won't regret it."

****

An hour later, Tim had been introduced to everyone and they had unloaded their gear. Dranko had given them all a tour of the structures and ground. The cabin was an impressive defensive structure. He'd pointed out how the logs had been treated with flame retardant and showed them how to access the basement that lay underneath. There, food, water, and a few firearms were stored; along with a myriad of other supplies. Dranko explained that he had a little over a year's worth of food for himself. With this many people, he expected it would last for two months.

"The grocery trucks will be running again by then, right?" Jake asked, knotted eyebrows.

Dranko shook his head slowly, "Hard to tell. We need to prepare as if not, though."

"We'll need to get our hands on some seeds and get the ground worked outside," Calvin added.

A grin lit up Dranko's face. He pointed to a row of metal cans lining one shelf, "I have plenty of seeds."

"You stored *seeds?*" Angela was incredulous.

"Damn straight," Dranko said. Cooper noted how his chest puffed up a bit, "For a few hundred bucks, I was able to put aside plenty of seeds for this kind of situation. I know some people would spend that much on *one* fancy meal at a restaurant. Here, I can grow enough food for *years.*"

Angela shook her head in disbelief, as did Calvin, "Amazing," his deep voice intoned.

"I have one question for you, Paul," Lily Stott piped up.

Dranko turned towards her, "What?"

"Have you ever spent a dime on something that *wasn't* about getting ready for the end of the world?"

The room exploded in laughter. Dranko was speechless. Cooper was shocked to see Julianne and Angela briefly clutch each for support while in riotous laughter. Calvin's laugh boomed off the basement's walls. Seconds later, Julianne and Angela looked at each awkwardly and then disengaged. *Tension down enough for them to embrace while they weren't thinking, but that's all for now.* When the laughter had subsided, Cooper couldn't resist.

"There was that time back in '98 you bought a candy bar and ate it right then and there with not even a thought to storing it for the end of the world?"

Dranko punched him in the arm, "Screw off," he said while passing him on his way to the stairs.

"Ah, c'mon, Paul. I love you like a tick loves blood," Lily called after him. The others added other calls of affection. Dranko continued stomping up the stairs. Just before passing out of sight, he lowered his head and gave them all a wide smile to show his anger was in jest. This induced another round of laughter, but lighter.

Their dinner that night was canned beans and instant mashed potatoes. *I guess I have to get used to mostly tasteless food for a while. His mind drifted to how Elena would often make him his favorite home cooked meal of turkey, mashed potatoes, and stuffing — outside of Thanksgiving.* His mouth watered and the memory made the dinner taste even worse.

They decided the women would lodge in the Airstream, while the men would fit themselves into the cabin. *I wonder how long it will be before sexual tension becomes an issue? We have a lot of people still in their prime without a good outlet.* "Don't borrow trouble," he muttered.

"What's that?" Calvin asked.

Cooper smiled, "Nothing. Just something my father used to say."

Chapter Seven

When Cooper awoke, he found Dranko boiling water for tea. It wasn't yet light out and the others lay in about the cabin, sleeping.

"Want some?" Dranko whispered to him.

He nodded and inclined his head to indicate Dranko should join him outside. Cooper opened the door, being careful to do so quietly, and stepped outside. The air was brisk, and he pulled the oversized green quilted flannel shirt tight around himself. Wood smoke greeted his nose. It smelled like it would at a campground. *More people using wood now, they're saving their propane and heating oil or are already out,* he guessed.

The door opened before him, and Dranko joined him. He took the steaming mug, welcoming the source of heat and the sweet smell of Earl Grey tea.

"Won't be long before boiling water for tea might be an extravagance we can't afford," Dranko observed.

Cooper nodded, "You were up late."

"Yeah, I was on the ham radio. I wanted to get the lay of the land, both regionally and nationally."

"Start locally," Cooper requested.

"Well, there have been scattered riots in Portland. Some over the news you released. Some over food. No news about areas around here, except vague references to various local officials 'establishing order' in their respective comm..."

"Strongmen," Cooper interrupted. Dranko nodded, face laced with concern. "Nationally?"

"Riots all over the place. Again, it's a combination of riots demanding the truth about what happened and the other half is over food. People are both desperate *and* pissed off."

"How bad is the unrest?"

"Pretty bad. Dozens dead in this city. Hundreds in another. Whole sections burning in others. Everything is still teetering. The plague has left a huge gap in the *human* infrastructure. The planes, trains, and trucks are still not running on time. But, honestly, they're not really running much at all."

"And news about me?"

"Brother, the hunt is *on* for you. The President and others in officialdom are continuing to declare you a liar to the thousandth degree."

"They still focused on California?"

"Seems like. I gotta tell you. I think the government and military are stretched beyond belief. I half expected a Blackhawk chopper to have been waiting for us here."

Cooper rubbed his chin, "I half expected one back on Lincoln Street!" He paused for a moment before continuing, "What's happening with the Chinese?"

"It's hard to figure. My best guess is that they *mostly* have sent over police and medical personnel to help out. But, it does sound like small military detachments accompanied them."

Cooper's eyebrows furrowed, "What do you make of that?"

"I'd guess they are here to scout us out. See the state of our military and defenses, post-Plague."

"Hmmmm...could be. What's the word on the international front?"

"Russia isn't just sabre rattling, she's pulled it out and is waving it above her head. I think they see this as a chance to *finally* win the Cold War. A few other countries have joined in their call for surgical nuclear strikes against us. Anti-American sentiment is off the scales. Tourists stuck overseas have been beaten and some killed. Embassies all over the place have been attacked. Most countries are demanding 'justice' but want a UN panel to determine what that means. But, Russia and her pals aren't waiting for any UN foreplay. No, they have a serious hard on for us."

Cooper rubbed his temples, "What a mess. I think I might have screwed up."

Dranko put his hand on his friend's shoulder for comfort, "Brother, I know you. You didn't have a choice but to let the truth out."

He looked back at him sternly, "Except for breathing and eating, everything is a choice."

Dranko looked at the ground, "There's one more thing."

"What?"

"A reporter from the *Philadelphia Inquirer* is making noise about the billionaire Karl Van Welton's link to the Brushfire Plague."

"I know that name." Both men whirled around, hands going to their holstered sidearms.

Julianne stood twenty feet away, eyes wide in shock, and putting her hand up in a defensive posture, one held a hunting rifle.

They exhaled together, "Don't sneak up on us like that," Cooper growled.

"I wasn't sneaking. You guys were just deep in thought. I was on guard duty and drifted over."

Dranko shook his head to clear it, "You know this guy?"

"That's a name you don't forget. I would periodically bump into him and other very wealthy men while working with Mitchell. He always described them as our 'wealthy benefactors'. What's the *Inquirer* saying?"

"A reporter there has found some links between Van Welton's investments in China prior the outbreak of the plague and his close ties to the President and to Admonitus."

"What does that mean?"

"He speculates that Van Welton knew about the pending outbreak, knew about China's apparent preparation for it, and bet heavy on them."

"What?" Julianne gasped.

"When a billionaire goes from zero percent invested in a country to almost one-hundred percent invested, it can raise eyebrows. And, it's no secret that China was one of the *least* affected countries. Van Welton was also invested in Admonitus. There *are* dots to connect."

"We need to get to the bottom of this!" Julianne was almost hysterical. "I need to know."

"Know what?" Cooper asked.

"Whether I got played like a damned, stupid fiddle!"

Dranko looked at her, nonplussed, "Well, I can get onto the Internet from here. You can research the other names you remember and see what you come up with."

"Good. I want to get started right away." She grabbed Dranko by the arm, pulling him inside. He looked at Cooper, helpless. Cooper shrugged. *That woman gets what she wants.* He finished his tea alone, enjoying the solitude and quiet. When the last warm mouthful fell down this throat, he went back inside to start making breakfast. *Boiled oats with a dollop of honey. Good times,* he mused to himself.

****

After breakfast, they gathered outside at Dranko's urging. Cooper was glad to see Freddie back on his feet. He moved gingerly, but he *was* moving. They gathered in a circle as Dranko reviewed a litany of protocols needed for security's purposes. He laid out the week's guard duty schedule.

"I'd suggest we swap Calvin on nights for Julianne. You're a natural night owl, right?" Cooper directed his question at Calvin. *Put people where their strengths are, nothing overcomes natural talent,* his father had often told him.

Calvin nodded. "Okay," Dranko responded.

"You might as well put me on the other night shift. I've done enough night ER shifts, I can handle it fine," Angela added.

Dranko scribbled onto his schedule sheet, "Done." He finished with a flourish of pencil on paper and then continued, "Let me turn to the more unpleasant topic of sanitation."

"Pee-yoooou," Freddie groaned, grabbing his nose and plugging it in exaggeration. Jake howled with delight. *So good to see him be a kid again.* The others chuckled.

Dranko looked annoyed, "I was set up for myself and my composting bucket system would have worked fine. But, with this many people, we need a better plan."

"Let me guess, we're building an outhouse," Lily asked.

"That's the short of it. I'd suggest we get started today. I have the dimensions we need right here," he said, foraging a piece of paper from his stack.

Cooper took a step forward, "Calvin, Tim, Angela, and I should get on this." The others agreed.

"Great. I need to work on our menu and estimate out our caloric intake…"

"Our what?" Jake asked, puzzled.

Cooper rustled his hair, "It means he needs to figure out how we can eat each day to make our food last the longest."

"Get ready to tighten our belts…literally, right?" Freddie added, his face turning serious.

Dranko frowned, "'Fraid so. We'll all be losing some weight, I'm sure."

"Well, I have twenty I would lose gladly," Calvin joked, patting his belly.

"Most of us have a few extra pounds, but being hungry isn't any fun," Dranko said, smothering the humor. Cooper's eyes narrowed as he glared at Dranko. *I'm going to have to talk to him. He's bringing everyone else down. Constantly. For no good reason.* Calvin's face fell and those who had been smiling were no longer.

"This afternoon, can we go and visit my son, please?" Lily Stott beckoned from the other side of the circle.

"Absolutely. It will be a good source of news and he can give us a good lay of the land, too," Cooper answered. "In the meantime, you and Julianne should be on guard and food patrol!"

Dranko shook his head, "Julianne's tearing through that research. You won't get her off the computer for nothin'." Cooper caught Angela frowning out of the corner of his eye.

"I can help Lily. We can shout if anyone starts coming up the road, or," Freddie paused, catching Jake's eye, "I can fart real loud!" Once again, Jake laughed loudly while the adults groaned. *Potty humor and eleven-year-olds!*

"Right. Let's do this. Everyone keep your weapons within arm's reach, alright?" They all nodded and began drifting off to work.

"Wait!" Cooper shouted. Everyone was startled and a few of them visibly jumped. "What's the air horn sign for come running and be ready to fight?"

They were startled by his outburst, just what he'd intended.

"Ah...one long blast!" Jake stammered.

He smiled at his son, "Good. I just wanted to test you. The surprise is the stress we all experience at a time like that. Or, at least a taste of it."

Dranko patted him on the shoulder, "Clever bastard."

"Best to test under stress."

"Who said that?"

"My father. Who else?" Cooper responded with evident pride.

"Your father was one smart bastard. I wish I could have met him."

Cooper nodded with a wistful look in his eyes, "Me, too."

Dranko showed Cooper and the others where he wanted the outhouse trench dug and reinforced how deep it would have to be for a group of their size.

"Shovels over in that shed," Dranko said pointing to a ragged wooden shed that lay next to the large gardening area.

"We got this," Cooper said, dismissing him. He ambled off, back towards the cabin. "Who'd like to dig with me first? I think if we work in pairs in fifteen minutes bursts, we'll get more done faster," he said to the other men.

"I will dig first. 'Work's begun is sooner done.' That's what my father always said," Calvin said as he marched off toward the shed to retrieve the shovels.

Within minutes, the two of them had fallen into an easy rhythm. Despite the chill in the air, they were both quickly bathed in sweat. When their first shift of fifteen minutes had finished, both men were stripping off their shirts as they handed their shovels to Angela and Tim.

"I'll get us a pitcher of water and cups," Cooper said before heading off to the cabin. Calvin nodded, gasping for air.

"I will go and see if there are gloves in the shed. My hands are already feeling it." The two men moved off in separate directions, as the first spadefuls of dirt began flying from Angela and Tim.

Cooper and Calvin returned at about the same time. Cooper carried a metal pitcher and four plastic cups, while Calvin had two pairs of worn gloves in hand. He tossed them to the two digging, who welcomed the pause while they put them on.

They watched in silence as the others dug, breathing deeply to get as much oxygen into their muscles as possible, before their next turn would begin. When it was their time, they took one last deep breath, donned the gloves, and set to digging at a furious pace.

Six hours later, minus a short break for a lunch of beans and baked bread, the trench was finished. The bread had been a delicious surprise, courtesy of Lily Stott. It even had nuts and raisins folded into a deep, tasty wheat flour. Dranko came to inspect their work.

He nodded approvingly, "Good. Tomorrow, we can build up some walls for privacy. I think I have enough wood and plywood to make this work."

The quartet of diggers smiled at one another. Their hands were raw, unaccustomed to manual labor. Their muscles hurt. *And will hurt worse tomorrow.*

"We did something good today, friends. We dug a shithouse. It's symbolic, too. We will face more 'stuff' together. But, guess what? We stick together, we can get through it, just like we did this together," Cooper observed and noted the agreement and appreciation from the others as they stretched and nodded. He recalled his father's words about using every chance you had to educate people about their purpose and build a team. *I must be getting better. I'm using his advice before I consciously remember it!*

As the group readied to walk back to the cabin, Cooper pulled Dranko's sleeve, "Can we chat for a second?"

Dranko looked at him, eyebrow cocked, "Sure." They moved away from the group, walking toward the gardening area.

"I need a favor from you," Cooper started.

"What's that?"

"I know you're just trying to tell everyone what to be ready for or offer that realistic viewpoint, but I think you're bringing people down."

Dranko turned to him with a confused frown, "Whatdya mean?"

"Like this morning, when Calvin was making light of the food situation and you went and told him that 'being hungry isn't any fun.'"

Dranko's eyes narrowed, "I was just telling them what I thought. They need to be ready. This is *serious* business. Not some camping trip."

Cooper's jaw tightened, but he fought to keep his voice steady, "I hear you. I'm just asking you to not *always* say stuff like that."

Dranko took a step back, "So, you want me to *lie*? That's a surprise coming from you."

Cooper growled, "I'm *not* asking you to lie. I just want you to *think* about what you say and how it will affect others."

"Look, it's not my job to hold anyone's hands. That's not my job," Dranko said shaking his head slowly.

"That's right. It's *my* job. That's why I'm talking to you and asking for your help."

A long pause passed between them as Dranko stared at the ground before looking back up, "Look, I'm gonna do what I'm gonna do. I ain't gonna sugarcoat things or hide the truth."

Cooper's hand exploded as he poked him in the shoulder and pushed his face to within inches, "What the hell is the matter with you?"

"I'm stretched out and now you're asking for more."

"What does *that* mean?"

"You wanna know? Do you?"

"Yes," Cooper answered with furrowed eyebrows.

"I'm tired. I've shared my stuff. The stuff that *I* bought over the years by giving up the vacations and meals and clothes that the rest of you were spending your money on. I've shared my knowledge. I've shared my time. I've shared *everything*. And, I haven't got a single 'thank you'! Not once. And, now you want me to start watching every word I say? Screw that!" By the time he'd finished, his head was boiling red, bits of froth peppered his lips, and his eyes glistened.

Cooper faltered a step back, speechless for several seconds. Dranko stood before him, fuming. He took a step back towards his friend and put his hands onto his shoulders, "You're right. I'm sorry. Let me be the first. *Thank you.* We wouldn't have made it this far without you. My boy," that word catching in Cooper's throat, "likely wouldn't be alive without you. So, words won't ever express how much I appreciate what you've done."

The color slowly drained from Dranko's face and he washed his sleeve across his mouth, wiping spittle away, "It's...ah..."

Cooper waved his hand, interrupting him, "Don't say anything. We *should* have thanked you more. Without you asking for it. And, I won't ask anything more of you. Say what you want. Just keep what I said in mind, is all." Cooper clapped him on the shoulder, turned on his heel, and strode back towards the cabin. *I need to do a better job of recognizing people for their work.*

Dranko looked at him walk away, a thin, awkward smile creeping onto his face, before he lowered his eyes and kicked at the duff on the ground.

Chapter Eight

Dranko steered them down the long driveway as tires crunched gravel. Lily, wearing a bright yellow housedress, sat next to him in the front seat. She had scolded Dranko up one side and down the other for not having an iron on hand. Dranko had fired right back at her, chastising her for wasting precious cargo space on a 'frivolous dress' and not something more practical. The rest of the group had found their respective earnestness a source of great humor.

She fussed about her dress, trying to stretch out the numerous wrinkles. Cooper had gathered that she was fiercely proud of her son, triggering her need to dress up for the occasion. On Lily's right was Angela, wearing hiker's pants and a loose-fitting flannel top. Cooper and Jake occupied the rear seat. Cooper's rifle was resting on the floor, ready at hand, but not drawing unwanted attention. Likewise, they had two M4s stashed in the cargo area, but covered with a blanket. Based on what they'd seen coming into town, they all wore their side arms holstered on their hips, save Lily.

The others who remained back at camp were engaged in various work and projects that Dranko had assigned. Meanwhile, Julianne was continuing her urgent search to learn more about the emerging conspiracy behind what had led to Brushfire Plague.

As Dranko followed the directions Lily was giving her, Cooper's mind drifted.

****

The acrid smell wafting up from the large Sharpie pens made Cooper's nose cringe up in a vain attempt to ward it off. His fingers were stained in many hues from his repeated attempts to make the perfect picket sign. He looked up when his father's footsteps clattered on the wood floor at the bottom of the stairs.

His father's eyes were quizzical as he surveyed the half dozen or so unfinished signs strewn about the floor.

"Whatcha doing' son?"

Young Cooper grimaced and shook his tight fists in frustration, "I'm making a protest sign."

A thin smile crept onto his father's face, "What for?"

"Mrs. Small!".

His father struggled to keep a smile from showing, "And, what has

Mrs. Small done to deserve your wrath?"

Cooper leapt to his feet and the Sharpie pens clattered against the floor, "She won't let me and Brian play basketball at recess!"

His father looked confused, "Why not?"

"**Because**," his son adopted the tone of someone explaining the obvious, "Samantha got hurt on Monday playing it!"

His father shook his head in exaggerated sympathy, "Well, that doesn't seem fair."

"I know! And, you taught me to fight against things that are unfair."

His father's smile grew wider, "So, what's the problem?"

The young Cooper stomped his feet, "I can't get good words for my sign!" His voice was plagued by a plaintive whine.

His father paused for a moment, "Well, I'm sure you'll come up with something good." He tussled Cooper's hair and moved to the living room where he sat down to read the morning newspaper.

Twenty minutes later, he looked up to find Cooper holding a sign proudly displayed for his review. The sign said, "The Ball Must Be Free to Fall!" A shaky picture of a basketball formed the bottom of the exclamation point.

Cooper's father looked up at him, a growing smile on his face.

"It rhymes!" Cooper declared proudly.

"I see that. Very nice work." His eyes gleamed with pride. Cooper never forgot the look he'd received that morning from his father. He also never forgot the week of detention he got from Mrs. Small when he brandished the sign when he'd arrived at school that morning. Cooper thought the look his father gave him that night was prouder still.

As Cooper mused, he was struck by how those brief moments when a son feels his father's pride could last forever.

****

At Dranko's request, they took a longer route to Lily's son's house so that they could avoid going through the center of town. As they approached, Lily's excitement grew. After twenty minutes, she exclaimed, "We're here! Just up there, take a left into that driveway!" Dranko obeyed and they were quickly past the thin screen of pine trees that shielded the house from the road.

Her son's house was really a hobby farm, about five acres. The house was a modest one, ranch style, painted nearly as bright yellow as Lily's dress. A neatly laid out orchard flanked the house on its right. A bright red barn and a variety of coops and fenced areas housed chickens, geese, at least two pigs, and what looked to be a dairy cow. A bevy of goats wandered about the property, grazing. Finally, stretching across the backside was a large area of at least fenced three acres in various stages of plowing and planting. In the midst of the fields, a man clutched his hat off his head and waved it at them in their approach. Cooper noted how the man's other hand went to his waist, where a pistol likely lay.

They pulled up in front of the house. The front door flung open and a fierce woman trained a double-barreled shotgun on them, "Move slow!" She shouted at them. Dranko and Cooper exchanged the same thought, *Lily can handle this.*

Lily opened the door very slowly, "Dear Beth! It's me, mama!" She climbed over Angela and stepped out, still moving tentatively until her face and what she'd said registered with Beth. The shotgun's barrel fell to the ground, as Beth's other hand clasped to her open mouth. Tears raced into her eyes.

"Oh my! Mama! You're alive! We thought…" she paused. "Oh, never mind! Get over here," she said moving down the steps of the porch. She clutched Lily in a firm embrace. Looking out past Lily, she cried, "Miles! Miles! Get over here! It's your mama!"

Miles had been walking steadily in from the fields, hand at his waist. As he saw the scene unfold, his pace had quickened, but Beth's words were electric. He began sprinting toward them, hat in hand, bouncing in a wide arc as he ran.

"I wish my mother-in-law had liked me as much," Dranko deadpanned as they watched Lily and Beth's lingering hug.

"You were married?" Angela asked, surprised.

"Hard to believe any woman could *love* him, isn't it?"

Angela looked hard at Cooper, "That's *not* what I meant."

"Don't worry about him. The man who insults others just doesn't like himself enough, you know?" Dranko mustered a dignified voice, as if he was psychologist rendering an official diagnosis.

"Thank you Dr. Know-It-All," Cooper rebuffed.

"But, to answer your question. Yes, I was married once. When I was in the military. It burned hotter than Eva Mendes in her prime. We loved each other like in the movies. It was just like that," Dranko's voice quivered.

"And then it burned out?" Angela queried.

Dranko paused before answering and then he swallowed hard, "I wish. That would have been easier. No, she died."

Angela's eyes flew wide, her mouth fell open, and her hand went to Dranko's arm, "Oh my God, Paul! I had no idea." Cooper had heard the story, but he lowered his gaze. Jake also knew, but his eyes were transfixed on Dranko as he talked.

Dranko's eyes searched the distance, "It was a freak situation really. I was deployed in Iraq and she was caught at home in a blizzard. This was when I lived in Minnesota, out in the sticks. Some neighbors found her body two weeks later. Heater had quit and she ran out of things to burn in the fireplace. The house was threadbare of things to burn. Her body was found a few hundred yards from the house; an axe frozen to her hand. I think she'd gone out to try and cut something down. I think hypothermia had already messed up her ability to think clearly."

Angela gasped, "That's horrible!"

Dranko slowly nodded, "If I'd put in the woodstove we'd talked about and laid in the wood before I left home, she woulda made it. A fireplace alone just doesn't cut it to keep a house warm." He looked away as his eyes filled with tears.

"You can't blame yourself! You said it was a freak thing," Angela countered.

He returned his gaze to look her directly in the eyes, "I know what part I played. But, I learned something good from it all. Don't get caught with your pants down." He snorted, as the tears welling in his eyes was making his nose run. He jerked the door handle, left the car, and slammed the door shut.

Angela looked back at Cooper, "Is this why he's so cynical?"

Cooper shook his head, "Maybe. I didn't know him before." His mind drifted to the time Dranko had first told him the story of how his wife died. He closed his eyes, picturing the summer night sitting in Dranko's backyard. He could still smell the pungent mix of burned lighter fluid and charcoal from the earlier barbeque. Elena had taken Jake back home as night fell, and the two men had stayed behind drinking. Hours later and slurring his words throughout, Dranko had told Cooper how his wife, Jennifer, had died. By the time he'd finished, he was sobbing uncontrollably. Cooper had embraced his neighbor who, in that moment, became his best friend. After that night, Dranko had never mentioned it again, until today.

"I guess we know why he's so into getting prepared for things," Angela reflected, pulling Cooper back from his musings.

He let loose a bellowing laugh. Angela looked at him, confused. Her hands splayed out, asking 'what'?

He shook his head in deprecation, "I *never* made that connection!"

"Really," she asked, with a cocked eyebrow.

"No. I never did. But, it's obvious!"

Outside the vehicle, the Stotts had finished their reunion greetings and were staring at them, surprised they were still sitting in the car. Galvanized, Cooper and Angela cranked their doors open and stepped out. Jake followed their example.

Cooper approached Miles Stott and shook his hand. *Firm grip.* Miles was of average height and weight, but muscled from farm work. His hair was blonde and lay raggedly cut by an unsteady hand. *Supercuts or his wife,* Cooper thought. Squinty eyes were deep set in a square face that looked friendly and welcoming.

"I'm Cooper Adams, great to meet you."

"Likewise. I'm Miles Stott. My mother just told me who you were, while we were waiting for you to finish talking."

Cooper offered a smile, "Yeah. Sorry about that. Your mother is quite the character!"

Miles flushed red, "That's not what I call it."

Lily poked him in the back with her cane, "Watch your tongue, boy!"

"You see? Try living with *that* when you're thirteen years old."

"I feel your pain, brother," Dranko added, apparently already introduced.

Cooper allowed the easy smiles to linger for a long pause before continuing, "More importantly than her personality, I trust her judgment and she has spoken highly of you as someone we can trust."

Miles cocked his head and he met his eyes firmly, "I like to think that's true." He pivoted and indicated his wife, "This is Bethany, my wife." She smiled at them in turn. She was tall for a woman, just an inch or so shorter than her husband, but heavyset. Stylishly cut, long, highlighted, blonde hair fell to her shoulders. Her clothing was fashionable, yet functional, a mix of catalogue collections.

She extended her hand, "Nice to meet you."

Her skin was softer than Cooper would have expected from a woman on a farm, even a small one, "Pleasure is mine." Miles and Bethany introduced themselves to the rest of the group. Lily was beaming as she watched the affair. When they were done, Bethany spoke again, "Let me introduce you to our kids." She called into the house.

"Come on out, kids!" Her words were met with silence and Bethany looked alarmed. Miles looked at her and started laughing.

"You got it backwards!"

She flushed and slapped her knee, "That's right!" She turned once more to cast her voice into the house, "Come on out, Baxter!" Cooper immediately heard the faint clatter of footsteps coming up from a basement.

"It's our simple code when strangers approach. Call for the kids, they don't come. Call for the dog, they come out," Miles explained. "Only problem is, our kids remember it better than my wife!" He poked her in the ribs when he finished. Cooper caught a brief glimpse of anger flash across her face before she stifled it with a mock smile and slapped his hand away.

A young boy and a girl came bounding through the door.

"This here is Aidan," he said, patting the boy on his head. The boy was probably seven or eight, blonde hair just like his father. His face was all teeth and sparkling blue eyes, beaming happiness. "And, this is Chloe." Miles wrapped his other arm around the girl. She was a couple years younger, very thin, and brown curls fell to her shoulders. Green eyes shined up at them from behind shy long eyelashes. She positioned herself to half-hide behind her father.

The adults exchanged greetings with the children.

"Where's Miles Junior?" Lily asked the question before realizing that the answer was evident. Miles eyes fell to the ground.

She closed with her son and embraced him, "I'm so sorry, son." Miles' eyes welled up as he accepted his mother's hug. Bethany snuggled her children, while Cooper and the others stepped back and averted their eyes, offering space as the only sympathy they could provide.

After a few minutes passed, Miles broke the awkward silence by clearing his throat and stepping back from his mother, "Where were we?"

Cooper looked at Miles, eyes full of sympathy, "We were hoping you can help us get the lay of the land around here."

"Sure. But, you know it's bad news?"

His face tightened, "Really?"

"Yup. We have our very own tin pot dictator here in Estacada."

"The Man?" Dranko asked.

"You learn quickly. You want to know the joke of it all? Sheriff Hodges was a staunch no-tax Republican before all this started. Now, he's demanding a very high 'levy'—just taxes in disguise—to pay for security and such. Worse part, we can't pay them in dollar bills, only goods."

"Power corrupts and absolute power corrupts absolutely, no

matter the party line," intoned Lily with an even voice. The others nodded.

"Let me guess, the goods are the hardest things to come by?" Angela asked.

He put his wide-brimmed hat back on and nodded, "Food, guns. And, of course, gasoline."

"What about gold or silver?" All heads turned to Dranko, who had asked.

Miles looked confused, "Sure. He'll take that, if you have it."

"You have something you want to say?" Cooper asked him.

Dranko shook his head nonchalantly, "Nope. Just curious." *Sorry, Dranko, I've beat you too many times in poker. I know you've got a stash of some kind, you sly one!*

"What else is he doing?" Cooper asked.

"Lots of rules, curfews, restrictions on movement. He's formed a security force that keeps everyone else in line. You can't criticize him. Several people have already been hauled in as 'undesireables'."

Cooper's lips curled up, "How'd this happen in just a few weeks?"

Miles cocked an eyebrow, "He acted swiftly and just stepped into the vacuum. It's almost like he had a plan."

"You think," Dranko asked.

"Either that or he was very, very smart and fast on his feet. For example, he took over the gas stations and the grocery store on the very first day that Brushfire went public."

"That *is* strange," Angela commented.

"He's a bastard for sure, but his son is even worse," Miles spat. Bethany shuffled her feet and cast her eyes downward. Cooper noticed the faintest flush of red onto her cheeks.

"Who's he?"

"Junior Hodges. He's in his twenties. Randy as a cooped up rabbit. Rumor has it he's built himself quite a little harem these past weeks. You don't want to cross his path. He shot Mr. Waters down in cold blood just last week. Claimed that ole' Walt was fixing to draw on him. I talked to men who saw it go down, complete hogwash."

Bethany glanced up, "He's got his problems, but he has kept us supplied with milk for our kids."

Miles scoffed, "That's just cause he's sweet on you, baby, and he's trying to get into your…" Miles caught himself, realizing his kids were there. Her cheeks turned unmistakably red this time and her eyes were downcast once more.

"If you're going to just talk politics, I'm going to take the kids and get to work in the garden," she said, before gathering the kids and moving off.

"Just don't touch too many of the seeds as you're liable to just kill them. Bethany's a good woman, but she's got the opposite of a green thumb," Miles said with too much edge to his voice. *A lot of tension between these two.* Bethany stalked off, ignoring him.

Miles laughed at his joke and motioned the others to move inside the house, which was a simple affair, with the kitchen off to their left as they entered and a large mixed family and living room straight in front of them. A hallway led to the bedroom to their right. A woodstove was burning in the corner. The familiar smell of it made Cooper long for his own woodstove back on Lincoln Street in Portland. The home was furnished with plain, worn furniture, except for a remarkable kitchen table. It looked to have been cut from a huge Cedar tree, stained, with remarkable grain patterns.

"I built that one myself," Miles commented with pride when he noticed their stares.

Toys were strewn about the floor and across the rooms, "Damn woman can't keep these kids in line," he scowled as he kicked a toy truck across the room.

"Miles, be kind. Mothering is always easier to the men who don't have to do it," Lily said, weighing in.

"Whatever Ma, you don't know the half of it," Miles said, staring at her sharply. Awkward tension filled the room.

The group took seats around the beautiful table, while Miles offered plastic cups and a pitcher of water. Cooper poured for the group and passed out the cups to everyone. As he took his seat he began, "So, what else do we need to know to get along here?"

"Avoid the downtown as much as you can. That's where Hodges and his crew do their worst. Whatever you do, stay out of the one bar that's functioning down there. And, be ready for a Levy Collector to come a calling as soon as they figure out your place is occupied again."

"We might as well get it over with then," Dranko said in a matter of fact manner.

"What?" Cooper asked.

"We need salt. I completely screwed up on that."

"Salt?"

Dranko nodded emphatically, "Yup. Your body needs it to survive."

"I never thought about it," Lily continued.

"Nobody does. We usually have a problem of *too much* of it with all the processed food we're used to. Now, we're going to have to make sure we have it."

"How'd you screw up? What do you mean?" Cooper asked his friend.

"Last month, I traded my salt supply for some tools I needed. I figured I'd get more salt easy enough. Then, Brushfire happened." He paused, and then shrugged, "At least I got a good deal on the trade. But, we need to get salt. As much as we can get our hands on. And, it's something that will just get more valuable as time goes on. Better to get it now, at whatever price Hodge is demanding."

Cooper nodded, "So, today?"

"Don't see why not."

"I should go with you, to make sure you get by okay," Miles offered.

Cooper shook his head, "I appreciate the offer, but you can brief us the best you can and then let us go. If we run afoul, it's best we can claim the 'we're new in town' defense."

Miles nodded at that.

"That's smart. Besides, you might not want to be associated with us, anyway," Dranko added with an impish smile.

"Why's that?" Miles asked, confused.

"Don't you know who this is?" Angela said, motioning toward Cooper. Miles offered a blank look in response.

"My dad told the truth about the Brushfire Plague," Jake blurted out. His voice was fixed dead between pride and sadness.

Miles' head jerked around to stare at Cooper, "What?!"

"You heard about all that?"

"Well…sure…hard to know what to believe."

Cooper stared at him intently, "Believe it. Every word. It's the truth."

Miles sank back into his chair, "Really? All of it?"

"All of it," Lily added.

"You mean my boy is dead because of some damned hippies?"

Cooper returned a measured look, "It's more complicated than that. But, yeah, Brushfire was no act of God."

Miles fists balled as Lily extended a hand to comfort his son. He was left alone to his thoughts for several seconds and then his eyes alighted, "You got trouble, my friend. Hodges would likely shoot you on sight!"

"Why's that?"

"He's been calling you a damned liar and a scoundrel. He says the entire conspiracy theory is a bunch of BS spread by the enemies of America."

Cooper sat back, arms folded on the table, "Interesting."

"You're going to have to use a fake name when you roll into town."

Dranko exhaled, "Well, *that* should be interesting."

Miles face grew clouded, "Why's that? No big deal. Just come with your own version of John Doe."

A sardonic smile infused his words, "Cooper don't lie. Never."

"Oh my. I see," Miles responded. "Why don't you just stay out of town?"

Cooper thought for a moment, "Two reasons. First, I want to get a feel for what's going on around here. I can't do that hiding up in Dranko's cabin. Second, since this whole thing started, I've learned that trouble is going to find me, no matter how I might try to avoid it." Cooper's attempted joke fell flat.

"Maybe you ought to rethink that," Dranko said, looking at him intently.

"We'll figure it out," Cooper said, irritated.

Dranko shook his head in resignation, "Ever the optimist, brother."

****

Dranko was at the wheel once again, with Angela sitting next to him in the front seat. Cooper sat in the back seat alone, Lily and Jake having been left at the Stotts'. Miles had finished briefing them so they had their pistols holstered, as it was very common in Estacada for people to be carrying. They had left their rifles behind, as well. Sheriff Hodges was fond of confiscating any long arms brought into town, especially military styled weapons. They had decided it wasn't worth the risk. Cooper felt agitated without them. *I don't like going into a potential bad situation under gunned.* He had his pistol out, trying to burn through his anxiety by checking the function and thumbing the rounds out and then back into the magazine. Miles had filled them in on what to do, how to act, and what to look out for as they made their way around the town. He had drawn them a rudimentary map, as well. This showed the key buildings and the main store that functioned as *the* place to buy and sell goods.

The drive into town was uneventful and silent. Apprehension gripped them all. Dranko was frequently grabbing his earlobe, which was what he did when was under stress. Cooper had won many poker hands against him by learning his 'tell' early on. Angela's lips were pursed tight and sometimes she whistled while breathing. Cooper kept his hands occupied with the pistol.

Estacada was a typical small town nestled off a secondary highway. The whole affair was maybe four blocks in any direction. Shops catering to passing motorists and tourists flanked the highway. Cooper had stopped at some of them in days past. The stoplight on the highway was out and a few scattered vehicles littered the roadway. Most looked to have been abandoned, but a few had been shot up. The stoplight had been replaced by two pickups parked head to tail and four men armed with rifles.

"Here we go," Dranko muttered as they were motioned to a stop by one of the men.

Dranko pulled up next to the man and cranked his window down.

The guard was dressed in warm hunting clothes and a red ball cap with the Budweiser logo emblazoned on it.

"How are you folks?"

"Fair to middlin'," Dranko said, deliberately clipping his words.

"What's your business in town today?"

"We come to see about gettin' some salt." *He's adding a bit more 'country' to his tone.* Cooper had watched his father do the same, varying his tone and inflection to reflect the groups of people he was working with. When he was twelve, Cooper had witnessed him doing this with some workers from India. He had been horrified, thinking his father was mocking them. When he had asked him about it, his father had shrugged his shoulders and said, "I didn't notice I was doing it." What Cooper had noticed was how his father had, in fact, not offended them, but established an easy rapport. From that day on, he saw his father do this often. As an adult, Cooper had a laugh one day when Jake asked him why he was mimicking a fellow from West Virginia who owned a hardware store down in Enterprise, Oregon. He'd chuckled, shrugged his shoulders, and said, "I didn't notice I was doing it!" He expected Dranko's effort was more intentional.

The guard nodded, "You got the right currency?"

Dranko's mouth curled up at the corner, "We'll see. Ain't gonna get fleeced in any trade."

The guard laughed, "Alright, good luck. Just don't forget to get a receipt showing you paid your taxes on the purchase. We'll be checking you out on your way out." He waved them on.

Dranko rolled up his windows and drove onward, slowly. Once they were a safe distance away, he burst out laughing.

"Did you hear that?"

"What?"

"There hasn't been a politician born yet that could get a sales tax in place in Oregon. But, wham, Brushfire Plague come along and BOOM Sheriff Hodges gets it going!"

Cooper smiled at his friend's comment.

"I hadn't even thought of that!" Angela said, chuckling.

"Good job, by the way," Cooper added.

Dranko's shoulders responded nonchalantly. "I like how you countrified your voice."

"Oh that? I seen you do that before when you talk to different people, so I thought I'd try it out."

"Well, you pulled it off."

"I was half waiting for you to blurt out 'git er done'!" Angela's voice cracked with laughter.

Dranko winked at her, "I'm saving that for the trip home!"

Cooper turned his attention to the town as they drove toward the trading center. After the last two weeks in Portland, he was immediately struck by the *lack of destruction.* Not a single building had been burned, or even looted. There were many scattered groups of people and individuals who walked along the streets, desultory, heads down. He noted how a few still wore ragged surgical masks or dirty scarves over their mouths, but most had abandoned the effort to protect themselves from the plague. Cooper was struck by how the amount of pedestrians on the streets was much higher — and the cars on the streets much less — than before the plague had struck. As people passed one another, they either made no effort at greeting or did so without much enthusiasm; a lazy wave or head nod. Miles had been right, at least half of the people walking around had pistols on their hips, but nary a rifle was to be seen. He also noted that no one was simply out strolling or 'window shopping'. Almost everyone was carrying loads of goods, or pushing or pulling a cart laden with the same. Foodstuffs and firewood were the most prevalent, but some had bundles of blankets or clothing that they were moving from one place to another. Surveying the scene, Cooper felt like he was watching old movie footage of downtrodden refugees from Eastern Europe.

"I guess Hodges moved quickly to secure things here. Nothing has been destroyed," Angela commented.

"And, he moved firmly. Look at how somber everyone looks," Cooper answered.

"Yeah, it's striking. Chaos would have happened slower here, in any event. Small towns, where people know each other, tend to be safer."

"Good point."

"On the flipside, they are also friendlier. So, everyone being so down on the streets is even *more* telling than it would be in a big city," he continued.

"Even better point," Cooper said.

The Jeep crawled down the main street, toward the store that Miles had indicated on their map. On their left, two men were clustered around a man laying curled up in an abandoned store's entryway. One carried a hunting rifle, while the other had a shotgun pointing at the man lying down. The man on the ground was homeless; dirty clothes, unshaven, with a worn backpack sitting next to him. The men were kicking him, in an attempt to get him onto his feet. The man was disoriented, flailing about with his arms. Cooper rolled down his window so he could hear what was going on.

"…up, you worthless slob! NO drunks in town!"

"Wha…lea-vve me…'lone," the man slurred back. He was rewarded with another round of stiff kicks to his legs and stomach. To their credit, the men weren't trying to hurt the homeless man, but to harass him until he got up and moving. The man's arms flailed down to protect his body, revealing his face for the first time. Cooper was shocked for a moment. His eyes shined in disbelief.

"It can't be," he exclaimed. His left hand grabbed Dranko's shoulder from behind, "Pull over!"

"Why?"

"I know that guy. It's the cook from Redmond! Buck Floy!"

****

Dranko glided the Jeep past the gathered men and over to the curb, "Who?"

"I'll explain later," Cooper shouted as he leapt from the vehicle before it came to a stop.

As he rounded the back corner of the Jeep, one of the guards directed his attention at him and gripped his shotgun with both hands,

"Hold up!" The gun wasn't pointed at Cooper, but was positioned as if to physically bar him from crossing.

Cooper stopped, palms up, "I'm just here to help. I know this man." He pointed at Buck, who was now lying on the ground, groaning.

"Well, then. You can do us all a favor. You get him up and out of here in two minutes, I don't care if you got a contract to kill 'im," the first guard said, relief in his voice.

Cooper nodded and took the final steps to kneel at Buck's feet. The second guard stepped back to give him room as he did so. Buck saw Cooper's approach and pulled back, curling his legs and arms into a defensive posture. His face had a gash across his left cheek and, although they were covered by clothes, he was likely bruised from the beating that had just been administered.

"Donnnn't hu-rr-t mme…" he stammered.

"Buck, I'm here to help you."

Buck shook his head, trying to clear it, "Whhaa…whoooo?"

He leaned in to whisper in his ear, "Cooper Adams." Buck reeked so badly, he had to fight his urge to recoil backwards. The first odor to assault him was the rank of too much alcohol, but the foul body odor of a man who hasn't bathed for a long time quickly piled on. The wafting smell of dried vomit joined the fray. Cooper brought the crook of his elbow to shield his nose from the affront.

Cobwebs hung on in Buck's mind, "Cooopp…who?"

With the guard so close by, Cooper didn't want to yell out his name and he struggled to find a way to help Buck remember him. Then, it hit him.

"Sicilian omelet, *double* helping of wheat toast!" Cooper exclaimed with the glee one has when they figure out the key to a puzzle. *If anything sparks him, it will be my unusual order!*

A smile started in the corner of Buck's mouth, but quickly took over, "Coop—! Doubb-llle the wh—eat! Healthy Portl-landers," he finished with a disdain-ridden muttering. His eyes had some clarity now, drilling into Cooper's.

Cooper smiled and clapped him on the shoulder, "Yup, you got it! The one and the same."

"You lovebirds gonna get moving or not?" The second guard said, prodding Cooper with the butt stock of his rifle. He stifled his anger, but not before his right hand moved a few inches back toward his pistol. Luckily, the guard did not notice the movement.

"Yup, we'll be moving along," was what he said instead. "Can you move?"

Buck moaned as he sat up, "Sure. Jusss-t might n-need help."

Cooper grasped him under the arm and helped lift him to his feet. Buck was unsteady and nearly stumbled. Cooper righted him. As he turned him towards the vehicle, Dranko was waiting, arms crossed. The vicious frown plastered on his face as he shook his head slowly from the side to side, made his statement unmistakable.

Cooper rebuffed him, "It's happening. One, I know him. Two, remember that homeless man from Hawthorne?" The reference to the man they had met in the first days of the Plague, who was teaching about the value of generosity while the world fell apart, deflated Dranko in an instant.

The frown turned into a sheepish smile, "Sure." Dranko moved to gather up Buck's belongings and throw them into the back of the Jeep. Meanwhile, Cooper manhandled Buck into the backseat, opposite of where he was sitting.

"Buck, this is Angela...Angela, Buck Floy, best cook east of Mount Hood."

Buck gallantly offered her a sloppy smile, "P...pl-eeased to meet you," and a dirty palm. Angela took it and shook.

"Pleased to meet you, sir!" She offered an awkward smile, but her nose involuntarily curled up.

Cooper closed the door on Buck and made his way around the back of the Jeep. He tipped his hand from his forehead to the guards, who pretended not to see him. Instead, they turned and walked away, dismissing him.

"He's a solid man," he said to Dranko as they met up at the rear of the vehicle.

"Sure looks like it," he smirked.

They opened their doors simultaneously as they got back in.

"Buck Floy, this is Paul Dranko. A very good friend of mine. And, Dranko, this is Buck Floy, a good man and a great cook from Redmond."

The other two men exchanged nods.

"You stink. Roll down a window," Dranko grunted. The stench was indeed *that* bad and Cooper wasn't annoyed at Dranko's blunt command. Buck fumbled with the window handle for several tries before getting the window down. Dranko didn't wait for him and resumed driving towards the store, a few blocks further up.

Cooper rolled his own window down and turned back towards Buck, "What happened? How'd you end up here?"

Buck looked more alert now, his green eyes looking much more like how Cooper remembered them from the restaurant, "Drove. Then, w-walked. Last bit."

"Why'd you come here?"

"Ex-x-w-ife and my son. Livv-ed he-rre."

"Lived," Cooper asked, mustering sympathy.

Buck's face tightened, "Yeah. P-l-ague got 'em. Both. 'Fore I got here. Got he-rre ye-ssterday and f-found out."

Cooper's eyes shot wide open, "Oh, Buck." He recovered and offered him a hand on his shoulder as comfort, "I'm sorry." Buck's eyes misted and he slammed his fist into his chest. *Using physical pain to hold back the emotion,* Cooper observed. He'd seen men do this before; from kids inflicting self-mutilation in high school to bar fights as he got older.

"I'll be a-lll-right," he said defiantly.

"How is Luisa?" He asked about the kind waitress at the diner and hoping to change the subject to a better one.

"Dead," Buck said flatly. Cooper blinked. It was hard for him to imagine her dead. She was a bundle of frenetic energy. *Gone?* He didn't want to believe it.

"Plague," it was less a question than a statement.

"No, g-got h-hit by a carr-r," Buck corrected.

Cooper's hand flew to his temple and rubbed it, "Seriously?"

Buck nodded and burped, "'Fraid so. Horrible. Coulda lived, but the h-hos-pp-ital was full up."

Cooper's fist slammed into an open palm, "Damn!" Buck stared at him with dulled, but open and sympathetic eyes.

The scratch of the emergency brake interrupted them.

"We're here," Dranko announced.

****

They were in a parking lot for the town's former main grocery store. The nondescript dusty white building was pockmarked in a few spots with bullet holes. The front glass doors had been replaced with plywood and sheet metal. The multitude of bullet holes framing the doorway made Cooper guess that they had been shot out. *Must have been a struggle for control. Owner and employees versus Hodges' group? I'll have to find out.* Two guards were stationed out in front of the doors. They wore body armor, police helmets, and carried M-16s. That they were also wearing sunglasses on a gray day told Cooper they were

150

trying to create an intimidating presence, as well.

The parking lot was mostly empty, there were only about a dozen vehicles in one that could easily hold over fifty. The Jeep had barely stopped when a gaggle of kids swarmed around them, offering all manner of cheap goods to trade. Cheap wood carvings. Handfuls of cartridges. Fishing implements. Hand tools.

Their catcalls varied about their various offerings. But, there was only thing they were all chanting for: "Food!" The kids were all dirty, hungry, some already looking thinner than they should have been. Cooper wrinkled his nose in disgust.

"Poor kids," Angela lamented.

"Looks like kids in Mexico when Elena and I went there four years ago," Cooper added.

Dranko scowled, "Stupid parents probably didn't have a single preparation, either!"

Angela punched him in the shoulder, "C'mon! Their parents could be *dead.* Have a heart, will ya?"

Dranko looked like he hadn't considered the possibility, "Good point. But, why don't you stay with these kids and Buck. Cooper and me will take care of business. You can keep an eye on everything." He wrenched the door open and stepped out, not waiting for an answer.

She glared back at Cooper, who flashed her a 'go figure' look and joined his friend outside. They had to physically push the kids back, worried that the buffeting could be a ruse to hide a pickpocketing attempt.

"We might have something for you when we come out. No food now," Cooper said. The kids drifted away, as Cooper and Dranko marched toward the entrance.

"Whatcha here for," one of the guards asked them when they walked up to the door.

"Trade. Mostly salt, but we'll see what else there is," Dranko responded.

"What do you have to trade *with?*" The other man asked, seeing no visible goods. *I'm getting slow, I hadn't even bothered to ask Dranko that!*

"Precious metals," he responded. Cooper concealed his surprise. *I figured back at the Stott's that you had some, but not on you!*

"What?" Another guard exclaimed.

"Silver and gold," Dranko said as evenly as if he was saying "Visa," when asked about his method of payment in the days before the Plague.

"We don't get that very much around here. Usually, that's only used with the Man when someone is making a big deal."

"Good to know, I'm guessing I'll get some good deals then," Dranko said.

"You just might. Barter deals are much harder to figure out. Anyone will take silver or gold these days. Much easier to work with," the first guard stated.

The guards proceeded to explain the rules of the establishment: no violence, no stealing, no touching merchandise, tax collector must be present at the time of sale, tax collector will tell you the amount of tax, it varies with each transaction, get a written receipt from the collector, incline your head in the presence of the Sheriff, firearms must be left here, and so on. When they had turned over their firearms and secured Cooper's and Dranko's understanding and agreement to the rules, they opened the door and waved them in.

"We're not planning to bother the Sheriff," Dranko commented when they mentioned the rule about him.

The second guard laughed, "Oh. You got precious metal? The Sheriff will come bother with you. Be sure of that!" The way he said 'bother' made Cooper's stomach tighten. His jaw clamped shut and his lips drew into a scowl when the guard's cohort guffawed.

****

They stepped into the former grocery store turned trading post and were greeted by dozens of pairs of eyes, sizing them up. The store was dimly lit, about every third panel of lights had been turned off. The back half of the store had been left completely dark. Rows of shelving had been removed and replaced with tables. *An indoor flea market.* The room had been subdivided into groups: foodstuffs up front, tools to the right, clothing on the left, and so on. Several armed men drifted through the room looking bored. *Inattentive too,* Cooper thought.

"Their boredom means this place must be calm," he whispered to Dranko, who grunted to show he'd heard him.

The store buzzed with the chatter of a few dozen customers doing business with the dozen or so vendors. Within a few seconds of watching, a man bellowed, "That's absurd," and stormed off. Off to his right, Cooper saw a woman gesticulating wildly as she tried to convince a merchant to agree to her price. From the looks of it, it wasn't working so well. Others talked too loudly. A man wailed and burst into tears. Another screamed, red-faced, at a seller. Several were conducting transactions as goods exchanged hands.

"This is chaos," Dranko muttered.

Cooper laughed, "Nope. It's education," he said, clapping his friend on the shoulder.

Dranko looked at him as if he had just said something crazy, "What?"

"They're figuring out how to bargain."

"People *know* how to do that. Who hasn't been to a flea market or a garage sale?"

He looked at Dranko, disappointed, "C'mon! You know better than that. Trying to figure out a deal on a used couch or a worn out toy is *not* the same as trying to get something you need to *survive*."

Pausing, he cocked his head to the side, "Yeah. I got you. Stakes are higher. Stress is higher."

"And, don't forget that there's not a commonly accepted currency anymore."

That made Dranko laugh, "True. How do you know how much your eggs are worth relative to sewing thread?"

"Exactly. It's a brave new world."

"I guess we need to go and figure out how much salt we can get for your gold?"

Dranko looked taken aback for a moment, "How'd you know?"

"Magic. The magic of knowing your sorry ass for far too long," Cooper said with a mischievous grin before walking off to the first vendor to find out if they had salt.

****

Twenty minutes later, they had identified two sellers of salt and were finalizing the price with the better of the two. The vendor was a woman in her sixties; white hair with a fading blue tint job. Cooper wished they had Lily with them. He guessed she could have charmed this woman in a New York minute with her Kentucky accent and witticisms.

She tossed her head back, laughing, "Fifty pounds? You wanna clean me out?"

Cooper laughed himself, jostling Dranko with his shoulder, "Look at her! You ever heard of a merchant complaining about selling *too much* of her product?"

Dranko refused the levity, "Nope." His face was serious, his

153

shoulders tense. *I need to teach him how to bargain!* From a young age, Cooper's father had taught him the basics of successful negotiations. "Rule number one, put the other guy at ease." Cooper had heard his father say that a thousand times.

The woman, Marjorie, laughed with Cooper, despite Dranko, "I ain't complaining. I just want to make sure that your trade goods give me something good to keep my trade going on."

"What's your price for fifty pounds of salt. In silver?" Dranko asked flatly. Cooper tried to hide his grimace.

"I bet you don't do foreplay either," Marjorie said, smirking. Cooper noted her deft attempt to hide her surprise when the word 'silver' escaped Dranko's lips.

"I just don't have time to waste," Dranko replied, edginess creeping into his voice.

"You'll have to forgive my friend's brusque nature, but we are in a bit of a hurry today," Cooper added.

"Let's see. Fifty pounds. Silver. Five ounces," she said, her voice turning sharp.

Cooper burst out laughing, "Five? You'd be doing well to get an ounce."

A sly smile crept onto Marjorie's face as she recognized the bargaining process had begun. "An ounce? You must be new in town, eh? I have two twenty-five pound bags. You want fifty pounds all at once? You obviously need it and I'm a kind hearted woman so I can let it go for four ounces."

"Let's go see if the other guy is more reasonable," Dranko said, beginning to move away. Cooper grabbed his arm to stop him.

"Hold on, Dranko. I'm sure Marjorie will come round. Right?"

Marjorie folded her arms and looked nonplussed, "I'm always reasonable, but I won't give it away. I made that mistake in my early twenties and ended up with three kids and not a one of their daddies done me right." She laughed at her own joke. Dranko stopped, but only turned halfway back toward facing her.

The back and forth continued for another few minutes as they dickered. Finally, they agreed to pay three ounces of silver, including the taxes, for the salt. Dranko fished the silver out from a pocket inside his jacket, handed it to her, and Marjorie began writing out their receipt.

The receipt had been pocketed and the salt put up onto her table for Cooper and Dranko when a group of men approached. Cooper saw them first and tapped Dranko's foot and directed his attention to them with his eyes.

A short man, listing to the stocky side, emerged at the front of the group of five men. He had black hair, likely dyed, given his age. It was kept short and greased back. He was in his fifties, with dark brown eyes.

"Afternoon, gentlemen," he said with a firm, commanding voice. "I'm Sheriff Hodges." He extended his hand and promptly attempted to crush Cooper's hand. Cooper pressed back to show him he could, but didn't go so far as to invite a contest.

"Good afternoon, Sheriff. I'm CJ and this is my good friend, Paul Dranko." The two men quickly shook hands, as well.

"You paying in silver, I see."

"Yes, we are. Is that a problem?" Cooper responded.

Hodges shook his head, "Of course not. In fact, we need more metal to come into circulation. Bartering for everything is very cumbersome."

"Glad we could be of assistance."

"Indeed. You new in town? I haven't seen you before."

"We just came in, staying at my property just outside of town," Dranko weighed, mustering politeness.

"Most excellent. We need more upstanding folks who can pay their bills in town." He rubbed his hands together while talking. "Dranko? Yes, I remember your name from the tax rolls."

"You must have a good memory," Cooper added.

"Well, Dranko's an unusual name. We were keeping eyes on the empty properties, keeping them secure until the owners arrived or we would declare them abandoned and award them to those families in need for a place to live. We have a number of refugees, you know?" Cooper watched Hodges sizing them up as he talked.

"I'm glad you remembered me," Dranko said, unsure of where Hodges was heading. Cooper knew. *Here comes the tax warning.*

"Thank you. I should let you know, there are levies that all who live in the area pay. For the costs of our collective security, I'm sure you can understand. The outlying areas consume more resources to patrol and there might be an issue with the work we've done the last few weeks keeping your place secure, as well." By the time he had finished, Hodges' smile was as greasy as his hair. His delivery was polished, and reminded Cooper of a very successful used car salesman.

Dranko stepped forward, "That's complete..."

Cooper grunted, and used his arm to bar his friend and interrupt him, "We'll certainly do our part for our collective security, but we will not need any special measures. We can defend our area. And, while we appreciate the efforts you've made thus far to keep it safe, we did have to deal with an interloper when we arrived. So, clearly there were some unfortunate gaps in the security, despite your good efforts. Which we appreciate. I'm sure you are a fair man and you'll keep that in mind in considering the costs of any past efforts by the town." Cooper returned the same wide, insincere smile he had received.

Hodges met Cooper's eyes and the two men stared at each other for a long moment. Cooper saw a resolute and cunning man. *Determined.* He looked directly at Hodges, his eyes steeled to show him he wasn't a man to be reckoned with lightly.

"Of course," Hodges said. "I'd be remiss in not introducing you to my son. He's essential to the good operation of our small town." A younger man stepped forward.

"I'm Junior Hodges, Undersheriff for Estacada." He stood a few inches above his father, with light brown hair, and bright blue eyes. His smile looked more like a snarl. *Not as polished as his father.* The men shook hands and exchanged pleasantries.

"It was a pleasure to meet you fine men, and again, welcome to our fair town. A team of my men will visit you in the next few days to do an assessment and explain our levy procedures."

Cooper nodded, "Understood. Let me thank you for having such an orderly town, Sheriff." He heard the nearly inaudible choke from Dranko on his left.

They hefted the bags of salt and exited the market, showing their receipt to the door guards on their way out. When they were out of earshot, Dranko asked.

"CJ? Where'd you come up with that?"

"My middle name is James. So, it was true, but also not flatly telling him I'm Cooper Adams!"

Dranko laughed, "Nice!"

They deposited the heavy bags of salt into the Jeep's cargo area and pulled out of the parking lot.

****

The loud rasp from Buck Floy's snoring in the back seat competed with the engine's growl as they drove back towards the Stott's.

"How'd you have silver on hand?" Cooper asked Dranko as

they rumbled down the road.

A wide grin crossed Dranko's face, "That's easy. If you think things might come unglued at some point, you gotta prepare that the currency won't work anymore."

"Were you betting against America, you SOB?" He was only half joking.

Dranko gave him a sharp smirk, "Nope. Just betting on probabilities. I knew something was going to happen that would upend things. Gold and silver are *hard* currencies. They outlast paper money every time."

"I was just thinking about that yesterday," Angela joined the conversation.

"What," Cooper asked.

"My 401k. I spent so much energy and worry building that thing up. Now, I wonder if it's worth a penny."

Dranko burst out laughing. Angela punched him in the shoulder from the backseat.

"Don't be an ass!"

He fought to restrain himself, "I'm sorry." He regained his breath, "I just always said that they shouldn't have been called 401k's." He paused.

"What should they have been called?" Angela asked, exasperated.

"401Cs. For 401 Craps. It was gambling pure and simple and you were destined to come up a loser. Even without the Brushfire Plague, it was a rigged system from jump street."

Angela's face drooped, the corners of her mouth downturned, "I guess you were right."

"So, E. F. Hutton, what was your investment strategy?"

Dranko inclined his head towards Cooper, "That was easy. The four B's. Beans, bullets, band aids, and bullion." The mock smug look and tone as he delivered his response made Cooper and Angela laugh and slap him on the shoulder.

They drove the rest of the way in silence, made it up the long driveway to the Stott's, and manhandled Buck Floy into the kitchen.

Chapter Nine

They gathered around the kitchen table. Cooper and Dranko relayed how they had bargained for the salt and of their conversation with Hodges about the levy. As they talked, Miles' face flushed until he exploded.

"He's pushing way too hard! People can't take it," he fumed.

"Is he overplaying his hand?" Cooper queried.

"Damn straight."

"He ain't so bad. Just trying to keep things safe," Bethany offered in a soothing tone.

Miles spun around and glared at her, "And, getting rich in the process!" He stormed past her and the door banged as he went outside. Cooper and Dranko exchanged a look and Cooper followed him out.

He found him twenty yards away from the front door, near the garden. A cigarette puffed from his lips, angry smoke blowing outward.

"You alright?" Cooper asked.

"I'm tired of her defending the Hodges."

Cooper grunted in agreement, allowing him the space to continue.

"I know she's sweet on Junior."

Cooper dropped his eyes to the ground and waited.

"But, I can't help but wonder if it's more than that." Miles' voice was filled with pain and embarrassment. Cooper was surprised at his admission to someone he'd just met. *But, I guess Brushfire Plague has shattered all sorts of social conventions. Rampant death has a way of slashing and burning them to the ground.*

Cooper placed a hand on his shoulder, "You got enough worries. I wouldn't take one on, unless you're sure of it."

Miles caught his eye, "You're probably right." He shook his head slowly from side to side, as if to banish the thought. "Nonetheless, Hodges is a problem." Cooper nodded in agreement.

The sound of rubber tires tearing through gravel as a pickup truck came roaring up the driveway made them jerk their heads around as one.

****

159

The pickup, a bright red Ford, lurched to a stop just a few yards away from them. It hadn't even fully stopped when the passenger leapt out. Miles' calm kept Cooper's hand from reaching for his pistol. The man was a shade under six feet and he wore sturdy work pants and a green flannel overshirt. A revolver was holstered at his side. His face was contorted and flushed.

"He's gone and done it now," the man roared at Miles. It was like he didn't even see Cooper.

Miles raised his hands, "Slow down, Keith. What are you talking about?"

The driver stepped forward to join them. He had moved slowly, more deliberately. He was dressed in a similar fashion to Keith, except his flannel was gunmetal gray. As far as Cooper could tell, he was unarmed.

"He's crossed the line," he said in tones as measured as his walk.

"Robert, why don't you tell me just what the hell you are talking about?" Miles answered, as Dranko, Angela, Buck, and Bethany approached from the house.

"He's trying to get my wife into bed!" Keith gasped, spittle flying from his mouth.

"What?" Miles responded, flummoxed.

"As a way to settle his levy debt," Robert said calmly.

Miles started laughing, "This is a joke, right?" Bethany's face grew dark, angry lines etching across her forehead and drawing her mouth up tightly.

"No! It's not a joke. Bastard said I could either give up my only rifle as my tax or let him have one night with Valerie. Dirty runt has had his eye on her since high school!" Keith was out of breath when he'd finished spitting the words out.

Miles looked at Robert, who nodded in confirmation. Miles staggered back. His hands came to his head and he grasped it in disbelief.

"Wow. This is a whole new ballgame."

"He's crossed the line, right?" Keith pleaded for agreement.

"You sure he wasn't just joking around? You know how he can get sometimes," Bethany proffered.

Both men turned on her in disbelief. "If you'd seen how he was looking at her, you'd know he wasn't joking. He was nearly licking his lips right in front of me," Keith responded, biting the words out between his clenched jaw. His words startled Bethany and she turned quickly and walked away. Cooper had seen the hurt that flashed across her eyes. *No doubt that something is going on between her and Junior.*

"What the hell are we gonna do?" Keith's voice was choked in desperation.

Miles and Robert looked at each other blankly. The voice of Cooper's father came back to him, "*Strength in numbers. It's all the little guy has against the big man. Follow those who unite the little against the strong. Be wary of any who divides.*" He didn't imagine his father had ever thought his son would be confronting a local strongman as part of a tax revolt. Nonetheless, his words came back, wise and strong.

"How many can we rally?" Cooper's voice was resolute, commanding. He deliberately said 'we' and not 'you'.

"Whatcha mean?" Keith asked.

"How many of your friends and family will stand against Hodges once they hear this news?"

Fear came and usurped Keith's rage in heartbeat, "How can we stand against him?"

Cooper's own face flushed and he drew his face up against Keith's, "How can you not? Didn't you *just* tell me he wants to take your wife into bed? *To pay your taxes, man?* You gonna stand for *that?*"

Keith's back stiffened, "Hell no."

"Good. Now you three tell me who else will stand with Keith. If it's his wife today, it's gonna be someone else's tomorrow. Or their daughter. Or, who knows what else he will begin to demand."

"Bullies push you 'round until you don't push no more," Lily Stott added. Cooper hadn't noticed that she had walked up.

Miles, Robert, and Keith started discussing names of others they knew in town. Cooper ignored the names. Instead, he kept a mental count of anyone that they all agreed would stand against Hodges. When his mental count reached twenty, he stopped them.

"That's enough. You have twenty. More than enough. He can't just kill twenty men."

"Why shouldn't we get more?"

"Two reasons. First, your first twenty are your best twenty. The ones you think of first are always the strongest ones. Second, twenty is big enough for protection, but not so big that it will feel like a mob."

The others nodded in agreement.

"Let's gather them all here, tomorrow at five. We'll make a plan. Sound good?"

Keith nodded his head vigorously, "Yeah. Sounds good. Junior said he'd give me three days to make my decision."

Robert nodded slowly and turned to get back into his pickup. Keith took Cooper's hand and shook it rapidly.

"Thank you, Mister. Thank you!" He turned and scrambled back into the truck. His hand stopped at the handle and he turned as if to ask something else, but then got into the vehicle.

"Something else, isn't it?"

Cooper turned toward Dranko, "What?"

"You can lead people who you just met and don't even know your name!"

He contemplated the comment for a moment, "Hmmm. I guess you're right." A self-satisfied smile crept onto his face.

"Oh no. I knew I shouldn't have said anything to make you even more arrogant!"

"It isn't arrogance if it's true," Cooper shot back.

"Dear Lord! Help me!" Dranko responded, drawing his hands into prayer and gazing longingly skyward.

"You guys are a regular Laurel and Hardy," Miles said, chuckling.

"Yeah, just remember, he's the skinny bird," Dranko said, jerking a thumb in Cooper's direction.

"And...he's the lardy one!"

"Ouch! I guess I walked into that one," Dranko lamented.

He shrugged his shoulders in response.

"Miles, we should get back to Dranko's place. Let's meet at four tomorrow to get ready for this meeting."

Miles nodded, "Right. See you then."

Cooper, Dranko, Angela, and Buck clambered into the Jeep and began driving back to Dranko's place.

"You just can't help getting caught up in the middle of what's happening, can you?"

Cooper looked at Angela, "Guess not. I see a need, I try and fill it. Been like that since I was a kid."

"It's admirable," her eyes shined with respect as she said it.

Cooper looked at her for a moment longer than he probably should have before looking away, "If you say so. I never could stand a bully, anyway."

"Yeah, neither could I," her words were laced with contempt. "It's going to be fun taking that bad boy on."

"Fun wasn't the word I was thinking of. It's going to be dangerous," Dranko disagreed.

Cooper turned to look at him, surprised, "You in?"

He nodded with drawn eyebrows, "'Course, I'm in. Hodges is a problem. His boy is worse. I'm just saying, we *are* playing with fire here."

Cooper nodded, "Yeah, I know that. But, there's no choice."

"We always have a choice, brother. Except for breathing and dying, everything else is a choice," he said, his mouth drawing up tight.

Cooper grimaced at his friend using his own words against him, "Well, I don't see much of a choice. If we're going to try and make a go of things here, Hodges will have to be confronted sooner or later."

"And, I don't disagree. I was just making the point that there *is* a choice."

Cooper shook his head, annoyed, "Whatever. You sound like a philosophy professor. And, that's no compliment."

He looked back at him, nonplussed, "Whatever, yourself." He kept his eyes fixed on the road.

****

They arrived back at Dranko's place by late afternoon. The sun hung low on the horizon, casting long rays across the land. Cooper loved this time of day; the light made everything appear peaceful, content. He remembered many evenings spent with Elena watching the sun fall behind the horizon. He'd never grown tired of watching her face, alight in the soft, warm light of the fading sun. She had looked beautiful in a thousand different ways. The sweet memory turned bitter in his mouth as he recalled the way the sun had faded that day when she lay dying; leaving her ashen. He spat deliberately, trying to clear the foul taste.

They gathered on the porch, all seeking the easy grace of the peaceful sunset. Julianne was off to his right, leaning against a post, gazing at the faltering sun. The lighting highlighted what was already there; her stunning face and glistening hair. She turned just then and their eyes met. Despite his resistance, Cooper felt his heart stir. *She looks angelic in this light.* The juxtaposition of his thoughts to her deeds made him chuckle to himself and turn away.

Angela was off to his left, looking out in the opposite direction. The soft light made her face seem even more kind, caring. Cooper felt comforted by having her so close by. While his feelings lacked the intensity of those with Julianne, they also lacked the deep conflict and tension that Julianne stirred in him. Angela was calming and exuded warmth he needed. He knew she'd make a good mother for Jake. That thought startled him. *Why am I thinking like this, with Elena so soon gone?* Guilt washed over him and his face drew into a self-reproachful scowl. He pushed those thoughts away.

"The end of the world has a way of shortening timelines."

He turned toward Dranko, who had crept up behind him and put his hand on his shoulder.

"Am I that obvious?" Cooper mused.

"Just to me. I know you, brother."

"That you do," he said, letting loose an easy laugh. When it ended, he turned serious. "Should we gather folks and make the plan for tomorrow and then have dinner?"

Dranko nodded. Thirty minutes later, they had a plan. They would all work to prepare the garden for planting. Dranko knew they needed to get seeds in the ground as soon as possible. Given the colder climate on the mountain, he was going to work on getting plants going in starters, indoors. The rest would work on the garden itself. They needed to weed, prep, and fertilize the ground.

After a bland dinner of white rice and lentils, they gathered in the living area of the cabin and listened to the radio. The news was dark. Widespread rioting continued across the country. The riots had turned decidedly anti-government. A dozen or so mayors and a handful of governors had declared themselves in open defiance of the national government for their lack of action in releasing more information about the Brushfire Plague and the allegations swirling about it. Cooper had the thought that such actions may have been a deliberate attempt to take their cities *off* the nuclear target lists that Russia was continuingly rattling its saber over. Nonetheless, haphazard efforts were being made to occupy key sites in the defiant locales and states. The slowness of the federal government's response made him suspect that desertion was a problem that existed but had mostly gone unreported.

"...and in sobering news, there are reports of house-to-house raiding in search of food in many, many cities. There have been numerous reports of violent and deadly clashes between gangs and neighborhoods that are defending themselves."

"I was afraid of that," Dranko intoned.

"The food is running out now," Calvin added.

Cooper nodded gravely, "It's going to get ugly. Very ugly."

"We have one interesting report out of Portland, Oregon. The city is the site of much controversy because it is home to Admonitus, the bio-tech

company that allegedly engineered and released Brushfire Plague onto the world. We will talk about that in just a moment, but the city leadership has commandeered two grain barges that were docked there when the outbreak began. They are using the grain to feed the city with organized distribution points throughout the city. So, far, Portland has avoided the food-related violence that is becoming common in far too many places. However, mayors from surrounding towns and cities, including nearby Vancouver, Washington, are demanding that Portland share those foodstuffs. Already, one armed vigilante group from Vancouver seeking to get the grain has been repulsed with dozens of dead. Vancouver's Mayor, John Stillwell, denies any official sanction of the incursion."

"I guess, 'Keep Portland Weird' won't be our slogan anymore. It will be, 'Keep Portland Fed!'" Freddie joked from the corner of the room.

"It's really funny," Dranko mused.

"What?"

"I had read many times over in the survivalist forums on the Web that Portland always had at least *one* grain barge in port. And, that such a barge could feed the city for a year!"

"Really?" Angela asked for the entire group. "I'd never heard that."

"Well, I'd heard it, but I never quite believed it," Dranko responded.

"And, they have *two*. I guess my friends *aren't* going hungry then," Jake commented, his voice the most optimistic it had been in a week or more.

"True. But people from other places are going to be coming for that food. The city government should have controlled that information better. As surrounding communities start to go hungry, that grain could become a curse," Dranko said.

"Or a great source of power," Cooper intoned flatly.

"What do you mean dad?" Jake queried.

"Well, if I were the Mayor of Portland, I would immediately use that food to make alliances with the immediately surrounding cities and towns. If they provide border defense for Portland, they get food. Dranko's right, they are going to have wolves at their door very soon, and hungry ones at that. Better to push those wolves further out by making those kinds of alliances."

"Good point," Dranko interjected. "And, he better be training and arming a defense force worthy of the name. Otherwise those surrounding towns might just ally themselves and take the food."

Jake blew out a loud exhale, "It all sounds confusing to me!"

The radio caught their attention once more.

"...for Cooper Adams continues. The President has declared him Public Enemy Number One for the 'grave harm his vicious lies are causing'. The Administration has also released a set of documents that they claim refutes the outlandish claims made by Mr. Adams. Those documents are being examined and reviewed by an International Team of journalists and experts."

"I wonder what that is all about?" Calvin inquired.

"People don't want to believe in the truth that I revealed. This will give them something to latch onto," Cooper observed, dryly.

"I'd like to know just who's on that team of journalists and experts. Were they handpicked by the Administration?"

They all nodded in agreement.

"...This shocking news just came in." The announcer's voice sounded genuinely shocked, rather than the faux emotion that they often evidenced. The room fell silent.

"The Governors of Idaho, Montana, and Wyoming have just announced their secession from the United States of America!" Radio silence claimed the air for several long seconds. Cooper imagined that the man on the other end was actually speechless after reading the newsflash.

"I repeat, it is confirmed that the States of Idaho, Montana, and Wyoming have announced that they are seceding from the United States. They are calling their new nation the Patriotic American States. The declaration of secession issued jointly by the three Governors cites, and I quote, 'the long-standing infringement of our inalienable liberties and freedoms by the overbearing and intrusive Federal Government....after an extensive review of all the proven information related to the Brushfire Plague, we have decided the government of the United States was complicit either intentionally or through wanton negligence in the commission of this horrendous crime upon our beloved land. We see no other course of action and honor our revolutionary forefathers in announcing our total revocation of our ties with the United States...'"

"Is this really happening!" Julianne exclaimed, hands grabbing her head.

Cooper just shook his head.

Dranko was notably calm, "There had to be contingency plans in place before the Plague even struck. No way they move all this so quickly otherwise."

"What are you talking about? You see a damned conspiracy under every rock!" Cooper scowled at Dranko.

Dranko raised his hands, palms up, "What me? I'm just stating the obvious. There had to have been some discussions and plans about this already on the books. In fact, there was a famous survivalist, James Wesley Rawles, who said those states should secede."

"You are making my head hurt," Cooper responded. "What does this all mean?"

"It means that the pitch of the cliff we have been travelling over just got steeper," Dranko replied smugly.

"It means the end of the United States," Julianne added dryly.

The door flew open so abruptly that everyone had pistols drawn and pointed at the door in a flash.

Tim's flushed face peered over the edge of the door, he recoiled when he saw the multitude of guns pointed at him. His face appeared a second time, this time more slowly.

"We got company."

Julianne hustled Jake into the basement, while the others grabbed their rifles and took up their pre-arranged defensive positions inside and outside the cabin.

Headlights stabbed through the darkness haphazardly as a single vehicle made its way up the winding driveway.

"Either a friendly or someone incredibly brazen to be coming up like that," Dranko observed.

He and Cooper were standing exposed in front of the cabin door. Someone had to do it. They had reasoned that if everyone was hidden away, that the risk of mistaken identity with someone who was friendly was very high.

As the vehicle rounded the tree line, they breathed a sigh of relief when they saw it was Mile's truck. That relief was very short-lived.

He piled out as soon as the wheels stopped, "We need you guys now!"

"What's going on?"

"That son-of-a-bitch Hodges came out to Keith's place tonight, drunk as all get out. He just *took* Valerie off, kicking and screaming. Junior's men held Keith down until she was good and away."

Cooper's face felt warm and his hand quickly ached from gripping his rifle so tightly, "So, what's the plan?"

"We're gathering at my place in thirty minutes. I want you guys to be there."

Dranko and Cooper exchanged a quick look and immediately knew their answer, "Okay. We're there."

They decided to bring Tim with them, since he was from the

area. Calvin and Angela would stay behind and split guard duty in case they were gone all night. They gathered their gear and got into Dranko's Jeep for the short drive to the Stott's.

****

When they arrived, the Stott's place looked like a parking lot at a busy summer fair. Cars, but mostly pickups and SUVs, were squeezed into every available patch of land. Drivers had long ago stopped worrying about boxing others in and the vehicles were parked nose to tail, and side to side. Cooper quickly counted over twenty. He noticed the wide range of vehicles, from old rusted out pickups that looked like they would keel over and die at any second to brand new trucks with extended cabs and shiny new paint. The handful of cars in the yard told a similar tale: from an old Dodge K car to one as new Cadillac. *You can always tell the economic background of who has come to a meeting by checking the parking lot,* his father had said more than once or twice.

Any pretense of holding the meeting inside had been abandoned and a crowd mingled in the chilly air. Cooper felt the electricity in the air and the hairs on his arms stood up.

"Feels like home, eh?" Dranko asked, winking.

He smiled back, "I guess you're right. Feels like an eternity ago when we gathered on my stoop and tried to figure out what to do next, doesn't it?"

Dranko grunted as an affirmative, paused, and then commented, "Good crowd."

"What do you mean?" He intoned, curious

"I bet we got more guns on hand up here than back in Portland." He'd laid the scorn so thick into his voice that Cooper felt scolded, even though he was a gun owner himself. Now, it was Cooper's turn to grunt in agreement.

Someone tugged on his elbow and Cooper turned to see Miles with a flushed face and small beads of sweat on his brow, despite the obvious chill hanging in the air. Cooper offered him a reassuring smile.

"Nervous?"

Miles gulped, "That obvious, huh?"

Cooper clapped him on the shoulder, "You'll be fine."

"I ain't never spoke to this many people before. What do I say?"

Cooper thought for a moment before responding. "My father

did a lot of public speaking in his day and he gave me precious advice when I asked him the same question."

"What was it?"

"Ask what you need to know. Say what you know to be true. And, most importantly, don't screw it up and embarrass me!"

Cooper exploded in laugher, hoping his boisterousness would carry Miles along in the joke and get him laughing, too. It didn't. Miles looked like he was turning a shade of green.

"Look, I'm sorry, Miles. Bad joke! I was just trying to get you to loosen up. If you get stuck, I'm here to help you," Cooper said as he clapped him on the other shoulder.

Miles nodded his head quickly a few times, "Yeah, Okay. I'll be fine." With that, he turned on his heel to make his way to the edge of the group. He was breathing so rapidly and shallowly that Cooper was worried he might pass out.

"Breathe! Deeply!" He shouted after him.

He watched with bemusement as Miles clambered up onto the hood of an old Chevy pickup that was bereft of a single flake of paint, as near as Cooper could tell. Rust had long since claimed its victory.

"Can everyone gather here along the fence line?" Miles shouted to the group.

"Hey, Miles, watch it. Don't scratch the paint on my beauty there," a gruff voice yelled. A round of chuckles ran through the crowd.

"Hell, Frank. Any scuffing he does will be an improvement!" This catcall got more laughter than it should have. *People venting their anxiety,* Cooper mused.

Miles began tentatively, his voice cracking from nerves, "I wish we could make jokes all night, guys. But, we got some serious business to discuss." Frosted air jerked outward from his mouth as he spoke in a broken, awkward cadence.

"Let's get to it," the gruff voice called out once more.

"Junior Hodges has crossed a line. Many of us have been complaining about the 'levies'…"

"Damn that word. Call it what it is. Taxes!" Someone interrupted him.

Miles took a long moment to recover, "Fine. Taxes. We've been complaining about them since they started. Now, he first demanded to have a go at Keith's wife, Valerie, or Keith had to give up his only rifle as payment."

A bevy of hoots and boos descended upon the crowd and grew

to a low roar. Colorful catcalls were liberally mixed in the general din. Miles raised his hands to quiet them. When the noise had subsided, he continued.

"It gets worse. He told Keith he'd have two days to think it over. Then, tonight, he came over, drunk, and took Valerie away."

The place was deathly silent. Miles looked confused and looked around searching for an answer. Apparently, he decided that they hadn't heard him.

"I said, he came and *took* Valerie away!"

The effect was catalytic. The stunned crowd erupted in a frenzy. The shouting was so loud that Cooper clapped his hands to his ears. People were yelling, stomping, banging rifle butts against the nearest vehicle, and crying out an indiscernible cacophony of protests. Miles was visibly shaken and took a step backward on the pickup's hood, trying to gain scant distance between himself and the mob's rage. Cooper turned to look at the man to his right. He was in his thirties, with black hair and a neatly kept beard. The man was screaming at the top of his lungs, but the noise was so deafening, Cooper couldn't make out a word. He lip read profanities lacing every third word, but could not hear those, either. To his left, Dranko was as dumbstruck as Cooper; gaping at those around him and the spectacle. Then, it hit him. *Junior's outrageous act is magnified because of the horrors everyone has just lived through. They are imagining their wife or daughter being in Valerie's place and what would have been unfathomable a month ago is now cause for the mob's ferocity. The enormity of their loss makes the crime shift to beyond heinous.*

Miles remained on the hood of the pickup for at least five minutes as the crowd vented its fury. Finally, after repeated attempts, he gained some semblance of order.

"The question now is, what do we do?"

"We kill the son-of-a-bitch," the man with the gruff voice yelled. That drew a loud round of clapping and yells of support for the idea.

As it subsided, a nervous voice chimed in, difficult to hear, "He's got a lot of armed men with him." Space cleared around the speaker. *Almost like you have the plague, ain't it?* Cooper half-expected to see a bespectacled frail-looking man, given the voice and the comment. Instead, he saw a stocky, well-muscled man, wearing a green flannel workingman's shirt and a Carhart tan jacket. Matching workpants and black boots completed his attire.

The man shifted his feet, gaining traction. His voice found greater confidence, too, "You know what I say is true."

170

His comment drew a spattering of support, before others rushed in to silence them. The word "coward" struck clean through the crowd.

The man reared up, "Who said that? Come say that to my face!" The man's brown eyes searched frantically for the offender.

Miles quickly lost control as the group splintered into a half-dozen animated arguments about whether or not taking on Junior Hodges was what they should do. Several of the groups were quickly moving beyond exchanging words and pushing and shoving started. Miles locked onto Cooper's eyes like a drowning man does the life raft. He beckoned him to join him on the hood.

Cooper saw that the situation was about to descend into abject chaos. He quickly climbed atop the pickup. His father's advice came to him once more. *When put in front of a group who don't know you, make a dramatic entrance. One they won't forget.* His father had offered all sorts of examples that were appropriate to calmer times. Cooper improvised.

He drew his pistol and fired at a low angle into the air.

Everyone froze, some in comical looking mid-grapple positions or in the middle of yelling at the person in front of them. All heads swiveled to look upon this stranger with the smoke drifting up from the muzzle of his pistol.

Someone spoke for the group, "Just who the hell are you?"

Cooper began, "My name's C.J. and…"

He was cut off by a familiar voice, "This man brought me out to Miles' from Portland. More importantly, he done got our neighborhood through the crisis a damn sight better than any other down there. You need help figuring out what to do next, I suggest you listen to him."

The same man confronted her, "If you don't mind me asking ma'am, who the heck are you?"

"Lyle, she's Miles' mother. Anyone who's been here for a while knows her. She don't blow smoke up anyone's…anything." This time, it was a man in his fifties, gray-haired, and wearing the clothes one would expect to see on a well-to-do hobby farmer.

He turned to Cooper, "So, what do you have to say?"

In a fractured group, find agreement first, his father called to him once more.

"Why don't we start with what we agree on?"

Murmurs of assent filtered through the group.

"Junior Hodges has crossed a line that every living soul here wants to make sure he doesn't ever think about crossing again, right?"

The crowd signaled its agreement with a deafening boom of

"hell yeahs" and "that's rights." Cooper felt the familiar feeling of capturing a group's attention and forging unanimity from it. An electric charge shot through him. *Damn, I think I'm starting to enjoy this!*

"And, we want to make sure he's held accountable for what he's already done, right?" Cooper felt the crowd joining him, accepting him.

"Now, one option that's been suggested is to rally ourselves into a posse and go and kill him." Once more, the sparks of disagreement began flying. Cooper held up his hands and was somewhat surprised that silence resumed so quickly.

"Let's evaluate that choice using cold logic. First, raise your hand if you have a gun of any kind." Nearly every hand shot up.

"Now, leave your hand up if you have a rifle or a shotgun." Three-quarters remained up.

"Finally, leave your hand up if you have a military-style weapon with a mag that holds twenty or more rounds." Only a dozen hands remained up.

"Alright. How many men does Hodges command?"

"About forty!" Someone shouted.

"That right?"

"Close enough," someone added. Seeing agreement in the group, Cooper continued.

"Next question. Most of his men have military-style weapons, right?"

This question was answered with a mix of enthusiastic and reluctant "yeses" depending on where people had stood in the original argument.

"So, the question is, do we really want to start a war when the numbers are about even, but the other side has us outgunned?" Mumbles and grumbles were the only answers he received.

"Good; this is progress. We *are* gonna respond, but we are going to be smarter than trying to bring a bolt-action to a machinegun fight." His joke received a few laughs.

"Let me try this on for size. We march on Sheriff Hodges tomorrow morning at nine. We come armed. We go with two simple demands. One. No more payments in *human* form for *anything*." Cooper choked out the word, as it felt so foreign in this context. He continued, "Two. The taxes are reduced by 10% permanently. On top of that, 10% of the taxes collected go to Keith and Valerie for the next six months."

"What about holding Junior accountable?"

Cooper paused before responding, "It's up to you all. But, my daddy taught me to always leave the other guy a way to save face when negotiating. I don't think someone like Hodges will publicly agree to do anything to his son." Cooper held up a finger to stifle the protests, "But, I'm willing to bet that you take twenty percent from Hodges, that Junior will get punished well and good."

A disturbance came from the back of the crowd. It was Keith. "Not good enough! He's raping my wife, for God's sakes! He's gotta get punished!" Cooper caught the glint of a killer in Keith's eyes and watched his muscles ripple as he struggled to free himself from those around him who were trying to restrain him.

Cooper had an idea, "Keith, I bet you'd beat the hell outta Junior if given the chance?"

That brought a baritone laugh from him, "I could have whipped that weasel in a bar fight a month ago. Now, I'll tear him limb from limb."

"Good. That's what I thought. You gave us our third demand. Keith and Junior go toe to toe in a fair fight. No holds barred."

The shouting and applause was so loud that Cooper felt like he'd just been elected the Mayor of some small town. Before he could enjoy the elation, he heard his father's voice. *When getting people to do something they will be scared to do, get them to commit to each other, not you. That will hold.* His father had been talking about workers confronting an abusive boss or going out on strike. Cooper was taking this group up against a boss with guns.

He quieted the group once again. "So, if you're in, raise your hand." Every single hand shot rapidly skyward.

"Now, stop looking at me. Look at each other. Look each other in the eye. Any one of you get cold feet tonight, you remember who you are committing to. It ain't me. It's to each other. It's to this community. It's to what's right. It's to saying you won't ever have to worry 'bout Junior coming for your wife, your daughter, or your mama next time he wants to." Cooper felt the weight of his words and saw them sinking in. He paused to let it all happen. When most of the crowd had turned back towards him, he continued, "You all in?"

Cooper had expected another chorus of yells and applause. Instead, he looked out onto the crowd and saw neighbors, relatives, and friends looking each other squarely in the eye with an unspoken promise. Jaws were firmly set. Some eyes glistened in the light cast by the moon and the headlights. Many had clasped hands or were holding one another by their shoulders. A few grabbed one another in tight embraces. A chill ran down his spine. *Now, I know what my father was talking about when he spoke of the 'electricity of that damned thing called solidarity'.*

"I know one thing to be true," he muttered to Miles, who stood next to him on the hood.

"What's that?"

"I wouldn't want to be Sheriff Hodges come the morning. There's a reckoning coming."

****

The rest had been details and the myriad of questions that took another hour to sort through. Cooper let Miles handle most of it, but jumped in when he had to. Miles had thanked him profusely after the meeting and a dozen men had come to introduce themselves and thank him for his help in getting things organized. He was offered, and took a few nips, from flasks containing alcohol of all kinds. The homebrews burned his throat like kerosene while the store bought whiskeys felt like sweet water going down. His belly and his head felt warm and light by the time the group had dispersed. Instinctively, he made his way to the Jeep.

Dranko stopped him, "I think we should just stay here."

"Really? Why?"

"Fuel. Things are set back home 'til the morning. We brought our gear. We need to start conserving anywhere we can."

Cooper didn't like the idea of being away from Jake for the night, but agreed with his friend's reasoning. *Before the plague, I could have just called and checked in.* Cell phones had been down for a while and the land lines were dead up in Estacada, as well as most places across the United States.

"Alright, let's bunk here. That fine by you, Miles?"

"Sure thing."

"There's one added plus to your plan," Cooper said, directing his comment at Dranko.

"I surely won't die tomorrow."

Dranko grinned at him, smelling the setup, "Why's that?"

"Because God wouldn't let my last night on this fine earth be spent sleeping next to an ugly mug like you. Even post-Brushfire, I don't believe he's that cruel."

Dranko clutched his chest, feigning a wound. Then, the three men fell into easy laughter.

Chapter Ten

Cooper and Miles awoke early the next morning, the nervous anticipation of the coming day doing its work. Dranko continued sleeping soundly, as did Lily, Bethany and the children. The two men crept quietly about the house while getting dressed and readying some hot water. With a steaming cup of tea and a dry slice of stove-toasted bread in hand, they went outside.

"You were lucky you were on propane up here," Cooper commented, his breath frosting.

Miles nodded, "Luckier still that we had just been filled up about two weeks before everything went to hell. Wood fired cooking would change a lot of things."

"It *will* change a lot of things. You'll run dry on propane soon enough."

Mile frowned, "Yeah, I know. At least I have a few months to get ready for it. Some of my friends already have. Chopping wood ain't no joke."

Silence lingered between them. Cooper sipped the tea, each time burning his lips. He welcomed the contrast between the cold air and the scorching tea. He breathed in the clean, frosty air deep into his lungs. It burned him, but it woke him faster than any cup of caffeine would ever do. He savored the morning quiet. He wished he could take the peace that surrounded him now and bake it into his body so that he could bring it with him. *Must be thinking about the conflict that's coming up today.* Cooper wished he could tell how it would unfold. He took a big bit of the dry, tasteless toast. He washed it down with a burning gulp of the tea. *I'd kill for some butter right now.* He laughed at his own thought. *But, I'd only maim for some coffee.*

"You have any idea how Hodges will react to being confronted?"

Miles sucked his cheeks in, thinking. Finally, he blew out the air before talking, "I think he'll be reasonable." He paused again, his eyes squinting in deep thought. "It's his son I'm worried about. He's a hothead. Has been since the day he was born."

"You ready for today?"

Miles laughed nervously, "Ha! That's a good one. "

He smiled back, "What makes you say that?"

"I just mean, how do you get ready for something like this? I feel a little like I'm about to deliver the Declaration of Independence to the King or something." He shook his head in disbelief when he'd finished.

Cooper finished a drink of tea, blew out a long exhale of steam, "Well, you sort of are doing that. Can I give you some advice?"

"Always."

"Keep what you say short. But, most importantly, pitch whatever you say to the people who are in the middle."

"What do you mean?"

"Think about those who are with us right now, but could be talked out of it. Think of those who *aren't* with you in the room, but could be won over to support you when they hear what you said. Pitch what you say to those people. What you say will be repeated on down the line."

Miles thought for a few moments, chomping down a mouthful of toast, "Why wouldn't I want to just fire up those who are *most* supportive?"

Cooper smiled, "Trust me. Those people are going to be fired up to just be standing up to that SOB. The people you need to think about are those who are there with you, but their knees are wobbling. That's how you keep and expand support."

Miles nodded, "Alright. That makes sense."

"So, you know what those kinds of people will want to hear?"

"Sure, I think so. They need to hear that they might be next. They need to hear that he's gone too far."

Cooper clapped him on the shoulder, "Very good! I think that's right. And, what do they need to hear about our demands?"

"That's a good question," Miles said, and thought for a moment. "Well, first, I'll present them as requests, not demands. Then, we just need to make them seem reasonable, which I think they are now — thanks to your help."

Cooper gave him a wide smile, "Not bad for a farmer boy from Estacada. You have good instincts here. Trust 'em."

Miles raised his mug in response, "Thank you. It's mostly just common sense. But, it's good you made me think it through. Not sure I would have done that on my own."

Cooper clanked his own mug against Miles', "You're welcome. Some people don't have much common sense in the first place."

Miles laughed at that, "True. We have a lot of them back in D.C., don't we?"

Cooper smiled wryly, "Maybe less now."

****

Miles whiled away the time by pacing about his property. Cooper watched him. At times, he would walk with intense, deliberate focus; head down and unaware of his surroundings. Then, he would gyrate into wild gesticulations and punctuating unspoken words with emphatic gestures. The contrast was remarkable. Miles went from a mild mannered college professor walking on a bucolic campus to a wild-eyed agitator up on a soapbox in front of a mob. Cooper expected the latter would be the more appropriate analogy today.

Cooper contemplated the various ways that the day could play out. He was most worried about Junior Hodges *being* there during the confrontation. He knew he was the wild card in the scenario. Junior was a hothead, there was no mistaking that. Then, he had Keith who was raw and emotional from the trauma he was experiencing. Putting the two in the same room was likely to result in an explosion. Last night, he had debated asking Keith to stay out of the fray today, but he had decided he didn't have enough cachet with the group to pull that off.

****

Dranko's Jeep rolled down the roadway that led toward town. Cooper was riding shotgun, while Miles sat upright in the backseat. He was quiet and the other two men left him alone. Cooper and Dranko had attempted their normal joke-laden banter to alleviate the tension, but Miles hadn't found any of it humorous, so they let it lie. Dranko peered ahead intently, focusing on the road and was soon lost in his own thoughts. His left foot was tapping out a nervous rhythm. Cooper fiddled with his Smith and Wesson pistol, checking the slide and trigger function.

The parking lot was much fuller than it had been yesterday. Their plan had been to arrive over the course of a half-hour, entering in separate groups of two or three men. They didn't want alert Hodges that anything was amiss. They had decided to confront him at 9:07am. Miles would lead the group. Cooper and Dranko, being new to town, were to remain separated from everyone else. They would disperse away from the group and provide some 'flank' cover. Their biggest tactical disadvantage was that they would all have only pistols because security didn't allow long guns into the marketplace. Meanwhile, the guards would have rifles and shotguns. Cooper knew that if gunfire broke out in a place like this, it would be a bloody mess. *At least we'll outnumber Hodges and his guards by 4-5 to one.*

The emergency brake scratched and the Jeep came to a stop. Cooper turned back to Miles.

"You ready?"

Miles looked up at him and nodded. His face was firm, the jaw set and muscles tense. *He's nervous, but resolute.*

"You'll be fine. Just remember *who* you are talking to," Cooper said.

Miles nodded once more and then exited the vehicle. Dranko and Cooper remained behind. They were going to give him five minutes to get inside and mingle before they entered as a pair. He looked at his watch; it was 8:56am. His stomach tightened. He grabbed his pistol once more and checked its function again.

"Leave it," Dranko said, irritated. *He's tense, too.*

Cooper re-holstered his pistol to placate his friend. They watched as other vehicles pulled in and men entered the marketplace in pairs and trios. Cooper spotted some familiar faces from the night before, including the man with the gruff voice who had spoken up several times. He noticed the outside guard watching them as they remained in the Jeep.

"We should go. We're drawing attention by sitting," he said and opened the door.

He gazed skyward as he exited. It was a rare cloudless day. The sky was azure and beautiful. Cooper's skin rose up in goose pimples, triggered by the frigid air, but sustained by the anxiety of what was coming. His feet barely touched the ground as he moved in rapid strides across the worn parking lot. Dranko was a step behind him. They crossed without incident into the marketplace.

Cooper surveyed the scene in rapid fashion. He spotted six guards spread out across the market's tables and floor. He saw Hodges on the upraised office area with three other men clustered about him; apparently his personal bodyguards. The guards were mixed between rifles and shotguns. Hodges had a pistol at his side. With the guards at the front entrance, that made a dozen guards. He sidled up next to Dranko and they quickly exchanged what they'd seen and confirmed it was the same. Cooper told him where he should go. If where Hodges sat now was the tip, he and Dranko would deploy as the outward edges of an arrow. Their crowd of men, led by Miles, would fill in the area around the tip. These positions would allow Cooper and Dranko to protect the backside of the crowd and cover the guards in that area. Last night, they had made additional plans to have the men in the crowd face outward in all directions. Someone had called it their 'porcupine defense.' Cooper moved deliberately to where he wanted to be when it all started. He pretended to browse the tables as he passed, but deflected conversing with the vendors, so that he wouldn't get delayed. He kept glancing up at Hodges, who was huddled over some paperwork. So far, their plan to go unnoticed was working. Cooper breathed a heavy sigh of relief.

It proved to be a hair's breath too soon.

****

The front door clattered on its hinges as Junior Hodges and two men flanking him came bursting in. He wore a self-satisfied smile on his face. He strode confidently across the marketplace, snatching an apple off of one of the tables without even a pretense of paying for it or even acknowledging the offended seller. With his entrance, the place had fallen silent, and Cooper could hear a sharp crunch as his teeth plunged into the apple's flesh, ripping a good-sized chunk from the core. Watching him from across the room, Cooper saw juice dribble down his chin before he wiped it away with his sleeve. Cooper found Keith in the crowd and was thankful that two of his friends were both holding him steady and shielding him from Junior's view. Hearing the silence, Hodges looked up from the table. He scanned the room and Cooper saw him surveying around with the larger than normal number of customers. Hodges eyebrows drew together just as Junior reached the stairs and climbed up to stand next to his father.

Miles moved into position. The men, moving like a school of fish, followed.

"Sheriff Hodges, we need to have a word," Miles' voice rose to fill the silence. His words were filled with anxiety at the start. But, by the time he'd finished the sentence, confidence had displaced that. *That a boy, Miles!*

Hodges looked confused for a moment, but then recovered. He moved to stand directly across from Miles, but from the higher position, looking down. The guards moved into a large semi-circle around the crowd of nearly forty men. Cooper and Dranko were outside of that line, giving themselves a strategic position. No one had yet drawn a weapon or unslung a rifle, but every hand was ready to do just that.

"What is this about?" Hodges demanded, his words coming out strong and forceful.

"We have a dispute to settle," Miles answered.

Someone from the crowd added, "Damn right we do."

Hodges mouth tightened and his eyes grew sharp, "Well, what is it? I don't have all day."

"We know you aren't aware of this," Miles started. *Damn smart to build in a graceful way for Hodges' hands to be clean in this, even if they aren't.* "But, yesterday Junior Hodges came and kidnapped Keith's wife Valerie as 'payment' for his levy. She hasn't been seen since."

Cooper saw genuine shock flash across Hodges' face. He could tell it was taking the man the force of will not to turn and engage with his son. His son lacked such discipline.

Junior's reedy voice rang out, "I didn't take nobody, she wanted to come along and have some fun…"

"You son-of-a-bitch! That's a damned lie," Keith shouted vehemently. A friend on his right grabbed his arm with both hands to prevent him from ripping his pistol from its holster. Cooper couldn't see his eyes, but he could only imagine how they burned in furious hatred.

Now, Hodges turned to his son, "Keep your mouth quiet, boy." Junior slinked down like a dog that had just been kicked across the room. He backpedalled until he disappeared behind a partition.

"Continue, Mr. Stott," Hodges said, turning back toward Miles.

"We have three simple requests, Sheriff. First, we want your commitment that people will never be asked for or accepted as payment for our levy. Second, we want the levies reduced by ten percent. On top of that, we want ten percent of the remaining levy to be diverted to Keith and Valerie as compensation for this terrible crime. Third, we want a fair, no weapons allowed, fight between Keith and Junior."

There was no hesitation from Hodges, "Done."

Like a popped balloon, the tension hissed out of the room.

Then, a shot rang out.

****

Cooper first saw Keith crumple to the ground in slow motion. His face went slack in surprise. Hands clutched to his chest. A rush of scarlet cascaded past his fingers and began forming a violent blood fall down his chest.

Then, the thunderous boom smacked his ears. His eyes swung toward the direction of the shot. Junior held a hunting rifle in his hands, the smoke curling haphazardly upward. He was racking the bolt to chamber a fresh round. The dull metallic clanging was heard from across the room. Cooper was surprised he could hear it, given the deafening roar of the single shot that had just been fired. Cooper's hand went for his pistol. He wasn't the only one.

Hodges' face went wild in panic. He waved his arms in a wide, circling, gesture. His lips formed the word, "No," but Cooper couldn't hear him.

At first, those wielding the faster-to-deploy pistols had the advantage. The room descended into a fusillade of gunfire. Cooper drew on a guard that stood less than twenty feet in front of him, to his left. The man, youngish-looking in his twenties, had a frail-looking growth of hair on his face. He had a shotgun slung on his shoulder and he was desperately trying to bring it into his hands. The sling got caught up on a metal stud that was protruding from his leather jacket. The man's head jerked around to assist himself in the detangling and his eyes drew back in shock when he saw Cooper's pistol muzzle bearing down on him.

He fired. He hit the man square in the forehead. A neat, dark hole appeared instantly and Cooper tried to avoid seeing what exploded outside the back of his head. The man teetered on his feet, his vacant eyes locking onto Cooper's for an instant before he slumped to the ground, like a puppet whose strings had just been cut. Cooper shuddered at the look the man had given him in death.

He wheeled to his right, anticipating that the guards from outside would come piling in. As he did so, he saw several guards falling down, apparently hit by the cavalcade of gunfire spitting across the room. Cooper knelt as he turned, to gain the scant cover offered by a nearby table, piled high with metal tools. As he'd expected, two men were swarming inside, pushing past the glass door and coming in with an AR-15 and a shotgun, respectively.

Cooper fired rapidly at them, not taking proper time to aim. His shots went wide. His fire, from twenty yards away, was close enough to force the men to go tumbling to ground, seeking cover.

From behind him, and to his left, the sound of an angry buzzsaw cut loose. It lasted all but a few seconds and then an odd silence descended upon the room except for the dull moaning of the many wounded. Cooper couldn't avoid turning his head. On the raised platform, Hodges stood out in the open, a smoking machinegun in his hands. The machinegun was a Thompson, straight out of a 1920's gangster movie with a fifty round drum magazine attached. Miles' group of men had been decimated. At least a dozen men lay slumped on the ground. Some were silent and unmoving, but most were writhing in throes of pain.

"Truce!" Hodges' voice thundered across the room, as he held up the machinegun above his head, using both hands.

Miles was still standing, despite the many fallen to his right and left. He echoed the word, "Truce!"

Hodges looked down upon them, "We are neighbors here. Let us attend the wounded!" It was then that he noticed that Junior was not among the standing. *Someone must have gotten the bastard. I hope for good.*

Cooper was mesmerized by the scene as it unfolded. Men who had only moments before had been shooting at one other were now gingerly moving past one another to assist the wounded from their respective 'sides'. The vendors formed a neutral group in this equation and some remained unmoving, while others helped those closest to them. He was amazed that the hastily arranged peace had even happened and more so that it was holding. He attributed it to the power of the bonds these men had held for a long time as residents of a common community. While recent events had quickly driven divisions between them, those bonds still lay below the surface.

Cooper's assessment was that half of the guards were either dead or wounded from the first wave of gunfire. He and Dranko exchanged a look and nodded to one another. They avoided joining the larger group, seeking to maintain their charade of not belonging with Miles' group. Instead, they dithered in place.

With hasty bandages applied to those still living, Hodges' deep baritone rang out again, "Retire with your dead and wounded, Mr. Stott. Meet me here at three today, in the parking lot. You and two men. I will do the same. We cannot let the sun set on this day without resolution."

Miles nodded to him, "Agreed." His voice was shaky and he looked to be unsteady on his feet. Cooper knew that seeing bodies riddled by bullet holes and the blood and gore usually untethered the uninitiated. He saw the dark stain down his pant leg and recalled reading once how common it was for soldiers to wet themselves in combat, but that was rarely talked about.

Cooper and Dranko exited ahead of the main group, but remained to hold the doors open as the wounded and dead were carried out. As Miles passed them, Cooper talked nonchalantly to him.

"Hitch a ride, we will go and get Angela to come help the wounded at your place."

Miles looked at him, and nodded. Cooper could tell he was in shock by the hazy look in his eyes. Miles was the last man from their group out the door and he promptly dropped to his knees and spewed vomit that splashed across the asphalt. As Cooper left the building, he saw a half dozen other colorful pools of puke that marked another common reaction to being involved in a violent, and deadly, encounter. The stench of it immediately assaulted him; the sour smell of bile mixing potently with the coppery smell of blood.

He lifted Miles up by the armpit, and pushed him onward.

Miles called out to the group, "Those with wounded, back to my place. Those without, gather medical supplies and join us there." He then jumped into a pickup truck, driven by the man with the gruff voice, Frank. There were several wounded cloistered in the pickup's bed. Dranko and Cooper ran to the Jeep, got in, and tires squealed as they raced back to Dranko's place.

****

The drive to the cabin was a blur because of the adrenaline coursing through their veins. Neither man spoke a word and it seemed like they arrived there in a matter of seconds. They spilled out of the Jeep and were met by an avalanche of questions from Angela, Buck, Jake, and Calvin.

Cooper let Dranko handle the adults, while he pulled Jake aside. He knelt down next to him, so he could look at him in the eye.

"One at a time, son."

"What happened?"

"There was a shootout at the marketplace between Hodges and our men," he responded, holding onto his son's shoulders.

"Who was killed?" Jake's eyes were heavy with worry, deep lines forming at the corners of his eyes.

"About a dozen men. No one you knew," he offered as comfort.

Jake transformed before his eyes. The worry was replaced by a boiling anger, his jaw grew tight, and his eyes went sharp, "I asked *who?*" His voice went flat, with a stiff edge.

Cooper looked at him confused, "I don't *know* their names, son. But, no one you knew died there."

Jake's voice rose to a high pitched squeal, "I want to know *who!*

183

Names matter. They *can't* be nameless!" Jake tried to wrestle out of Cooper's grasp, but he held on more firmly.

"What's the matter, son? I don't know these people well enough yet to *know* their names."

Jake continued squirming to get free, "Don't you get it? The dead can't be without a name. It's wrong!" He yelled into his father's face.

Jake's irrationality suddenly made sense to him. He released the grip on his son. "You're right, son. It's wrong."

His rant continued, "The names matter. I won't forget Antonio. Or, Leroy. Or, Peter. We need to know their names so we *remember*." He dissolved into a wash of tears as the last words came out. Cooper pulled him into a tight hug.

His son sobbed into his chest, "We can't forget. *I* don't want to be forgotten."

Cooper pulled him back, so he could look him into his read and tear-stained eyes, "Jake. You won't *ever* be forgotten. No matter what. You hear me?"

Jake nodded meekly and sought the refuge of his father's chest again. It pained Cooper to see his son like this. *Grief and stress come out in all ways.* Cooper knew that, but it still tore at his heart to see Jake like this. *No eleven year-old should have to go through this.*

He answered a debate he had been having in his head, "You want to come with me to Miles'? We'll be tending the wounded."

Jake nodded, "Yeah. Better than sitting here and wondering what's going on and if you're okay." He wiped his sleeve across his face and breathed deeply, collecting himself.

"Let's help Angela and Dranko collect what medical supplies we can spare."

Jake nodded and they moved off. Within minutes, they had piled back into the Jeep and drove to the Stott's. Calvin and Buck remained behind.

****

They were forced to park on the roadway next to the Stott's entrance, given the pile up of vehicles along his driveway. Seeing two guards posted made Cooper inwardly praise Miles' foresight. They rushed past, carrying the supplies they had brought in two small duffle bags. People were dashing up and down the gravel driveway. When they crested the small rise and reached the opening in the trees where

Miles' house and small farm lay, the scene that greeted them was little more than organized chaos.

They quickly spotted Miles, who was besieged by questioners pleading for his attention. Cooper quickly saw that half the people were relatives of the dead or wounded pleading to find out what had happened to their loved ones. The other half were people trying to organize things.

"Where's the triage area?" Angela's clear, firm voice cut through the din.

Miles looked at her blankly.

"Where do you have the critical patients situated?"

He shook his head, "Adam is over there; he got one in the chest," he said while pointing to a pickup under a tree. "Jerry is inside the house, he got it..."

Angela grabbed him by his shoulders, "Look. This needs to get put together. And, now."

Miles looked at her with a vacant look, nodding.

"You know where the critical patients are?"

He nodded.

"Good, round them up. Move them *all* into the house. Now." As Miles moved off to comply, she called after him. "We have any other medical personnel here?"

"Not really. Couple EMTs. Doc Jones is supposed to be on his way."

Angela shook her head.

"Cooper, find those EMTs and get them to me." He nodded and moved off to move through the crowd to find them. He heard her barking orders as he left, Jake following in his wake. It didn't take him long to find the EMTs and get them to report to Angela. He also found a practical nurse who was wailing over her dead husband's body. Cooper was able to get her up and ambling towards Angela. He sent Jake with her to make sure she got there. He continued surveying the people there for medical skills or supplies that could be mustered. The last person he saw was a man wearing a white coat. He was sitting on the passenger side of a Jeep Cherokee, staring at the ground and rubbing his legs furiously.

He approached slowly, "How goes it?"

The man, gray hair glimpsing from underneath a ball cap, looked up.

"I said, how are you?"

The man nodded, shallowly and in a flurry, "Ah. Good, I

185

guess."

"What's your name?"

"Raymond. Raymond Harrison." The man's voice was reedy, unsteady.

"I'm CJ. What do you do?" He continued, pointing at his coat.

"I'm a vet. Jimmy asked me to get over here. But, I...I can't help."

Cooper moved in and pulled Raymond to his feet. He brought his face in close. "Yes! Yes, you can!"

Raymond tried backing away, "No. Too much. I'm not trained for this!"

Cooper grabbed him by the collar, "You can. Just do *what* you can. You *will* save lives."

"I'm not trained. Not ready for this. I take care of dogs and horses for God's sake!" Raymond yelled at him, fear shredding his voice to a raspy, thin wail.

Cooper burst into laughter, "Yeah. And, I was a travelling salesman before I had to become a damned combat leader!"

"Huh? What do you mean?"

"It doesn't matter. The point is, you *gotta* get in there and help. However you can. Right *now!*" He threw Raymond in the general direction of where Angela was. He stumbled and fell to one knee. He looked back at Cooper, incredulous. But, he rose to his feet and began ambling off in the right direction. Cooper's hope grew when he saw him straighten up and begin to tug at this white coat as he walked. His gait became more firm with each passing step. *Damn, fear is an evil thing.* He collapsed into the car seat that Raymond had just vacated, he folded his hands around his head and breathed heavily. He counted to ten and then rose up to rejoin Angela.

****

Upon returning, Cooper was surprised at how quickly Angela had brought order from chaos. The EMTs were triaging the wounded in an area to the left of the house. Angela and Raymond were, apparently, inside the house tending to the most critically wounded. Doctor Jones, a man in his sixties with a mane of white hair draped to his shoulders, showed up just as Cooper arrived. He was quickly directed inside by one of the EMTs.

Cooper approached the other one, "I have some training in Wilderness first aid. It ain't much, but do you guys need help?"

The EMT, a woman in her thirties with chestnut brown hair that fell to her shoulders, shook her head, "Thanks, but we got it under control."

Cooper nodded, "Alright, but give a shout if things change." She answered him with a quick nod and went back to work.

Cooper drifted a few paces away and leaned up against a Chevy Bronco. Jake soon joined him, as did Dranko and Miles. They milled about, breathing in a collective sigh of relief, as they watched the medical personnel work.

"Thank God for Angela, eh," Miles asked.

"You can say that again," Cooper answered.

"I wasn't up to this," Miles commented, shame clouding his voice.

"Don't be so hard on yourself. It's a long way from farmer to running a MASH unit!" Cooper offered in support.

"But, still..."

"Ah, shut it, will you? You done what you could. What man can do more than that?" Dranko lashed out at him.

Miles recoiled, taking a step back, "Well...thanks...I guess?"

"Sorry. It's been a long day. But, you know what I mean, right?"

Miles nodded, "Yeah. I do. Thanks."

"You ready to talk about our 3pm appointment with Hodges?"

Miles exhaled loudly, "If I have to."

"'Fraid so."

"I'm hoping you can join me. I was thinking you and Frank."

Cooper shook his head, "I think it's best if I keep my distance. I don't think Hodges knows yet that I'm linked to you. That element of surprise is something we should keep in our back pocket."

Miles thought for a moment, "Yeah, that makes sense. What do you think is the play?"

Cooper shrugged his shoulders, "I think your leverage is stronger than it was this morning. He knows this town will stand up to him now. His nose is bloodied. So, I think it is to stick with the demands."

Miles folded his arms across his chest, "Sure. I was thinking the same. I'm damn proud of these guys. We paid a price. I need to make it worth something."

"I don't want to rain on anyone's parade..." Dranko began.

"But, you will," Cooper interrupted.

Dranko raised his eyebrows, "Yeah, well. Someone has to. The wild card in all this is whether Junior was wounded or killed. If he's dead, you might be dealing with one pissed of Hodges. He may not be rational. We best hope that he's only wounded."

"Good point," Miles said.

"You could find out before the meeting," Cooper offered, a sober look in his eyes.

"What do you mean?" Miles asked, with furrowed eyebrows.

"Bethany," Cooper's one word answer was ripe with risk. He knew he was *almost* saying what Miles most likely knew already. But, there was a big difference between a man suspecting, or knowing of, his wife's infidelity and him admitting it out loud. A long, tense pregnant pause hung in the air.

Miles shuffled his feet and dropped his eyes to the ground, "Yup. She could find out." Miles drew a deep breathe, pausing for another long moment. "Can one of you guys ask her to?"

"I will," Cooper offered, softening his voice to a whisper.

"You all set, then?" Dranko asked, adroitly changing the subject.

Miles looked up at them again, "Yeah, I think so."

"Let's get everything ready and meet back up at one?"

Miles and Cooper nodded in response. Miles drifted off and the other men watched him with sympathetic eyes.

"That's gotta be rough," Cooper mused.

"At least he's being smart about it and not being an emotional moron."

"Yeah. I just wouldn't want to be facing something like that during the apocalypse."

"Would there ever be a good time for something like that?"

"Nope, I guess you're right," Cooper responded, chuckling morosely.

"What are you guys talking about," Jake asked.

"Nothing, son. Nothing."

"Oh, I *hate* it when you do that!" Jake groaned.

"What?" Dranko asked, knowing already.

His eyes grew sullen, "Nothing. Forget it."

Before all of this, Jake would whine about not being included in adult conversations and he never gave up this easily. His resignation today disturbed Cooper.

He began with an apologetic tone, "It's just that Miles and…"

"I said forget it," barked Jake before he turned and walked away. His tone lacked any whine and was instead as flat as the

Nebraska plains.

"Just one more symptom," Cooper mumbled just barely loud enough for Dranko to hear.

"Of what?"

"That he's using anger to keep away the pain," Cooper's voice drifted.

"He'll be alright," Dranko lamely offered, not a shred of confidence in his voice.

"Yeah, thanks. Let's go do what we gotta do," Cooper said unenthusiastically.

****

Cooper found Bethany boiling some sheets in the kitchen, making bandages no doubt. A man Cooper didn't recognize was helping her. She looked up as he came into the room. He inclined his head, indicating he wanted to talk to her alone. She paused for a moment, and then nodded. She untied her apron strings and addressed her assistant.

"I'll be back in five."

The man nodded and moved into position to tend the boiling cauldron of sheets. Cooper moved aside as Bethany whisked past him. She was digging furiously in her front jacket pocket as she passed. He followed in her wake as she exited the front door.

They moved to the side of the house. The cigarette was already lit and the first burst of smoke was blowing out as she turned, combative.

"Whatcha want? I'm pretty busy." Her feet were splayed wide, her posture matching her aggressive tone.

"We need your help," Cooper said, attempting to soften the mood.

Curiosity gripped her face, "Really?"

"Yeah. In the firefight today, we're pretty sure that Junior Hodges was hit."

Her hand made it halfway to her mouth before she stayed it. She awkwardly tried to conceal the reflex by switching the cigarette to a new hand. Her face went slack in surprise for an instant, as well. Then, she forced it back to a devil-may-care look. She didn't say a word, but kept staring at him.

"We don't know if he was wounded or killed. And, we need to know." He looked at her intently, awaiting her response.

"Why m…" She started to ask the question, but stopped herself. *She doesn't really want me to answer that.* She stared at the ground, took two long drags on her cigarette before answering.

"So, you want me to go find out?"

"That's about it. Miles needs to know before the three o'clock meeting. It's very important for him to know Sheriff Hodges' mental state right now."

"So, Miles knows?" Her tone told him how her question had more than the obvious meaning.

"Yes," he responded. He paused before look into her eyes, his own narrowing, "I'm pretty sure he does."

Her eyes glistened and she blinked back tears. "That's too bad. I never wanted that."

Cooper just looked at her. Something in her eyes weighed on him.

She looked again at the ground and lit another cigarette. Her feet shuffled and she folded her arms. "Why's it all so complicated?"

"I'm not here to judge you," Cooper said, hoping to stifle the conversation. They stood in silence for a long while. What was bothering him finally hit him. *This is what a lost soul looks like. She's lost, involved in an affair during the apocalypse.* He shook his head, weighing what that must be like.

"So, will you do it?"

She looked up at him with sad, weary eyes. Cooper understood her reluctance. *Saying yes will peel back one of the last veils of deniability between her and Miles.* Cooper guessed that eventually those layers would get so thin that they would have to face it.

"Yes, of course I'll do it," she finally said, forced firmness lacing her words. "Tell Miles I'll be back soon, will you?"

He nodded, "Sure. And, thank you. I know this isn't easy."

She laughed, exhaling nervous tension, "You can say *that* again!" She blew out the last puff of smoke, crushed the butt under her heel, and walked off. Cooper watched her walk away. The way her shoulders drooped and how her steps plodded, he could see she carried a heavy load.

****

"So, she gonna do it?" Mile's words dripped with heavy meaning.

"Yeah. She said she would find out for us." Cooper answered, not knowing how he'd react.

Miles squinted. His eyes drifted to the tree line, and he fixated there for several seconds. "At least some good may come of it all." His words hung in the air, unanswered for a long moment, then he turned and walked away.

When he was safely out of earshot, Dranko spoke up, "I feel for him. He has a heavy load to carry."

Cooper nodded. Suddenly, he felt wearied by the events of the morning. "I'm going to try and catch some sleep. Can you keep an eye on Jake for me?"

"Sure. The seats in the Jeep are pretty comfortable."

Cooper smiled, "Nice to hear your optimistic side. Wake me when Bethany gets back, alright?"

Dranko grinned and nodded. Cooper walked off and found the Jeep. Within minutes, he was asleep.

****

Knuckles rapping on glass startled him awake. His body jerked and a hand went to the pistol laying in its holster on the seat next to him. He wrenched his neck, finding the source of the noise.

Jake's smiling face was perched in the door window's frame, "Wake up Sleeping Beauty! Bethany's back."

Adrenaline shot through Cooper and he was instantly awake and searching for the door's handle. He snaked the belt holding the holster on as he slid out of the Jeep. He buckled it as Jake led him to where Bethany must have been waiting to be debriefed.

He found Dranko, Bethany, and Miles standing in a semi-circle filled with awkward silence. Bethany and Miles assiduously avoided eye contact with one another. Dranko stood between the two of them, arms folded.

"We wanted to wait for you, brother," he said as Cooper walked up.

"Great, what'd we learn?" He fixed his eyes on her.

Her eyes drifted up to his, "Junior is wounded. But, badly."

"Good. Bastard deserves it," Miles interrupted vehemently. *He's trying to bait her.*

Bethany gritted her teeth, "They expect him to survive, but he might lose an arm."

"Anything else?" Dranko asked.

"I couldn't get a word in with the Sheriff. But, there are already notices up around town recruiting new 'deputies' to join him and..."

"Whew, he doesn't waste time, does he?" Miles interrupted again.

"Well, this is good news, all told," Cooper said.

"How so?" Miles asked.

"His son is alive, so he shouldn't be crazy-mad. And, the wounding might be good in the sense that Hodges knows there's a cost to be paid by a war. It should put him in the mind to negotiate."

The trio surrounding him nodded in agreement.

"So, our plan at three remains what we discussed," Miles asked.

"Yup." Cooper said.

****

The caravan of three vehicles meandered down the highway toward Estacada. The lack of haste was reflective of their collective apprehension. In the lead vehicle, Miles and the two men he had hand selected to attend the meeting with him set the pace. Dranko, Cooper, and two other men were in Dranko's Jeep. Bringing up the rear was a minivan filled with six men. The plan was for the last two vehicles to listen in on the meeting via walkie talkie. If anything went wrong, they were to come rushing in. The men were all fully armed, rifles or shotgun in hand and a pistol, or more, strapped to their sides.

Cooper had become adept at smelling the fear of those around him. The Jeep was filled with that faint, familiar odor once more. He fell into his comforting habit of checking the action of the weapon in hand. He racked the bolt on the FAL repeatedly until Dranko told him to knock it off. Then, he shifted to checking the action on his pistol. Dranko exhaled in exasperation. The men in the backseat were similarly preoccupied with their own pre-combat rituals. One was lost, deep in prayer. The other was quietly repeating to himself the various tactical situations they had reviewed as a group before leaving. Dranko was tense.

"Will you shut it? You sound like Rainman getting ready to storm the beaches of Normandy," Dranko exploded at the whispering man.

The man startled, gave a sheepish look to Dranko, and fell silent.

"Thank *you!*" Dranko muttered in frustrated appreciation.

Cooper stopped his own fidgeting with conscious effort. He

looked out the window and saw the trees whipping past at a steady forty miles per hour. The sky was clouded and the light fighting its way down was dull and gray. Cooper's mind drifted to a day much like this one when Elena had been driving up to a wedding being held up at Government Camp. He remembered how her hair had shined even in that dull light and how...

He was interrupted by the whispering man resuming his mumbling tactical cant. Cooper looked at Dranko, who was rolling his eyes. Cooper couldn't restrain the smile from breaking across his face. Dranko saw this, raised his hand, and flipped him a long and steady bird. In response, he shrugged his shoulders in the classic 'what did I do' way.

Thankfully, Dranko made the last turn and they were moments away from their destination.

"Alright, boys, look sharp," Dranko said as he cranked the wheel, turning the Jeep at the light.

"Sure thing, Sarge," the praying man remarked, doing his best to imitate a New Yorker's accent.

"Hey, those introductions flew fast and furious back there and I know my mind was much more focused on our planning. But, if we gotta charge in there, guns blazing, it'd be good to know each other's names. I'm CJ."

"I was thinking the same thing, but I was too embarrassed to say anything! I'm Michael," the praying man said. "Like the Archangel!"

"Yeah, I'm Rusty," the whispering man said.

A long silence passed as Dranko sat silent. *I guess he's mad about something.*

"Our esteemed chauffeur to this confab is Dranko. His Christian name is Paul, but he's so surly that it's best to call him by his last name. Otherwise, you risk charming him out of his sour attitude," Cooper offered, a wry grin crossing his face and imbuing his words.

"Screw you," Dranko muttered, gravel in his voice.

Cooper looked back at the two men in the backseat, as if to say, "See?" Both men chuckled. Dranko made a production out of turning the walkie talkie to the agreed upon channel, as he pulled the Jeep up next to a curb about two hundred yards from the parking lot, but where they could see it. This brought silence to the group.

"This is Red One. Do you read? Ten Four," Miles voice crackled over the speaker.

Dranko fingered the mic, "This is Blue One. Copy. Ten Four."

Then, the man leading the group of men in the van, "This is Blue Two. Copy. Ten Four."

They watched Miles' pickup truck lurch into the parking lot. A black Cadillac Escalade crouched in the middle of the lot. Cooper used binoculars to scan the rooftops surrounding the parking lot. He exhaled when he saw nothing. In fact, he didn't see another vehicle in sight. *Hodges must have cleared them out.*

"He's probably got his men inside the store," Cooper observed for the group.

Miles' pickup came to a stop about ten yards away from the Cadillac. Over the walkie talkie, they heard the rustling as he opened his door and got out. The men in the Cadillac imitated them and soon the two trios faced one another. Hodges was resplendent in a freshly pressed Sheriff's uniform. The normally dull green uniform was almost shining. He was even wearing the full tassel on his Cavalry-style Sheriff's hat. *I guess he's going for every ounce of authority to bolster his leverage.*

"Howdy Sheriff," Miles began.

"Afternoon, Mr. Stott," Hodges responded.

"I've got this walkie talkie on. My men are listening in. If anything goes wrong, they will be here in seconds," Miles informed him.

Hodges chuckled, "Wise security. Yes, I see their vehicles over there." He pointed in their direction. "My men are inside and will be out here faster than yours."

Miles grunted, "So, let's make sure nothing goes wrong then?" Cooper smiled on the inside at how Miles adeptly handled that one.

"Indeed. I believe we are here to negotiate an end to the hostilities."

"We think of it as a justified rebellion."

Hodges guffawed and then his voice turned deadly serious, "Let's not get into a rhetorical bullshit fest."

Miles voice faltered, "Sure. Our demands have changed." Cooper cringed and looked at Dranko. He shrugged, indicating he was as surprised. "Junior fired first, killing Keith. Valerie must have more compensation, as do the other men who were killed in the shootout."

"Valerie is dead," Hodges' voice was flat.

"What?" Miles' shocked voice rang out over the tiny speaker.

"She's dead. She attacked Junior this morning and died in the scuffle."

Cooper saw Miles pace around in a tight circle and then come face to face with Hodges, "Your boy is a load of trouble!"

"And, *I'll* deal with that."

"You aren't doing a very good job lately!"

"Watch it, Miles."

They could hear a loud and long exhale as Miles gathered himself. "Alright, here's the deal. For the next six months, one-third of the levy is distributed to the men's families who were killed today, on our side. After that, the levy is reduced by ten percent permanently. And, we need a civilian oversight board so excess use of authority can be addressed. Finally, Junior is to be stripped of all authority."

"Done," Hodges answered without a pause.

"Really?" Miles' shocked answer made Cooper shudder. *Rookie negotiator.*

"I just have one condition."

"What's that?"

Despite the static on the hand held radio, Hodges words came through as clear as a lightning bolt on a sunny day, "I want Cooper Adams."

****

Cooper's eyes shot to Miles. Over the walkie talkie, his voice came through firm and steady, "I want him, too. That bastard screwed the pooch for all of America."

There was a long pause. Cooper watched as Hodges first sneered and then took a step closer to Miles and leaned in. He whispered something in Miles' ear, which they couldn't hear. Miles' face remained flat, controlled. Cooper's stomach tightened. He looked down and saw that his knuckles were white around the pistol grip of the FAL. He deliberately relaxed them.

He watched as the two parties separated, got back into their vehicles, and drove away. Cooper shot Dranko an apprehensive look as they fell in line behind Miles' pickup. He responded with a sympathetic look. Cooper cursed the men in the backseat for preventing him and Dranko from talking freely about what had just happened.

The drive back was interminable for Cooper. He knew his fate was in another man's hands and he hated every second of it. Anger flushed his cheeks and his heart was racing. He was much more comfortable when he was able to take action. The enforced idleness and the unknown was killing him. He reflexively balled his fits and

195

uncurled them repeatedly.

His mind burned. *What had Hodges said to him privately? Would Miles sell me out to save his own family? Had Hodges made such an offer? If so, what the hell was Miles thinking about it? Miles hardly knows me. He may not even believe that what I've said about the Brushfire Plague is true! Had Hodges figured out from Miles' body language or facial expression that Cooper was in town? Or, had Miles' thrown him off with his lie? If he hadn't, how soon would Hodges come for me?* These thoughts tormented him as they drove.

He breathed a sigh of relief when the tires crunched gravel and they were churning up the driveway toward Miles' house.

****

He was at Miles' side as soon as he clambered out of the pickup. Miles held up one finger, signaling him to wait. Cooper grinded his teeth, but turned away to give him space.

"Frank and Michael, round everyone up. I'll tell everyone what happened in five minutes." The men ambled off in opposite directions to spread the word.

Miles grabbed Cooper by the arm and led him around the side of the house. Dranko fell in line behind them. When they stopped, they realized that Jake had appeared, as well.

"What'd he say?"

Miles' eyes were full of concern, "He said he knew who you were and that you were with us."

Cooper spat, "How the hell does he know?"

"Who knows? But, he sounded pretty confident."

"Bethany?" Cooper asked, no longer concerned with Miles' feelings about his wife and their delicate situation.

His face flushed, "Maybe. We could find out."

"Does it really matter," Dranko asked. "He *knows*. The rest are just details aren't they?"

Cooper nodded, "You're right. The only question now is what are you going to do?"

Miles rubbed his temples, "Well, he gave me forty-eight hours. We meet again at the same time, same place, day after tomorrow."

"That's not an answer," Cooper said, squaring his eyes with Miles'.

He looked helpless, "I don't know, Cooper. I owe you. For what you did for my mom and what you did for us, here. But, it's that obligation versus risking an all-out war."

"He could be bluffing," Dranko added.

Miles shook his head. "I don't think so. There's more. Jake, can you give us a minute?" Cooper waved Jake off with his hand. Jake stomped off, shooting them the sharp dagger looks that only an eleven-year-old can master.

"What is it," Cooper asked, as soon as Jake was out of earshot.

"Hodges said that he has help on this one. He said that if I say no, it won't just be us against him."

"Did he say what kind of help?"

"Nope. But, it could be the Feds."

"Or the Governor," Dranko added.

"Or, he's just a damned blowhard," Cooper cursed. He kicked a clump of forest duff in frustration, "So, Miles. You gonna give me up or not? I need to know?"

"I don't know, Cooper." He looked him with imploring eyes. "I'm sorry. I think I should tell everyone what happened and make it a group decision."

"That's not good enough," Cooper's eyes blazed.

"What do you mean?"

"What are *you* going to recommend? What you say will matter a lot."

Miles looked down at the ground for a moment, and then looked up. The face that greeted Cooper was a tortured one, "I don't know, Cooper." Their eyes caught for a moment before he turned and left.

"Coward," Cooper whispered in rage. He started to walk away, but Dranko grabbed him by the arm.

"Ease up, brother. He barely knows you. It's a big decision on shoulders that aren't used to it."

He looked up at his friend, relaxing a degree, "You're probably right. But, it still sucks."

"That it does, brother."

"I don't want to end up on the run again. We just got here."

"We'll figure it out. We always do. Now, I have to get ready."

"For what?"

"I have to do what I hate the most."

Cooper's brows furrowed deeper, "What?"

"One, make a speech so these good people don't throw you out like the morning trash and two is something even worse." A wry smile crept onto his face, "To accomplish this grandiose feat, I *also* have to say something nice about you."

That brought a smile to Cooper. Then, the two men walked to where the group was assembling.

****

Miles climbed onto a hood of one of the pickup trucks and waved his arms to quiet the group gathered around him. Cooper estimated it was close to a hundred people, mostly men. Miles licked his dry lips and then rubbed his hands down the sides of his pant legs. *Nervous.* Slowly, the talking faded to whispers and then to silence.

"I got a lot to say, so hear me out," Miles began, his voice raspy. "First, the good news. Hodges agreed to our demands, but..." Miles was drowned out by hearty applause. He waved his arms to quiet them.

Finally, a robust voice bellowed out from the crowd, "What's the condition?"

"He wants Cooper Adams."

"Who?"

"The man," Miles said, pointing at Cooper, "who helped us plan this thing in the first place."

"I thought his name was CJ," a young woman queried, confused.

"Wait, Cooper Adams? Isn't that the guy that has everyone squawking about how Brushfire Plague started?" This time it was Frank, who was bemused by the thought.

The group devolved into a chaotic frenzy of shouted questions and loud assertions. Mile's efforts to calm everything down failed. He turned to Cooper, helpless. As Cooper ascended the hood of the pickup, the yard fell silent.

"I'll answer all your questions. Yes, I'm Cooper Adams. I'm the guy that told the truth about how the Brushfire Plague started."

Several people shouted out in derisive mockery and yelled obscenities.

Cooper locked eyes with one of the offenders, "Look. I wish it wasn't true. But, it is. You can either believe the facts. The facts I revealed to everyone. Or, you can believe the government that is denouncing me. But, I'll just ask you one question: what did I have to gain by making it all up?" Cooper's eyes burned with the intensity born of conviction and only available to the zealot or the truth teller. The other man wilted. *My father always said a sincere man is a powerful man*. No one else answered his question.

A raised hand beckoned for his attention and he pointed at a short man who was made shorter because he was flanked by two tall, lanky men, "Let's put that aside for a moment. Why'd you introduce yourself as CJ?"

"My middle name is James, so it's true they are my initials. Why'd I use them? Frankly, I was hoping to stay hidden here. Telling the truth to the world about Brushfire Plague is what forced me, and my son, from our home." *Gain the sympathy of a hostile crowd whenever you can*, his father had advised. Cooper pointed down at Jake and the group paused a moment, taking him in.

"So, the question before us is whether we hand Cooper over to Hodges or we tell Hodges to pound salt," Miles said. "Personally, I think we tell Hodges to go take a bath in the Clackamas River."

"C'mon, Miles. You can't be serious?" It was Rusty, one of the men who had ridden with them just a short time ago to the meeting with Hodges.

"And?" Miles retorted.

Rusty looked up at Cooper, "No offense, man. But, he's not from around here. You want us to risk a war with Hodges to protect one man? And a stranger at that?" Cooper struggled to keep his face calm. He knew lashing out at the man for saying what many must also be thinking would be a mistake. Silence hung in the air after Rusty finished talking. Cooper saw a dozen or so heads nodding in agreement. *Less than I would have thought.*

"Hell, I don't like that Hodges is in cahoots with the government in trying to *get* their hands on Cooper," Frank took a step forward as he began. People moved away to give him space. *More importantly, people are leaning in, listening to him.* His father had told him often: If you want to know who the leader is within a group, watch who gets listened to. "We are *smart* people here in Estacada. We know if the government says it's bad, it must be good. If they want Cooper, it tells me we *should* protect him." Cooper was impressed with the man's oratory; his words shifted from flattery to indignation effortlessly. A number appeared to agree. Cooper noted that they were the better armed in the group.

A large man who Cooper didn't know raised and then threw his arms down in dismissal, "C'mon, Frank. That's a bunch of hogwash. The government wanted to kill Osama bin Laden. You sayin' that means it was a bad idea?"

"The *military* wanted and got bin Laden, not the government.

Why are you changing subjects, anyway," Frank shot back, undeterred.

That brought the house down in another furious and chaotic round of shouting, insults, recriminations, and near fistfights. Cooper wanted to drop off of the hood of the pickup. He really wanted to drop off the edge of the world. *Why the hell did I tell the world what I learned? What good has come of it?*

The rapping of a wooden cane against a metal car body roused him from his thoughts. He knew before looking that Lily Stott was going to make a speech.

"Listen here," the group quickly fell silent. "You listenin'?" Lily's playful question, delivered coyly, caused a ripple of laughter.

She made a deliberately pained effort to climb onto the hood of a Buick sedan parked in the yard. People next to her reached out to help her, but she rebuffed them. Her progress was painstakingly slow as she crawled onto the hood, before slowly standing awkwardly upon it. *Talk about garnering sympathy,* Cooper thought and almost started laughing.

"First, you know what I said about Cooper already. I won't repeat it. Second, you got it *all* wrong." She drew out the word 'all' in an elongated Southern drawl. "This ain't about Cooper. It's about us." She paused and took a deep breath. Cooper suspected on purpose.

"What do you mean?" Someone asked.

"We need to be honest with ourselves. You all been living under a King. Hodges has been doing what he wants and how he wants since this whole thing started, right?"

A strong murmur of assent was her response. "And, it's kept getting worse. And, harder. Until, a few days ago, his son felt such *disdain* for us that he come and took one of our women. And, ain't she *dead* now?" Lily surveyed the group, taking time to look everyone in the eye.

"Then, what happened? When confronted, Junior shoots down, in cold blood, that woman's husband." Cooper felt the crowd shift underneath his feet. *She has them now.*

"But, get to the point," Rusty called impatiently.

She gave him a long, hard stare before continuing. "Yes, Hodges has agreed to our deal. But, just like the shining moon on a lake's surface doesn't tell you what's in that lake, you gotta look deeper. His demand for Cooper is *really* about him reestablishing his power over us all. You've broken free. *That* is what this is really about. Are you ready to give him that power back? Are you ready to go back to where Hodges' son or his men feel like they can take what they want? No, take *who* they want? When they want?"

The group was stunned. The silence, complete.

Then, Miles' voice cut through, quiet, somber, and strong, "No. I'm not." The effect was like an avalanche of rocks coming down a mountain as one "No" after another came roiling up from hearty throats.

"I guess it's revolution," Frank said with a grin plastered across his face.

"I want a vote," Rusty challenged. When he saw the number of angry looks his words invoked, he hastily added, "If we're going to war, we should vote it. That's all I'm saying."

Frank started to shout him down, but Miles stomped his foot on the hood to stop it. "Rusty's right. Let's vote."

"All in favor of standing up to Hodges and keeping our freedom, say 'Aye'," Cooper never thought the word "Aye" would make him feel so good, as the word washed over him now, shouted out in a full-throated roar.

"All in favor of bowing down again to Hodges, say 'No'." Miles' face beamed and his words were sure as he said them. Cooper was surprised when Rusty and a handful of others were brave enough to say "No."

"Alright, it's decided. I will convey our answer to Hodges." Cooper almost didn't recognize the man who was standing next to him. He was smiling from ear to ear and it seemed like he was a foot taller. *My father once told him that circumstances could elevate an ordinary man to do extraordinary things. I guess they just did.*

"And, he certainly comes from solid stock," Cooper muttered without realizing it.

Miles leaned in, "What'd you say?"

"Nothing, Miles. Nothing at all," he said as he clapped him on the back and jumped down.

Cooper was greeted by introductions and handshakes and was forced to wade through the crowd. Before he knew it, he was looming over Lily.

"You have a way with words, Ms. Stott," he said.

"I'm just like you, Cooper. Just tell the damned truth and the rest takes care of itself."

"Well said," he responded, before pulling her into a warm embrace. It finally hit him. This group of strangers had stood by him. While he worried about what was to come with Hodges, he was overcome with relief that he wasn't going to have to flee into the unknown, with Jake in tow. It struck him how different this felt than the night his neighbors in Portland had turned against him. Tears stung his eyes as he whispered, "Thank you," over and over into Lily's ear. She patted him on the back to soothe him.

****

A while later, he found Dranko waiting for him by the Jeep. He wasn't one for crowds, so Cooper suspected he'd been waiting since the meeting ended.

"What happened to your big speech?" Cooper jested.

"Did you need it?" Dranko's response was flat.

"No, I guess not," he responded, his attack deflated.

"Unlike you, brother, I learned a valuable lesson a long time ago."

Cooper bit, "Yeah, what's that?"

"It's as important to know when to shut the hell up as it is when to talk," Dranko said, satisfied.

Cooper pantomimed turning a key and locking his lips shut in dramatic fashion. Dranko grinned and then they both got into the Jeep, with Jake climbing into the backseat.

Cooper dozed off as Dranko drove them back to the cabin. The day's events had caught up to him. A day's worth of stress and adrenaline made him crash immediately, until the screech of the emergency brake startled him awake. Like him, Jake had fallen asleep, but he slept the child's deep slumber and did not wake when the Jeep stopped. He opened the back door and scooped his son into his arms. A contented feeling struck him to his core. This mere act reconnected him back to when Jake had been allowed to be a child. It was only a few weeks ago, but the absence of it felt like it had been years. He stopped himself, closed his eyes, and breathed it in.

Dranko opened the door to the cabin for him and whispered to him as he passed, "I'll take care of our weapons."

Cooper nodded and carried Jake to his bed, laying him into it gently. His son breathed peacefully, a slight grin on his face. Cooper watched him sleep for a few minutes, enjoying every second. He looked up. *Elena, this is when I miss you the most. I need your help keeping our boy a boy.* Cooper suspected his plea was futile, that it was far too late for that, but he knew he had to make it.

He found his own bed and was asleep very quickly.

Chapter Eleven

Over a dull breakfast of plain oatmeal and dehydrated apples, Cooper and Dranko informed everyone else on what had happened. It took a while to get through everything, as there were a lot of questions. When they had finished, the table fell silent.

Suddenly, Calvin struck his hand to his forehead with a loud smack, "Oh my!"

"What?" They collectively asked.

"The decision you all made last night is going to leak back to Hodges. Do you think he is going to wait for the forty-eight hours for Miles to come and formally tell him the answer?"

Cooper and Dranko looked at each other in stunned silence. Dranko's mouth drifted agape.

"What?" Julianne broke the quiet.

Cooper shook his head to clear it, "I can't believe we hadn't thought of that. Calvin's right, that's the question."

Dranko chuckled in disbelief, "I'm still in shock here. I'm the king of paranoid thinking. How'd I miss that?"

"The only question that matters now is, what will Hodges do?" Buck joined the conversation.

Cooper rubbed his chin and thought, "He could come for me now."

"Or, it could be more about what Lily said and he'll crush his insolent subjects as part of it," Dranko added.

"Or, he might just wait 'til tomorrow. He might need the time to regroup after his losses," Angela said, thinking aloud.

"Could be any of the three," Julianne summarized.

"I'm not sure we have much choice but to sit and wait," Dranko intoned.

"What makes you say that?" Calvin asked.

"We *need* these two days to get seeds in the ground. Otherwise, it won't matter because we'll be starving come the winter."

His words sobered the group instantly.

"We should at least get word to Miles and then keep our weapons handy here while we are working," Cooper declared.

The others nodded.

"We need to save our fuel," Dranko said.

"I will take the motorcycle over to the Stott's. It won't take much time," Cooper offered.

Dranko nodded and then launched into giving directions to everyone on what tasks had to be completed over the next two days, to get crops planted and expand their food supply. When he had finished, Angela patted him on the shoulder.

"Can I just say again, how lucky we are that you stored *seeds*! I mean, who thinks about that?"

"People like me," he deadpanned, but Cooper saw the trace of a smile that he was trying to hide creep onto the corner of his mouth.

Cooper decided to exploit the moment, "Let's give Dranko a round of applause for saving our asses, now and tomorrow!" The room broke into hearty applause and Dranko lost his fight. A wide smile lit up his face for several moments before he managed to bring it back under control. He waved his arms to quiet them, which had the effect of making them redouble their efforts. Cooper stood and the others followed. Dranko turned red-faced at the ovation and hustled himself out of the room as quickly as he could.

When the front door had shut, the group looked at one another, smiling.

"Mission accomplished!" Cooper shouted and then everyone started laughing again. *I embarrassed him* and *thanked him for his wise sacrifices and preparation.* A self-satisfied smile lit up his face.

****

The high whine of the motorcycle's engine pierced the otherwise peaceful forest walls as Cooper sped toward Miles' place. Cooper was paying close attention to operating the bike, as he was not an expert. He enjoyed the thrill of riding in the crisp early morning air, as the wind buffeted past him. He had to fight the temptation to push his speed past what he could safely handle.

When he arrived at Miles' house, he found him sitting alone outside. He barely looked up as Cooper drove the bike up to the house. He looked like he hadn't slept all night.

Cooper dismounted, "What's wrong?"

He looked up, haggard, "Bethany's gone. She took my kids, too."

Cooper's stomach dropped to the ground. *No question that Hodges knows our plan.*

"I'm sorry, man."

He shook his head, his lips tight, "It ain't about me. She ain't loved me in quite a while. I know that." Miles paused, gazing intently

204

at the ground. "It means something worse than all that."

"What do you mean," Cooper asked.

"That woman is a survivor. War is coming. She went to the side she thinks is going to win."

Cooper chuckled, "We'll have to see about that. I guess the news I came over here to tell you isn't news anymore."

"What was that?"

"Calvin realized that the decision made last night was going to leak to Hodges well before tomorrow."

Miles nodded slowly, "Yeah, I figured that out as soon as Bethany flew the coop. I'm not sure it matters all that much."

"How so?"

"Hodges is a methodical man. He won't do anything crazy until our meeting. The reason for *that* is he's also a bit arrogant. He's most likely to think we are going to get cold feet or that he can talk me into giving you up when we meet."

Cooper thought for a moment, "I hope you're right. We'll be doing some work at Dranko's to get seeds planted and the like, but we'll be keeping a lookout too, just in case."

Miles pursed his lips, "Makes sense." He stood up slowly and reached out to shake Cooper's hand, "So, I'll see you tomorrow?"

"Sure thing. And, I'm sorry about Bethany."

He grimaced, "Yeah, it's a damned thing. But, what are you gonna do?" He turned and went back inside his house, the door coming to a quiet close. Cooper remounted the motorcycle and rode back to Dranko's place.

****

They spent the day at a furious pace. Clearing. Weeding. Digging. Planting. They needed to make use of every square inch of Dranko's land for food. And, they did so. Dranko's seeds came out of cans so that they would last for many, many years and displayed an amazing variety of plants.

"These are Heirloom seeds. None of that Monsanto Frankenseed," Dranko had informed them when they were getting started with the seeds.

"What's Heirloom mean?" Jake asked.

Dranko's face lit up like a Christmas tree, "Oh, Heirloom are seeds that have been around a long, long time. So, we know they work and we know they are right for this part of the country, too!"

"What's a Franken-whatever you said?" Jake pressed on.

Now, Dranko's face grew grave, as if he was about to tell a scene from a horror movie, "Some companies have started to modify the seeds to make them better. But, they do some crazy things."

"Like what?"

"Like make it so the seed won't reproduce. That way, you have to buy the seeds *every year* from the company. They make more money, but it is unnatural."

Jake's face drew back in surprise and he visibly shuddered, "That wouldn't be so good now, would it?"

"Nope."

There had been another round of praising Dranko's acumen when he distributed the hand tools for work. He had stockpiled not only extra sets of every tool that would be needed to run a small farm, but the quality of the tools was striking.

"I knew I was buying tools that needed to last a long, long time," he responded when Calvin commented on them.

They had to stop working when the light faded from the sky. As Cooper rested his hands and chin on the handle of the hoe he had been working with, the smell of freshly turned earth wafted all around him. Sweet. Damp. Earthy. He breathed it in deeply. Already, muscles unaccustomed to such manual labor were sore. *I know I'll be hurting tomorrow.* The smell comforted him. And, a day of solid, good work, always made Cooper feel good. He lingered for a while, before grabbing the hoe and heading back to the tool shed.

Dranko had to stop them from simply putting the tools back and calling it a day.

"We have to *clean* these tools every day before putting them away. And, when they are going to sit for a week or more, we are going to have to lightly oil them. We can't let rust consume these tools."

Calvin laughed, "You know, it is funny, is it not?"

They all looked at him.

"When you can no longer run down to the store to buy things; it changes everything."

"It's not a bad thing that one lesson we'll learn is how to take care of stuff," Angela intoned.

"Like our planet?" Julianne dared. Angela glared at her, but held her tongue.

"My daddy taught me how to take care of hand tools when I was a kid. I'm pretty good at keeping them sharp, if you want," Buck offered.

"You are deputized as our Chief Sharpener, then," Dranko said, smiling.

They finished with the tools, ate dinner, and then gathered by candlelight and kerosene lamps around the table. As expected, Dranko had his list of things they needed to discuss.

"We made good progress today on the planting. If Cooper, Julianne, Angela, Calvin, and Jake keep working that tomorrow, we should finish before we have to leave for the meeting."

"What's everyone else doing?" Cooper asked.

"We need to expand my chicken coop. I know a farmer down the road and I can trade for some more layers from him, I hope. Also, I want to build a rabbit hutch."

"Rabbits, cool!" Jake sat up and exclaimed. Cooper reached over and put a hand on his shoulder.

"Not for pets, son."

Jake looked up at him, "For what then?"

"Meat," Dranko said flatly.

Jake leapt up, "Eww…you can't eat a rabbit!"

Chagrined, Cooper looked down at him, "Yes you can."

"Rabbits are the fastest, and best way, to create protein. You can feed them a lot of scraps and they breed like…well, rabbits," Dranko explained.

Jake had a patented look of disgust planted on his face and folded his arms.

"Trust me, son, when you haven't tasted meat in a few weeks, rabbit will taste like your favorite hamburger."

"So, that's what the rest of us will work on until we have to get ready for the meeting. Any questions?"

"Yeah, what is the news from the *rest* of the world?" Calvin asked the question that was on most everyone's minds.

Julianne sat up straight, "Well, I have learned quite a bit from digging into the connections that people have had with Brushfire Plague. Beyond Admonitus." Her voice dragged, weighed down.

"What'd you learn?" Cooper asked with knotted eyebrows.

"It's a fair mess, to be sure. But, there are numerous heavy hitters who did the same thing Van Welton did…"

Calvin raised his hand, "Can you back up a bit? Who is Van Welton?"

Julianne proceeded to explain to the rest of the group the suspicious Chinese investments billionaire Karl Van Welton had made just prior to the outbreak of the Brushfire Plague. She told them how she had spent the last few days doing further research into Van Welton and a few other names of prominent men she had met during her work at Admonitus.

"Were the others invested like Van Welton?" Calvin asked when she had finished the overview.

"Not exactly like him. Van Welton went all in on China. Most of the others had investments in other countries."

"Like where?"

"Africa, mostly. Some in New Zealand and Australia," she answered.

"Well, those countries were also less affected than everyone else. Africa was barely hit at all, especially sub-Saharan," Dranko added.

Julianne nodded, "Yeah, I know. I knew the plan was always to not release it in Africa, Australia, or New Zealand. We knew they'd get some secondary exposure, but not primary impact."

"Why?" Buck leaned in and asked a question.

"Africa was easy. They produced hardly any greenhouse gas emissions..."

"So, they didn't commit the sin, so they shouldn't suffer," he reasoned.

She nodded, eyes downcast.

Angela leaned heavily back in her chair and placed her hands behind her head, "Wow, you guys really were playing God!"

Buck ignored her, "And what about Australia and New Zealand?"

"Well, like every other industrial country, they certainly contributed to the problem of climate chaos. So, we didn't spare them for that. We spared them because they have already been hit hard with droughts and it's going to get worse in the coming years."

"Because of their proximity to the pole?" Buck asked, intently interested.

"Yes. The effects of the planet heating up are most pronounced near the poles." Julianne then stopped a moment, confused. "Buck, most people don't know that..." Her voice trailed off in the unasked question.

Buck smiled, "I might just be a fry cook from a two-bit town in central Oregon, but it doesn't mean I'm dumb. I paid attention to global warming long before it became trendy with the liberals."

"Why?" Several people asked at once.

Buck became agitated, moving in his seat and rubbing his hands together. He stood up, pushing the chair back quickly, and eyes fixed on the table, "I don't know. I've never talked about it much. I guess you'd say I'm a true conservative. I think conserving the planet makes a ton of sense and flipping Mother Nature off is pretty damn stupid." His voice had risen to a loud crescendo before he finished. When he did, he looked up and saw the group all looking at him in wonder. He waved his hands, "Hey, don't you get me wrong. I also think it's damn stupid for the liberals to try to take our guns away and tear up the Constitution and I would punch every single pompous ass from Hollywood driving their Prius and trying to tell me how to live right in their damned face." Once again, his voice was filled with passion. He thrust his hand into his shirt pocket, grabbed a pack of cigarettes, and then stormed outside.

The table sat in silence for a pregnant pause.

"He's one of a kind," Cooper intoned. "Especially nowadays." The others nodded either in agreement or in lingering surprise.

"So, what do you make of it?" Dranko asked, turning the attention back to Julianne's investigation.

"Well, it could just be that those who had insider knowledge of Brushfire Plague switched their investments to make a big profit off of it," she said, unconvinced.

"And, what else could it be?" He continued.

"I don't want to think about it," she said, folding her head into her hands and resting it on the table.

"Have you made any connections to other investors or the government?" Dranko pressed on.

"Not yet. The trail gets murky, but I'm still digging." Her voice barely rose above a murmur and the others had to lean in, straining to hear her.

Cooper clenched his fists, blood rising in his temples, "Yes, please do so." His stomach tightened. *I need to* know why *Elena died.* The uncertainty gnawed at him like a lazy rat nibbling a worn rope.

"Did you see any news about the states that seceded from the US?" Cooper asked, anxious for updates.

Julianne's face fell, "The President is talking fire and brimstone toward the Patriotic American States, but so far there has been no military moves to speak of. In fact, dozens of counties in eastern Washington, eastern Oregon, and northern Colorado have officially petitioned the PAS to join them!"

"It's unbelievable," Cooper exclaimed.

"Not really," Buck intoned.

Cooper looked up at him, "Say more."

"Well, those states and areas had very different politics than the rest of the country. With the Federal Government so weakened, it only makes sense that some might seize the opportunity. In fact, I think we'll see more secession movements arise very soon."

Cooper digested what he had said, "I think you're right. And, with the United States facing nuclear attack now, that would sweeten the pot to get the hell out."

"Exactly," Dranko said.

"You men should really learn not to interrupt a woman," Julianne admonished them.

"What are you talking about," Dranko asked.

"You didn't let me finish. You are both right and wrong. More states are going to secede. In fact, it's already happened."

"What," the men exclaimed as one.

Julianne was grimacing, "Texas announced its secession last night. The Lone Star rises again. There are rumors of other states, cities, and areas that may secede."

"How'd we miss that?" Dranko exclaimed.

"Maybe you've been busy," Julianne offered. Her smug smile revealed she was happy to have been one step ahead of Dranko on this issue. He glared back at her, but worried lines appeared across his brow.

The group spent the rest of the night discussing what it all meant that the United States was falling apart all around them. Finally, they turned to discussing the work to be done tomorrow.

****

They woke up early and settled into an easy routine. Freddie and Angela made the familiar breakfast of boiled oats, once again leavened with dehydrated apples. They still had coffee and Dranko brewed it strong.

"While we have it, we might as well run it full strength," he commented as he poured a round of cups for the adults.

"In that case, can I have a Grande?" Calvin's joke brought a smattering of chuckles and lamented stares at their eight ounce cups. There would be no seconds.

"I'll get right on that, after I make Cooper's double low-fat latte with soy milk and no whip," Dranko said, pouring. The laughter swelled.

Cooper returned a cocked grin, "To hell with you. You know darn well I only like my coffee one way: simple and black."

"Just like I like my women..." Calvin's retort earned him a roomful of laughter and a playful punch in the shoulder from Angela.

"I'm not only offended by your racism, Calvin, I'll confess to some disappointment," she said with an amused tone and winking at him. He returned an upraised eyebrow as they fell into easy laughter.

Cooper inhaled the aroma before he took his first sip. He liked the pungent smoky smell that Dranko's coffee held. *When this is gone, I'm going to miss it.* As he swirled the hot liquid in his mouth, savoring it, his thoughts turned dark. *I miss much more than this already. The caress of the woman I loved. The easy innocence of Jake. Being bored!*

He noticed the silence surrounding him. Looking around, the others were lost in thought, too. Dranko looked worried. Julianne's eyes were red and moist, as she fought back tears. Calvin's jaw was firm, eyes closed, and the muscles in his face tight. Freddie's back was to Cooper, but it looked like he was staring out the window. Angela had a coy smile as her eyes danced surveying the others, as well. Jake caught Cooper's eyes. Sadness consumed his son's eyes for a brief moment, before he forced it away and mustered a weak smile for his father. He looked back at Jake, eyes full of sympathy. Jake gave him an understanding nod before walking to the window and looking out. Cooper mused at the enormity of what could pass between two people in a simple glance.

The thoughtful quiet lasted for a few moments before they clustered around the table to eat their breakfast. While they ate, Dranko reviewed everyone's assignments for the day, to their annoyance. Breakfast was finished as rapidly as they could eat. Jake and Cooper cleared the dishes and washed them quickly, before anything could dry. He hated washing dishes in cold water, but they were conserving their fuel. Each person had been assigned a cup, plate, bowl, and silverware to minimize any unnecessary sharing of germs.

"Let's work until two. Then, let's gather before some of us have to leave for the meeting at three," Dranko instructed as they left the cabin to their respective tasks for the day.

Cooper fell into the work with abandon. His stiff muscles loosened quickly as he set to it. He welcomed the distraction that the work provided. *Everyone with a task*, the sound advice echoed. Cooper knew there was more to it than that. *Knowing that being fed depends on their callouses and sweat is a powerful motivation.* He marveled at how no one complained about the work, especially since most of them were not used to manual labor.

He worked his rows, hoeing and then seeding. He was surprised when Jake tapped him on the shoulder.

"It's two o'clock." His voice was full of dread. Cooper gave him a reassuring pat on the head as they walked back to the shed to turn in their tools. Buck was at the ready for cleaning.

While others made lunch, Cooper, Dranko, Calvin, and Angela made ready to leave. They did so in silence, readying their weapons, donning body armor if they had it, fastening their gear, and checking one another's preparations.

"We are getting far too good at this," Cooper's attempted joke fell flat amid the tension strangling the room.

Those heading off gulped down a few mouthfuls of the beans and rice that had been prepared. Dranko had approved adding scant chunks of preserved turkey meat from his stores. To Cooper, it tasted like desert sand going down his throat. He knew it wasn't the food, but the stress robbing him of its taste and texture. His stomach was tight and he didn't feel like eating. He handed his leftovers to Jake, who spurned it.

"Eat up, damn it!" Cooper barked and immediately regretted it. *I am too keyed up for my own good.* He apologized to him as Jake fell into sullen compliance. He grimaced with each mouthful.

"It's time," Dranko said.

Those leaving were wished a round of "good lucks" and hugs or handshakes. The four of them got into the Jeep, as Dranko cranked the engine to life. The others were arrayed on the porch, waving to them. As Dranko began inching backward, Jake broke from the group and ran towards them.

"I love you, dad!" His frantic yell reached Cooper's ears as a muted cry, muffled by the closed windows. Cooper smiled and waved to his son.

If he had known what was about to happen, he would have stopped the Jeep, gotten out, grabbed his son in a bear's embrace and never let him go.

Chapter Twelve

The Jeep growled onward toward the center of town. The plan was essentially the same as before. Miles and two bodyguards would have the meeting with Hodges while two carloads of others would park nearby and listen in on the hand held radios. Cooper felt better that he was now in a vehicle with those he knew well and trusted. The grip of the FAL rifle gave him comfort. Surrounded by the stress of uncertainty, the firm familiar grip was reassuring. Cooper reviewed their plan in the event the meeting turned violent, as much to relieve the pressure as anything else.

Dranko parked in the designated place, different than the other day, but still where they could see the meeting location. They were ten minutes early and the seconds ticked by.

Miles' truck pulled up right at three o'clock. He and his two men piled out, forming a loose triangle so they could observe all approaches.

"You there," the radio squelched.

Dranko and the other group returned their call signs and fell silent once more. Time slowed even further. Minutes crawled. Cooper constantly checked his watch, growing more anxious with each passing second.

At five minutes past, Miles came back over the radio, "How much more time do we give him?"

Cooper took the radio from Dranko, "No more than ten minutes longer."

"Roger that. Agreed."

They resumed their uneasy wait. Cooper's skin crawled and his throat tightened. Blood rushed into his head as adrenaline flooded his body.

"This ain't right."

Dranko nodded, "I don't like it, neither."

"Maybe he's just hit traffic," Angela joked, without affect.

Cooper balled his fists and gritted his teeth. He was reaching for the radio to tell Miles it was time to go when the Escalade pulled into the store's parking lot. Cooper exhaled. He watched Hodges and two lieutenants leave the large SUV and move into positions opposite Miles and his men.

"My apologies for being late," Hodges said without elaborating.

Miles greeted him with stony silence. Cooper was impressed. He saw Hodges shift his weight. *Uncomfortable. That's good.*

"So, what is your answer?"

"I think you know it. We know this isn't about Cooper Adams. We won't divide ourselves over it. He isn't ours to give up. I'm hoping we can reach a..."

"I figured you'd say that," Hodges said, interrupting him. "The good news is that I don't want to make this town come to blows over an outsider. Especially not one as irresponsible and unpatriotic as Cooper Adams." Hodges lingered on the words, drawing out his disdain.

"So, we have a deal without Cooper?" Elation perked Miles' words.

"We do," Hodges said, extending his hand. Miles took it and the two men shook.

"I just have one small favor to ask," Hodges continued.

"What's that," Miles asked warily.

"Tell Cooper Adams that he'll want to come and see me on his own accord."

Miles laughed, "Oh, I somehow doubt that!"

Hodges voice was steady, cold, "When you tell him that I have his son, I think..."

****

Cooper didn't wait to hear the rest.

"Go!" He shrieked in Dranko's ear and grabbed the steering wheel, locking it straight ahead.

Dranko gassed the Jeep, lurching forward. Just as suddenly, he slammed on the brakes. Cooper's mouth fell open, ready to scream at his friend once again.

"Look!" Dranko yelled, pointing forward.

Cooper tore his gaze from Dranko and looked toward the parking lot. Hodges had disappeared and the Escalade was careening away from the parking lot. Already, at least forty men had come spilling out of the store and were deploying into defensive positions.

"We can't!" Dranko yelled, his face, inches from his friend's. Cooper's eyes were wild, his ears unhearing.

He began to climb into the driver's seat, trying to push Dranko out of the Jeep. The two men grappled. Cooper's muscles strained, emotion making him much stronger than Dranko. He shot out a hand

214

and opened the door. Dranko was halfway out when Cooper caught a flash out of the corner of his eye. The rest happened in slow motion. He got a glimpse of Angela's tormented face, tears streaming down it, just before the rifle butt smashed into the side of his head. Cooper felt the shock of pain, his vision went white, nausea washed over him and then darkness found him.

****

Cooper awoke, woozy, when they were halfway to the cabin. Dranko clenched the wheel, driving like a man possessed. The tires squealed at the slightest twist in the road. The Jeep would lean precariously to the side as they did so. Dranko expertly pushed it to its limits.

Cooper shook his head to clear it.

"I'm sorry," Angela said from the backseat, leaning into the front.

Cooper waved her off dismissively.

"You woulda got us all killed, brother," Dranko added in between navigating an S turn.

"Just get me there," Cooper seethed.

"We will get your boy," Calvin added from the back, his voice matter of fact.

Cooper looked back at him. The resolution in Calvin's eyes broke through. It was reassuring. His father had often told him there was no better feeling than knowing someone had your back. Cooper felt it just then. His father had called it solidarity. The military called it camaraderie. Right then, Cooper just called it good.

"Thank you," he more mouthed to Calvin than said it.

Calvin inclined his head.

Tires belched gravel as they sped up Dranko's driveway. Cooper was out of the vehicle before it had even slowed appreciably. His rifle was at the ready as he scanned the property. His stomach somersaulted as the thick smell of cordite assaulted his nostrils. No smoke lingered. *Gunfire here, but it was a bit ago.* A figure stumbled out of the shed and Cooper's rifle was up and aimed in an instant.

It was Buck. His hands were zip-tied and he staggered. Blood ran down from his scalp and sheathed half of his face in crimson. Cooper lowered his rifle. The door to the cabin had been blown off its hinges. Black burn marks and splintered wood told him that.

215

"On my ass," he commanded Dranko as he moved in a low crouch to the entryway.

Dranko fell in step behind him, his M4 tightly gripped in his hands.

Cooper entered the cabin, swinging his rifle to quickly scan the inside. Timothy's body lay at his feet. His head had caught either the blast from the explosives used on the door or a shotgun shell. There wasn't much left of it, except the side of it and one perfectly preserved eye.

"Jake!" Cooper called out.

Silence.

He moved over Timothy's body and proceeded to search the cabin's main floor and then the basement. Dranko kept watch. Nothing.

Cooper bounded up from the basement. His face told Dranko the search had been fruitless.

"Freddie's here!" Calvin called from outside.

Cooper brushed past Dranko as he raced to exit the cabin. Angela was kneeling next to Buck, tending to his wounds. Calvin was pointing to the tree line just past the garden area.

Freddie was ambling towards them, slow on his feet. The three men sprinted toward him.

"What happened?" Cooper shouted as soon as he was within earshot.

Freddie looked up, seeming surprised. He collapsed where he stood. There was no sign of any wounds, but he fell into an awkward seat on the ground. His hands clasped to his face, hiding it.

Cooper knelt beside him and shook him, "What happened?"

"They came. Too many...happened...so fast," he stammered.

"In cars or on foot?" Dranko asked.

"On foot. From the woods. All sides. Two pickups...right after."

"They took Jake?"

"Huh...Jake...I don't know," he said, lowering his hands and looking up at them. His face was dirty, tear-stained.

Cooper grabbed him by the shoulders, shaking him, "What do you mean you don't know?"

Fear and shame clouded his eyes, "I...I...ran."

Cooper's eyes blazed and threw him backward, jumping on him, "You ran! You let them take my boy!"

His right hand reared back to smack Freddie in the face, but a steely grip caught it. Cooper glared over his shoulder to find Dranko constraining him. Dranko used the leverage to throw Cooper off of Freddie.

"C'mon Cooper. Knock it off!" Dranko yelled at his friend. The two men stood facing other, both falling into natural fighting stances.

They began circling each other before Cooper lunged forward, trying to get past Dranko and get his hands once more on Freddie. Dranko caught him and stood him up. Then, Calvin jumped into the fray and they wrestled Cooper to the ground, each pinioning an arm to the ground.

Cooper struggled mightily before exhausting himself and then collapsing.

"OK, I get it. Let me up!"

Calvin and Dranko eased up cautiously. Cooper sat up, with Freddie across from him.

"I'm sorry, Cooper. I panicked when I saw how many there were."

Cooper glared at him.

"I didn't know they were coming for Jake. I just thought they were coming to kill everyone," Freddie continued pleading.

Cooper dropped his gaze to the ground and waved an open palm towards him, "Fine. I get it." His shoulders dropped and he took a deep breath.

He sat there for several moments, letting the situation absorb him. When he got up to stand, he rose slowly and heavily. Calvin reached in and offered him a hand up. Cooper took it gratefully.

"Sorry, Freddie."

He climbed onto his own feet, "No worries. Me, too. Do we know *who* took Jake?"

"Hodges' men," Dranko informed him.

"What are we going to do now, boss?" Dranko asked, turning to Cooper.

"First, I'm going to talk to him to get Jake back." Cooper trailed off.

"And, then?"

"Then, I'm going to kill him." The deadly mirth in his voice made the other men shiver.

****

Cooper and the others staggered back to the cabin, rifles sloppily slung over their shoulders. Freddie's banged up and down as

217

he dragged it along the ground. Cooper didn't have it in him to chastise him. He was back in a daze, overwhelmed by all that had happened so suddenly. When he reached the porch, he clung to one of the poles and stared blankly ahead.

Suddenly, his eyes flashed, "Where's Julianne?"

Dumbly, heads jerked to survey their immediate surroundings. Bewildered, they then looked at Cooper blankly.

"You see her?" He snapped at Freddie.

"No," Freddie said, eyes downcast.

"Where is she?" Calvin asked.

"Where *haven't* we searched?" Cooper asked and then answered his own question, "The Airstream."

Calvin and Freddie were in motion before he was. Freddie's younger legs carried him and he dashed into the Airstream trailer at least ten yards in front of the others. By the time Cooper pulled the door open again, Freddie was already on his way out.

"Nothing," he lamented.

Cooper's hand cradled his jaw as he thought, "Where could she be?"

"Who?" Angela asked, walking up, while supporting Buck with her arm hooked around him.

Cooper turned to face her, "Julianne's missing, too."

"And?" Angela replied coldly.

"Enough," Cooper flatly replied, cutting her off with his fierce eyes as much as his tone. "She's the ticket to getting to the final truth about the Brushfire Plague."

Angela rolled her eyes, "Whatever you want to tell yourself, Cooper."

They conversed as the group slowly migrated back to the cabin. Dranko took over supporting Buck's gingerly steps from Angela. She retreated to the shed to clean up the supplies left lying about when she had tended to Buck. Dranko helped him sit on one of the crude benches that fronted the cabin. Buck fished a cigarette out from his shirt packet and lit it. Cooper noted his still shaky hands.

"Why would they take Julianne, but tie Buck up and leave him?" Cooper mused.

Buck blew out a blast of smoke, "That's easy. She's a damn sight better looking than me!" The others laughed for a moment.

"Timothy's dead. They let Freddie retreat. They knock Buck upside the head. They take Julianne and Jake. Doesn't add up," Cooper continued.

"Could just be the simple fact that no plan survives the point of contact with the enemy," Dranko answered.

"Ah, what's that mean?" Freddie asked.

Cooper looked annoyed, "It just means that maybe this wasn't their plan. Maybe it just happened."

"That makes sense to me. They probably only came for Jake and then Julianne got rounded up with them, somehow."

Cooper looked unsure, "We'll figure it out."

"I'm gonna miss these when they run out," Buck said, having ignored their conversation. He was holding out the cigarette, blowing a stream of smoke, and gazing at it all longingly.

"I picked up the habit in the Corps, but quit cold turkey the day I got serious about being prepared," Dranko responded.

"Why's that?" Calvin asked him.

"You can't really be prepared and be addicted to anything."

"Because it would run out?"

"Exactly. I used to laugh my ass off at others who were getting ready for the end of the world, but would be puffing away on a Marlboro while loading up their bulk food," Dranko extolled as he laughed.

Cooper, Freddie, and Calvin smiled politely. Dranko saw the others' muted reactions and waved his hand to dismiss them. He turned and headed back into the cabin without another word.

Moments later, he returned from the cabin with a white piece of paper in hand. Seeing that stirred Cooper.

"Ransom note?"

"Looks like it. It just gives you a radio channel to contact them."

Cooper snatched it from his hands. He scanned it, confirming the contents.

"You going to call them?" Calvin asked.

"In a minute. I need to think about it for a minute," he said, before moving off toward the garden area to give himself time to think.

****

He clutched the paper that held the radio channel in his hands. It felt rough against his fingertips when he rubbed them together. He studied the handwriting, wondering if it was Hodges' or not. He studied it for a moment to see if he could divine the personality of the writer. *You're stalling*, his inner voice warned him.

219

Cooper shook his head and then looked up, "Alright, where are you now?" He beckoned the Heavens for advice from his dead father, closed his eyes, and breathed deeply to clear his mind. He heard the murmur of voices from back at the cabin. The wind rustled the leaves of the trees that lined the property. An insect buzzed by his left ear. He inhaled the sweet smell of the pine trees clustered off to his right. His mind drifted.

****

The young boy eased the black leather shoes off of his Father's feet. For the seven year old, it took straining his muscles to get it done. Once the shoes were off, Cooper made a big display of fanning his hand across his face, "Peee-Yoooo. They stink!"

His father rolled with laughter, despite having seen this ritual many times. His father's laugh infected him and Cooper fell into wild, gleeful, laughter. As it subsided, they both sat in the glow found in the shared moment that had become their routine. Cooper splayed his legs out on the floor and unzipped the shoeshine kit. As he always did, he brought the kit to his nose and inhaled. He loved the smell of the polish, cleaning cloths, and the horsehair brush. He was especially proud of the brush: a gift he had bought for his father.

Looking up, "What were you doing today, Papa?"

His father arched his back, groaning, "Negotiations."

"Nego-what?"

Cooper began to apply polish to one of his father's shoes, setting to work diligently working it into the leather. His father smiled down at him.

"Negotiations."

"What's that?"

His father cocked an eyebrow, "Tough to explain. Let's see. It's when two sides come together and try to compromise."

Cooper stopped his work, "Huh?"

His father laughed heartily again, "Sorry. It's like when you try to figure out who gets to watch their TV show with your brother."

Satisfied with that explanation, Cooper set back to polishing, "Arrgghh! So, it's no fun!"

"Yes, sir. It's not very much fun."

"Are you good at it?" The child's words held the tone of assurance that every seven year old has that his father is a god, omnipotent.

"Yeah, I think so."

"What makes you good?"

"It's simple, really. Know what your side wants. Know what the other side wants. Try to work it out."

"What if you both HAVE to watch a show at the same time?" Cooper *squealed.*

His father chuckled, "Then it gets hard. Do you want to know what my secret is?" He had a devilish look on his face as he leaned down to whisper in his son's ear. Cooper's face exploded into a smile and a furious nod.

His father made a display of looking to his left and his right, as if to ensure no enemy agents were lurking nearby.

"I act a little crazy. Out of control. The other guys always hate unpredictable things!" His father cackled at delight of a joke his son had no way of understanding at that time. Confused, Cooper settled into shining his father's shoes and the rest of the talk was easy banter.

A week later, when Cooper smashed a lamp against his brother's head during a heated exchange over a TV show, his father fought to restrain his laughter when his wife told him what Cooper had said, "I was just acting crazy in my negosheeayshuns!"

As Cooper's attention came back to the present, he was chuckling to himself.

****

He strode confidently back to the cabin, knowing what he had to do now. Raise Hodges on the radio. Plead for this son's life. Act more unhinged than he was. Present himself unpredictability to throw Hodges off his game. He was mentally rehearsing what he would say when the throb of an engine whirring up the drive disturbed him.

His pistol was drawn before he even realized he was doing it. The others spilled from the cabin and took up defensive positions, rifles at the ready. The light was fading from the sky. *Better cover for us, who knows the terrain here.* He welcomed the sight of Dranko sprinting across the open space to take up a position opposite the cabin's entrance, near the Airstream trailer. Cooper ran to his left and took cover behind a water barrel about fifteen yards to the left of the cabin's doorway. His muscles tensed and he forced himself to take a deep breath to try and relax.

A beat up Corolla came churning around the last bend in Dranko's driveway. The driver brought it to an abrupt stop in front of the cabin, gravel spitting from the front tires.

Cooper drew a bead on the driver side door. The door swung open and a woman emerged. It took Cooper a second to recognize her. Bethany. He exhaled in surprise, "What the…"

"Cooper," she yelled, her call so loud it echoed off of the

221

cabin's walls.

He stood up, holstered the pistol, and walked forward.

"Yeah?"

She pivoted from looking at the cabin's door and immediately rushed over to him. The others slowly stood up from their hidden positions. She stopped for a moment, surprised.

"What do you want?" Cooper asked, coming to stand a few feet from her.

"I know where they have Jake," she panted excitedly.

Cooper did a double-take, "What?"

"I know where they have taken him!"

The others drifted in to stand around them. Curious looks adorned their faces.

Cooper's mind whirred.

"Where?"

"It's an abandoned hunting cabin up in the hills. Just above 224, a few miles outside of town. In the Mount Hood National Forest." Her words came in a rush.

Dranko stepped in, "Why are you telling us?"

She turned to him, confused, "What?"

Cooper stepped in and grabbed her by the collar, "You're with Junior, ain't you?"

Her head snapped back to face him, "Well...yeah...but..." she stammered.

"But, what?" Cooper growled.

She grabbed and wrenched his hands away from her. He didn't resist her efforts.

"What's that got to do with anything?"

He just stared at her in disbelief.

Her eyes blazed, "That's between Miles and me. Yeah, I love the nasty son-of-a-bitch! It's true. But, I know what I'd do if someone took one of my kids. It ain't right!" Her tone struck Cooper like someone explaining an obvious thing to a stupid man.

Cooper stared at her for a long moment. Her eyes burned back at him, unwavering. Finally, he nodded.

"Alright, can you show us on a map?"

She nodded, "Sure. I don't have much time. I don't want Junior to know I went missing."

Cooper caught Dranko's skeptical look out of the corner of his eye.

****

Fifteen minutes later, they had finished debriefing her. She had indicated where the cabin was on one of Dranko's maps of the area. She told them that the place was heavily guarded. Eight to twelve of Hodges' best men had been sent up to guard the place; she couldn't be sure of the exact number. She knew that there was at least one machinegun in the mix, but likely other automatic weapons. She had clambered back into the Corolla when she was done, wished him luck, and quickly drove away.

Dranko and Cooper watched her tail lights round the first corner and disappear.

"You believe her," Dranko grunted.

"I do."

"Could be a trap," he retorted, eyebrow raised.

"I don't think so. I made my living reading people. I saw truth in her eyes," Cooper said evenly. "Besides, if Hodges wanted a shootout, he could have just stormed us here."

Dranko nodded in agreement. "Alright. Enough said. So, what's the plan?"

"Let's convene the war council," Cooper raised his voice so the others could hear him and then turned back toward the cabin.

Timothy's body had been moved out at some point, but the hasty cleanup effort had left smeared bloodstains across the floor near the entryway. Cooper dipped his head in respect as he carefully stepped over them. *I owe you, Timothy.*

Cooper moved to the head of the table as the rest of the group drifted in and stood around the table.

He cleared his throat, "Here is what I'm thinking. I want to go and get my boy."

His short, obvious statement elicited awkward laughter from around the table.

"We need more firepower," Dranko said matter of factly.

"Yeah, I know. I figure we could probably get Miles and a few others."

"That's not enough," Dranko responded curtly.

Cooper looked at him sharply, his voice rising, "You got any solutions or just problems?"

Dranko didn't back down, "I won't apologize for stating the facts."

"Go piss out your testosterone in the bucket outside, will you

223

two?" Angela chastised.

"Where can we get more men?" Cooper asked, thinking.

"Or women," Angela added.

"Michael Huynh." Calvin said, slowly, resignation clouding his words.

"Who?" Buck Floy asked.

"He leads the Vietnamese Protection Society in Portland. He hires out armed men, for the right price, of course," Cooper answered.

"He is a gangster," Calvin said with disdain. "Let us call it what it is. I do not like it one bit, but he is the only resource right now."

"Good idea. But, we don't have time to get back and forth to Portland. We need to make this happen tomorrow morning," Cooper responded.

"I know how to reach them over the Ham radio," Dranko said.

"What? How?" Cooper asked.

"I pay attention. I know who talks on what frequencies," Dranko responded, his voice full of self-satisfaction.

Cooper took a step backward, "Alright. What can we pay him with?"

"That's easy. The weapons we take from Hodges' men. I can sweeten the pot with some gold," Dranko continued.

Cooper looked at his friend with warm, thankful eyes. After a moment, he turned to the rest.

"This will be beyond dangerous. I can't ask you to come, but I'd welcome…"

Calvin looked at him askance, "Really? What are we surviving for if it is not to go and save a boy from this madness?"

As Cooper surveyed the table, the others nodded agreement with what Calvin had said. Cooper was nearly overwhelmed by their support. He choked out a "Thank you."

"So, what are you going to say to Hodges? You going to tell him we're coming for his sorry ass?" Buck Floy asked, eyes alight.

Cooper shook his head, a wry smile fleeting across his face.

"Just the opposite. I'll follow the advice from Sun-Tzu's Art of War."

"What's that," Calvin asked.

"I forget the exact quote, but it's something like, talk sweetly before waging war. Bark loudly when preparing to retreat. So, I'll act distraught and beg for my son's life. I'll agree to anything he says. Try to lull him a bit."

******

Cooper fingered the handheld speaker for the ham radio set. Earlier, Dranko had radioed Hodges' men to arrange a call over the radio between Hodges and Cooper at eight o'clock. The black plastic was cold in his hands. He turned it in his hand, changing the grip, getting its feel. It was a good distraction as he gathered his final thoughts.

Angela and Calvin had been dispatched to Miles'. They were going to find out how many more would join them in the attack on the compound where Jake was being held. He knew the pool was small. They could only talk to a few highly trusted people. If Hodges got wind of their plan, it would he hopeless before they even started.

He knew this call to Michael Huynh was critical. He *needed* more men for this attack to succeed. He wanted to know the answer from Huynh before he talked to Hodges. He hoped that he could raise him quickly and get that answer.

"You ready?" Dranko asked as he turned the radio on.

"Yeah."

Dranko powered up the unit and fiddled with the dials. Random bits of conversation floated through the speaker as he searched for the station where he had heard Huynh's men talking before.

The distinct sharp staccato of Vietnamese told them they had found the right channel. The conversation between two people was animated, stressed. They waited for it to end before transmitting.

"This is call sign Hammerdog. We wish to talk to the leader of the VPS," Dranko said, slowly pronouncing out the initials VPS.

A long pause ensued. Dranko repeated himself, this time adding, "We were referred by Joe Vang. Repeat, Joe Vang."

"Moment please," the accented voice returned. Cooper and Dranko waited for more than a minute. Each second grew longer than the one before and Dranko's foot tapped nervously. Cooper clenched his jaw and looked at the clock. They still had an hour before the call with Hodges. *We'll be fine if we can get Huynh on the line before then.*

The radio cackled, "State again your business." The voice was clearer, without an accent.

"This is Hammerdog. We are friends of Joe Vang. Talked to the leader of VPS before. Need to do again. Business proposition."

"We do not talk business over the radio in English."

"This is lucrative. Very."

225

Another pause, "OK. Leader can talk tomorrow morning."

Cooper cringed and the two men exchanged a look, "Must be within hour. I repeat, very good business."

"Give me a minute." They waited.

"OK. This channel at seven forty-five."

"Thank you. Wilco."

Dranko leaned back heavily in the chair and exhaled, "Phew! I think that may have been the hardest part."

"I hope so," Cooper responded and then yawned. "I'm going to crash. Wake me in thirty minutes." Cooper stood up and headed for the stairs.

"How do you fall asleep before and after big moments of stress? I'm wired as a junkie right now!" Dranko marveled.

"Dunno. Just can. Heck, Tom Brady fell asleep right before the first Super Bowl," he called over his shoulder.

****

A little later, he was woken by the sound of Dranko kicking his shoes. Cooper rose, stretched, let out a loud yawn, and then followed him back downstairs.

He stared at the battery-powered clock on the wall as the last minutes ticked by. At seven forty-five exactly, Michael Huynh's clear, strong voice bellowed into the room.

"This is who you wanted to speak with. Who is this?" Cooper could picture him sitting at his ornate desk, talking on a portable unit.

Cooper fingered the call button, "This is a friend of Joe Vang's. We came to you a few weeks ago about protecting our neighborhood. You never heard back from us."

There was a pause. Cooper guessed that Huynh received a lot of requests for such things.

Finally, he said, "Are you the popular one?" Cooper appreciated Huynh speaking in code.

"Yes, sir. The very one."

"Ah, good to hear from you. What can I do for you now?"

"I need six very well trained and very well armed men. First thing in the morning. Estacada."

"That is a dangerous journey," was Huynh's response.

"Yes. Three or four hours, I'd guess."

"You told my man this was lucrative. How so?"

"I have gold."

"So do I," he laughed.

Cooper smiled. *Negotiations underway.* "It's always good to have more, yes?"

"Certainly. What is your offer?"

Cooper eased back into the chair, "Three ounces. Plus six M4s, automatic, when it's done."

Huynh laughed. "That would buy you a toothless old man with a squirt gun."

Cooper forced a laugh himself, "But, I'm sure it would be a handsome old man."

"I like a man with a sense of humor, but let's get serious." Huynh's voice turned cold as a corpse.

Cooper matched him, "Yes, let's."

"You are far away. Any men I send will face danger both coming and going. Plus, they will face danger on the assignment itself, of course," Huynh's voice was steady, dripping with confidence.

"You speak truth I cannot deny. However, you see what's happening around us. Since we last discussed, ah, business, the value of gold has increased has it not?" Cooper matched the other man's demeanor.

"It is good you agree with me about the peril my men will face. And, yet you offer me machineguns which you do not even yet possess."

Cooper countered, "True. But, you've heard of the spoils of war, no?"

"Of course," Cooper knew he was striking a nerve as irritation crept into Huynh's voice.

"Well, that is a sound basis for our deal. I'm able to tell you that with success, what portion of the enemy's loot shall be yours."

Huynh paused so long before responding that Cooper almost panicked and asked him if he we still on the line.

"I see your point. It is valid. I will accept five ounces of gold and all of the automatic weapons liberated from our adversary," Cooper could almost imagine Huynh at his desk, hands folded in assurance of getting what he wanted.

The tense negotiations continued back and forth. Cooper's blood rose as the minutes ticked by. He was violating one of his father's cardinal rules of negotiating: *never be the only person in the room with a time deadline.*

At seven fifty seven they hadn't made much progress. Huynh had agreed to two men for four ounces and the weapons.

"Let me have a second," Cooper said to Huynh and huddled with Dranko.

"How much gold can you put to this?"

Dranko rubbed his chin. "It's your son, brother. You can have it all if you need it."

"How much do you have?"

"Ten ounces." That was worth almost $20,000 before the Plague.

Cooper touched his shoulder, "Thank you."

He clicked the handset. Seven fifty-eight. "I want to save us both busy men time. Here is my final offer; for six well-trained and well-armed men, I will give you six ounces of gold, a dozen M4s, and a heavy machinegun."

Seconds ticked by in silence.

"Alright. You have a deal. I can have my men there by nine in the morning. Where shall they meet you?"

Dranko gave them the map coordinates for a road junction a half mile from his property.

Eight o'clock. Cooper mopped his brow with a rag and had Dranko begin turning dials to reach the station that Hodges was on.

****

Static. It hissed over the speakers as minutes ticked by. Cooper forced himself to take rapid, shallow breaths. He wanted to sound like he was on the verge of panic when Hodges came on. Dranko made a few attempt to raise Hodges on the radio and the only response was the disturbing scream of dead air. As the clock changed to 8:05, Cooper's fear turned real. *What did this mean?*

He looked at Dranko, whose eyes were full of concern.

"Maybe he just wants to take you off guard?"

Cooper nodded, hoping, and kept up his practice of breathing quickly, so that he would sound out of breath.

"You there?" The voice actually startled him at 8:08. "Sorry I am late. I had a situation to deal with." Hodges voice was flat, emotionless.

"I want my boy," Cooper responded, deliberately sounding firm, but letting fear seep into his words.

"That's easy. Just turn yourself in to me. I'll release your boy to anyone you want."

"What do you want me for? What would happen to me?"

228

Cooper let a false panic rise in his throat.

Hodges laughed on the other end. "*I don't care a bit for you. But, some people I know want you pretty badly. Bringing you in myself will not only give me a lot of money, but it will help my standing with them. They just want to question you. Probably have you take back the things you've said. Then, I'd guess you'll be on your merry way.*"

Cooper held back the scoff that leapt into his throat and instead played the part, "Yeah, sure. I just want my son to be safe. Can I talk to him?" Cooper's voice quivered on the last words.

"Sorry, he isn't with me."

"How do I know he's safe then?"

"You'll just have to trust me."

"OK," Cooper gulped.

"Can we make arrangements to meet then?"

"Sure."

"Tomorrow. Noon. At the Ranger station just outside of town."

"Alright. I'll be there. I want to warn you."

"Warn me," Hodges exclaimed indignantly.

"Yeah. You harm my son, and all hell will rain down upon you!" Cooper's false bravado was pitch perfect.

"I have no desire to harm a hair on his head. You come in, nice and easy…he goes home nice and easy."

The channel went back to ominous static.

Cooper leaned back in his chair and exhaled.

"You played that well, brother."

Cooper pressed his fingers into his forehead, kneading the flesh.

"I guess so. Big day tomorrow, eh?"

"Indeed."

Cooper rubbed his temples, "This is driving me crazy."

"Yeah," Dranko grunted sympathetically.

"I can't believe Jake is in that bastard's hands. How'd I let that happen?"

Dranko leaned in, bringing his face closer to Cooper's, "Hey, now. Don't go there. This ain't your fault."

"But…"

Dranko waved his hands dismissively, "But, nothing. You can't carry him around in a backpack twenty-four seven. Can you?"

"I guess not," Cooper said, unconvinced.

"This just happened."

Cooper brought his eyes from the floor to look Dranko squarely in the eye, "It didn't just happen."

"What?" His friend asked, confused.

"I could have just kept my mouth shut about what I'd learned about the Brushfire Plague. Look at what's it's caused. More violence. Threatened war. Riots. Jake being kidnapped. It's all a damned mess." Cooper's hands slid behind his head and he dug his fingers into his neck, massaging the tense muscles.

"Yeah, it's a mess for sure."

Cooper chuckled, "Thanks for making me feel better."

"You didn't let me finish. Yes, there's been a high price for the truth getting out. But, can I ask you a question?"

"Sure. What?"

"Does water in a creek flow downhill?"

Cooper wrinkled his eyebrows, "I don't see what..."

"Just answer the question," Dranko demanded.

"Yes, it flows downhill."

"Why?"

Cooper looked at him dumbly, "Duh. Because it has to. Physics."

"And, does Cooper Adams tell the truth? *Always*. Even when it's annoying and frustrating. Or stupid."

He turned sheepish, "Yes, he does."

"Why does he?"

Something swelled up from deep inside Cooper. Impotence at not being able to lie when it would help him so much. When it would help Jake. The hurt from what had happened to his father and his lost childhood. It ran together with the pain he now experienced watching the same thing happen to his son. A devilish froth of pain and rage overwhelmed him. His face flushed red, his jaw clenched, and his fist thundered onto the table. The ham radio bounced.

"Because I *do*. Because I'm trapped inside of this!" His hands motioned his body.

Dranko was surprised at his friend's reaction, but let him go. Cooper stood up and paced the room in a wide circle. Dranko watched. Waiting. He knew him well enough that words would come.

After his fifth rapid cycle around the cramped basement room, Cooper stopped and looked at Dranko.

"I do have a choice, that's the difference."

"Do you really though, brother? Really?" Dranko stood so that he was at eye level.

"Hell, I don't know. Maybe you're right. But, it doesn't help with how I'm feeling. I *did* all of this.

"What'd you say about Julianne?"

Dranko's question stopped him cold, "What?"

"What'd you say to Julianne. Didn't you say she made the best decision she could with the information she had?"

"Me or Angela said something like that. Yeah."

"So, didn't you?"

"Yes, I suppose so."

"So, stop this baloney about guilt. You *are* who you are. You made the best decision you could. What more can be asked of any man?"

"To make the right decision."

Dranko's arms flew into the air, "You're impossible."

Cooper put his hand on his friend's shoulder, "Thanks. It does help. Why don't we get our gear set up for tomorrow?"

Dranko nodded and let his friend lead them upstairs to the main floor of the cabin.

As they prepared their equipment, Cooper whispered to his friend, "I wish I knew what was happening inside Jake's head. He's been on a roller coaster these last few weeks. Sometimes he sounds like a grizzled, emotionless, and cynical war veteran. Other times I see the little boy like nothing has happened."

Dranko's eyes shined with concern for his friend, "Yeah, he's been through a lot."

"I just wish I knew how this was affecting him and how it's going to turn out." Cooper's hands grasped his head before he continued, "I mean, he's seen *so much* death and destruction. My God, he couldn't even have time to properly grieve his mother's death yet. What's going to happen to his *mind*?"

Dranko stepped in so he could put a hand on his friend's shoulder, "Look, Cooper. Try not to think about it. There's nothing more you can do right now. He knows you love him. You keep trying to talk to him. What more can you do?"

It was as if Dranko had said nothing, "And, what are those bastards *doing* to him right now? I swear to God, if he's been harmed I will put a goddamned bullet into the brain of every last man involved in this!" Cooper's voice shook and thundered as rage overtook him. His fists were tight balls by the time he had finished.

Dranko's words were stern, "If they have harmed a hair on his body, you'll have to beat me to it, brother."

Despite his feverish wish to the contrary, Dranko's words were not helpful to Cooper. He just nodded to his friend's sympathy, then shook his head and returned to topping off one of the magazines with fresh rounds. The two men continued their work in silence. Cooper's thoughts continued in torment as circular thoughts of worry, rage, and desperation went unabated for hours.

Chapter Thirteen

The first rays of sunlight drifted into the room where Cooper slept, waking him. He was instantly alert and tense. He had slept fitfully, worrying about where Jake was and whether he was all right. He had doubted his decision to wait until morning to attack. The advantage of a surprise night attack versus the advantage of having more men to even the odds battled in his head all night. But, the risk of having Jake accidentally shot in the darkness was too much for him to bear.

He dressed quickly, slipping into the same camouflage clothing he had worn on the night that they had attacked Ethan Mitchell's compound. It had only been weeks since that day, but it felt like a lifetime ago. He crept downstairs and worked his way outside, carefully closing the cabin door behind him.

The brisk air assaulted his lungs when he stepped outside. They stung as he inhaled deeply, the scent of the pine heavy in the air. He strode across the open ground, walking toward the tree line. The ground was saturated from an overnight rain. His ears heard each 'squish' as he tromped toward the trees. When he reached the trees, he surveyed the area looking for a suitable spot for privacy.

He spied a copse of four pine trees clustered in a tight circle and made his way there, about fifteen yards into the forest. He cloistered himself in their cover and knelt, one knee on the ground. He fished a photograph out of his breast pocket and looked at it intently.

Elena looked back at him, cradling a newborn Jake in her arms. It was taken a week or so after his birth. Her face was radiant, the glow of newfound motherhood emanating from her. Jake's face was scrunched into a grimace that looked like an evil smile, but Cooper smiled to himself every time he looked at this picture.

"I need your help today," he said to the photograph. His voice was quiet, barely making it to the edge of the trees that surrounded him.

"I *have* to succeed in bringing our son home."

Cooper's throat tightened as he thought about the alternative, which wasn't something he thought he'd survive. He'd known too much loss already. If not for Jake, he thought he would have laid down beside Elena when she had died and willed himself to die with her. Without Jake, he there would be no reason to struggle onward in this world turned upside down.

Tears did not come to his eyes. His heart stayed just shy of that. *Maybe this is all making me harder,* Cooper thought when he recalled how easily the tears had flowed when he had knelt beside Elena's grave before his last mission.

He looked into Elena's eyes, "I'll do whatever it takes to get him back safely. I promise you that. Or, I'll die trying." His words were firm, stronger. They rang out into the forest, but went unanswered by the trees and animals that scurried about. He *felt* her answer in his heart, though. Warmth rushed in. The love they had shared came back. Her confidence in him had never wavered that he would do what was needed for their son. Now, it came back to him from her grave. His nerves vanished.

Cooper stood up. He gave a last look at Elena and Jake in the photograph and nodded to it. No words were needed now. He put it back into his chest pocket and began walking back towards the cabin. He was peaceful, relaxed.

He made it about ten yards past the trees before a plaintive wail ripped all of that away from him.

****

"Oh my God! Oh my God!" Angela wailed as she came flying outside. She was running in haphazard fits and starts, changing direction constantly. Her arms flopped up and down unevenly, akimbo. Her eyes were unfocused, wild.

Cooper raced towards her, just as she collapsed into a heap on the ground. The others came rushing out from the cabin and clustered about her. Everyone else was confused.

Cooper slid down beside her, grabbing her shoulders, and tried to make eye contact with her, "What, Angela? What?"

His eyes caught hers. Terror owned them. Her words came out jumbled.

"Nuked. They. So many dead!"

Cooper looked at the others, but received nothing for his trouble except blank stares.

"Okay. Slow down. What are you talking about?" Cooper responded.

Angela took a deep breath, closed her eyes, and then looked up at him again, "I was listening to the Ham radio. Honolulu. It was nuked. It's gone!" She began sobbing again.

The air whooshed out of his lungs and he immediately felt

dizzy. He fell backwards and landed in an awkward seated position.

He shook his head in disbelief, "Honolulu? What? Who?"

Seconds ticked by before Angela could respond. "Early this morning." She shook her head slowly, "No one knows."

Dranko recovered fastest, "Could be the Russians or the Chinese."

"Why Honolulu?" Cooper asked, looking up at him.

"If it was the Russians, it's a good warning shot to the U.S. Limited fallout to the rest of the country. If it's the Chinese, it's good for weakening our power in the Pacific," Dranko's tone was analytical.

Angela climbed to her feet, "Oh my God. I can't believe it."

"What's gonna happen now?" Freddie asked.

Cooper shook his head, "Who knows?"

They all stood in shocked silence for a long while. Freddie fell to his knees. Calvin paced around, wordless. Cooper remained on the ground shaking his head in disbelief.

Freddie finally spoke, "The world needs this like we need a hole in the head."

Suddenly, Dranko's face alighted, "Is there any news of a retaliation?"

She shook her head, confused, "No. Why?"

"There will be a hue and cry for one. And, it could lead to an escalation."

"My lord," Cooper exhaled.

His father's words returned to him: *in a crisis give people a shared challenge to rally them.* Then, he shook himself out of it, "There's one upside here. At least for our little tiny corner of the world."

"What's that?" Dranko asked.

"This might have Hodges and his men distracted. If *we* can stay focused."

He received a series of mumbles for the response.

He looked at each of them sharply in turn, "*Can* we stay more focused than Hodges' men and bring Jake home safely today?"

Calvin squinted his eyes to look at him intently, "Yes, we can."

Freddie nodded vigorously. Angela fell into his arms and gave him a firm, confident, hug. She stepped away, drying her tears. Dranko simply nodded at his old friend.

The butcher's bill for the truth I told just keeps growing. Cooper brushed his tormented thoughts aside as he went back inside to grab his gear and weapons for the work that lay before them today.

****

He had laid everything out the night before, so it was a simple matter for him to don his body armor, the belt and pouches that held the magazines for the his FAL rifle, and then to hoist it into his arms. He checked the function several times out of habit more than necessity. He liked the heaviness of the rifle in his hands. He knew that there were disadvantages to carrying a rifle that weighed more than ten pounds; namely that fatigue could set in during combat. However, it was the weapon he was most familiar with and that counted for a lot, too, in the stress of battle. But, the biggest reason he carried the FAL was that he welcomed the hard-hitting power of the .308 cartridge.

Around him he heard the sharp snick of metal hitting metal and sometimes the louder bangs as metal crashed against metal. His friends were readying themselves and their equipment, as well. Everyone else, except Angela, was carrying the M4 rifles that they had taken from the men who had attacked them. The selective-fire M4s might make the difference in their attack. Angela was cradling a hunting rifle in .308. She would provide sniper fire during the attack.

"So, how did it go at Miles'?" Cooper asked.

Calvin finished snapping a buckle before responding, "Good, I think. In addition to Miles, he thought he could round up another four or five trusted men."

Cooper nodded, "That is good. What kind of weapons would they have?"

"That part wasn't so good. Mostly hunting rifles and shotguns."

He rubbed his chin, thinking, "We can put the ones with hunting rifles as our sniper fire support team and those with shotguns can join one of the assault teams."

"That makes sense," Calvin answered, while hoisting his rifle into his arms.

"What's the general plan, anyway?" Angela asked.

"We'll review it in more detail later once we have all the people together, but it's a simple plan. We will have the sniper team infiltrate on the left side of their position to provide suppressing fire. One assault team will approach from the front and to the right. The other will hook around and come in from slightly behind their position and from the left," Cooper responded.

The others nodded and then Calvin spoke up, "What happens if, during all this movement, we have contact with them early?"

"I'm hoping they will mostly be buttoned up in their defensive positions. But, if not, we will have to crash it."

"What's that mean?" Freddie questioned.

"From point of contact, everyone moves quickly to engage the enemies' positions as soon as possible."

Cooper continued to jam magazines into their waiting pouches and turned back towards Calvin, "Where are Miles' men supposed to meet us?"

"I told him that I would meet back up with him at nine."

"Perfect. I'm meeting the men we hired from Portland at nine, as well. Hopefully they are on time."

"Yeah, travel from Portland to here is iffy at best," Freddie added.

Cooper nodded and continued. "So, let's meet here," he said pointing to a road junction on the map. Calvin leaned in to see it.

"At ten," he asked.

"Sounds good," Cooper responded.

Dranko slammed home a magazine into the M4 he carried to get their attention.

"As much as I hate to waste the gas, we will need to move out of here in a haphazard fashion."

"Why?" Freddie asked.

"Well, if Hodges has an ounce of brains, he'll have us under some kind of surveillance. If we all tear out of here at once, it will be too easy for them to follow us and too easy to know something is up."

Cooper agreed, "That makes sense. You and I should drive out first. If someone is doing some tailing work, they will follow us. Then, Calvin and Buck should drive out to Miles' spot. Finally, Freddie and Angela should leave last and just meet us at the ten o'clock rendezvous location. Sound good?"

"Sure. I will wait twenty or so minutes after you leave," Calvin added.

"That's good. If you see someone tail you out of here, do your best to lose them," Dranko said, stating the obvious.

"Same will need to be done at Miles' place. Leave in separate groups. He probably would have them under the microscope, too," Cooper said.

"I will handle it," Calvin answered.

"Everyone ready," Dranko asked.

Cooper cleared his throat.

"I want to say something before we go out there," he said. He paused for a moment, looking each of them in the eye. He liked what he saw: friendship, sympathy, and support. *There is no greater feeling in the world than being with people you know will have your back in a life or death situation.* His heart swelled.

"I just want to thank each of you." Others immediately tried to stop him, but he plowed through their protests.

"What you are doing today, I will never forget. You are risking your lives to save *my son*. You aren't just fighting for your own survival. You could walk away. From this moment forward, I owe each of you my life. If it is ever needed, it is there for each of you." Despite his efforts, his voice cracked as he finished.

A long silence filled the room. They looked at each other, soaking the moment in. Warm smiles that spoke volumes without a word were exchanged across the room.

"Heck, I woulda settled for a Big Mac, but I'll take it!" Freddie broke the silence with a deadpanned delivery and the room exploded in laughter before the group devolved into a flurry of hugs and high fives. Eyes were wet and hearts were warm by the time they had finished.

"Let's do this," Cooper said as he and Dranko left the cabin and scrambled into his Jeep.

****

They drove toward the rendezvous location with the hired men from Huynh's gang. Silence ruled the cab, as neither man had anything to say. Cooper was preoccupied with reviewing the plan of attack over and over in his head. His stomach was tight. Thinking about his son in danger maddened him. He worried about what was being done to him. He wanted him safely back in his arms. He cursed himself for not being there when the men had come to take him.

A black Toyota Forerunner was parked at the intersection when they got there. Two men remained inside the front seats, while the other four had dismounted. They were dressed in green camouflage; pant legs bloused at their boots. They all wore bulletproof vests, while three had additional body armor on their legs and arms. Each wore a helmet on his head, with goggles affixed to the front. The weapons they carried were an equal mix of AK-47s and M4s. Vests carrying multiple magazines for their respective weapons were strapped over their body armor and their faces were stern, emotionless. Cigarettes dangled from half the men's lips. They were taking deep drags and blowing clouds of smoke upward or to the side.

Dranko tapped his horn gently, flashed his headlights a couple times, and approached at a slow pace.

"You don't want to surprise armed men," he mused as much to himself as to Cooper.

He pulled the Jeep in behind the Toyota. Once they were at stop, they exited the vehicle.

One of the other men stepped forward from the others. He lifted his goggles up, so that he could make eye contact with them. He was young, in his later twenties. He had sharp, dark, eyes that surveyed Cooper as he extended his hand.

Cooper took it and the man's grasp was firm, "I'm Cooper."

"Nice to meet you. I heard a lot about you from Mr. Huynh. I'm Jason."

Cooper mustered a smile, "What'd he say?"

Jason demurred, "Just that you were a man of your word. A straight talker."

He nodded in response, "Fair enough. He's a good man to deal with."

Jason cocked his head to one side, "And, he's a good boss to work for. Should we get down to business?"

Cooper motioned Dranko forward and the trio walked to the hood of the Jeep. Dranko spread out the map that showed the area where Jake was being held. They reviewed the plan with Jason first. He had a few questions that they answered in turn. Then, he brought his men in for a briefing. They talked through the plan.

Cooper pulled out a picture of Jake and showed it to the gathered men, "This is my son, Jake. Take a good look. I don't need him getting killed in the attack. Be careful, please." The men who were clustered about him were a hard-looking lot. It was clear to Cooper that Huynh had sent some of his better men. Experienced. Still, he saw them nodding in rapt attention. He guessed several of them had children of their own and hoped that connection would compel them to be careful during the attack.

Jason spoke, "Our men will pay good attention, but you know there's a risk."

Cooper nodded gravely, "I do. Thanks."

Dranko explained to them the location from where they were going to jump off into the attack.

"Any other questions?" Cooper asked the men.

"We need the gold now. Weapons after the attack," Jason's

voice was firm.

"Sure thing," Cooper said and motioned to Dranko to retrieve the pouch holding the gold from the Jeep.

Dranko handed it to Cooper. In turn, he motioned Jason to step away from the other men with him. They slowly walked side by side down the asphalt.

"I have to ask you one thing," Cooper began.

"What?"

"Why aren't you just hauling me in? I'm worth far more than this bit of gold."

Jason laughed, "That's a good question. The boss would have to answer it. But, my guess would be that you have been very good for business. The greater the chaos, the greater the business opportunity. You get into the authorities' hands; the chaos would probably go down. You get it?"

Cooper smile was rueful, "Yeah, I don't like it, but I get it."

"Now, I have one question for you."

"And?"

"If you were that worried about us just nabbing you and turning you over for the reward, why'd you even call us?"

Cooper didn't miss a step, "That's easy. I had no choice. We didn't have enough firepower to get my boy out. I had to take the risk and hope."

Jason's smile withered from his face, as he turned serious, "I get that. I have a six year old son and I'd risk anything if he was in danger."

"Thank you. I need the best from your men."

Their eyes fixed on one another, "You'll have it. Mr. Huynh was very clear about that. He wants our work to be solid. Always. And, most of my men have children of their own."

He reached out and handed him the pouch full of gold. When Jason took it, he extended his hand and they shook once more. The grip was firmer this time. Then, they separated and made it back to their vehicles.

Dranko was already sitting in the Jeep when Cooper got back in.

"What was that all about?" He asked.

"I had to find out why they weren't just hauling me in for the reward."

Dranko grunted, "I was wondering about that myself. I figured it was a very high risk, but didn't want to bother you with it."

"You went into this, thinking it could be a trap?" Cooper's tone revealed his surprise.

"Sure did, brother."

"Damn, you are a good friend."

Dranko shrugged, "Nah, I just know something to be true."

"What's that?"

"You'd have done the same for me if the shoe was on the other foot."

Cooper gave his friend a warm smile, "True."

"So, what'd he say?"

"He said I'm good for business because of the chaos I've caused. And, I'm better for business while on the loose." Dranko heard the sorrow in his friend's voice.

"Sorry, brother. But, look at the bright side."

Cooper turned to look at him, "*You're* telling me about the bright side? The apocalypse must truly be upon us!"

"That I am. As much as you don't like it, it *is* keeping you from getting kidnapped and turned over to the government."

A forlorn grimace took hold of Cooper's face, "I guess. But that's gotta be the worst 'bright side' I've heard in my entire life."

Dranko made a mocking low bow, "Forgive me, sir. I don't have much practice."

That brought a chuckle from Cooper.

****

Their vehicles were stacked upon the side of the road, about a half-mile from where Jake and Julianne were being held. Cooper closed his eyes deliberately and sniffed the air, trying to calm his nerves. The pine was heavy with a faint hint of lavender mixed in. He was pacing up and down the line of pickups and SUVs. They were waiting for one more, carrying two more men from Miles' group. Cooper couldn't remember being more amped up before an action than he was now. *A lot more at stake than any time before.*

He edged up to Freddie, who was puffing on a cigarette at the end of the line.

"Can I have one?" Cooper asked.

Freddie's eyes opened in surprised, but he quickly recovered, "Sure. The first one's free. The second will cost you a pound of gold!" Freddie's quip was nearer the truth than not. Cigarettes were quickly becoming very scarce and expensive. Dranko was endless in

241

pontificating about the stupidity of being addicted to any substance.

"I won't be having another. I just need something to calm my nerves before we do this thing," Cooper responded seriously.

Freddie fished the pack out of his pocket and handed a cigarette to Cooper.

"Yeah, that's what I said two weeks ago. Now, I'm hooked like a heroin addict."

Cooper took the cigarette into his mouth and leaned in so that Freddie could light it with his Zippo. He inhaled deeply. He hadn't smoked in a long time and coughed loudly. Freddie smiled at him.

"Been a while?"

"Not since basic training. I tried it then but it never took." Cooper's cigarette glowed again as he pulled in another drag. The rush from the nicotine was already hitting him. *I need every advantage today.*

Freddie saw the pleasant look on his face, "You feeling it?"

Cooper nodded, "I figure it will make me a bit more alert. I need anything that will help today."

The two men puffed away without saying another word. By the time he had finished his, Cooper's head was buzzing. He felt more *awake* than he had. As his heel crushed the butt on the roadway, the final pickup came whining over the hill and eased into a spot behind the last vehicle.

"Right on cue," Freddie mused.

"Thanks," Cooper said as he strode toward Dranko's Jeep, where the map was spread out. This was where they would do the mission briefing. As he walked down the line, he called out to those around him to gather round. The word quickly spread down to the farthest vehicle at the head of their queue. Men quickly finished cigarettes, adjusted their gear, were woken up by their friends, and assembled around him after a few minutes' delay.

Dranko had taped the map up onto the Jeep's driver-side door and everyone crowded around it. Cooper motioned the front rank to kneel or crouch so that the second rank could see it clearly. The groups clustered by those that they knew best. The Asian gang members were off to Cooper's left, in the second row. Miles' group, which included seven men and a woman, were to his right, evenly split between the two rows. His friends did the same, filling up the space directly in front of him.

He reviewed the plan once again and liked that it was simple. He knew no plan survived the point of first contact with the enemy. So, he reasoned, a simple plan was even more needed with a group of

242

largely untrained people. He was hoping that Hodges' men were also inexperienced. If they weren't, it would likely be a bloodbath in the wrong direction.

He was having Huynh's men perform the flanking move around the left and to attack from the rear. He remembered reading somewhere, possibly in Sun Tzu's *Art of War,* that men fighting for money should be used in a way that minimized their casualties. Mercenaries usually didn't fight as hard as men fighting for kith and kin or their homes. Angela and two men from Miles' group would form the sniper group. Angela was placed in charge of that group. The rest were divided into two fire teams that would attack from the front. Cooper would lead one made up of Dranko, Calvin, Buck, and Freddie. Miles would lead the other, composed of the people that had come with him. Cooper's group would be front and center, while Miles' would be to their immediate right. Cooper took a few questions before concluding the briefing. He saved the most important for last.

He gave a quick description of Julianne and asked them all to be alert for her. Then, he paused for affect and pulled something out from his chest pocket. He held up Jake's picture and let silence take hold.

"This is my son Jake. This is who we are after." Cooper paused again and handed the picture to the person nearest him, Freddie. "Please take a good look and then pass it along. I've already lost his mother and I *can't* lose him. Jake is eleven years old. Before all this, he was just a normal boy. Probably like your son, if you have one about his age. He liked to ride his bike, read, and play video games." Cooper wanted to personalize his son in timid hope that it would encourage those around him to fight harder to bring him home safely. His emotions came through clearly in his voice. He stopped again, collecting himself, before continuing.

Now his voice was strong, deliberate. "For those of us who live here. We *have* to win. We need to show Hodges that *our families* are off limits. All power must have a boundary. If we don't draw the line *here,* where will it *ever* be drawn? Can he come for our children? Our wives? Our daughters?" Cooper let the words fall and hang in the air. He wanted Miles' men to know that they were fighting as much for their own families as they were for Jake. He looked into their eyes and saw the intensity that he had hoped for.

"Any questions?"

Jason spoke from the back of the group, "What is our jump off time?"

Cooper looked at his watch, "Eleven. That should give you enough time to loop around the back of their position."

Jason nodded. He gathered his men in a short huddle and they set out first.

"We move out in ten," Cooper called to those that remained. He could feel the tension and nerves hanging in the air. He couldn't tell if it was real or he was imagining the sharp tang of nervous sweat bleeding into the scent of pine. There was no denying the acrid smell from those clustered in a small group that were nervously puffing on cigarettes like steam locomotives. Cooper used the time to double-check his equipment and weapons.

Dranko sidled up next to him. He leaned in and pulled the flap from one of his pockets back so Cooper could look inside.

"I got one left," he said, as Cooper saw a fragmentation grenade cradled in the pocket.

Cooper smiled, "I'd forgotten about that. You'll know when to use it."

Dranko frowned, "I hope so."

He chambered a round into his pistol and then did the same for his rifle. He found the sounds reassuring.

"Lock and load," he called out to the group and then waited as the sharp sounds of metal hitting metal resonated as each worked their bolts. He didn't want anyone doing this when they were in position and have the sound give them away.

"Now, safeties off." Again, he waited as they complied.

"Alright. Now, your safety is your finger. Keep it *out* of the trigger guard until you are ready to shoot. These guns won't go off by themselves. Don't get nervous and put your finger in until it's go time. If you see someone getting lazy or stupid, nudge them. An accidental discharge might kill your friend and it definitely will blow our surprise. Got it?" Cooper delivered the lecture because he knew he was dealing with inexperienced people who needed to be walked through it, point by point.

Anxious heads nodded around him. He saw how they deliberately pressed their trigger fingers against the outside of their trigger guards. Some did it so hard that their fingers turned white. Nervous tongues licked dry lips, hands tightly gripped their weapons, and color drained from their faces as the adrenaline was dumping into everyone's bloodstreams. *This is it.* Cooper decided on one last piece of advice.

"Now, everyone take a long, deep breath. Remember to

244

breathe!" He saw chests rise and fall as they did so. *I have to hope they hold together and no one panics* before *the bullets start flying.*

He recalled something else he'd heard once. He couldn't remember if it was from his father or his drill instructor. *When the bullets start flying, men do not fight for country or for any cause. They fight because they don't want to let their buddies down.*

Cooper called out, "Remember, we have to count on *one another*. If we do, we will get through this." He made sure he made eye contact with each of them, to drive the message home. "Alright, let's move out."

"Right, Sarge!" Freddie called out with a mocked up tone of bravado. Most everyone laughed. Cooper guessed it was more to release nervous energy than the humor.

As they walked down the road, they separated into the three groups. Angela and the other two sharpshooters were in front, Cooper and his team in the middle, and finally Miles' group. There was some small talk as they first set out, but it quickly disappeared after a few minutes. The only sound from the group was the rustle of clothing as they walked and the occasional clang as metal touched metal. Whenever that happened, the person repositioned the offending object so that it wouldn't happen again or became more careful in how they carried their weapon. Cooper was impressed when he saw them doing this without being told. *Self-preservation is a powerful motivator.*

They had button hooked across the road and were making their slow advance through the trees and underbrush to get into position near the cabin where Jake was being held. Their progress was painstakingly slow. Movement was limited to crawling and the occasional crouched jog. Cooper kept a steady eye on his watch as the minutes ticked by. *We're gonna make it.*

He and his team reached their position at 10:50. Miles' group had safely taken cover a few minutes before. Meanwhile, Angela's group was still working their way down the opposite side of the road and hopefully would cross and get into position in time.

Cooper lay on his back and did his best to follow his own advice and keep breathing deeply. He had exchanged a few breaths when he heard something that made his stomach leap into his throat.

The high whine of a truck's motor roaring closer.

Chapter Fourteen

Every muscle in Cooper's body tensed. All his senses immediately heightened. The green foliage around him became a deep emerald forest of trees, ferns, and brush. The scent of pine turned to an invigorating rush. His clothing turned to a raspy mess against his skin. The engine's whine was a roar assaulting his eardrums and he could hear the nervous breath of those around him.

A pickup truck crested the hill to his left. It was moving so fast he half-expected its wheels to leap from the pavement as it did so. His vision sharpened. He saw a white haired man behind the wheel. He thanked God that its bed was not full of armed men. His mind raced furiously, recalculating their plan and trying to assess the best path forward. He clamped the fear that rose in his belly as frantic thoughts of Jake and doubt about the rescue plan cascaded up from deep within.

The truck sped across the asphalt and his field of vision. Break lights flared red; tires screeched and white smoke leapt from the tires as it reached the driveway that led to the cabin. The pickup careened as it made the turn and the body leaned precariously to the side; a threatened rollover that was narrowly averted. Cooper's brain told him to drop his focus and to scan the area. A man was running towards a sandbagged position set up to guard the entrance. A makeshift gate made up of a felled tree on a metal swivel blocked the vehicle's path. Two other men were moving into flanking positions on either side of the truck.

It skidded to stop just inches from the tree-made barricade. A cloud of dust flew past the truck as it stopped. The nearest guard waved his arm about him and sputtered with a coughing fit. Cooper's line of attackers looked toward him expectantly as a group. His gut screamed at him to hold and he held up one finger signaling them to wait. Still, he cursed himself for his indecision. *Act for Christ's sake,* his mind assailed him.

He spurred his gaze back to the pickup. The guard had recovered and was holding his rifle at the ready, pointing it at the driver. He was dressed from head to toe in hunting camouflage, but the rifle was of a military-pattern that Cooper did not recognize. A long, slender magazine butted out from underneath.

"Help me!" The voice screeching from inside the cab was a woman's. "Someone's chasing me!" The shrill cry of distress pierced the forest floor.

Cooper blinked, did a double take, and looked again at the driver. She was yelling, tossing her head back and forth in clear panic. As her face turned in Cooper's direction, it hit him.

It was Lily Stott! His mind reeled to process the information. *What the hell?*

The guard was taken aback by the elderly woman's plea for aid. The muzzle of his rifle dipped a few inches. Cooper could make out the curious frown that alighted on the man's face. He took a few cautious steps toward the pickup's cab.

"Help me, please!" Lily's voice fell from the loud scream to a plaintive cry. "I've been shot! I'm going to die!" The last word fell away into the air. Her hands left the steering wheel and fell toward her body. Cooper presumed to staunch the bleeding. *Who shot her?* His mind struggled to catch up to the swift moving drama unfolding before him.

Her last cry catapulted the guard into action. He ran the last few steps to the driver's side of the truck in response to her desperate plea. His look of confusion had transformed to one of deep concern for the injured old woman. As he drew alongside the vehicle, his eyes went wide in surprise.

BOOM! Cooper's body jerked in surprise. A cloud of smoke erupted from inside the cab. Crimson spray spouted out from the guard. His rifle dropped from his hands, which jumped towards his throat. The guard fell backward, stumbling. *Lily shot him,* Cooper's mind registered. The door of the pickup swung open and a glint from a revolver hit his eyes as Lily brought it to bear on the other guard, positioned about fifteen yards to her left.

"Now!" Cooper bawled at the top of his lungs.

****

He went to a kneeling position and drew a bead on the guard to the right of the truck. The man was turning toward the truck in a confused, jumbled reaction. Doing so exposed his profile to Cooper for an easy shot at fifty yards.

Cooper squeezed the trigger, the adrenaline coursing through his veins. His rifle thundered, the deep-throated roar of the .308 cartridge exploding. Flame and smoke bellowed from its muzzle. His shot went wide. He had rushed the shot. *Damn!*

To his right, another rifle fired. This one missed, too. The man was pivoting toward the newly found threat. He fired wildly as his rifle turned. Fire spewed from the muzzle of his AR-styled rifle with each haphazard shot.

Cooper drew a quick breath, steadied his rifle, aimed, held his breath when it was half released, and deliberately squeezed the trigger. A puff of white down burst outward from the guard's chest. A blank look of shock gripped the man's face for a moment. In that split second, every detail of his face etched its way forever into Cooper's mind. Piercing green eyes. Crow's feet running outward from those eyes. Thin lips, chapped white in chaotic lines. Flared nostrils. A short, jagged, scar on his left cheek. Hazelnut hair tufted out from underneath a green stocking cap. His eyes looked right at Cooper. A distant, sorrowful, dying look as the light ebbed out of them even before he was dead. Then, he slowly collapsed onto his side. He knew he would see this nameless man's face in countless dreams in the nights to come. Despite the claims from Hollywood, killing another person always exacted a price.

He rotated to his left to check on Lily. She had dispatched the guard to her left. He lay sprawled over a set of logs that had formed his defensive position. He was face down, but still moving from side to side. It looked like he was trying to regain his feet, but weak arms pushing against the logs failed to succeed. Blood oozed from his mouth and dripped onto the forest's carpet.

He lost sight of Lily as she withdrew from the driver's side door. He saw a glimpse of white hair above the bed, halfway to the truck's rear. A cascade of shots rang out and the truck paid a heavy price. Glass shattered as bullets peppered the cab. He heard the sharp, metallic puckering sound that shells will make when piercing metal. Lily emerged once again, taking up a prone position behind the pickup truck. *That crafty, smart woman.*

Cooper turned back to the front of their position. To his left, Dranko had already moved up about ten yards, taking cover behind a fallen tree, ferns growing upward from its body. Muzzle flashes flared from two of the cabin windows and from several positions scattered on either side of it. That sound was then dwarfed by another that made Cooper's skin crawl.

The shrieking buzz saw racket made by the machinegun came to life. It was set up about thirty yards in front of the cabin, in a carefully arranged sandbagged position. Flames that looked to be ten feet long leapt from its muzzle. Cooper was surprised that he could hear the sharp tinkle as spent shell casings ejected out and clattered against the metal tripod or ammunition boxes below the sandbag line.

The machinegun spat destruction at the pickup truck. It seemed to visibly wither and shrink under its fire as its heavy-caliber bullets struck home. True enough, the cab collapsed on its right side as the pillars supporting it were torn off or destroyed by the machinegun. Two men manned the machinegun, one firing and the other feeding the belted ammunition. It had a voracious appetite as countless rounds sped through its jaws. They wore the visage of the confident look of men feeling invulnerable behind such a fearsome weapon. Cooper imagined, more than saw, malevolent smiles creasing their camouflage stained faces. He involuntarily cringed when he saw them both wearing helmets and body armor.

His morale sagged for a moment as the heavy odds against them hit him square in the belly. His heart cried out against his fear-gripped gut. He summoned courage by willing himself to remember the feeling of his son's embrace and then screamed a guttural battle cry that sounded like that of a rabid animal. His brain came back into the fray and he knew they had precious seconds before the machinegun crew turned their attention towards them.

He disregarded caution and scrambled across the distance to where Dranko lay, fully exposing himself, trading speed for safety. A sole bullet whizzed past him, splitting the air as it did so.

He thudded heavily onto the ground next to Dranko, his ribs crying out in pain as he landed.

"We gotta get that machinegun now, give me the grenade!" He yelled into his friend's ear.

Time slowed to a crawl. Dranko's face turned towards his. Confusion turned to resolve as he processed Cooper's words. Their eyes held each for what seemed like an eternity. Cooper saw something deep shift in Dranko's eyes. He shook his head almost imperceptibly. When he saw the fatal, resigned look mixed with the depth of a friend's love in his eyes, his own cried out *No* before his brain could force the word out of his mouth. Dranko's rifle fell from his hands as his right shot into his pocket, pulling out the grenade. His feet churned as he clambered to his feet and then Dranko was gone, racing pell-mell towards the machinegun.

Cooper's mind whirred as he stifled a myriad of emotions that were rushing through him at what was unfolding. He scrambled to his knees, bringing his rifle to a firing position to offer what aid he could to his friend.

"Cover him!" Cooper's shout to the others sounded like the desperate plea of a heartbroken lover.

Dranko was rushing towards the machinegun nest. His run was frantic, stumbling across the uneven ground of the forest. Cooper sighted in on the men manning the machinegun and rushed shots in their direction as fast as he could pull the trigger. His shots smacked into the front of the sandbag and then into those behind the men. The smoking barrel was silent now, swinging towards Dranko. The range was pointblank for a machinegun. They couldn't miss. The others in their line were a second behind Cooper, but their guns were now blazing furiously at the machine gunners. Two rounds simultaneously hit the man feeding the ammunition and his hands fell from the belt. The gunner was undeterred and the muzzle kept coming.

Dranko's left arm jerked as an unseen defender's bullet struck home. He didn't pause and kept racing forward. He was almost in throwing range and his right arm drew back in the beginning of a throwing motion.

Cooper squeezed more shots in futility at the machine gunner and the sting of tears hit his eyes as he imagined the sure and imminent death of his friend. From the corner of his eye, he saw the small dark stain against the gray sky as Dranko hurled the grenade. Then, the machinegun spat death once more. Dranko flinched more than once as he was hit, and he fell face forward, his body slumping to the ground, bouncing once and then coming to a rest.

The world exploded with a sharp BOOM! Then, the machine and its crew disappeared under a flash of light, smoke, and debris. It had landed squarely inside the sandbagged walls. Dranko's aim could not have been truer.

****

Cooper used the deafening lull that the grenade's explosion caused to race to Dranko's side. His stomach had dropped out, a sickening feeling of emptiness that started there and extended to make his legs and arms feel numb. He scraped his knees as he slid to the ground, coming to a stop next to Dranko. He wasn't moving. Two baseball-sized bloody and bleeding exit wounds were on his backside. One was near his right shoulder and the other near his waistline, on the left. Cooper's heart leapt into his throat when he saw his body rise and fall in a shallow breath.

He dug out the ersatz first aid kit he carried and tore out the plastic-sheathed maxi pad and ripped it open. He jammed it firmly against the wound that was bleeding the worst. He was in the middle of securing it in place with a long piece of cut linen that he had when a face appeared at his side.

It was young, pink, flushed, and sweating. Blond hair fell haphazardly down his head down to his shoulders. It was one of Miles' men. Cooper couldn't recall his name.

"Let me take this!" The man was digging into what looked like a medic bag. Cooper's brain caught up. *Doug. That's his name. The EMT.*

He shook his head fervently at Doug, "I gotta make sure he's okay!"

Doug looked back with desperate eyes, "The attack is bogging down! You need to *lead* it!" His mouth was inches from Cooper's as spittle punctuated his words. They both ducked instinctively as a bullet split the air to their right, ripping past them.

His words catalyzed Cooper into action. As Doug started working on Dranko, he surveyed the area. It was true; his attackers were caught in a rough stalemate with the defenders. The advance had stopped. Given the superior cover that the guards enjoyed, a stalemated shooting contest was not a good thing. Cooper knew this. *I have to get things moving!* He glanced at his watch: 10:56am. *Had this all happened in six minutes? Where the hell are my snipers and Huynh's men?*

His heart tore at him and called him a baleful scoundrel when he turned to Doug, "Don't you dare let him die!" Doug nodded with determined, squinting eyes. Cooper crawled away, saying a silent prayer for his friend's life. It salved his conscience little.

Cooper made it about ten yards before he found a log he could peer over and assess the situation. As he was crawling, he heard the wail of one of his other men cry out behind him. *Another casualty.* He hoped it wasn't one of his friends. He focused on counting muzzle flashes and figuring out the enemy's defenses. He heard the first deeper-throated cracks from his left as the sniper crew joined the fray. They were firing heavy-caliber hunting rifles with scopes. The first volley found at least one victim. A lamenting, shriek of "Mama!" told him that.

The cabin held at least a half dozen defenders, with at least one weapon firing from both of the two windows on its front side and several gun ports that had been cut through the walls. Spread along the forested area were at least ten other men, clustered singly or in a few pairs in hastily built defensive positions.

Calvin was at his side now. His dark face glistened with the sweat of exertion.

"What is the plan?" He asked. He rolled over and began

readying himself to fire upon the enemy's position without waiting for an answer.

Cooper rolled onto his back and fished the hand held radio out of his pocket.

"Hook One, this is Eagle One. You read? Over." He used the call signs that they had developed before the attack.

Seconds passed and then he repeated himself.

His radio squelched, "Eagle One, this is Hook One. Over." Jason's voice was calm on the other end.

"Where the hell are you? Over." Cooper abandoned the radio protocol in the heat of the moment.

"Encountered resistance. Eliminated. ETA is 3 minutes to engagement. Over." Jason maintained radio formality.

"Hurry. Need Aggressive flank attack. Over."

"Wilco. Over."

Cooper rolled back over and put his mouth next to Calvin's ear. He was steadily firing every couple seconds. Cooper was impressed with his fire discipline.

"Work your way down the line. Huynh's men attack in three minutes. General aggressive advance forward to take advantage of the surprise."

Calvin nodded and then backed away until he was under good cover. Then, he turned around and crawled back toward the others. Cooper replaced him and began looking for a target of opportunity. His vision narrowed and sharpened. The firing had died down considerably and lonely shots rang out every five seconds or so. *Most of these men are untrained and are interested in hiding more than in fighting.*

Movement caught his eye. To the left side of the cabin, mottled clothing moved against a bevy of green ferns. The position was oriented to defend the cabin's right side and it had inadequate cover from the angle Cooper had. He sighted in the FAL. The man opposite him was facing in the other direction, working the bolt on a hunting rifle, readying himself to shoot back at the snipers hidden amongst the trees to that side. The range between them was about a hundred yards.

Cooper drew a bead on the man's back, breathed in, released half of it, and then squeezed the trigger steadily until the rifle bucked against his shoulder; surprising himself when the rifle finally roared. He'd kept his focus on the front sight while firing, but shifted to the where the target lay. He'd missed just inches to the man's left. The man quickly rolled to the other side, onto his back, and was desperately searching for the source of the new threat. Cooper didn't give him time.

253

The way he had rolled and lifted his upper body off the ground to search for his adversary, now gave Cooper an even better target. He lined up his sights and carefully fired again. This time, the bullet struck the man. It hit him in the chest. His face went wide in shock and then he stared at his chest for several long seconds. It was like he couldn't believe that he had just been shot. Then, his face went white, blood dribbled out of the corner of his mouth, and then his body went limp.

Cooper didn't pause to reflect, but resumed his search for another target. Gunfire was sporadic all around him, but he could not get a good look at anyone. He grounded himself, eyes barely peering over the log. Instead, he figured out the next place of cover he would advance to once Huynh's men attacked. The wait was interminable. Adrenaline was thick in his blood, every muscle grating at the inactivity forced upon them, and his heart raced in anticipation. He pulled the bolt part way back, visually double-checking that a cartridge was chambered. Dull brass stared back at him, confirming it. He knew the act was unnecessary, but he was desperate for something to do while he waited. He took the opportunity on a more needful task, pulling out the partially spent magazine and inserting a fresh into the rifle. He loaded each magazine to nineteen rounds, instead of the twenty it could hold. In his experience at the firing ranges, loading them to capacity made jamming more likely.

Suddenly, a man was running across the open ground, back towards the cabin. *Madness! He must have panicked.* Sure enough, the man carried no weapon. Cooper gritted his teeth, cursing the necessity of what he had to do. He drew a bead and fired. He'd guessed the man's speed wrong and led him too much as the bullet whacked a tree a few inches in front him. A sane man would have hit the deck and sought cover, but he kept running. Cooper re-sighted, breathed, and fired again. The man fell to the ground abruptly, as if his legs had suddenly given out. The puff of fibers spilling into the air showed Cooper he had hit him squarely in the side, just above the waistline. Bitterness flooded Cooper's mouth at shooting a fleeing, unarmed, man. *That man might have made it to the cabin, been rearmed, and come back into the fight.* His rationalization calmed his piqued conscience, at least for now. He gritted his teeth in renewed determination, *everything for Jake.* Yet, his conscience would not be silent: *Even a part of your soul, Cooper?* This time the answer came back with no hesitation. *Yes, anything. Even that.*

A fusillade of gunfire rang out from slightly behind the cabin and Cooper knew their best chance to advance and take the cabin had arrived.

****

He gathered his legs underneath him. Fear screamed at him to stay put and hug dirt, but his mind won.

"Charge!" Cooper yelled with encouragement from the top of his lungs, to benefit those around him.

He rose up and fired blindly, his rifle at his hip, as he ran forward. He knew his chances of hitting anyone was zero, but he hoped that bullets flying through the air would keep at least some of their enemies' heads down. Around him, he heard similar fast-paced gunfire, as his men mimicked the tactic, just like they had discussed before the attack.

His boots pounded the ground, making the best time he could over uneven ground. His ankle cried out in pain as it was nearly turned when it slipped into a hole. He jerked it free and pressed on. He leapt over another fallen log before a bullet zinged by his right ear. He fell to the ground on reflex. In front of him, he saw a muzzle flash from the cabin. Someone was firing at him from a porthole of sorts. The rifle's barrel poked out and eyes peered out from behind it. Cooper gave a silent prayer of thanks when he saw the barrel was quivering slightly.

A mini-fireball leapt from the muzzle and a round hurtled over him, to his right. Cooper aimed his rifle and fired a half-dozen snap shots at the porthole. He hoped to either hit the man behind it or at least scare him enough so that he'd withdraw from the position. When he peered through the smoke, the muzzle of the enemy's rifle lay resting in the dirt. He could not tell if he had, in fact, hit the man or if he had simply pulled back and left the rifle. Cooper charged forward.

Gunfire rang out all around him. To his left, and behind him, he heard someone cry out in agony as one of his men was hit. He did not waste the time to look behind to see who it was. To his right, he heard someone yelling, "I surrender, I surrender!" Behind the cabin, he heard the racket as Huynh's men lay down a barrage onto the cabin's defenders. His lungs burned as he sprinted towards the cabin. His heart felt like it was going to explode. His legs were lead weights and his muscles protested his commands to lift them again and again, but he pressed on.

He was surprised when he crashed into the cabin's log walls unscathed. His back pressed into the logs. To his right, another defender lay completely exposed to him, unaware anyone had made it this far. He was quickly dispatched.

A barrel poked out from another porthole to his left. Cooper stepped back, jammed his own rifle into the hole, and fired. A shrieking scream was the response. Those in the cabin were now in a very bad tactical situation. Up close, it was easier to shoot in than shoot out.

Cooper crashed the butt of his rifle against the door.

"Surrender and you'll live!" He yelled, trying to get his voice to rise above the din.

"Surrender and we will let you live!" He shouted again.

Someone else had heard him from outside the cabin and the same cry was raised to those who defended the cabin on the outside. There were several seconds of confusion as shots continued to ring out, but gradually lessened to silence.

A tentative voice emerged from the cabin, "How do I know we can trust you?"

"You don't. But, you're going to die for sure if you don't throw down. Like shooting fish in a barrel, you ever hear that?" Cooper yelled back inside.

Seconds passed as a hurried conversation took place inside.

"OK, we're coming out! Hodges don't pay us enough for this shit!"

"Come out, arms up!" Cooper instructed them loudly.

He positioned himself so that he could cover the door well. Slowly, the door edged open. The first man that came out was in his fifties, gray beard with a shemagh covering his head. Piercing blue eyes blazed from a man who did not like losing.

"You got us good, you bastard," he said as he exited, hands up.

"Where's my boy?"

"That sniveling brat yours? He's inside. We didn't hurt him," the man responded.

Cooper snarled at the insult, but his joy at the rest of what he'd said was overwhelming. His impatience overtook him.

"Get out quickly, hands up!" Cooper yelled. A half-dozen others filed out, hands up, heads down. Outside the cabin, the surrender was proceeding apace as the defenders emerged as individuals or pairs from their defensive positions.

Once the last man was out, Cooper left them under the guard of Calvin and rushed inside the cabin.

The stench nearly overwhelmed him. He spotted two dead bodies. One on the side he had advanced from and the other on the rear of the cabin. Blood pooled with defecation on the floor near the dead men. He guessed some of the other men had urinated, or worse, in their pants as the battle unfolded. Light cascaded in from the gaps in the wooden boards that had been nailed to cover the windows.

There were two chairs in the middle of the room. Their occupants wore hoods, had gags jammed into their mouths, and were tied down. Jake and Julianne! Tears filled Cooper's eyes as he raced to the smaller of the two figures. His rifle clattered to the ground. His pocketknife was in his hand when he got there.

He ripped the hood off of him and untied the gag in one fluid motion.

Jake's eyes blinked. His face was dirty. Dried blood ran down from the left side of his mouth and his lip was gashed there. His eyes were puffy, from crying and lack of sleep, no doubt. At first, he shrunk backward when he saw a tall imposing figure standing over him. His eyes dilated to the light and then his eyes grew wide. His mouth moved, but no words came out. His eyes filled up and glistened, wet.

Cooper knelt to the ground and sawed at the bonds that held his arms behind him and then those against his feet. His wrists and ankles were chafed and bloody. Cooper scooped his son into his arms and lifted him from the chair. He felt like a feather in his arms. Jake pulled his head back, looking at his father's face in disbelief, as if he was trying to convince himself that his father was truly holding him in his arms.

Cooper's heart was torn in two when sound finally came from Jake. He wailed like a wounded animal. He sobbed deeply, his body wracking against Cooper's hold. Relief gushed from him. The shock of rescue overwhelmed him. He held his son tightly against him, never wanting to let go. Someone else came in and tended to releasing Julianne. He saw it from the corner of his eye.

He knelt down and placed Jake's feet on the ground. He cradled his face in his hands, "Are you alright? Are you really OK?"

Jake nodded slowly. His own eyes were still wide with disbelief.

"I thought…I was…going to…die," he sobbed between each painstaking word.

Cooper pulled him into his arms once again, "I know, son. You are safe now."

Jake's body pulsed against his as the tears continued.

Cooper turned to Julianne. Her face was a bloody mess of caked blood, swollen eyes, and deep purple bruises. Her lips were swollen and cut in several places. Tears ran down her face. A puddle of urine lay under the chair.

"What happened?" He asked purely from shock.

"She fought for me," Jake surprised him by answering for her.

Her eyes were clouded by fear, but she nodded slowly.

"What?" He asked, confused.

"When they came for me, she fought. She punched. She bit. They had to hit her in the head to get her to stop." Jake's words came staccato.

Julianne's eyes simply pleaded, like an animal in pain.

He softened his look, "Thank you." His heart stirred. "Thank you," he said again, absentmindedly. Their eyes locked for a long moment. Something passed between them that hadn't yet. It scared him and he looked back at Jake.

Jake continued, excited, "She was like an animal. Clawing, hitting, biting, screaming. She scared *me!*" He exclaimed.

He looked once more at Julianne, in wonder. "Why?"

Her words came muddled by the pain and swollenness around her lips and jaw, "I just did. Something came over me. Like if I could save Jake it would make up for..." Her voice trailed off as she descending into a fit of sobbing. Cooper knew the rest.

"I understand," he said, reaching out to place his hand on hers.

She shook her head furiously, "You don't. You don't! I had to. I owed you. I owed the world! One bit of good is all I wanted!" She was frantic and yelling.

He rubbed her hand, "You did. Jake's alive. Who knows what *could* have happened."

This calmed her for a moment, but then her eyes flew wide open.

"We have to get Hodges!"

Cooper's hand dropped from hers, "What?"

She cast a gaze at Jake and worry clouded her eyes. She leaned in to whisper in Cooper's ear, so he wouldn't hear her.

"He told me he wasn't going to stop until he got you. Said he had help coming."

Cooper took a step back, buying time to think.

"Where is he now?"

She shook her head, her eyes turning morose. "I don't know."

His face turned hard, "Keep Jake inside."

He turned to Jake, "I need you to stay in here for a few minutes with Julianne. I'll be right outside."

Jake reached out and grabbed his father around the waist, "Don't leave me!"

He dropped to one knee so he could look into his son's panic-stricken eyes. Cooper wanted nothing more than to wrap Jake in the world's longest hug until his tears, fear, and pain left him, but he knew Hodges stood in the way. "There's something I need to do that I don't want you to see. I'll be just outside and I won't be in any danger at all. They've surrendered and are all disarmed."

Jake looked unconvinced, fear gripping him. Cooper stood up, plying his son's fingers from their grip on him. He looked at Julianne, who stepped in and cradled Jake in her arms, holding him back. Cooper gave him one last reassuring look and then turned to go outside.

****

The prisoners had been lined up, their weapons stacked up alongside the cabin's front wall. Angela and the snipers were clustered off to the left. Jason and the man from Huynh's gang were waiting for him. Cooper raised a finger to him, asking for a minute. Jason nodded and pulled a cigarette out from his pocket, lighting it, and walking his men a few paces further into the distance.

Cooper turned to the prisoners, "Who's in charge here?"

The men looked at the ground; no one would step forward.

Calvin caught his look and inclined his head to indicate the man with the gray beard and shemagh. Cooper stepped to where that man was and grabbed him by the collar, pulling him roughly from the line of prisoners.

"I'm guessing it's you."

The man looked up at him with fierce, defiant blue eyes.

"Whatcha want?"

"I want to know where Hodges is," Cooper said, meeting his eyes full on.

"I don't know," the man nearly spat the words at Cooper.

"Really?"

"Really."

"I don't believe you." Cooper ripped his pistol from its holster and held it next to the man's temple.

"I'm going to ask one more time. Where is Hodges?"

The man glared back at him stone faced. "He's my brother." It sounded like an excuse.

259

Cooper shook his head, "I'm going to count to three. One!"

The man flinched, emotions warring.

"Two!"

"Just tell him. Dad!" A voice screeched from the end of the line of prisoners. The face of the man in front of him fell.

"Shut your mouth, you damned pansy!" The man admonished his son.

Cooper grinned, "Well isn't this interesting? I need to know where Hodges is so that I can save my son once and for all." He walked down the line to where a younger man, in his twenties, had yelled. "Now, you can decide whether to save your son right now."

Cooper raised the pistol once again.

"Alright, I'll tell you!" The gray-bearded man said in a crestfallen voice.

Cooper walked back towards him, "Tell me."

"He's at his place. I can tell you how to get there." Cooper didn't like the tone of his voice or the way his eyes shifted when he said the word 'place'.

He looked intently at him, "Before you say another word, I should tell you. I'm going to bring your son with us. If you're lying, a bullet into his brain is the price you'll pay for dishonesty."

The man angrily kicked the dirt, "Damn you! You son-of-a-bitch! Sure, you got me. He's at Roscoe's place. He's got the Ham radio."

Cooper sneered in disgust, "Where's that?"

"I know where that is," Miles spoke up from behind him. Cooper did a half-turn towards him and nodded.

He turned back to the gray-bearded man, "You know I don't like liars. At all."

"Good for you." His voice had turned obstinate once more.

Cooper's elbow crashed into the man's face, shattering his nose. The man yelped and fell to his knees. Cooper's lips curled in disgust and his voice was icy, "No, good for you."

****

After directing Calvin to keep everyone under guard, he walked over to where Jason was waiting.

He extended his hand, "Thank you. My son is safe."

Jason shook his hand, but his face was hard. "We have a problem."

"What's that?"

"We were promised a machinegun, but it was wrecked by the grenade."

Cooper kept his face placid, "We can get you more gold. Later today."

Jason shook his head, "I don't have the time. We'll take all the M16s instead."

Cooper paused for a moment, feigning thinking, "Sure, you can have everything from these guys." His hand swept over the prisoners.

"Most of what they had were semi-auto. Not good enough. I want *all* of the M16s." His men's weapons were raised and suddenly pointed at Cooper and the rest.

Cooper cursed himself for not seeing this coming. His blood rose in anger, but he steadied himself.

"C'mon, man. I still gotta deal with Hodges. He's going to keep coming for me." His eyes pleaded.

"How's that my problem?" Jason asked, unmoved.

"At least let us keep two of them."

Jason looked at him and shook his head.

"One of them belongs to Dranko and he was shot to pieces. At least let me keep that one."

Jason's face softened, "Alright, I can do that."

"Thank you," he said grudgingly.

Everyone else had heard the conversation and, under gunpoint, the arms were exchanged. Jason let them keep the semi-automatic weapons from Hodges' men. Apparently, they weren't worth his time.

After he had the weapons in his possession, Jason approached him again.

"I hope you know this isn't personal. It's business. I do hope you get Hodges."

"Thank you. Our odds would get better with one more M16..." he smiled warmly at him, hoping for sympathy.

Jason offered a sympathetic smile, but shook his head nonetheless, "Give us a five minute head start and then you can go back to the cars."

Cooper nodded. Jason and his men retreated, keeping their weapons fixed on them until they were out of sight.

He directed his attention back to his people and sidled up next to Miles.

"Can you join me on this next thing?"

Miles nodded, "Assumed it."

Cooper clasped his hand, "Thank you. Can you find one more of your men to join us? And, can you send some men back to your place to keep an eye on Jake and Julianne?"

Miles nodded and moved out to discuss things over with his people.

Cooper only needed to exchange looks with Calvin and Angela to see that they were in.

"What do you want to do with these guys?" Calvin asked, referring to the prisoners.

"We'll lock them inside the cabin. Someone will come and find them before too long, but it will give us the time we need and they won't be able to warn Hodges."

Calvin nodded.

Cooper ran over to where he had left Dranko. He shuddered at seeing his friend wrapped in a bevy of bloodstained bandages. Doug was still with him.

"How is he?"

"He's a tough son-of-a-bitch. Honestly, I'm surprised he's still breathing. That *is* a good sign."

Dranko's eyes were closed and his breathing was shallow, raspy. Cooper had never seen him prostrated before. He looked smaller.

"How do we move him out of here without killing him?"

"Get me a few men. I will rig up a travois. That's the best we can do."

Cooper shouted, "Miles, we need three men over here. On the double!"

He turned back to Doug, "Make it happen. Get him back to Miles' place. I need to get going. Gotta deal with Hodges once and for all."

Doug nodded. Other men rushed up as Cooper darted back to the cabin.

Jake and Julianne had been brought out of the cabin and the prisoners were put inside. Two men were at work, securing the doors from the outside.

Miles, Angela, Calvin, and another man were gathered off to one side. They were readying their weapons and gear.

Cooper went to Jake's side, dropping once more to his knee, "Son. There's one more thing I need to do. To make us safe, once and for all."

Jake looked back at him, resigned. His voice was cold, "You've never lied to me before."

Cooper looked back at him, shocked, "What do you mean?"

"We won't ever be safe again." His voice was toneless, empty of feeling. His son's eyes looked vacant.

Cooper's heart dropped into his stomach. "I've got to try!" His desperate plea was as much to convince himself as his son.

Jake's voice was faraway, morose. His eyes fell to the ground. "Yeah, I know you do." They were the words of a person devoid of hope. Cooper's mind railed against the notion that his son had become that person. He struggled for something to say. He desperately wanted to inspire his son. To make him see it *would* be safe again someday. But, he could not even convince himself. And, he would not lie to his son. Finally, he gave up.

"I've got to go," he said as he stood up. He gave his son a futile pat on the head and stumbled away.

"You ready?" Calvin asked him has he approached.

Calvin's words made something click, "Oh, man. Where's Lily?" He looked about, expecting to see her standing nearby.

Calvin's eyes clouded and he slowly shook his head from side to side, "Miles found her."

Cooper pushed past him, and made a beeline to the pickup truck.

His hand came to his mouth as he rounded it, near where her body lay in the dirt, hastily covered by a rain poncho. It only covered the top of the body and her skinny legs were exposed and cast at awkward angles.

He dropped to his knees beside her. His mind was insisting there had been some mistake as he jerked back the poncho from her head.

Her head had been pulped by a direct hit from the machinegun. His lips curled back in disgust. He pulled the mess to his chest and wailed. His mind protested. *Lily was the most alive person I'd ever known. She can't be dead!* He rocked back and forth, struggling to grasp what had happened. The poncho fell away from her torso and he saw another gaping wound in her belly where another machinegun round had found a home. Grief consumed him.

"Why'd you come out here, Lily? Why'd you do that?"

"She would have wanted to die doing something worthwhile," Miles' words from behind shocked him. His words were even, emotionless. Cooper gently set her body back to the ground and covered it once more.

"I'm so sorry…" He began, but Miles waved him off.

"Later. We have work to do. You ready?" Miles' voice was steady and he met Cooper's eyes.

Cooper's mind was far away. He didn't answer, paused for a moment and then simply started walking back to where the vehicles were awaiting them. His gait was like that of a drunken man, uneven and unsteady. The quartet fell in step behind him.

Lily's death shocked him. Grief laid its consuming claim to him and he struggled to push it all away.

Jake's words deeply troubled him. So much of his son's childhood had been sluiced away in large swaths. He was unsure if any was left now. He shuddered to think of what being kidnapped and held hostage had done to him. He raged to think he had *one* more thing to do, rather than just being able to be with Jake and care for him right then. He knew he had to turn his sadness to anger and focus it on finishing the job with Hodges. His mind continued wandering as he walked. The others could tell he was deep in thought and left him alone.

A surprise was waiting for them when they arrived back at the vehicles. On the hood of Dranko's Jeep were an M16 and a bandoleer of magazines for it. When it came into view, Cooper smiled to himself. He saw a white piece of paper flapping in the wind, pinned beneath the hood and the rifle. He picked it up.

Scrawled in black Sharpie: *Use this to protect your boy.* It was signed, "Another dad."

Cooper picked up the rifle and bandoleer and held them aloft.

"You see this Dranko? Even now, even among gangsters, there is some goodness left in this world!" Cooper was beaming and laughing. Then, when he realized his friend wasn't in the group, his face fell. He was so used to him being there. Always there. He shook his head in disbelief and embarrassment. Calvin came by and put his hand on his shoulder.

"It is alright. I miss him, too."

Cooper nodded and slowly his puzzled look turned back to normal. Calvin took the rifle and the bandoleer from him. He let them go, in a daze. He shook his head in exaggerated fashion to clear it and focus back to the task at hand. The others clustered around him. He turned towards Miles.

"So, what is the best way to get to Hodges?"

"I can get us there easily enough. The trick is how to get close enough to him to *get* him."

"Can you act?" Cooper answered.

Miles' eyebrows furrowed, "What do you mean?"

"Could you convince him that you have me? That you are tired of me tearing up your community and you want it to be over?"

A wry grin spread across his face. "You thinking about that scene from Star Wars? The pretend prisoners?"

Cooper shook his head, "I don't remember that, but it is one of the oldest tricks in the book. Use your opponents' desires against them. They *want* to believe that what they want is coming to them, all nice and tied up in a bow."

Miles mused for a moment, "I can make that work. Hell, I *am* tired of you messing up our nice little town. I'm just going to solve it a bit differently than I'll be saying." Cooper smiled at him.

"We take two vehicles. You go up with your man. You tell Hodges you have me. Make sure you *ask* for something for giving me to him. That will help sell it. Then, radio us, and we'll come up. Their guard should be down a bit. Once we roll up, guns out and blazing. Everyone got it?"

The determined faces and nodding heads surrounding him told him the answer was affirmative.

"I'll say 'bring him up' if everything is going to plan. If not, I'll say, 'Get Cooper here'. Make sense?" Miles offered.

"Great idea," Cooper said, nodding and smiling.

It was odd for Cooper to see Angela behind the wheel of Dranko's Jeep. It made the world off-kilter, like the way he felt when he temporarily misplaced his car keys because he *never* lost his car keys. The ground underneath him shifted and he felt unsure of his footing. He hoped to God that Dranko would make it. It was incomprehensible to think of him being gone. Since the outbreak of the Brushfire Plague, Dranko had been such a key to their survival that he could not imagine trying to move forward without him.

Focus. A word his father had drilled into him a thousand times. *Only a focused man accomplishes anything.* His father had abhorred men who flitted from one pastime to another or who could not accomplish one task before moving on to another one. He had talked ad nauseam to Cooper about the need for focus. His father's words came now in full force. *I'm about to go into combat. I can't be thinking about Jake or Dranko.* He pushed those thoughts aside and set his mind to getting ready for the task at hand as Angela started the Jeep and fell in behind Miles' truck.

He inserted a fresh magazine into his rifle. Then, he made sure the other full magazines were in the pouches closest to his hands. This way, his reloads would be faster and he wouldn't mistakenly push in a magazine that was only half-full. He pulled his pistol out and checked it. Then, he checked it again. He continued with his anxious ritual of his equipment review. He ended by racking the slide on his pistol and working the bolt on the rifle. Both unnecessary actions, except they helped calm his nerves.

Outside, the world raced by as Angela sped to keep up with Miles who knew the roads and drove them expertly. Angela struggled to keep up with him, but managed. The sky was gray, oppressively so. He watched her face intently. It was screwed up in a look of focused determination. Eyes locked on the road. Her hands gripped the wheel tightly. The muscles on her forearms stood out in stark relief as she worked the wheel and her sleeves would pull up from time to time. He found himself smiling as he looked at her. He realized how close he felt to her. She was always *there* for him. She stirred a decidedly different set of passions within him than Julianne did, but stir them she did. She caught his gaze and an awkward smile lit across her face.

"What?" She demanded.

Cooper looked away sheepishly, "Nothing."

She smiled. He could tell she knew what was on his mind. He was surprised when he realized he was actually all right with that. Unlike Julianne, he felt no need to pull away from her. His mind drifted as he thought about...

Focus. He punched himself in the chest to break the chain of thoughts that were beginning to form in his mind. The rifle was glued to his white knuckles.

They rounded another bend in the road and Miles flashed his hazard lights several times as he slowed.

"Pull over," the radio lying on the seat between them buzzed. Miles' voice was tight, anxious.

Angela pulled the Jeep over to the side of the road. Her hand went to turn the ignition off.

"Don't," Cooper said, reaching to stay her hand.

"We need to save the gas," Angela countered.

"Not right now," Cooper responded. Angela answered by withdrawing her hand.

They watched Miles' truck travel another quarter mile and then turn sharply into a driveway. It disappeared among the trees.

"Now we wait," Cooper said evenly. He fixed his gaze straight ahead, trying to will time to speed up. His body was rigid, muscles tensed. His breath was shallow.

He was surprised when he felt Angela's hand clasp his. Her hand was warm against his hand, which was chilled by nerves.

"Breathe," she whispered. He looked at her, deep concern in her eyes. "It's going to be okay."

"Yes, it is," Calvin's deep voice resonated from the backseat.

He inhaled deeply and offered her a meek smile. He did not want to wander into her eyes, so he returned a steely gaze forward. He left his hand in hers; welcoming the comfort it brought him. They sat in silence as the moments passed.

Seconds turned to minutes as they waited. His blood pressure rose and sweat beaded across his brow. He willed the fear to stay in his belly to keep it at bay. *What's going on? Did Hodges not buy it? Is he not here?* The tumult of unanswered questions plagued him. He hated not *knowing*. He wanted to move. To act. To settle things once and for all. He could smell the fumes from the idling engine. His stomach turned.

"What is…" he started, but the radio interrupted him.

"Bring him up," Miles' voice rasped. *Everything to plan so far.* Angela put the Jeep into drive and rolled forward. She withdrew her hand. Cooper's body underwent a transformation as it always did once the action started. He breathed deeply and the anxiety dropped away like a snake shedding its skin.

"It's go time," he said. His voice was steady and sure. His eyes narrowed. His hearing sharpened. He wiped the sweat from his palms and forehead.

"Speed and surprise are our friends. No hesitation. Attack and keep attacking until it's done," he said as much to himself as to remind Angela and Calvin of the strategy.

"We will get him, Cooper," Calvin said, patting him on the shoulder from the back.

As they turned into the driveway, Cooper felt the muzzle of Calvin's pistol pressed against the back of his head. He almost spun around to knock it away from reflex, but caught himself just before.

"We have to sell this," Calvin explained. He held the pistol so that its silhouette would be prominent by anyone viewing from the front.

"Good idea. Just warn me next time," Cooper said in a weak joke.

****

Hodges' driveway was paved and the Jeep's tires found sure purchase as they drove forward. Trees crowded the driveway, blocking out the weak sun. In the distance, about two hundred yards ahead, the clearing beckoned them. Much closer, two guards toting rifles stepped onto the asphalt, blocking their approach and motioning for the Jeep to stop.

Damn! There was no time for Cooper to conceal the weapons he carried. His mind spun and decided all in a split second.

"Keep it steady and slow. As you pull up, gun it," he said to Angela.

"Calvin, take the guard to the right. I'll get the one on the left. We'll all be deafened after that," Cooper continued.

He was counting on that one-half second of delay in the guard's reaction time to get them through this. *That's all surprise buys you. One half of a second.* He hoped Miles could deal with what was about to happen on his end.

They rolled forward. The Jeep was travelling about ten miles an hour, but it felt as if they were travelling at ten inches per hour. *C'mon!* Cooper's mind cried out. The guards did not raise their weapons as they approached; they only kept them at the ready in their hands. Cooper thanked God for that. He could see their faces now. The man on the right was young with pimples emblazoned across his face. He carried a shotgun, was dressed in Carhart work clothing, and a black baseball cap with white stitching spelling out 'CAT.' The guard on the left was older, probably in his thirties. His clothing was a mottled camouflage jacket and black pants. A green knit stocking cap struggled to keep curly brown hair covered. He had a pistol on his hip and an AK-47 style rifle in his hand; likely semi-automatic.

Angela craftily slowed the vehicle down as she approached them. Cooper lifted his pistol from its holster, keeping every muscle above the dashboard still as he did so. The guards took a half step forward, closer to the Jeep. Angela floored the accelerator and the engine revved loudly. Time slowed.

Cooper lifted his pistol up and rushed off two point-aimed shots at the guard. The pair of .357SIG rounds punched through the windshield in front of Angela. Puffs of clothing exploded outward from the man's chest and he collapsed to his knees before toppling over. The sound was deafening and concussion from the pistol firing resounded within the cab. Cooper felt the muzzle of Calvin's pistol leave his head and his pistol boomed just a few inches from his left ear. Flame shot outward in front of him, his left cheek feeling the heat. This shot was even louder than his had been. Stabbing pain shot through his left ear. He guessed his left eardrum had just been ruptured. Out of the corner of his eye, he saw the guard drop out of view.

His head was ringing and pulsed from the massive concussion. His hand went to his ear and came back bloodied. The Jeep sped towards Hodges' home. He shoved the pistol back into its holster and grabbed the FAL from where it rested on his lap. The reek of cordite and the haze of smoke filled the cab. He cranked his window down. Calvin had done the same in the back. Cold air rushed in. The Jeep gathered speed and the trees to either side whipped by. In mere seconds, they were into the clearing and the light. He squinted.

Angela slammed the brakes and the Jeep came to a rapid stop about ten yards from the front of the house.

Cooper spilled from the Jeep, coming up on one knee with his rifle at the ready. His eyes scanned the porch in one fluid motion. His mind cursed in frustration.

Hodges was on the porch, just above the front steps. An antagonizing smile was impressed across his face. His feet were splayed out wide. His posture was strong, confident. Miles was standing next to him, Hodges' arm wrapped around his throat. His face was riven in fear. His eyes pleaded with Cooper's for forgiveness and mercy simultaneously. Glistening beads of sweat covered his face and neck. Hodges had a pistol muzzle pressed firmly against his head, just behind his right ear. A two-man team was facing them from the other side of Hodges. Their weapons were a mix of military-style rifles and shotguns—both deadly at this short range.

Cooper saw Hodges' mouth move, but could hear nothing of what he'd said. His could hear some muffled noises through the ringing in his left ear, but nothing out of his right.

"You'll have to yell, I can't hear a thing!" Cooper screamed.

Hodges looked confused for a moment, but then yelled. Cooper saw the veins popping on his neck.

His words were barely discernible to Cooper, despite his exertion, "Nice to see you, Cooper," Hodges said. His sanguine tone irritated Cooper. *The confidence of a man holding a Full House in a high stakes poker game.* He ached to wipe that grin off his face, preferably with a paint scraper.

Instead, he forced a smile onto his own, "Likewise." He kept his rifle up, aimed. By the actions of Hodges and his men, he guessed that Angela and Calvin were doing the same on the other side of the Jeep.

"You really do need to lower those rifles if we are to have a civil conversation," Hodges said.

Cooper's mind spun in overdrive. The flurry of options and probabilities raced through. He kept coming up empty.

"What guarantee do we have that if we throw down, you won't just kill us?" He cared less about the answer than in buying himself time. Time to think.

Hodges belly rolled in a deep laugh, "*You* have the guarantee that the Governor wants you alive. Your friends, well, they'll just have to trust me."

"That sounds very sketchy to me," Cooper willed ease into his voice.

Miles caught his eyes again. If they had been hands, they would have been gesticulating wildly. *What the hell is he trying to tell me?* Cooper couldn't discern the intended message as he saw desperation, despondence, and panic roll across Miles' face.

Hodges impatience, however, came through clearly, "I'm going to give you five more seconds and then Miles and your friends are going to get very messy."

"What does Miles think I should do?" Cooper opted for the direct route.

Miles' eyes narrowed to slits full of anger and he yelled back at Cooper, "Bethany and Mama would know. Ask them!"

Looking perplexed, Hodges turned toward Miles. For Cooper, it all fell into place. *Bethany's recent revelation of infidelity. His mother, Lily's, violent death within the hour. Miles' inconsolable depression over it. He knew Miles was telling him to take the shot while keeping Hodges in the dark.*

Cooper's own eyes squinted. His sights lined up on Hodges' head, on those gleaming teeth. His finger began depressing the trigger. Hodges knew what was coming, but he was a split second too slow to react. Cooper's rifle fired. He hit Hodges in the right shoulder. At the same time, Hodges' pistol went off. Miles' head disappeared in a ruinous red splash. Blood, flesh, and brain sprayed across and onto the two guards to his left. They both cringed under the impact. These were the men opposite Cooper, so it saved his life, buying him precious seconds to delay on their part.

He heard gunfire from the opposite side of the Jeep as he pivoted and fired at the two other men in front of him in rapid succession. They both disappeared under the fusillade of the half-dozen rounds he'd fired. Cooper ran through the haze of smoke that lay about him and ascended the stairs. He looked to his left and found the other guards down and moaning. *Calvin and Angela had done their job.*

He rushed to the downed men, kicking their weapons out of reach. The porch was awash in blood and he almost lost his footing twice as he skidded through the ooze. Two of the men were already dead. Angela or Calvin had hit one of the men in the head, while one of the men he had shot had been hit three times in the chest. The other two men were badly wounded and moaning in abject misery. Once he had ensured they posed no further threat, he looked at Hodges. He was also down, but conscious. Cooper assiduously avoided looking at Miles. He knew if he did he would be haunted forever by that image of carnage.

Cooper stole a look behind him, while shouting, "We need to secure the house!"

"In a minute!" Calvin called back. His back was to him. Angela lay on the ground and he was tending to her. Cooper was shocked to see her lying so. In the furious action, he had not seen it happen. Cooper bit the inside of his cheek to fight the worried thoughts about her condition and his desire to run to her side.

Cooper knelt to the ground, next to Hodges. He kept an eye watching the door. He wanted to move through the home and see if other threats awaited them inside.

"You're going to kill me, aren't you?" Hodges rasped through clenched teeth.

"Can you tell me why I shouldn't?"

Hodges laughed shallowly and grimaced in pain, "Probably not. Except you might need me." Through his grimace, a faint outline of the confident smile returned.

"Need you for what?" Cooper asked, taken off guard by his assertion.

"The Governor," Hodges answered, his smile turning into a smirk.

"I'm listening."

"First, the Governor knows you are here. He's sending men from Salem for you." Hodges fought for breath before continuing, "Second, you've only scratched the surface of the Brushfire Plague. I know so much more. You let me live, I'll help you avoid the Governor and tell you everything there is to know about the *real* conspiracy behind the plague." Despite the obvious pain, his smile kept growing in confidence and contempt as he spoke.

Before he could react, he *felt* the presence of someone standing over him. He had been badly distracted by Hodges' talking. He glanced up and was shocked to see Bethany standing over him. She held a bloody knife in one hand and a pistol in the other. She looked at him vacantly. Her eyes were bloodshot, tear-stained. Blood was smeared across the white blouse she was wearing.

"What are you doing…" he began, but his voice trailed off as he saw her look over at where Miles lay. A chill ran down his spine as she looked at her husband *vacantly* and devoid of reaction.

Her mouth moved automaton-like and her eyebrows furrowed, "There's nothing left, is there?"

"What do you mean?" Cooper asked.

"Everyone's dead. Everything's gone." Her voice was flat.

"Bethany dear, it will be alright," Hodges said, offering comfort.

She looked down at him, as if seeing him for the first time. Her eyes grew curious.

Cooper saw the hand holding the pistol move a few inches and she fired before he could react. He looked down in horror at Hodges' face. A neat hole was quickly pooling with blood where his right eye had been. A second pistol shot and the sound of Bethany's body falling to the ground sent Cooper over the edge. He scooted himself backward until his feet found the stairs and then he stood awkwardly, backing away from the horrid scene that had just unfolded. His brain struggled to make sense of it all. He could not connect the dots.

Instead, he turned around and focused his attention back towards to Angela and Calvin. He was still hunched over her, so Cooper bounded to her other side, kneeling down when he got there.

"How is she?" He asked. Calvin was pressing a bloodied and makeshift bandage over her right arm.

"She will be alright. I think it passed all the way through." Calvin was in the process of wrapping the bandage with a strip of his t-shirt that he had torn. Angela's face was sweaty and pale.

He reached down to stroke her cheek and her eyes fluttered open.

"You're going to be alright," he said, offering her a reassuring smile.

"I know," she responded, her mouth dry. "I'm just resting, waiting for Dr. Little here to finish me up." She managed a brief smile before a painful grimace forced it away.

He stood up in a daze. His mind raced to absorb what had just happened. His feet were numbly ascending the stairs once more, before he was even aware he was doing so. He plodded forward, step by painful step. He reached the top of the stairs and looked down. Hodges lay before him. The blood had overflowed from his eye socket and had made a neat river down his right cheek and pooled next to his head on the porch. His other eye was staring blankly skyward. Cooper shuddered; it looked so eerie. One side of his head a bloody mess, the other looking as it had in life; untouched and serene.

He could not avert his eyes from Bethany and his gaze slowly drifted to her. Her face looked peaceful in death. Her eyes were narrow slits, like she was about to doze off into a nap. She had landed on her left side. He was thankful the messier exit wound was shielded from him. On the right side of her head, a neat hole was surrounded by powder-burned flesh. Her head lay in a puddle of red, her hair matting in the coagulating blood. The bloody knife was still clutched tightly in her crimson stained left hand, while the pistol had fallen from her right. He looked once more at her placid eyes. The contrast was jarring. A chill ran down his spine and he shivered. Nausea threatened and he breathed deeply to keep it at bay.

Then his eyes went to the door that lay ajar. He knew what awaited him inside the home. Dread washed over him. Unconsciously, he shouldered the FAL and took his pistol out of its holster. He struggled for focus as he entered the home. His effort to clear the living room was lackluster and his legs ambled forward and toward the hallway that most likely led to the bedrooms. His mind called to him to make sure no other threats were in the kitchen or the dining room that lay off to the right, but his body refused him. A door at the end of the hallway beckoned him. The door was open and the doorknob was stained in blood. Muddled and bloody handprints stood out in stark relief on the door's alabaster paint.

Cooper wanted to turn around and leave. He wanted to desperately avoid seeing what he suspected lay beyond. But, the other part of him *had* to know, so he staggered onward. His pistol fell to his side.

When he reached the door, he stopped to gather himself. He sucked air in a futile attempt to calm his racing heart. His palms were sweaty and blood rushed into his head. He closed his eyes and then stepped into the room. He opened them reluctantly.

A flood of macabre images assaulted him. The coppery smell of blood overwhelmed him. He fell to his knees and retched. His hands clasped to his eyes and tears flowed.

"No...no...no," he mumbled in misery. He shook his head in denial. He did not know how long he remained on his knees, forlorn.

When he lifted his hands from his face and slowly opened his eyes once again, reality still awaited him. Bethany's children were arrayed neatly on the bed. Their hands were folded on their chests, but tied. Their throats had been slashed and blood had sprayed about. Each child was ghost white. Cooper cursed Bethany for doing such a thing and his mind sought to understand why and how she could kill her own children. Hoping against hope, Cooper forced himself to rise, walk to the bed, and check for any remaining heartbeats.

There were none.

His hand came away blood-stained and he furiously wiped it clean on the bedspread. He was a man possessed until his hand was clean once more. He ripped the closet door open and rifled through it until he found an unused blanket that he used to drape over the children before stumbling from the room.

He re-emerged into the dull gray sunlight and squinted for a moment. Calvin was on the porch, finishing up bandaging Hodges' wounded men. He stopped when Cooper stepped past the front door. He looked at him expectantly.

"The children," Cooper whispered, disbelief clouding his words.

Calvin looked confused, but asked nothing else.

"The entire Stott family dead. In one day," Cooper continued, trying to convince himself that it was real.

Calvin went back to his work, affixing a bandage, and left him in silence. Cooper looked out, past all the death that lay about him, to the tree line that fronted Hodges' property. The wind blew through them and tall evergreens swayed at their tops in the wind. In shock, his mind drifted. *Why can't I just go walk among those trees? Their sweet smell could erase the stench of blood and gore that is all around me.* He spotted a hawk circling just above the trees and was hypnotized by its graceful flight. He followed it as it circled and circled until it suddenly dropped out of sight behind them. That moment catalyzed him. *Jake and Dranko.*

"Let's go," he said abruptly, startling Calvin.

"I'm almost done," he replied.

Cooper leapt off the porch. Angela was still on the ground, bandaged, and with her legs propped up. She was resting. Her eyes fluttered open at his approach.

"Can you walk with help?"

"Yes," she answered.

He gently lifted her to her feet and slowly walked her to the Jeep, his arms supporting her. She moaned and gritted her teeth as he helped her in. As he quietly closed the door and turned, Calvin was at his side. His arms were full of the weapons from Hodges' and Miles' men. Cooper helped him stow them in the Jeep's cargo area.

"Hodges said the Governor was sending people for me. We need to get back to Jake and Dranko. They are at Miles' place."

"The ammunition," Calvin said simply.

"Right. Let's hurry."

"Wait, was Junior Hodges inside?"

Cooper stopped in his tracks and shook his head, having not even thought about him, "No. I wonder where he has slunk off too?"

"Probably still too wounded and hiding like a hurt animal."

"And, with the same moral code," Cooper finished and Calvin nodded in response.

Then, both men returned to those who had fallen on the porch and gathered up the ammunition they carried. They rushed through their work and returned quickly to dump the bandoleers and loose magazines into the back of the Jeep. Cooper bounded into the driver's seat and fired up the engine. He was jerking the transmission into 'drive' when he stopped suddenly.

"Damn!"

"What?" Calvin asked.

"It's on empty."

"That is not good."

Cooper yanked the door open, "Dranko has a siphon in here, I'm sure of it."

The small gas can was easy to find. Then, he clawed through the firearms, ammunition, and other gear in the back.

"Where is it?" he asked frantically.

"Would he hide it? You know, to keep it out of sight?" Calvin asked, at his side once again.

Cooper pointed two fingers at his head and mocked shooting himself, "Duh. Of course he would!"

He pulled open the cover where the tire jack was held. Sure enough, a siphon hose with an attached hand pump lay within. Within ten minutes, they had siphoned the two other vehicles on Hodges' property and managed about seven gallons of gas into the Jeep. The two men were moving fast, so they were bathed in sweat by the time they finished. Cooper was back in the driver's seat as he sped away from Hodges'.

"So, what did Hodges say? Exactly." Calvin asked him as they pulled onto the main road.

"Just that the Governor was sending men after me. And, that the conspiracy behind the Brushfire Plague was much bigger than even I knew."

"Did he say how many men?"

"No."

"What are we going to do? We are not exactly in fighting form right now."

Cooper thumbed his temple, "I don't know." He turned the Jeep through a tight turn before continuing. "We can't run with the wounded, either."

"Do we know how much Hodges' told them about you? Where you were staying? Things like that?"

Cooper shook his head, "No. Bethany shot him before I could interrogate him more. They might know of Dranko's place. On the other hand, Hodges' might have been keeping the information to himself. To get paid in person. Hell, I don't know if he was even interested in the reward."

"Where does that leave us, then?" Calvin asked.

"In a bind. And, a bind of unknowns."

"We should assume the worst. That they know of Dranko's place," Calvin added.

Cooper nodded slowly, "You're right about that."

"So, where can we go?"

He started to shrug his shoulders, but then his eyes sparked, "Miles' place."

Calvin took a moment to go from confusion to understanding, "Right! That is good."

"We can move as many supplies from Dranko's to his as possible. He's got crops in the ground. It's a well-supplied mini-farm. At the least, it will buy us some time with anyone the Governor sends in. At the best, it might work long-term."

"We need some disinformation," Calvin said, his voice mischievous.

He grinned at him, "What are you thinking?"

"Maybe we send Buck into town to make a squawk about you having went in and killed Hodges and that you were last seen racing out of town or something like that," Calvin was animated as he talked.

Cooper smiled, "Great idea. We could have Buck stay at Dranko's. If the Governor's men show up, he could repeat the story."

"One final thought."

"What's that?" Cooper asked.

"At Miles' place, we could try to keep you and Jake hidden as best as possible. If the Governor's men show up there, Angela and I could say that we took that place over after you skipped town on us."

Cooper grimaced and Calvin looked at him, perplexed.

"Dranko isn't dead yet," Cooper responded.

Calvin frowned, "I did not mean that…"

"I know you didn't." Cooper gathered himself. "I think this is the best plan possible. Hopefully Buck will be up for it."

The rest of the drive was in silence. Cooper was plagued by thoughts of how Dranko was doing and he raced to get there as fast as possible.

Chapter Fifteen

Cooper bolted from the Jeep as soon as they had come to a stop outside of Miles' house. He found Doug standing on the porch, smoking a hand-rolled cigarette. It smelled like pipe smoke.

Doug caught the odd look on Cooper's face, "Yes, that it is. Beggars can't be choosers."

"How is he?"

Doug's face grew grave and the corners of his mouth turned downward.

"He needs surgery. I've sent word for the best doctor we have around here…who isn't licking Hodges' boot, that is."

Cooper gritted his teeth in frustration, "When will he or she get here?"

He shot a glance at his watch before answering, "Soon, I'd guess."

"Does he have that long?"

Doug's eyes grew worried and he shrugged his shoulders in response.

Cooper staggered backward. Doug's response stole his breath and he struggled to inhale. His heart fell into his stomach and his head grew fuzzy. He grasped the nearby table to keep his feet steady.

He felt Calvin's hand on his shoulder, "He is a tough one. He is too ornery to die on us."

Cooper turned to Calvin, inhaled, and then spoke. He nodded slowly, wanting to believe it. "Thanks." He paused, before continuing, "Can you put our plan into motion?"

Calvin nodded, gave his shoulder a squeeze, and left to find Buck.

****

Dranko was sprawled on the living room couch. He was either asleep or unconscious. His face was ashen and waxy and his breath fell in uneven fits. His body was pockmarked with several bandages. Cooper gave silent thanks that they, at least, were not soaked through.

Cooper fell into a chair that was next to him. He found his friend's hand and pulled it into his. The hand was clammy and cold. Tears welled into his eyes upon seeing his friend prostrated and clinging to life. Despair consumed him.

279

"Please don't leave me, brother," Cooper mumbled. Tears fell from his eyes when he closed them. *There's been too much death. Too much.* "I can't do *this* without you," he breathed in a shallow whisper.

"About time," a weak whisper responded.

Cooper startled to hear Dranko speak. His eyes flew open. Dranko's eyes were slits.

"You're awake," he dumbly answered.

Dranko grimaced in pain, "For now." He managed a mockery of a grin. "About time you said it."

Cooper offered a warm smile, "I'm gonna tell you every day, from now on."

"Jake okay?"

His smile grew wider, "Yeah. We got him. Thank *you*."

"Good. It means something now." The tone was ominous, the words carrying a finality that jarred Cooper.

"Don't talk like that."

"You're the optimist, not me." A cough replaced his attempted laugh.

"There's a doc on the way. You just gotta hold on."

Dranko's eyes had closed as he had been talking and there was no further response.

He clutched his hand more firmly, but only silence remained. He sat for a long while, lost in his thoughts and watching Dranko. He didn't know how long he remained there.

The door flew open and he whirled around. Another man, middle-aged and bald, followed Doug. He was a short man, carrying two bags.

"Get outta the way," he commanded as soon as soon as he saw Cooper.

"Cooper, this is Doctor Jamison," Doug offered as Cooper quickly retreated from Dranko's side.

He stood off to the side, arms folded, as the doctor examined Dranko. He sat over him, intently checking vital signs in a flurry. Moments later, he was jabbing a needle into his arm and attaching a bag of plasma.

"Get me that coat rack," he blurted.

Cooper raced to the entryway and grabbed the coat rack, bringing it over. Doug attached the bag of plasma to it.

Jamison spoke again, "He needs blood. Now. You guys know his blood type?"

"A positive. He bragged once about his 'A plus' blood," Cooper answered.

Jamison looked exasperated, "Well, anyone here have that type?"

"Doug, go check Calvin and Buck!" Cooper barked.

Doug shook his head, "They left a while ago."

"Damn!"

"Angela's still outside, I'll go ask her," Doug responded, racing to the door.

Cooper's mind raced. He knew Jake's was like his own, B negative. *Julianne!*

He ran to the back of the house and called out, "Julianne!"

"Down here," her voice resounded from the basement.

Cooper took the stairs down two at a time and landed hard at the bottom. She was hunched over the computer.

"You won't believe what I..."

He cut her off, "What's your blood type?"

"Wha..." she answered, confused.

"What's your blood type," he yelled.

"I don't know. Hold on. Let me think," she said, holding up both her hands, palms out to him. She closed her eyes, thinking hard. Cooper stamped his feet in frustrated impatience, but he held his tongue.

Her eyes opened, clear, "A positive. That's right. It was years ago I had it tested. But, A positive."

He stepped in and grabbed her by the hands, "C'mon! Dranko needs it. Now!" He pulled her to her feet and then ascended the stairs as quickly as he had descended. She ran after him.

"Got it!" Cooper called to Jamison, pulling Julianne in front of him.

Jamison's face turned quickly to her, "You're A positive?"

Julianne nodded excitedly.

"Alright, he needs it now." Julianne was already rolling up her sleeves.

"You there. Move the kitchen table to the middle of the room and then clear out. We need to get this blood into him and then I have to operate." Jamison directed Cooper brusquely.

He started to object, but Jamison's stern look stopped him. He stepped to the kitchen table, ripped the tablecloth off of it, sending a few odd dishes crashing to the floor, and manhandled it to the center of the living room. Doug came back inside, his face brightening when he saw Julianne with her sleeves rolled up.

"Found some?"

"Yup! Doc told me to clear out. I'll be right outside if you need anything," Cooper responded as Doug passed him to assist Jamison.

He ran to the back of the house once again. He ripped open the doors to the bedrooms, looking for Jake. He found him in the rearmost one.

Jake was asleep, curled into a ball, oblivious to the world around him. Cooper shook him awake and then lifted him into his arms. He struggled against the weight of his growing son.

"What..." Jake said, groggily.

"A doctor is going to operate on Dranko. We need to wait outside." Cooper dragged him from the room, grabbing his son's coat as they left.

****

He and Jake were outside. It had taken Jake a few minutes to fully wake up. He had been in a deep slumber.

"How are you?"

Jake stiffened at the question, "Alright." *There it is again. The distant voice.*

Cooper's eyes clouded in concern and he reached to hold him by the shoulders, "Really?"

Jake shook his arms loose from the attempted embrace, "Does it matter?" He bristled.

"It does to me!" Cooper responded.

Jake shrugged his shoulders, "I'm alive. So, that means I'm okay, don't it?"

"I mean, *how* are you? You just went through a lot."

"Does it matter? I gotta deal with it, don't I?" His son's eyes were as dead as stone.

Cooper's heart sank, "Jake. Don't do this!"

"Do what?" His reply was cold.

"Shut down. You have to talk about what's going on. What's going on *inside*."

"Fuck that! The *outside* is a stinking pile of shit. What's inside don't count for nothing."

Cooper was shocked by the venomous profanity spewing from his son's lips. "*Please*, son. Don't." His words were desperate.

Jake looked at him like he didn't know him. He shook his head dismissively and turned on his heel and walked away. Cooper looked after him, paralyzed by what he was seeing. Jake's feet tromped across the yard. Cooper closed his eyes in despair.

"Give him some time," Angela's soft voice came from his left. She had been at the far end of the porch.

He turned to her, raised his hands up in frustration, "I just don't know what to..."

She approached him, "You don't have to know, Cooper." He shook his head, refusing her words. He paced furiously up and down the porch. She moved aside to let him pass. She went back inside. Eventually, he sat down on one of the chairs on the porch.

Julianne came outside, saw his look, and sat silently next to him. She reached out to hold his hand, but he withdrew it.

****

Doctor Jamison came outside, wiping blood from his hands as he did so.

Cooper was on his feet, "How'd it go?"

Jamison met his eyes gravely, "We got the bullets out and stopped the bleeding."

"Is he gonna make it?"

"I don't know. He lost a lot of blood. Luckily, the internal damage could have been a lot worse. His major organs are intact."

Cooper extended his hand, "Thank you, Doctor." Jamison refused the hand.

"Thank me if he lives, alright?" Jamison moved off, breathing the fresh air in.

Julianne was at his side, "Can I tell you what I found out?"

Cooper exhaled in resignation, sitting back down, "Sure."

She started to speak, but paused, emotion choking her.

"What is it?"

"We were used."

"What do you mean?"

"Mitchell and I. We were played like a damned fiddle." Her words were jagged, stopping between tears.

"Can you just tell me what the hell you are talking about?"

"This whole thing was about money. Not to save the planet!"

"What?"

"Well, I don't have smoking gun evidence yet, but the people that were working with us at Admonitus, those men I was researching, they had disinvested in America. I could write you a damned book on

283

it. Our debt. Our fiat currency about to crash. They dumped everything into China. Every dollar they had. This was about ensuring their ascendance as *the* new world power. I'm pretty damn sure of it!"

Cooper shook his head, "This can't be. What are you talking about?"

"Plainly speaking?"

"Yes, please!" Cooper nearly shouted.

"The wealthy elite gave up on America. We were a mess. Debt up to our ears. An unraveling economy. They all bet heavy on China as the place to invest. But, they just *made sure* it wasn't a bet. They *made* it a sure thing, with Brushfire Plague! Don't you see?" Her words were tear-stained.

Cooper shook his head in disbelief, "No, I don't. How'd you learn all this?"

"I've just looked into the investments these guys all made. I started with the inner circles and then I worked outward to their closest friends and so on. What I found is that there were maybe a few hundred of America's wealthiest families who all made this same bet!"

"How could you figure out they moved their investments into China?"

She smiled, "A lot of it was public record. For the rest, I had a few friends do some digging for me who had connections. I was able to get to some of them via email—that's still working sometimes. People I met working at Admonitus. Well, the ones that are still alive..." Her voice drifted.

"But, what? How'd this happen?" Cooper was tired and his mind was struggling to keep up with everything Julianne was telling him.

Julianne took a deep breath, composing herself before continuing, "Looking back, I think it started a long time ago. Think about it. We watched our manufacturing go offshore for decades without doing anything. You can't have a strong economy without it. It didn't matter which party was in control. We kept our economy propped up by debt...debt...and more debt. I think the dollar was about to collapse and become worthless. Those at the top just pulled out."

"But what did Brushfire have to do with it?"

"Think about it. China is the *only* country that seemed to be ready for it! They were hardly affected. The rest of the globe is in a world of shit. China stands ready. It was a way to *speed up* their rise as the world's new superpower! Remember America after the Second

284

World War? The rest of the world was in a shambles and we benefitted from it. We became the world's *only* Superpower."

Cooper felt the blood surging across his temples, "You mean..." He was unable to even form the question.

Julianne's face was alive with the excitement of explanation, "Yes! They wanted to just make China happen *now! And*, if you had invested everything you had there, guess what? Your wealth wouldn't just be protected, it would multiply beyond belief!" She finished, breathless.

"I don't want to think about it. It's too much." Cooper said, waving his hands. He stood up quickly and walked away.

"But you have to, Cooper. The websites still up are on fire about the Chinese sending troop ships over. Right now! They will likely start landing in a few weeks."

Cooper shook his head in despair, "What?"

"Well, you know how we've had scattered reports of police and military with their medical personnel?"

He nodded wearily.

"I think those reports were favorable enough for the Chinese to green light a full-blown invasion," she was breathless.

Cooper could muster only a lackluster nod of his head. "Well, at least there is some good news?"

Julianne cocked her eyebrows and drew back in surprise, "What's that?"

"The bastards gave the world too much of a dose and the planet that China will inherit is a big stinking pile," Cooper's words dripped with dark sarcasm. Julianne shuddered when she saw the black look on Cooper's face.

He went back inside. His heart ached and he was despondent. Angela and Doug were still cleaning up from Dranko's surgery. They must have moved him to one of the bedrooms because he wasn't there or on the couch. He stormed past them, not wanting to talk to anyone right then.

Angela's hand caught his wrist and stopped his attempted escape. Their eyes met. Her eyes pleaded with his to tell her what troubled him and what feelings consumed him. He saw the welcome comfort that she offered. He desperately wanted to embrace her, open up to her, and bathe in the solace he knew she could provide. But, as his heart began opening to Angela, he recalled the ferocious intensity of his attraction to Julianne. His desire and connection to Julianne defied logic and vaulted the obstacles that should have made his heart a dead stone to her. And, he could not forget the way her lips had felt on his just days ago.

Their eyes remained locked. He watched her gain hope at his first thoughts and then the disappointment as she could tell his thoughts had drifted to Julianne. He felt miserable at his indecision and the hurt he caused her.

"I'm not ready," he whispered to her. She nodded, but disbelief at his words clouded her eyes.

He descended the stairs to find some solitude in the basement. His mind raced. *I'm losing my son to the ravages of despair and hopelessness. My best friend is clinging to life. Julianne tells me that my wife and a billion others died for the cause of money? I'm torn between two women and I cannot make heads nor tails out of it!* His head sank into his hands. He wept futile tears.

The ham radio crackled. Julianne must have left it on.

"Sheriff Hodges, you there?"

Cooper looked at it for a moment, confused. But, then he deliberately picked up the handset, "Yes, I'm here."

"Do you have the package?"

Cooper's confusion was replaced by clarity, "Yes."

"Good, the Governor will be pleased. Meet at the rendezvous as planned."

The cold comfort of revenge stiffened Cooper's heart and he welcomed it. His mind raced to a possibility, "That's a no go. It is compromised."

"Say again?"

"The rendezvous is compromised."

There was a long pause. "Please authenticate with the password."

He cursed them for having good Operational Security in place, but then his grin turned sinister, "Three. Oh. Eight."

Another pause, "What? Say again."

"Tell the Governor. Three. Oh. Eight. That's the caliber of the bullet I'm going to bury in his goddamned brain for what he's been a part of."

"Who is this?" the voice on the other end asked, indignant.

"Nobody. Just a man who is going to get to the bottom of the truth."

"How dare you! Threaten our Governor. Who the hell is this?"

"Just tell the Governor that I know just what he did for a new fistful of dollar bills...or Chinese *Yuan*. And, he's going to pay for it."

Silence lingered for a moment, "What? Who is…"

Cooper clicked the radio to 'off'. He smiled at the rage rising in his belly, which was pushing away the confusion and despair. He knew what he had to do next. He resolved on Elena's soul and his son's childhood that the Governor and the rest involved in the Brushfire Plague's conspiracy would be burned. Yes, his mind churned, *burned by a brimstone fire that only the truth can stoke.*

CPSIA information can be obtained at www.ICGtesting.com
Printed in the USA
LVOW10s2328080514

385005LV00012B/245/P